Samantha Spük:
PARANORMAL WEDDING PLANNER

Samantha Spük: PARANORMAL WEDDING PLANNER

ALEESE LIN

SAGA PRESS

LONDON NEW YORK TORONTO
AMSTERDAM/ANTWERP NEW DELHI SYDNEY/MELBOURNE

SAGA PRESS

AN IMPRINT OF SIMON & SCHUSTER, LLC

1230 AVENUE OF THE AMERICAS, NEW YORK, NEW YORK 10020

First Saga Press trade paperback edition June 2026

Interior design by Milly McKinnish

Manufactured in the United States of America

1 3 5 7 9 10 8 6 4 2

Library of Congress Cataloging-in-Publication Data is available.

ISBN 978-1-6682-0519-8 (pbk)
ISBN 978-1-6682-0520-4 (ebook)

DEAREST, MOST LOVELY READER,

YOU'RE MY PLUS-ONE!

ENJOY THE PARTY.

JUST DON'T EAT ANYTHING WHILE YOU'RE HERE.

BOOK INK IS REALLY TOUGH ON THE BOWELS.

1

IN WHICH MY DEAD GRANDMOTHER FRAMES ME FOR A MURDER, POSSIBLY, I THINK

HAPPY FUNERAL DAY, GRANDMA ROSE: I HOPE YOU'RE WATCHING this from the cloudy heavens, stuffing your face with home-cooked ziti, perfectly pleased with yourself. You did it. You roped me into returning to Salem, my hometown and personal nightmare. I've just spent a whole afternoon with your wannabe-witch cabal of friends, and now that I'm back at your house, they still won't leave me alone. They're determined to blight me with threats of their dysfunctional friendship forever.

Okay, so technically, the six of them are busily undressing Grandma's pink flamingos, divesting the little birds of their festive black funereal finery. My point remains. Clearly, this is a cover for them to watch me. To *linger*. Grandma didn't ask to be buried in a lacy black veil, so why would she have wanted a Gothic makeover for her garden ornaments? When I direct a glower out the window at the crones in their campy cloaks, one of them waves back.

Dropping the blinds shut, I wheel back to face the living room. In spite of my genuine efforts this past week, the cluttered, hectic space remains a mess. If I were the dramatic type, I'd sigh at it with anguish. Instead, I hack a little, because the blinds have unleashed enough dust to kill all the crops in Kansas. Also because I'm harboring a tiny bit of irritation at being dragged here the week before I start the job of my dreams—a job that has nothing to do with landscaping hags and spooky whimsy.

I'm not like the other women in my family. I'm like everyone else. Normal. Lame, even. I'm not a witch, or a witch stan, or a crunchy queen who drops homemade sage oil into her water bottle. You definitely wouldn't know I'm from Salem, Massachusetts—the witch capital of earth—by looking at me. In fact, on a good day, you might not notice me at all, because I'm so unnoteworthy. I'm not just wallpaper; I'm a goddamn human Magic Eye puzzle. At my NYU graduation, my old RA asked for my name three times because I didn't leave a strong impression. Last week, I was at a food hall eating spaghetti while studying for my CPA exam when a tourist sat on me by accident.

This was The Problem, in Grandma's mind.

It's why I was so shocked to find out she'd named me sole heir and executrix of her will. Of all the people who might inherit her apothecary and her pink, cake-sliced triangle of a house, she chose me: the one person determined to sell them off immediately. It was uncharacteristically generous. And strategic. Obviously, it was a Trojan horse–gift, forcing me to come back to my hometown and pay my respects. As unpleasant as I found the prospect of returning to Salem, I knew that selling off the Spük estate would pay off my college loans and leave me with a nest egg of ostrichesque proportions. And if I learned one thing from my summer accounting internship, that was to choose financial security over emotional well-being.

It's also why I've embarked on this house clean-out project. Originally, I planned to hire a company to do the honors. But before I bolted from the post-funeral reception, Grandma's best friend, Matilda, patted my arm with her gnarled old hand and croaked cryptically about a surprise awaiting me in the house. I'm 99 percent confident she was trying to inform me of buried treasure. As a fledgling accountant, it's practically my *job* to unearth hidden funds. That, or hide funds. It seems kind of client dependent.

Anyway, when I resume my treasure hunt, I don't uncover gold doubloons hidden among the antique cuckoo clock collection. Or a stack of Benjamins behind Grandma's life-sized cutout of Colin Firth. The shelves of medicinal herbs and that ceremonial dagger . . . a little triggering, sure, but all in all, probably less valuable on eBay than a vintage Taylor Swift CD. I pause to scrutinize a mysterious bucket of water by the door labeled with a Post-it that reads *BULAN* in Grandma Rose's scrawled lettering. I'm not sure when or why she started naming her buckets. Grandma and I haven't had "quality time" for a decade, barring a brief summer visit three years ago. Aside from exchanging annual birthday cards, we were essentially estranged. Who knows what new habits she picked up? I've already learned from her lawyer that she was ignoring her bills and using them as kindling for the bathtub-cauldron in her illegal backyard firepit.

Oh, Grandma. You were always a multitasker. And slightly too fond of setting things on fire.

When I catch myself sneezing, I pop into the kitchen. Under the sink, I find a box of tissues and a bunch of spray bottles with home-made, scribbled labels like *Witch Hazel* and *Unwitch Hazel*. Arming myself with rubber gloves, paper towels, and what I hope is cleaning fluid, I resume my search in Grandma's bedroom. I flick on the light switch and make for the closet, prepared to uncover anything from a pile of oversize black panties to love letters from the Gothic mime who performs on Front Street.

I crack the closet door open. And—I hold it there. Ajar.

Observing the severed head on a shelf that is screaming at me. That's right: a *head*.

. . . Goddamn it, Grandma. *This* was the surprise, wasn't it? A murder victim, just for me! It's what I always wanted!

Well, thanks.

At least it's not a decomposing screaming head. In fact, it's so fresh and not-yet-stinky, I can tell it must've belonged to a (probably) burly mountain man. Or an old millennial, visiting from a hipster enclave in Vermont or Maine, based on the well-coiffed and waxed nature of his thick red beard. And the clear evidence of more than thirty years of not using sunblock. It troubles me slightly that I can't see what's going on beneath the fuzzy chin—my eyes kind of slide around, avoiding the area where a neck should start. Is this magic? It must be.

Gross.

Anyway, when I pick the head up with my rubber gloves, I only feel smoothness at the bottom. No hints of jawline. It's kind of like the rest of its body got soldered off, leaving behind a giant, anatomically deficient, plastic Ken head. Which is both creepy and offensive.

But not as offensive as the fact that the head keeps shouting at me.

"Don't spray those icky chemicals on me!" it says, blue eyes fixated on the spray bottle beneath my arm. "My eyes will burn terribly! I'm allergic to Windex!"

"You'll be fine. This stuff's organic." I think. I have no idea what this particular concoction is made from, but it made a satisfying fizzy sound when I tested it on the kitchen counter. "Anyway, you have a lot of audacity complaining about what is and isn't natural."

The head exchanges yelling for thoughtfulness.

"You know, I've heard that before."

"I can imagine."

"You're Sabby, aren't you?" says the head as I carry it into the living room. "I've seen your picture around here somewhere. Though I don't recall you being a brunette."

"Shh, shh," I say. Then I drop the head into my duffel.

He protests, understandably, but at least he doesn't seem unhappily murdered. Good. I don't feel in the mood to play paranormal Nancy Drew, or anything else paranormal, for that matter.

I am so past this, Grandma Rose. I've graduated college, I've spent the summer completing the last credit hours for my CPA license, and I'm *finally* less than a week away from starting my best, basic life as a first-year associate at EFG, one of the Big Four international accounting firms. Imagine a kitchen pantry filled with handsomely shelved cereal boxes. That's me, and this is my perfectly mainstream life, ready to be consumed with the bland, unsweetened nut milk of my choosing. Back in Manhattan's Midtown East, my first post-college apartment is a postwar walk-up stocked with Target, HomeGoods, and Kirkland furniture. I have a new roommate named Jane Willoughby, who I like to think of as Jane Doe—we roomed together at EFG's onboarding weekend—and I've nominated her to be my normalcy life coach and mirror. I'm going to copy every single thing she does. Which *should* mean spending my days curled up in bed with matcha-vanilla bubble tea and soaking in the angelic voices of BTS. Melting into the sheets to the sound of "Butter" played on repeat while eating flaky pastries made from butter. Or dressed in athleisure, pretending to run along the East River, while harmonizing to the chorus of "Blood Sweat & Tears." Or studying for my CPA licensing exam. Basically, doing anything but . . . whatever this is. I've put myself on track to become a white-collar keyboard jockey with a steady job and stable future. In other words? The polar opposite of everything you stand for, Grandma Rose.

Which apparently might include murder?

I bet you left this head in the closet as a sinister postmortem machination. That's why your kooky friend was in on it! You hoped I'd be so desperate to avoid police involvement that I'd deliver the head to the cabal; that I'd ask them to dispose of it for me. Well, as happy as I know it'd make you if I burst open the metaphorical door of paranormal friendship between me and your bizarro friends, it's not happening, Grandma Rose.

I zip the duffel bag shut, step back, and ponder it—along with my options. My spooky, non-magical options.

"Please don't do this," the head moans from within my bag. He presses its face against the fabric, creating a woeful indentation. I wince, because ugh, I liked that bag once. "Let me go. I'll be good. A good doggy. Arf."

"Sorry, Head," I say. "Grandma made me an offer I can't refuse. If you know what I mean."

"I don't. What *does* that mean?" replies the head, muffled.

That I'm not sorry about what I'm planning to do, obviously. If I'm going to sell off Grandma's house and return to my New York City life, I need to get this head out of here posthaste. And I'm willing to do whatever it takes.

Even if that means briefly dabbling in criminal activity.

2

A JUSTIFIED BREAKING AND ENTERING

I'M AT THE CEMETERY, SCOPING OUT THE DARK, GRIMLY MANIcured lawn riddled with tombstones and bent-over, judgy trees. So far, I think I've done a decent job of clearing the graveyard perimeter. I wouldn't usually be caught dead in a place like this. Right now, I'm mostly concerned about being caught, period. Being forced to return to Salem has been enough of a prison sentence. I don't want to get locked up for real.

I tuck away the pair of heavy-duty scissors I bought to cut the security camera wiring, then launch myself up the stabby-topped iron gate. The duffel on my shoulder gets jostled as I ascend.

"Oof," says a voice in the bag. Which I ignore, appropriately. I know I'm doing the right thing by not turning this severed head in to the Salem Police Department. The town's reputation notwithstanding, the Salem homicide department has zero experience with magical murder cases. Trust me, I looked it up.

Besides, dead people and dead things in general belong in graveyards. It's science.

I finally topple over the iron gate onto grass, the duffel bouncing a bit until it stops against a grave marker—more annoyed sound effects ensue—and I scope out my path.

"Please don't do this," the head whines. "I don't want to be buried again. It's so dark and wormy down there!"

I scowl. This brings up so many questions, and I literally do not want to know.

"My name is Bulan, by the way," adds the head.

So is that what was going on with the labeled bucket in Grandma's living room? Was she keeping this head as a freaky pet? Either way . . .

"I don't care," I mutter under my breath. I shoulder the bag again and retrace my steps to my destination: Grandma's grave. It was hardly ten hours ago we laid her to rest. The only ones gathered for it were me, Grandma's witch cabal, the probate lawyer, the undertaker, and some unhinged tourists who claimed to be LARPing and wanted in on the fun.

"Oh, come on," says the head. "You have to care a little, Sabby. You're a nice girl. I can see it in you. I also heard you singing karaoke before you found me. No one who sings BTS that passionately is heartless."

I'll show him heartless. "You can sing to the worms."

"They're a terrible audience. Even the beetles—"

"Listen. With the exceptions you just mentioned, dead things go in the ground," I say. It seems safest to assume that despite the talking, the attitude, and the fact that he has a name, Bulan the head is dead. "I'm selling Grandma's house, and I'm not letting the inspector find any part of a corpse in there."

The head harrumphs. I harrumph back. Mine's grumpier, and it settles our argument for the moment.

"If it makes a difference," Bulan says, "you only found me because I wanted to get caught by you! I'll hide better next time, I promise!"

He says more after that, but I tune him out.

Filtered light of the full hunter's moon guides me through the graveyard, illuminating tombstones in patchwork states of disrepair. When I get to Grandma's over-the-top resting place, I drop the duffel bag and step back to observe the spectacle of her magnum opus. I'm talking a black marble gravestone, with an oversize skull and crossbones over her name, *Rosamund Spük*, scrawled in a decadent swirly font. What is this, the Constitution? Of course there's more. A fresh wreath of black-dyed roses and black dahlias crowns the top of the tombstone. A low iron fence stabs at the sky. And lastly, black irises lie strewn across the dirt shoveled atop her coffin.

If I were still the little girl who adored her grandma, I'd clap in awestruck appreciation. Maybe I'd clasp my pointed hat to my chest and recite some Edgar Allan Poe. These days, I'd do practically anything before being caught dressed like Grandma, in a witch hat and intentionally mismatched socks. But my chest twinges with unexpected sadness to think she won't be traipsing through Salem in her funky outfits anymore. I guess even a thorn in your side can get familiar enough that you don't want it gone.

Anyway, don't worry, Grandma—I won't mess with your macabre memorial. In fact, I'll clear off the chipper yellow ash leaves that fell over your flowers, ruining your perfect Gothic vibe. That'll be our compromise for me desecrating your burial site with your unknown victim.

I unzip the duffel, ignoring the head's doleful, pleading eyes while I search for the gardening trowel.

"Hello?"

I whip around.

There's a guy standing a stone's throw away. He's come out of nowhere, a tall, solid-looking guy, rocking a fade haircut and a jawline that's gift wrapped in either shadow or stubble. His face places him somewhere near my age, early twenties, but his shoulders could rival the wingspan of an eagle's. Yes, I'll admit it: graveyard boy is hot. He's got a great body and "sensitive man" eyebrows, the kind that are currently drawing together with empathetic, masculine whimsy. But what's he doing hanging out here in the middle of the night, like me?

Oh god, what if he's a security officer?

In a denim button-down and rolled-up jeans?

Hmm.

"Hey!" I say casually. As if I'm not in the process of committing multiple well-reasoned crimes. "What's up?"

He gestures to his bespoke leather knapsack. "I'm collecting pine cones."

Wow, okay.

I feel my shoulders drop with relief at the revelation that he isn't a security officer in woodsy camouflage. It's possible he's a groundskeeper or maybe a lumberjack model-in-training. Yeah, that could be it. Too bad his *Vermont Magazine* cover-boy body is wasted potential, because I'm 1,000 percent sure "pine cones" is some kind of slang for magic mushrooms.

"Pine cones, huh?" I say. "What are you, a squirrel?"

"Ha. Funny. You out foraging too?" As he closes the bag, he smiles at me the way people do when they're smiling back at someone. Fun fact: I'm definitely not smiling. I'm offended to my core at the suggestion I might have such a crunchy hobby. Which I don't, because I'm 100 percent normal and boring. I've been working on it for years.

"No," I say through clenched teeth. "Nothing like that."

"Uh," says something behind me. The head?

I push my duffel back, hoping that'll keep the head from sight—and more importantly, *quiet*—so naturally the scissors wedge themselves out of the duffel at my rough handling. Okay, technically, they're a pair of wire cutters. Still not great. I can't let this guy think I'm the most suspicious person on the planet. Desperately, I explain: "I was arranging the flowers on this grave."

"Huh. I did think they looked messy earlier." He nods. "Nice work."

Wait a second. What kind of person even notices that about a grave? Maybe a grave robber. If this guy's a criminal, he definitely won't report me for deviant behavior. But then again: that would mean he's a criminal. And that means it's time to nip our conversation in the bud.

"Thanks," I say. I get down on my knees and hum to myself, gathering the yellow leaves and roses and laying them out in the shape of an inverted pentagram. It's what Grandma Rose would've wanted.

The guy bends to investigate my work. "Is that your job?" he asks. "To arrange flowers?"

Oh my god. Why won't he just walk away? And why does he smell so good?

"Yeah," I laugh as I shuffle over to the tombstone. "I'm a florist."

"A florist? For funerals?"

Why not? I nod. "And other events."

"Do you do weddings?"

"Oof," says a voice behind me. A voice from within my duffel bag, presumably, because of course the head won't let me flirt OR bury him in peace.

The guy cranes his neck, searching for the source of the sound. "Oof?"

I laugh tinnily. "*Oof* course I do weddings! Ha ha. Ha. It was a joke."

The guy's confused smile makes my heart beat faster. I feel light and fluttery, like whipped sugar and butter flying out of a hyperactive stand mixer, which is ridiculous. He's at best a forager, most likely a magic mushroom addict, and at worst a grave robber. Yet all I want is for him to keep taking an interest in me.

Sometimes I really, deeply, truly resent myself.

"So tell me," Graveyard Guy says. "What kind of weddings do you—"

"Agh!" says the head behind us, louder now.

"Agh!" I echo. In desperation, I grasp onto Grandma's death-wreath and cough. "Keh, kleh. Something caught in my throat!"

"Are you okay?"

The guy looks like he wants to help. I kind of want that too, but I throw out a hand to keep him at bay while I replace the wreath on the tomb. "Yeah, ahem, *agh*-s it happens, I plan lots of weddings. It's like that show *Chopped*, but for events: give me four weird ingredients, and I can pull off anything. That's me, that's my brand."

Why am I talking about wedding planning? I thought I was a florist. Oh well, doesn't matter. Amazingly, the guy doesn't notice my slipup or hear the bag rustling again behind me.

"I knew our meeting was lucky!" He snaps his fingers. "I have some friends getting married next weekend."

I feel like I missed something. "Umm . . . okay?"

"And they're in a real bind," he continues. "They're looking for last-minute help. But none of the planners in town have the unique vibe they're going for, you know?"

Oh no. No. This cannot be happening. I cannot be actually kneeling six feet above my dead grandmother's body, in the process of covering up a murder in the middle of the night, getting recruited to help some random guy's friends' wedding. Except it *is* happening, obviously. This good-looking, late-night lumberjack wasn't flirting with me; he was interviewing me for a job.

Well done, Sabby. You let your lumber-lust lead you into a weirdly embellished cover-up story. And now you've tied yourself to an anchor that's sinking you into a nightmare.

"Cool," I manage out loud.

The guy seems pleased. "I think they'll like your style. I'll be in touch soon. See you!"

Whoa, wait. Absolutely not.

"Hey!" I interrupt his attempted exit. "You can't do that. You don't even know my name."

"You're Samantha Spük," he answers. I follow his gaze to my duffel—where my name is monogrammed, courtesy of EFG's HR department. Before I can make a snappy comeback, the guy shoots me one last sensitively eyebrowed smile.

"See you soon," he says.

"But," I try in vain. He's already sauntering off to the entry gates, as chill and hot as ever. Well, I'm not. Chill, at least. Listening to the callously enthusiastic graveyard crickets, I realize:

1. Someone has seen me in the middle of the night messing with Grandma's grave. And,
2. Said someone knows my name.

Shit. There's no way I can bury the head here now.

With a groan, I toss the wire cutters back into the bag and zip it up. Then I slip the duffel back over my shoulder far too easily.

My breath stutters in my chest. When I drop the bag again, there's no bounciness or muffled protests. The fabric merely sags emptily, horrifically, in front of my feet.

"Hey!" I whisper-shout. "Head! I mean Bulan! Where'd you go?"

A wind tickles the ash tree over Grandma's grave, and its dead leaves seem to giggle. At me, at my predicament. I have no idea how this is possible, but Bulan the head is gone. Could he have rolled away, maybe, while I was talking with that guy? Is this why there'd been so much grunting? But how could a head unzip a duffel and escape on its own?

I search the grave mound, kicking up flowers. It's no good. I can't find the head anywhere.

Maybe it's just me—or maybe it's Grandma's frozen pesto lasagna, threatening to climb back up my esophagus—but I'm pretty sure having a severed head go missing is even worse than walking around with a severed talking head on your person.

Cool cool cool cool cooooool.

3

LATE-NIGHT DECISIONS ARE ALWAYS REGRETTABLE

PER THE PARCHMENT SIGN GRANDMA AFFIXED TO THE DOOR with egg yolk and horse hair, the Spük Apothecary of downtown Salem opens at noon. Per a new sheet of cheap printer paper I've affixed with Scotch tape—a significantly less noxious adhesive than Grandma's favorite multipurpose potion—Spük Apothecary now opens never.

Ideally, I wouldn't have to attend to the shuttered place at all. But in case the chaotic contents of the shop harbor another "surprise" on the scale of a talking head, I'm taking on the task of organization myself. I've also asked Grandma's lawyer to meet me one last time before I head back to New York, to discuss what's left in settling the estate. For better or for worse, he agreed, and here he is: the day after Grandma's funeral, at exactly 7:59 a.m., Baldy the probate attorney rolls up to the shop.

I try not to be impressed by his slick black Tesla or his punctuality. It's early October, and a Saturday, so the holiday traffic is already threatening to stack vertically. Car exhaust battles the scents of spilled pumpkin spice lattes and moldering leaves crunched into Salem's bloodred brick sidewalks. It isn't easy to navigate this witchy town, is what I'm getting at. But I refuse to acknowledge that Grandma's lawyer does it well, because even the impressive things about him are off-putting and lumpy.

Case in point? He double-parks.

And now, as I let him in, Baldy awkwardly clears his throat. His checkered bow tie stifles the noise from reaching its true potential.

"Do you need some water?" I ask. Unlike Baldy, I was brought up with social graces. If I had a car, I would have at least attempted to introduce it to a curb.

"Unnecessary," he says. "You and I have bigger priorities to address."

Oh, goody. "As long as I don't have to lick any envelopes."

"No envelopes are involved."

Baldy surveys the shelves of Grandma's occult-leaning pharmaceuticals, probably to avoid sighing over me again. He and I have known each other for a week, and he couldn't make it clearer that I grate at the scratchy wool fibers of his being. I suspect he has an eldest daughter he's projecting onto me. At least this would explain why he's so invested in micromanaging my handling of Grandma Rose's last will and testament.

"So," I say, hoping to keep his visit short, "funeral's done. Peachy. Now that that's over, the probate should all just be downhill from here, right?"

Baldy rubs his unpleasantly wet-looking, stumpy nose. "Not quite."

Rather than simply explaining like a normal person, Baldy drags himself theatrically into the center of the room. He settles for standing directly beneath the giant, dusty, and low-hanging chandelier. A blinding sheen bounces off his head. I consider grabbing sunglasses. Or SPF 50+ sunscreen. But I don't, because that would be rude, and I'd prefer to stay in Baldy's good graces. He holds my future in his pale, sweaty hands.

"There is a . . . hiccup," he says at last.

Oh, crap. I can see from Baldy's face that he's about to do it again. He's going to cruelly code-switch out of English into the foreign languages of Business and Law.

"It has," he begins ominously, "come to my attention that your grandmother confirmed receipt of a creditor's validation notice. A collections agency has petitioned the Massachusetts probate courts for possession of a portion of Rosamund's estate, requiring us to follow the judge's order to set up a payment plan to resolve the debt. Being that this is the case, I will need to intervene with a legal motion of . . ."

"Uh-huh," I say. "Yep. Uh-huh."

These are lying noises.

Because as might be expected of a twenty-two-year-old girl fresh out of college, I am lost. Completely in over my head. I have no idea how to read wills or contracts or IKEA instruction manuals, and not for lack of trying. The fact that I have been hired to perform audits at a professional level remains deeply mysterious to me.

Also, I suspect Baldy rambles like this to pad his legal fees.

". . . and of course, that stipulation is magically binding."

I blink. "Sorry, what?"

"This requirement of Rosamund's will and testament is magically binding," Baldy repeats, sniffing emphatically. I'm tempted to offer him a Kleenex and pretend I didn't hear him mention magic, but with yesterday's head discovery, I can't let this go.

"Explain," I demand. "But simply."

"Until the will releases you, you will have to remain physically, corporeally in Salem."

I take a moment to process this.

"No. I can't do that," I say once my blood remembers how to carry oxygen through my body. "I'm not staying."

"You said you would uphold the requirements of this role, Samantha, when I called you to inform you of Rosamund's most sorrowful passing—"

I interrupt. "My *mom* informed me of Grandma's death. And if I said yes to staying here, I meant for a few days, a week at most. It's been a week. You told me I would be named executrix within the week, and guess what, I was! What more could she want?"

"Part of the instructions for the executor include guarding Rosamund's spirit until it ascends."

"You can't be serious. That sounds like a quote from a nineties goth rock ballad!" Baldy shakes his too-shiny head at me. "Why hasn't she ascended yet?"

"Per the wording of her will, 'Once I am returned to the earth, my appointed must guard my spirit until the passing of seven tides, low and high, twice over.'"

"I don't remember you reading that part to me in your office a few days ago. Why would you leave that out?"

Baldy leaves my question unanswered as he rambles on mercilessly. "As I mentioned, the matter of the debt is indubitably keeping your grandmother's spirit here. I suspect that she will need to remain until that piece is resolved. And of course, she must be waiting for the passing of the—"

"—seven high tides," I finish with a groan. Then I groan again, louder, when it doesn't improve my mood. So I turn my back to the lawyer, take up a broom, and start sweeping.

Grandma Rose, why would you do this? Who puts a magical stipulation on a will!? Or who *claims* to do so, I should say? Because I know you weren't magical, Grandma.

To be fair, this is all par for the course. My grandmother's loony lunacy looned deep.

Pretty much every summer of my childhood, Mom spent a couple months test-driving a new boyfriend in Canada or wherever. She would drop me off in Salem with Grandma. Taking advantage of the situation, Grandma leaned hard into the kindly matriarch schtick: she fed me a diet of home-cooked food and gingerbread cookies laced with medicinal, possibly illegal herbs; she took me shopping, outfitting me in a black and purple Gothic wardrobe; she regaled me with legends of our eccentric and paranormally inclined clan. When I was little, I ran with it. Sure, kids at the playground stared at us in our Addams Family cosplay, and the librarian banned us after Grandma kept sneaking in stray, flea-trafficking cats. But Grandma Rose encouraged me to ignore them all. After all, weren't the little families she invited to her house cute and fun and accepting? Even if they were unusually hairy or had pets with tentacles, not arms?

I can't believe I trusted Grandma when she said that was normal for homeschoolers.

Everything changed the last time I stayed with Grandma. Mom was excited about her most recent boyfriend, so she extended her vacation time with him into September. This meant Grandma had to enroll me in one of Salem's public middle schools for the fall. I must've been handling the transition too well, because Grandma's friends persuaded her that this meant it was time to introduce me, an innocent and unsuspecting twelve-year-old, to their favorite local community event. On Halloween night, Grandma brought me to a "very special" party in the Salem Woods. There, her best friend, Matilda, unsheathed a dagger and held it against my heart, her silvery eyes boring holes into mine. This is it, I thought. I've been Hansel-and-Greteled. Fattened up and dressed up and now I'm going to be dinner. I was sure I was going to die.

Of course, I didn't.

No one ever planned to sacrifice me. It was all a joke they were playing while Grandma picked up pizza. When she returned, Grandma didn't notice my shaking, my terror. The fact that I'd peed myself. She just cackled around the fire with her wannabe-witch coven while I stress-vomited into a barrel of bobbing apples. I still wake up sweating from nightmares about it, sometimes. The dagger part, sure—but the pants-peeing part especially, because on my way home from the forest, I bumped into a popular kid who witnessed my wet-jeans waddle of shame. His discovery ushered in new and horrible humiliations. Between every class period, I was afflicted by water bottles "accidentally" squeezed in the direction of my pants. In math, the substitute let us play hangman, and the answer was "Only gross girls pee their pants." Thanks to social media, even the kids who'd skipped school nursing candy hangovers knew what happened and joined in the mockery. Overnight, I'd become something worse than "the new girl" or "another strange Spük."

I'd become an actual pariah. A pee-riah.

After that, I decided to stay as far from Grandma—more specifically, from the unstable people orbiting her—as I possibly could. I called Mom, pleading with her to come pick me up. She sacrificed the nascent bud of whatever was happening with her then-boyfriend to rescue me and move us all the way to the West Coast. To the far-flung city of Portland, Oregon.

Unfortunately, life with Mom was only two degrees saner than with Grandma. That's when I drew a line in the sand: I gave myself a nickname, less witchy-sounding than Samantha, and I made it my mission to become as un-Spüky as possible. I'm holding to that, too. By the time I'm thirty, I aim to be as boring as Baldy. To be the wallpaper of people, an owner of 2.5 children and/or dogs living in a suburban McMansion. To be graced with a back-buckling mortgage and a partner with no ambitions beyond making money and watching Sunday football.

The dream, basically. The goddamn, paranormal-free American dream.

Which I can't achieve while I'm stuck in this dysfunctional witch shop. In this dysfunctional witch *town*. When I need to be starting my new job elsewhere *in two days*!

"Samantha," says Baldy. "Would you kindly refrain from sweeping dust over my feet?"

I'd rather not. I feel a flicker of joy at the pained bob of his Adam's apple above his bow tie.

"You're a true believer," I say, sweeping more dust over his shoes. "I can tell. You really bought into the whole witch-town tourist package. But the joke's on you, Baldy."

"Bhauldeen."

"Like I was saying, my grandma was a cosplayer. The furthest thing from a witch. There's no magical binding on the will, no matter what she said, but if it helps, I'll pay you to figure out a legal workaround to Grandma's request—a magical workaround, if you will. Just call me before you send the invoice. I expect there will be a reasonable fee. And when you need me to do anything with the courts, I'll come back. As of tomorrow, though, I'm—"

I wiggle my index and middle fingers like they're running away. Baldy watches with intense, if pallid, concern.

"That is not possible, Samantha."

"Believe me, it is. I know a lot about quasi-legal wiggle room."

"Your continued presence in Salem, guarding your grandmother's spirit, was one of Rosamund's last requests. It deserves to be honored."

Good lord. What does he think Grandma was, a Gothic saint?

"Well, tough for her. I've told you, I can't stay here," I say firmly. "I start work Monday. In Manhattan. You might have noticed that's not in commuting distance."

From his blank expression, Baldy does not comprehend distance. This must be an advantage of owning a self-driving car.

"Don't you kids all work from home these days?" he asks.

"I'm twenty-two, not a kid. Besides, aren't you here in person?" I remind Baldy. "Same deal."

"I see," says Baldy, unaware it's not even close to the same deal. I didn't gun for a job at an accounting firm with a remote work model. I chose EFG New York *because* it insists on its employees living locally and working on-site. While I build up my suburban home savings fund, New York is where I have to be—mainly because it's a place you can't help blending in. In the city, no one will flag you down and expect you to stop walking. You can cross at an intersection wearing nothing but a brazen rainbow beach towel and the oiled-up pecs of a god and *still* get hit by a taxi. I would know. I've seen it happen. The oily man got away largely unscathed, if more naked.

Besides, it's a big deal to get to work at a corporate headquarters in the world's financial hub. The way I see it is, most people want the best job they can get. That's why I wanted it too. Because I'm so average. Average-zilla.

But I'm obviously not going to bare my soul to this Grandma Rose sympathizer.

"How about this, Baldy. When I'm done cleaning, we can resume this chat on a call," I say. "All right? Off you go. On to a new lawyering adventure."

I make shooing movements with the broom. Once he realizes I'm putting him to best use as a human dustpan, Baldy sighs with resignation and shuffles toward the door.

"Very well," he says as he comports himself. "I will find you when you do not call, since you don't answer your phone."

At last, the world's lumpiest lawyer dips out of the shop. Good riddance to him, to his resistance to oil-cleansing scalp products, and to his allegedly magical contract that I'm not buying a word of.

As loath as I am to admit it, watching Baldy drive away, I feel a pang of longing for my mom. I wish she were here. Or more accurately, I wish she had the presence of mind to be here in Salem, performing the role of executrix and alleged spirit guardian instead of me. The way a daughter should. Grandma was a lost cause, but sometimes I wonder what Mom would've been like if she hadn't surrendered to the paranormal life.

When I was a kid, she cycled through a zillion crunchy jobs she could do from home: reading tarot cards, selling MLM leggings and mouthwash, filling our living room with homemade soaps that she claimed were cupcake-scented, but mostly smelled like yeast and toe lint. She was weird even by Portland, Oregon, standards. I learned to hide my friends' existence so Mom wouldn't besiege their parents with invitations to join pyramid schemes. Still, we got along pretty well, the two of us, with the help of my mostly AWOL dad's child-support checks.

Until Mom discovered plants. Supernatural, succulent ones. This led to another quick packing of bags and the purchase of a one-way ticket, and suddenly, I was living alone in our apartment, dodging child services while Mom pursued her paranormal dreams in Mexico. After she stopped paying rent—having apparently forgotten that parents are supposed to house and feed their children—I sold everything I could and finished my senior year of high school while crashing on pullout sofas at random friends' houses. I swore to myself I'd never go through houselessness again. Or insecurity in general. Benjamin Franklin once said, "Nothing can be certain except death and taxes." It's what inspired me to become an auditor.

The weird thing is, Mom's been staying in a Baja California hotel ever since. She hasn't come home for my graduations or birthdays. She didn't come to Grandma's funeral. At this point, it's kind of unclear if she can even leave.

All the more reason to complain to the room, with Grandma's knobby broom in hand.

"Who knew that dying could be so damn complicated?" I ask the air.

"That's why I declined," says a voice behind me.

I nearly die right then.

But instead I turn around and bop what I find—the stupid head from Grandma's house—with the end of my broom.

"What the *hell*!" I say. Then I bop it again, twice, for good measure. "How did you get here? How did you get away from me last night? I figured an owl got you. Or a raccoon."

"I asked some crows to drop me off," Bulan the head replies buoyantly. He seems relatively unharmed, considering he's missing most of his organs. Which is unbelievable. Possibly less believable than his existence.

"Some crows," I repeat.

"They're quite friendly."

I stare at him until he laughs. "Don't look so angry, Sabby."

"I'm going to drown you in a sink."

"I like baths," he replies.

"Then how am I supposed to get rid of you?"

"I'm not going to give you *suggestions*," the head whines. "I came back because . . . Well . . ."

Because what? Is his gluttonous masochism the reason he's dead, or undead, or whatever? And why would he come find me after narrowly escaping being buried against his will? He better not think I'm going to keep him as my pet. A body-impaired, lighthearted curiosity *cannot* replace a golden retriever.

Our conversation, stilted as it is, gets cut off by the door opening. Two strangers stride into the apothecary clutching huge black parasols. They distress me in a way I can't identify. It's probably the outfits.

The woman has a long neck, like a giraffe's, wrapped tightly in about a half foot of fluffy, purple-feathered boa. She has bound the rest of herself in a black dress that might actually be a spray-painted roll of Bubble Wrap. Her nails are bright red, but not with polish.

She's still *kind* of pretty beneath the mess. I give her face an 8/10.

Meanwhile, the man is dressed in a blazer with joggers and hiking boots. His handlebar mustache seems to be twitching. Did a very slender mouse crawl onto his face? Or is it a fake mustache that's losing its stickiness and about to fall off? I think about the one and only time I tried wearing sticky boobs. No idea why you would do that to yourself.

All in all, I don't know why they're giving me weird vibes. A good half of the pedestrians in downtown Salem are parading around in absurd outfits right now.

Maybe that's my salvation. The spirit of the season might keep these weirdos from thinking my whole head-pet situation is too abnormal.

"He's a Roomba," I explain. "The head. Happy Halloween."

"I can be of assistance," says Bulan instead of acting like a Roomba, which would actually be helpful.

The visitors stare at me, then the head, then smile close-lipped in unison. I feel my hackles rise. Nothing good can come from such synchronicity.

"What do you two want?" I ask. "Because this shop is unfortunately—"

"We're friends of Hanry's," says the man.

I frown. "Henry who?"

"*Han*-ry. Hanry Burleson," says the woman.

With that, they devolve into silence. I refuse to be the first to speak. It's not my responsibility to push this conversation along. *They're* the ones who traipsed in here like misguided migratory parrots. I seriously should have remembered to lock that door.

After a painfully drawn-out minute, the woman says: "He said you help with weddings."

Oh, shit. Hanry must be the name of the forager-guy I met in the graveyard. This is his doing, inviting these people to come visit me—presumably, the couple in need of help with their wedding. Why is he friends with such weirdos?

Because he's one too. Obviously.

At my feet, the head starts making vacuuming noises and rolling around the floor.

Maybe I'm not really in a position to judge.

"I do like these," says the man, motioning toward a selection of brittle, browned lotus pods.

"You have great taste," I say dryly. "Want them?"

"Mmm, yes. We can pay up to four thousand dollars for all you have to offer."

"Do you mean . . . the shop?" As I try and calculate the value of dumping Grandma's inventory on her, the woman crosses the room. She steps over the head casually as it pretends to suck up dust in its mouth. Carelessly, she passes Grandma's floor-length, vintage mirror.

One of the first times I remember visiting her shop, Grandma was waving sage smoke over this gaudy thing. I thought it all impressive and mysterious until she accidentally set it on fire. So the shabby-chic charring on the frame, the cloudy stains in the glass? They're the real deal.

Also real? The way the mirror reflects the contours of this dark, square room and its exposed brick walls. And me, in my grocery-store-dyed brown ponytail and my beige, basic pants and top I bought on Amazon. And my fake Roomba.

But there is no reflection of the woman. Or the man.

I drop my broom, banging Bulan as he passes underfoot.

"Vroom-ouch," he grunts.

"Does that work with your rates?" the reflectionless woman asks, oblivious to my stunned silence. "I recognize this payment may not result in lavish, floor-to-ceiling decorations, but the room will be dark."

"Yes, very dark," says the man beside her.

"Like a tomb," she says.

"Ooh," he says.

"Ohh," I say, connecting the dots.

"We realize this is last-minute," says the woman. The not-quite-exactly-human woman. "But would you consider helping us ornament the wedding? And performing any other tasks as required? We can offer cash."

"Very dark cash," adds the male, his mustache twitching.

Putting aside the fact that all I want is to be a hundred miles away from Salem and its macabre dessert tray of non-delights, I'm not actually a wedding planner. Nope. Not in any shape or form whatsoever. I have zero interest in considering their offer. I am *not* making floral arrangements for vampires.

Because that's what these customers are. They're vampires.

Dead-on.

4

A GLASS HALF-FULL . . . OF IRONY

"THOSE TWO WERE NOT HUMAN," I SAY THE MOMENT THE VAMpire couple leaves.

The head rolls himself on the floor, seeming happy to continue functioning like a Roomba on a dry-mop function. Right, of course this revelation wouldn't impact him; he's not a real live human himself. At least, not anymore.

"I thought you wouldn't notice," he says.

"I'm not an idiot. I know that more than humans live in Salem."

Knowing and seeing are different things, though. It's rare for vampires and other paranormal beings to interact with humans. Grandma always said they keep out of sight, avoiding human notice by wearing magical jewelry with markings called runes. Unless, of course, you're friends.

I bolt the front door and slip the vampires' contact information into my pocket. Not to save it, though. The phone numbers for Dave and Amanda, whose names *hardly* suggest creatures of the night, now join a wad of lint and rubber bands in transit to the trash can.

"So this must be why you took my presence in stride!" declares Bulan the deviant head. "You *do* share Rose's predilection for the supernatural. In spite of your attempt to bury me—"

"I am taking nothing in stride. I am severely traumatized and masking."

The head laughs because he thinks this is a joke.

"Also," I add, "if you're trying to make me think you knew Grandma Rose, it's not working."

"How come?"

"I don't share a *predilection* for anything supernatural."

"I suppose it was a poor choice of words. A penchant, perhaps? A partiality? As I understood from dear old Rosie, your family line is fully human and non-magical yet has been allowed to dabble in the paranormal world ever since your ancestor was scapegoated in a witch trial for an infestation of albino pigeons."

"Crabs," I correct. "It was crabs."

"Be that as it may, with a name like *Mortifie*, who's surprised he got targeted? Not me! Ha!"

I fold my arms as I consider the head-turned-dust-collector and his knowledge of my sordid ancestry. "Fine. So maybe you did know Grandma personally," I allow. "And you two seem to have ended on good terms, in spite of your dismemberment."

"Of course we did! My limblessness was a preexisting condition, nothing to do with dear Rosie. So if you don't mind, I'd appreciate it if you refrained from another burial attempt. It's rather rude."

"Noted," I say, although it's not a promise or anything.

Maybe Grandma's possession of the head wasn't a convoluted scheme to make me to befriend her little cabal, like I'd suspected. But why is it, or he, still here?

"What do you want?" I ask the head. "Seriously."

He looks up at me earnestly.

"At present? To know why you aren't thinking of helping the happy couple," he says.

Nope. We're not revisiting that.

"You must be aware already that there's nothing to fear," he says as I actively ignore him. I am instead busying my hands with herb organization. It's concerning how many of these vials are labeled *Poison*. What's *more* concerning are the ones labeled *Poison, Maybe*. "Vampires aren't all bad. In fact, they're kind of wimpy. I've heard of their victims biting them back and winning. Of course, they still turned into vampires afterward."

I pick up a concerning vial of *Balm of Kitten*. What does that even mean?

"I'm not calling them," I tell the head. "Or taking on that job. Or staying in Salem."

"Hmm. So if it's not a predilection you have, is it fear?"

I roll my eyes. I'm not afraid of the paranormal itself. But do I harbor a fear of falling into Salem's paranormal world? Of it consuming me, destroying me, making me an irresponsible and inadvertently cruel mess of a person, like it did to my mom and my grandmother and countless Spüks before them?

Maybe.

Also, I would never extract the balm from a defenseless kitten. I'm morally flexible, not a monster.

"All your misgivings aside, Sabby, I think the idea of a paranormal wedding business is magnificent!" says Bulan. "Getting paid four thousand dollars for a handful of bouquets is a good living, especially if you don't have to pay taxes. And you do have a knack for design. Look how neatly you lined up your belongings on that table. Such effortless style. Mmm."

Internally I wince. Generally speaking, it's my goal to avoid compliments. They mean you've stood out instead of blending in.

"Design skill or not, I won't be sticking around to plan weddings," I say, bumping said table so my sling bag slumps a little less artistically. "You might not have heard, but staying in Salem puts me at risk."

"The vampires wouldn't—"

"At risk of losing my job," I clarify. "My real one. In New York. That I start on Monday."

With this revelation complete, I retreat to the back of the shop and behind the wooden door to Grandma's office. Bulan has the audacity to follow, rolling and bouncing with a smile unabated by contact with the dirty floor. I'm not sure how he propels himself, but I don't know how cars work either, and that hasn't affected my life or anything.

I sweep aside clutter and loose potpourri to sit on the edge of Grandma's desk, only to stare into a framed four-by-six of me and Mom. This must be how Bulan recognized me. Mom and I are on a weather-worn dock in coastal Oregon, eating hot dogs and smiling messily at the camera behind windswept blond bangs. That was my thirteenth birthday. The year Mom taught me how to dye my hair from blond to a mousy, run-of-the-mill brown. The year I started to go by "Sabby."

Considering that Grandma Rose wasn't with us at the beach, and was in fact supposedly out of contact, I'm not sure how I feel about her having this photo. Maybe a little bad? As much as Grandma aggravated me, I suspect she might have actually *liked* me.

Or at least, the idea of me.

I tip the frame over so it lands face down, *splat*. I wait for the guilty feeling to go away, and when it doesn't, I focus on Grandma's knickknacks.

"Look at you go," says the head, apropos of nothing.

"Excuse me?"

Chuckling as he eyes the newly rearranged desk, Bulan says, "You're making this office more appealing already, Design Queen. For you, decorating would be a cinch. As for the rest of your new wedding planning enterprise—"

I draw my hand back and slide off the desk.

"Here's the deal, Bulan," I say. "If you're going to stick around, I'm putting you to work."

"As a Roomba again?" he asks hopefully.

"You'll find out."

In short order, I enlist Bulan to roll me around the shabby little shop, then later, around Grandma's house, introducing me to her favored drawers for tucking away money and random papers, her indexing files and Post-it Note novels, her knitted scarf collections—which are definitely getting donated—and her plastic shrine of Dave & Buster's prizes. Straight to the trash with those. He helps me log on to her computer and regales me with tales of her overzealous use of spelling and grammar checks. I spend a good five minutes holding the door open to Grandma's freezer, toying with fate. For all I know, tossing out overcooked pasta might trigger some kind of ghostly conniption fit. The last thing I want is to be haunted by oily zucchini pesto.

By the next afternoon, I manage to consolidate all the family heirlooms Mom might want into two storage tubs, slap sticky notes on four boxes of questionably valuable collectibles that might get sold to some sucker online, then lock both the shop and the house up tight. In a few weeks, I'll come back and do a massive eBay push and prepare the place for a Realtor.

For now, I'm satisfied with a job complete—or at least, complete-enough-for-now—and so I settle atop Grandma's leaf-strewn porch stoop, dial Baldy, and wait.

"He's not answering." Hypocrite.

Bulan, who I had to forcibly remove from Grandma's house along with the scarves, wobbles around my feet with relief.

"Oh, that's too bad. I guess you should stay."

I side-eye him. "Do you know something I don't?"

"I *may* have overheard that oddly top-heavy man tell you about a magical contract keeping you here until the passing of seven tides, twice—"

"It's a will, not a contract," I correct. "And you said it yourself. Grandma Rose had no actual magic. Baldy might have bought her play-acting, but you should know better. Anyway, my work here is done, at least until the next court date."

"It didn't sound that way to me."

At my pointed glare, he explains: "I meant that lovely vampire couple. They'll be sorely disappointed."

"All the more reason to nip out of town fast." I bend and pat the head's dusty crown. He's wearing a big-eyed pout, endearing enough to make someone forget he's an undead abomination. For a split second, I can see why Grandma Rose let him live in her closet. "Good luck with everything, Bulan. By which I mean finding somewhere else to live rent-free."

5

AN OCTOBER BREEZE OF VILLAINOUS INTENT

Having said goodbye to Grandma's freaky yet slightly charming head, I depart for Salem's central train station. The night air's growing chillier—that's fall for you—and within a few minutes, I'm surrounded by a swarm of goths, which is Salem for you. Usually I like scrolling on my phone while I walk, but it's nighttime. Also, since it's the first weekend of October, the shops have littered the sidewalks with Herculean pumpkin displays and treacherous cobwebs. It would be safer to jaywalk into oncoming traffic.

I duck beneath a shop awning to send Jane a voice message, letting her know I'm heading home. Prior to signing for our walk-up apartment in Midtown East, we really only spent one weekend together at EFG's epic orientation retreat to Busch Gardens. From the little I've seen, Jane's personality is flatter than a paper doll's. Ergo, she is flawless. She hails from the New Jersey suburbs. She fondly remembers visiting the Olive Garden with her family for birthdays. She doesn't like spicy food, has a knack for B-list celebrity sightings, and visits Target for fun. She listens to K-pop, like me, but not too much. She doesn't do *anything* too much. When we first met, she was drinking coffee from the hotel canister and couldn't tell me if it was good or not. Most incredibly of all, she exchanged phone numbers with a bland, wall-faced guy at our first orientation breakfast.

I have so much to learn from her.

The rest of my walk graces me with an absence of eventfulness. That is, until I'm buying my ticket for the next southbound commuter train and the music in my earbud speakers cuts out for an incoming call.

"Hey, Bhauldeen." I say the lawyer's full name with emphatic correctness. That should put him in a favorable mood. "Great timing. I finished packing up the good stuff in Grandma's estate and set aside what she designated to Mom. I left the keys under a yard flamingo—the one wearing an Egyptian mummy headdress, not the nun. Everything should be good to go."

"Not quite," he says.

So much for getting on his good side.

"I know you think I have to stay here to guard Grandma," I edge in before the floodgates of recriminations creak open, "but I think her spirit will feel light and frothy about what I've set up. I've hired a junk removal team to come next week to—"

"It pains me that I have to do this," Baldy says over me. "I'm sorry, Samantha."

A shot of dread punctures the bland, agreeable balloon I've had floating inside me all afternoon, and the feeling drops straight to my toes. It's a cold, frosty terror, like I'm about to be subjected to the ice bucket challenge.

"Sorry about what?" I ask, suspicion leaking into my voice. "Baldy?"

"Iggo Spiggo Diggo Biggo. Tiggo, Liggo bee dud Driggo. Doop."

"Are you having a stroke?"

"By attempting to leave prematurely, you neglect your responsibilities to your grandmother."

I climb the platform staircase, lugging my suitcase behind me. "I just told you, I'm getting very ascendant vibes from her right now. And very subpar scatting vibes from you. I really don't know what genre you're going for, Baldy, but I suggest you workshop it with someone else."

"Doop Doop," repeats Baldy, his tone ominous now. A little . . . otherworldly, if I'm honest. "It is done. When your grandmother's soul ascends, the magic will remove its hold on you, allowing you to travel where you please. Until then, Samantha, you shall remain."

I look around, hoping against hope I'm being live-stream-pranked for TikTok content. No luck. I fight to keep my breathing normal. The air is villainously cold. The other passengers, ignorant of my dilemma. According to the digital sign above the platform, my train arrives in five minutes. And I have to board that train. I *have* to.

Grandma didn't have any real magic. I've got no reason to believe Baldy is truly activating some binding on a magical will. Clinging to my cringey hope, I pull my bag close to my chest and say, "Nice try. You nearly had me, Baldy. Better luck next time."

"Excuse me?" he asks.

No. I'm done with this.

I bang at my earbud until I've hung up on him. BTS's "No More Dream" floods back into my ears. Fighting a raw, shaky feeling, I turn to the tracks. Passengers cluster like drunken vultures near the platform edge, which means my train must be about to arrive.

Good. That's good.

I'm not going to fall victim to your bizarre ploy to keep me here, Grandma Rose: I'm getting on this train. I can make out its headlights in the distance: they're like concert lights sweeping through an audience before the main act comes onstage, and I can't think of a more glorious sight. I feel my breath catch, my knees going weak.

Oh no. I . . . don't feel like I can stand.

The train pulls up to the platform. My heartbeat syncs with the chorus of the song. I tug my suitcase forward.

At once, my knees buckle. And I fall like a heap of laundry with my suitcase toppling over me, the handle smacking the back of my head and knocking out an earbud, to add insult to injury.

I stay that way, a human puddle, three feet from the platform, as the train screeches to a stop. The doors hiss open.

Why can't I get up? Why must my legs fail me now, of all moments?

Weirdos, predictably, pour out of the train. They awkwardly pick their way around my undignified form. Should I ask one of them to help me up? To throw me onboard with my luggage?

Is it worth it, to force them to make eye contact with me when I am basically indistinguishable from a wrung-out towel?

I can't even move my mouth to ask. Also, I think drool is trickling down my jaw.

One by one, passengers step onto the train. I'm forced to watch as the last one hefts a bag with a skeleton print up the carriage steps. One, two, three, four . . . and then there's no one else. A yellow-light-backed hole looms before me, like the light of heaven held out to a dying man. It's calling to me. *Get on, Sabby. Come on.*

Then the doors clamp shut. The machinery grouses as the engines pick up. Only as the train whirs past and air whooshes against my eyeballs does my nausea subside. My breath normalizes. And I regain a sense of having bones.

All too late.

"*No*," I whisper, because my jaw has remembered how to work again.

No. No no no no. The words resound in my skull. The train moves on, abandoning the platform for more heavenly locales, leaving me here in hell. I swear that's what this is, because I feel the flames licking at my newly reusable feet, scalding me as they incinerate my hopes and dreams.

If I can't be in New York by morning, it'll be a disaster. If my senior—the person who is supposed to be my direct supervisor—thinks I'm ghosting on my first day on the job, I'll be let go. Worse, I'll be blacklisted from every major accounting company worldwide. And then what? I worked my ass off to be a top-three student in high school, despite spending over a year living on friends' couches. I worked part-time catering jobs during college, crammed into student housing with awkwardly touching beds. I single-handedly carried our group projects to completion. I got an A in Intermediate Accounting 1! And I abandoned my mattress for weeks, applying for internships. I can't let all of that toiling and misery go to waste.

All one has to do is look at Mom to see what happens to a Spük woman whose dreams of normalcy are thwarted.

It can't be too late to bargain my way out of this.

"Call Baldy," I demand of my phone after plopping my earbud back in. It rings too loud in my ears.

He picks up, and I start talking before he can say anything.

"What if I paid you to make a teeny-tiny amendment to the will? Would it take a hundred bucks? A thousand? I can set up a payment plan with you," I say, fighting to sound calm and measured and businesslike. The bad news is, it sounds more like begging. Okay, so it is begging. I've used up all my savings and was planning to live on credit until getting my first paycheck from EFG. But maybe there's a chance. "I can ask my mom. Not that she has a thousand dollars on hand. Pesos, maybe. Could I send you pesos?"

"Samantha, the will's terms are clear, and you accepted them. I will visit soon to discuss next steps."

Baldy hangs up, and it takes everything in me not to shake my fist at the sky—a sky snuffed out of stars, and moonlight, and any sign of hope whatsoever. I want to let the tears prickling at my eyes embark on a feeble journey to my chin. I want to weep like a destitute medieval maiden who's had her beet harvest stolen by a villainous rogue. Instead, because I'm in public, and because I've already sacrificed all my normalcy capital by temporarily turning into a human puddle, I refuse to become more noticeable in my shame.

I instead resign myself to mentally screaming at Grandma Rose as I crawl to a bench where I can lick my wounds. Another vile October breeze flutters past, prompting a shiver. I squeeze my hands together, annoyed at the crisp fall note in the air. I can practically hear Grandma Rose cackling from above—where, I continue to suspect, she's already ascended, unbeknownst to Baldy and this indecently magical will.

Less than an hour after my train leaves for Penn Station without me, I'm back staring at the feature-flush facade of Grandma Rose's house. Even in the dark, it screams for attention: the two-story home is crammed onto a triangular lot, shaped and painted like a pink piece of pie. Mom never could explain the decision-making behind this. I always assumed someone liked strawberries.

As I wriggle the house key out from under the flamingo's

woven-sandaled foot, Bulan rolls out from a flower bed filled with weeds. Of course he's grinning wildly.

"I knew you weren't really going to leave!" he crows. "A Spük never spooks."

It pains me that I can't prove him wrong.

"I think a worm's stuck in your beard."

He gives himself a solid shake, flinging the poor earthworm to the wind. "Better?"

"Uhh, sure."

"Good. I prefer sleeping on pillows to peat. It's much less squirmy."

Bulan follows me to the front door and bounces up the stairs in hyper little bursts. I don't want him staying with me, exactly, but what kind of person leaves a stray outside on a cool night? It's in the fifties. Though my experience having a beard is limited, I'm guessing that when it comes to warmth, it's no substitute sweater.

"So, so, so," Bulan huffs. "You're back! Does this mean we're doing the wedding after all?"

"Just because I'm here, I'm not—"

"Dave and Amanda are expecting you to do it," reminds Bulan.

"That sounds like a *them* problem," I reply.

After the radiant heat kicks back on in Grandma's house, I settle onto a scruffy, pistachio-green armchair and stare into the dead-eyed gaze of Colin Firth, pondering what I'm going to tell my senior. And taking a moment to review my cruelly manipulated fate in general. Baldy's unnecessarily ornate, and therefore very Grandma-esque, words echo in my ears: *Once I am returned to the earth, my appointed must guard my spirit until the passing of seven tides, low and high, twice over . . .*

It's simple enough to parse the meaning: if the tides roll in and out twice on a twenty-four-hour cycle, then basically, a week after Grandma's funeral, my spirit-guarding work should be complete. Grandma will be ready to pass into the afterlife—and I can leave.

Grandma's funeral was two days ago. If I only have to miss a week of work—most of it basic corporate training—then I'm sure I can figure something out with my company. It has to happen to a lot of people, right? I can't be the only one. I can't be fired over this, surely. Except that when I pull up my firm benefits guide, I find out there are specific exclusions for new employees who haven't accrued PTO. In other words? I'm at the mercy of my senior.

Desperately, I compose an email designed to garner maximal sympathy:

Dear Steve, I have caught a horrible illness . . .

It's not even an exaggeration. My illness is a paranormal curse, and considering that it's come from my own kin, that's pretty horrible.

As I type, I can't help imagining Grandma's unascended soul hovering behind her beloved British actor in this moment. She's rolling her unascended eyes at me. *Tut-tut! You're being dramatic again, Samantha! Just stay here and make the most of it, you lazy girl.*

Offended, I throw a slipper over Colin's shoulder, where I assume Grandma might be.

And yet, I'm considering the point.

I'm considering it because I've spent too long being poor not to realize I have the opportunity to make the best of this situation financially. Haven't I learned that financial security is worth some emotional pain? Not to mention occasional humiliation. Like that time when the fridge died, and my friends caught me storing groceries from the community food pantry using a bag of ice in a bucket beneath the sink.

Four thousand dollars is a *lot* of money. More than enough to cover a few weeks' rent in New York, should my job decide not to pay me.

Realistically, all Dave and Amanda want is for me to arrange a few bouquets and decorate a few tables. Even vampires deserve a nice wedding, right?

Assuming I don't get eaten—or worse, bitten—what's the worst that could happen? It's just one wedding. One toe dipped into Salem's unhinged paranormal world, and then, after the high and low tides are done with their poor tidings, I can go back to New York City like nothing ever happened. Assuming I can pull off a wedding planning gambit, that is. But how hard can that be, anyway?

Seriously, how hard? I haven't attended a wedding since I was five, but the last three years I spent working for a catering team at a hotel in Midtown East, the weddings didn't seem too bad. Sure, there were occasions I dodged angry brides and mothers by hiding behind food carts or extra-leafy ferns. The upside of this is that I have a vague inkling of what wedding planners do.

I don't know the first thing about what to expect from a vampire bride, though. I guess I'm going to have to learn that fast if I want to help pull off a wedding with such high . . . stakes.

Or no stakes, I guess. Those are probably tacky.

As loath as I am to admit it, Bulan isn't the first to praise me for my artistic abilities. When it came to skills with scissors, I was top of my class in pre-K, and I was the well-established corsage-tying person and boutonniere-pinner in my high school friend group. Not to mention that Mom's plunge into plantophile wonderland left me with realms of otherwise useless flower knowledge. I'm organized too—I *had* to be to juggle school and part-time money-earning gigs for the last four and a half years. So, handling florals, décor, and the catering? In other words, the bulk of a wedding planning gig? I can probably manage that okay.

What I'm not ready to do is grapple with all of Salem's more . . . paranormal quirks. So as soon as I finish emailing Steve, my senior, and cc'ing the HR admin who's been helping with my new-hire paperwork, I corner Bulan. Really this just means I place him on a dusty floral wingback chair and loom over him with my hands on my hips.

"Bulan," I say with an air of importance. "If you want to keep living here, you're going to have to help me out. I need you to give me a glow-up."

"A what?"

There's no way he's unfamiliar with these. "You know, a makeover? Like in old chick flicks. Do my hair. Pluck my eyebrows. Lips—"

"Pluck your lips?"

"What? No. I meant put on lipstick. But not like, regular makeup. Give me a *paranormal* makeover. Along with the lowdown on the town's vampires. The witchy ways of witches. Make me Salem-savvy. I've spent almost a decade away. I need to know what I don't know."

How ironic, that I'm having to reacclimate myself to Salem in order to leave it. But it's fine, and temporary. Soon I'll be in the land of no surprises or strangeness, strictly enforced by my new building's community guidelines. And someday, by the forced conformity of my suburb's HOA. I'll look back at this mostly purged memory and see this wedding-related debacle as a sign of my dedication to my dreams.

"I shall happily assist you," Bulan announces. "I do have one condition, though. You must give me a nice hat."

That's absurd. "Why?"

"So that when we're walking in public and I'm talking to you, everyone will think I'm your dummy."

"Oh, I think that already."

"Thank you," says Bulan. "I will choose to take that in the most magnanimous way. BUT WAIT."

Pained, I do. It's now Bulan's turn to put on an air of importance. His ruddy eyebrows flare up, and he pulls himself up to an additional quarter inch of height.

"I require payment," he says.

Of course he does. "Isn't it enough I haven't buried you?"

"I want to binge-watch the first season of *Bridgerton* tonight."

I raise my eyebrows as I consider this. How long has it been since I had time to binge something without needing to do other work at the same time? I've been waiting at least three years to catch up on *Crash Landing on You*, Jungkook's all-time favorite K-drama. My shoulders unknot a bit.

"That's . . . a surprising choice, but doable," I say. "I'd shake on it, but I'm not sure how."

"To the streets!" Bulan calls out, as if I weren't standing directly in front of him. And as if he has a say in the matter, which he doesn't.

Because while I may be temporarily adopting my grandmother's pet talking head and enlisting him in my regrettable schemes, I can hold off my paranormal-adjacent life for business hours tomorrow.

Before that, I'm going to order dinner delivered straight to Grandma's house. You know, a Last Meal, like prisoners get before execution.

A Last Meal with a side of *Bridgerton*.

6

THE ONLY NORMAL PERSON IN SALEM

WHILE IT'S TRUE I'VE DECIDED TO HELP TWO LOVESTRUCK vampires enter a state of bloodless nuptial bliss, and I'm missing out on my first day of work—the day I've dreamed of for years—there is one silver lining: I get to attend an extra session of my Becker live online class. This licensing exam review is a critical trauma-bonding experience for all new CPAs. So I join the Zoom room five minutes before 9 a.m. on Monday, settling in as usual with my phone, a spiral notepad, and less-than-as-usual, with one of Grandma's gaudy skull-capped gel pens. Come on, Grandma Rose—haven't you ever heard of Bic? Number 2 pencils? Sharpies?

I do admit the nub glides smoothly.

Anyway, it's midday once I'm done streaming the lecture, reorganizing my notes, and reviewing my daily flash cards. I still haven't heard back from anyone at EFG about my illness or the fact that I haven't come in for my first day of work.

So that's encouraging.

I should probably try and block it out.

Outside on the streets of Salem, a cold front has breezed across the sidewalks. My walk crackles with unnecessarily crisp, earthy, autumnal scents. The witchy, woo-woo foot traffic picks up steadily as I approach downtown. To make myself feel better, I decide to think of the experience like a Target run the week before Christmas: a lot of bustle, a bit of tired, a hint of manic, and a pickle-juice shot of weird.

Not that I'm helping the situation by walking around with a severed head under my arm.

"Let's start with Derby Square," Bulan says, because he's merciless.

"Eww."

"What's wrong with that?" he objects against my backpack strap.

"That's where all the ghost tours meet up."

Never mind that we're essentially going on a paranormal tour of Salem too. Here's what's different: I'm not in Halloween socks, vaping herbal medicine, or carrying a hand-carved pagan wand. Already I hate that my lack of seasonal fervor makes me stand out against the crowds and the moody, burgundy-hued brick buildings—my just deserts for being the only normal person in Salem.

Also, this alley smells like pee.

Nose twitching, I nonetheless carry Bulan, who is proudly wearing a purple-sequined bucket hat, to the stately rear of Old Town Hall. This is where we are assaulted by a tourist holding a wet gyro wrapped in a map.

"Are you here for the two p.m. crypt tour too?" he asks. He looks like he's been couch surfing. No judgment there. Having slept on countless sofas myself, I can churn up a sense of kinship for this tourist. We both know what it's like to test the limits of dry shampoo.

Inexplicably, before I can answer the disheveled brunette, Bulan announces: "We're here for an exorcism!"

"Wow." The tourist laughs around his sloppy cabbage. "You're an amazing ventriloquist!"

There goes the kinship. "Thanks."

"Do another!"

"Well, how about—" says Bulan, but I bustle us away before the cabbage eater asks how far my puppetry skills go. Or how I'm performing with both hands visible. I wonder if Bulan enacted some kind of magic when he held a Sharpie in his teeth and drew on the inside of his newly acquired hat. It would make as much sense as anything else he did.

As I leave the tourist and Derby Square behind, Bulan dolefully turns his eyes up at me. They're annoyingly blue and adorable and devious, like a husky puppy's.

"Aww," he says. "I had a good joke lined up, Sabby."

Of course this is what I get for being nice and taking him out of my bag. Under my breath, I hiss at my fake-puppet overlord, "Why did you want to start here anyway?"

"Because this lovely place is where my ship first landed in 1803!" Bulan says. "Back then it was dreadfully boring. The homes had no central heating. Or plumbing. And most witches were still hiding from Puritans in the woods and befriending the Algonquin, who sadly found me terrifying. All I had for company were mermaids and—"

"Stop. I don't want your life story, Head. I need to know more about vampires so I can pull off a wedding for them. That's it."

"History is important." Bulan sniffs. "It explains why we are the way we are, as a community and as individuals. Aren't you the least bit curious about me?"

"Nope," I say. "Mostly because I think you're having me on. The water line's over five hundred feet away. People would've noticed mermaids flopping across the pavement."

"Well, obviously the waterline moved over several centuries, Sabby. They're not here anymore, anyway; they've retired to Winter Island. We used to have a pickpocketing merm at the wharf, though. Your grandmother would bring trinkets for her to steal on purpose whenever she felt like cleaning out the junk drawers.

"As for that particular mermaid," he goes on, hat slipping over his thick eyebrows and heavily lidded eyes, "plenty enough rubbish is carried on the currents these days, so she doesn't come out much. I hear she's built a small junk kingdom down in the bay. Also, that she summers in Nantucket."

"Uh-huh," I say absentmindedly. Since Bulan isn't in the mood to supply me with useful information, I allow myself to meander backward into childhood memories. Grandma sometimes took me fishing around the wharf, back before she let her friends attempt to kill me ritualistically. Around the corner was a secret garden I loved. I wonder if it's still intact, or if the city turned it into a tourist trap with fake headstones and skulls.

". . . and that's why the merfolk and the kelpies are now thickest of friends with the— Sabby, are you listening?"

I lift the floppy, sparkling brim of Bulan's hat so we can get eye-to-eye.

"I told you, I want to know about vampires. Not this other stuff."

"Why?" he whines. "I never had to explain anything so basic to Rose."

"Right, but I'm Sabby. Different person. My mom and grandma loved the idea of vampires and anything that had to do with"—I throw up finger quotes with my spare, un-head-laden hand—"'*the Community*.' I was never interested."

"Whyever not?"

"Seriously? Why would I want to know about your super-weird paranormal world when I could break the generational cycle, attend college, and have a safe, predictable life? With steady meals and a couch that has never doubled as a mushroom farm?"

"Rosie always hoped you would outgrow your beige phase."

Of course that's what she called it. I turn to avoid the caress of a maple-leaf-addled breeze and say, "Vampires. Now."

Bulan relents.

"All right," he says. "Vampires are not, in fact, undead, nor are they humans suffering from an unfortunate medical condition. What are they, then? Their own species—with beautiful bone structure, a gift with words, and *terrible* osteoporosis. Their teeth can't handle heavy chomping, so they prefer a liquid diet."

"You mean blood?"

"True, they are known to drink blood, but not for the reasons you might think! Vampires are quite sustainably minded and they prefer to consume as eco-consciously as possible. Blood is a renewable resource, you see."

"Unless you over-drink and kill your victim."

"Oh, certainly," my spherical tour guide agrees. "It's best to avoid that. Alas, vampires have been known to farm humans from time to time. It's led to a bad reputation."

"Shocking," I say. I find myself picturing two vampires in overalls, holding pitchforks: an undead *American Gothic*. "What about sunlight? Is that a problem?"

"Indeed. Their skin is about as weak as their bones."

"That's rough. They're not good at much, are they?"

"They do live forever," points out Bulan.

"Yes, but so do jellyfish."

"I didn't know that! I should visit the beach and start a conversation with one soon. See if they have any tips for longevity . . ."

We've arrived at my secret garden at this point. I'm pleased to see it's remained intact, and better still, no one lurks nearby. Inspiration striking, I set Bulan on a bench, dig into my backpack, and break out my wire cutters, gloves, and folded duffel bag.

"Sabby," says Bulan with a nervous twinge to his voice, "why do you have that?"

"I came prepared to work. With what you've told me about vamps, I'm starting to have a floral vision. A budding wedding concept. So I'm going to nab a few plants while we're here." Shriveled-up flowering ones. I've a feeling they'll please my undead couple. It'll remind them of their coffins, right? So earthy. So dead.

"I see," says Bulan.

"The flowers here are organic and local, so they should be vampire-ethics approved."

"It *has* been a while since I had legs, so I may not be up to date on human culture at large, but I'm fairly certain florists purchase the items they require, rather than steal them."

"I'm broke."

"You could use your down payment for the wedding instead of resorting to theft," Bulan says.

A down payment? I could've asked for one of those? Crap.

"Well, never mind that now," says Bulan with an over-the-top sigh. "I'll chirp if I see the police."

"Thanks a mil."

The first plant I snip at the stem is wilted aconite. Bulan peers over my arm, brushing his fuzzy mustache and nose against my wrist.

"Is that wolfsbane?" he asks. "It is. Why, Sabby, I suspect you knew that!"

"Every spring and winter break, my mom force-fed me books about her favorite herbs. She called it 'science class.' She continued the tradition until she ran off to Mexico."

"Oh, when was that? After you finished your education?"

"More or less." I carefully lay the toxic plant in my bag and turn my attention to a pocket of red-leaved New England asters. "Mom put the bills on autopay. I'm super independent, so I was fine by myself."

It's mostly true. I mean, there *was* that late August night when Mom's credit card defaulted, the power got turned off, and the food in our fridge spoiled. And when I opened the freezer, some of her weirder plant seeds had sprouted legs. They were running and sliding around on a half-frozen puddle of Ben & Jerry's. Which should've stopped me from eating them, but I was a starving teen.

They tasted better than you'd think.

Once I left for college, it became easier to rely on myself. I manipulated my course load, cramming in classes back-to-back so I could maximize the number of shifts I took at the hotel. Being a working student meant joining fewer college clubs than I might've liked, and I ended up with a social circle very much on the smaller side of small, but my NYU meal plan wasn't going to pay for itself. Besides, I really didn't want to fight rats for pizza slices. Or scrounge around inside the dumpsters behind my dormitory hall. People vape back there. They would've *noticed*.

Having no home to return to over break was only lonely the first few times. But you can make bank working at a hotel during a peak season, like the holidays and summer. The best part was, I always ended up taking home an absurd amount of leftover turkey and cranberry sauce in Tupperware. By the time I graduated, I'd saved enough plastic containers to build a small airplane, or possibly a boat. On the last night before move-out, I bequeathed it all stealthily to the second-floor hall populated by engineers. It's quite possible I created a fire hazard. But I like to think of it as me having offered them a hands-on learning opportunity.

Mom didn't send me a graduation gift, but theoretically she understands I've accomplished a milestone and is proud of me for cinching my internship and job offer to EFG. I know this because I call her once a week and she answers about once a month. At times, the connection can be a little shaky, almost like her voice is coming from behind an electronic curtain, but it's fine. For all I know, it's a consequence of dropping her phone repeatedly in the resort pool.

In spite of her flakiness, I really thought Mom would make an effort to attend Grandma Rose's funeral. I can only guess that, like me, she never expected her mom to die. Maybe she hasn't come to terms with her grief yet.

Or maybe it's something else. One of her herbs? Is she a cactus juice addict now? Maybe she's found a form of it that sprouts whole bodies instead of just legs and has made herself a nice big surrogate succulent family.

Bulan coughs, alerting me to the fact that I've gone tellingly silent.

"I now see why you had so little sympathy when you found me alone in that closet," he says.

Is Bulan pitying me? I detect pity. Nope, not having that. Rather than look at him, I survey the withered plant zoo in search of my next moody specimen.

"You were fine," I say, reshouldering my bag. "You escaped my duffel, didn't you?"

"Consider the difficulty I encountered! You have arms. I miss arms."

"They require sunscreen. It gets expensive."

"Hmm. An interesting point."

As Bulan mulls this over, I refocus on my procurement task and aim for the rosebushes. After all, roses *are* Classic Romance. To my annoyance, most of the branches have already been cut back ahead of first frost. Hmm. Would it be terrible if I uprooted the scraggliest of the scraggly bushes? Probably not. I'd be doing the gardeners a favor.

As I get on my knees and prepare for some dramatic deadheading, a squirrel twitters in a tree above us, rustling acorns to the ground.

At this, my mind turns to the mysterious Hanry Burleson.

It's unexpected, yet I can't help it. It's all this foraging. The fact that I'm breaking and entering again. And the fact that Hanry, in spite of being rugged and the size of a tree, had eyes that caught in the moonlight with an endearingly boyish glint, and I thought I'd never see him again, but now, if I'm stuck in Salem—for a few more days, anyway—who knows?

"So, Head," I say in an intentionally offhanded way. "What did you think of that guy we met in the cemetery Friday night?"

"I didn't officially meet him," says Bulan. "You know, with my being in a bag, escaping your murder attempt and all."

I scrape aside dirt. "I'll rephrase. Should I be worried he's sicced vampires on me?"

"I wouldn't be! From the sound of it, he was desperate to help his friends. And as far as I know, there isn't anyone else with your alleged talents on the North Shore."

I allow that thought to simmer for a moment. "So . . . you're saying he's a gentle, sociable giant?"

"I'm saying that I should warn you: news travels fast in Salem's circles. I'm sure you'll have a good number of visitors this week, hoping for similar services."

"I hope you're wrong," I say.

It's EOD when my phone finally blows up with calls from a New York City area code.

Steve chews me out in a twenty-minute-long, unsubtly misogynistic tirade. Yes, of course I understand my ratings will take a hit before I've started my first day. I do realize my colleagues will be forced to take on a heavier workload for our tech client, MicroOrange, in my absence. As punishment for getting sick, it's only fair I miss out on the pizza party later this month. These are the burdens we must bear when horribly, yet ambiguously, ill.

I promise to send a doctor's note to HR. Then I squeeze my eyes shut, repeating affirmations to myself in a desperate attempt to drop my heart rate. *A year from now, no one will remember this, Sabby! You'll be seen as a predictable employee! Actually, you won't be seen as anything at all, and when it's time for ratings, Steve will have mistaken you for Jane and forgotten to fill out your assessment.*

Unfortunately, I'm catching notice amid the paranormal community too. Over the next two days, I'm forced to talk to no less than two more vampires, a werewolf, a druidess, a scuba instructor named Joe, and a polyamorous trio of banshees. They track me down at Grandma's shop, ignoring the closed shutters. The sign that reads OPEN: *NEVER*. It's possible I could have avoided them by staying at Grandma's house, juggling studying for my CPA exam, making floral arrangements, and dialing increasingly frantic calls to Dave and Amanda under the lustful gaze of cardboard Colin Firth. Their wedding night, Saturday, is closing in fast.

But Grandma's house isn't a better option. Every morning, her friends reappear in the yard to dress the flamingos in new outfits. Once, Matilda has the audacity to knock on the door and caw something about "checking on me." Provocations from the witch cabal aside, Grandma never installed Wi-Fi—whereas her shop neighbors a kitschy café with free Wi-Fi under the moniker HEEBYJEEBIES. Hopefully that's not how you're supposed to feel when you eat their sandwiches.

I tough it out all the way into Wednesday. By this point, Bulan no longer registers as a part of my day-to-day weirdness. I find myself forgetting he's bodiless more often than not. He seems to have warmed up to me too, and he supports and advises me through the visitations from paranormal characters. He chirrups helpful prompts to keep me from saying or doing anything too egregiously offensive. Once, he proves utterly invaluable: I'm not sure what it is, exactly, but The Unmentionable Thing that slides up to the storefront has the general build of an overstuffed garbage bag. Its stench reminds me of a fire ring at a summer beach party: a noxious tornado of dancing adolescent beach sweat, stale beer, and burnt marshmallows. Even though we're separated by windows and a door, the affliction to my sinus cavity is extreme. I crouch closer toward my laptop, determined to stay focused on my MCQs.

Bulan acts like he's dying.

"Closed," he gasps at the door, "for—business!"

I glance up.

"Don't make eye contact!" Bulan croaks. Then, furiously, he whispers: "As a general rule, if a being smells like fire or destruction, it's best to keep away. Even Rosie did that."

Grouchily, I say, "I'd think the appearance of that Thing would be telling enough."

"I'm teaching you principles."

"You're interrupting my studying," I say. Then I shove my bump-bridged nose deeper into my McGraw-Hill review book.

Bulan rolls his eyes, then his whole head-body for good measure. I pretend not to be amused, much less grateful for his help with The Unmentionable Thing. Same as I pretend I'm not existentially jarred by encountering a heaving bag of doom.

By Thursday, my anxiety is becoming unbearable. It wouldn't be so bad cobbling together the décor for Dave and Amanda's dream wedding if they would just accept my phone calls. Instead the most I get are sporadic and random disorganized texts, with them attempting to describe their wedding vision and complaining about their previous wedding planner either dropping out or dropping dead—I'm not sure which, but either way, it's too dramatic. They refuse to come back to the shop in person, because *the sun is too draining*, and they won't Zoom because video calls are *too novel*. The only clear desire they successfully share for their wedding comes from Dave, who wants everything to be *dark, so very dark*.

When I finally manage to reach Dave and Amanda on Thursday night, the call feels like an exercise in futility.

"Do you want a rehearsal tomorrow?" I ask. "After dark, right?"

"No, no, it'll be hard enough to get everyone there for the

wedding," says Dave. I nod, understanding. I'm familiar with this kind of friend group.

"No problem. Can we rehearse on Saturday? In the early evening?"

"I don't like the word *hearse*," says Amanda.

"Fine. We'll wing it."

"Winging it is perfect," moans Dave. "We have the right equipment."

I think he's missing the point, but hey—not my wedding, not my flying monkeys.

Or bats. It's probably going to be bats.

"So just checking, you don't have any preference for where you stand during the ceremony?"

"No," the couple says in unison.

"And you don't care about the order of the ceremonies?" After a pause, I correct myself. "Ceremony?"

"No, we don't, so long as we're carried into the room in our coffins," says Dave, giving me new information he could've shared earlier. "The coffins are very important."

Amanda puts in, "He needs it to be dark."

"Very dark."

"Noted," I say, rubbing my temples.

In desperation, I ask ChatGPT: "What do you need to do to prepare for a sixty-head wedding that's last-minute? Also, I have no budget and the guests aren't human." Its answer is . . . questionable. Thankfully, I find super-detailed DIY checklists on Pinterest for brides planning their own weddings. And I scour my memories of the handful of events I'd catered at the hotel. It's a total headache, and by this point I'm not sure that the four thousand dollars is going to be worth it.

If I ever see Hanry Burleson the graveyard forager again, I am going to give him a piece of my mind. And possibly hurl a bunch of pine cones at him.

By the end of Friday evening, I feel as ready as I can be. I've pulled together: a bridal bouquet, replete with dead beetles; an assortment of bridesmaid bouquets and boutonnieres, with the pins replaced with Command hooks and Velcro so no one gets any ideas about stabbing; centerpieces for the four banquet tables; and, because I'm an overachiever—make no mistake, that accounting degree from NYU was nowhere near a cakewalk—a garland for a wedding arch, composed of vines stripped from a spare lot nearby; and finally, lumber for the arch itself. Plus hammers, nails, and scissors and stuff. Pulling out my credit card with the greatest regret, I rent an SUV to carry everything to the wedding venue. In a moment of generosity, I suggest wedding singers. One of my NYU friends who moved to Boston for work moonlights as lead guitar for his cover band, the Vampire Weekenders. Judging by his sad posts on social media, they've been suffering for opportunities to play gigs. What am I, if not a good friend?

As I'm perfecting the last centerpiece, ensuring it looks genuinely spectacular—if you're into Gothic nightmares—I get a final unexpected visitor to the shop: Baldy.

"Samantha," he calls from outside. "Samanthaaa. Samaaaaaantha!"

I don't look up, too busy shaping Oasis, the professional-grade floral foam that holds arrangements in place. YouTube tells me that once you chip the green stuff off, there's no going back. But I'm precise. I'm focused. I'm a goddamn floral Michelangelo.

"Samantha, since you haven't checked your mail, I've brought documents for you to sign."

I jump from my seat, flinging the Oasis aside. Anything that must be done on paper has to be Serious.

"One second," I call out. I scramble to find the keys to the door—until I think better of finding them. Here's my problem: it wouldn't be good if Baldy laid his eyes on the torso-impaired head near my laptop, slurping Diet Pepsi through a straw. It's not just Bulan I need to protect, either. I don't trust Baldy to ignore me running a business in violation of local tax law. So I settle for shouting, which is, frankly, rewarding in and of itself. I've more than earned some stress relief.

"What are the papers for?"

"They affirm your understanding of the estate's debt and all its outstanding bills."

"Amazing. Could you let Grandma's creditors know I'm going to have the money to start paying them back by Sunday night? And let the courts know too? Also, the . . . magical courts? Also, question. When Grandma's soul ascends, how will I know?"

"I suspect there will be confetti," he says.

"Really?"

"No," says Baldy. "I have not witnessed such an event myself."

He presses his oily forehead against the glass, marring it horrifically.

"What are you doing in there, Samantha? The tables, they're looking . . . fuller than before. On our call, you said you had finished inventory and clean-out, so why—"

"Happy Halloween! See you."

I pull the curtain closed on him.

"Thank you," says Bulan. He squints up at me with gratitude. "The glare from his head was hurting my eyes."

"So true," I agree. "Now, hold this butcher paper between your teeth and help me wrap this up."

7

NATURALLY, EVERYTHING GOES WRONG THE ONE TIME I'M AT RISK OF BEING EATEN

ON SATURDAY MORNING, I WAKE TO THE SOUNDS OF SCREAMING outside the guest room window. A quick survey later, I've determined it's a flash-mob re-creation of *Moby-Dick* on e-scooters. I can almost appreciate that, for its novel lack of witchery.

Rubbing my eyes, I observe the street performers in their pop-art-inspired costumes, simulating a harpoonist and a dying whale. Are they less dignified than me and my paranormal wedding planner charade for two vampires? Debatable.

Buoyed by the thought, I drop the blinds and get to work. Today's the day of Dave and Amanda's wedding—and more importantly, it's the day Grandma should theoretically ascend, following the final high tide peaking in Salem Harbor at 9:02 p.m. I finish the last of the floral arrangements, pack the rental SUV with décor, plunk Bulan in the front seat, and get going.

Around two p.m., two and a half hours before the ceremony is scheduled to begin, I roll up to the wedding venue on Salem's outskirts. Dave and Amanda told me they'd chosen a traditional venue. The place was invisible on Google Maps Street View, so I'm startled by our arrival at a gray, three-story Victorian mansion. Maybe calling it a mansion is too generous. The word "mansion" implies a building you can live in. If I'm being nice—just kidding, I'm definitely not—this place has the look of a bed-and-breakfast that's fallen on the wrong side of a Hallmark movie treatment. The trees are withered, the flower beds chronically neglected. The roof is . . . gone. It's the kind of disaster that would make a jaded heroine realize her city job *is* the shit after all.

"I've never been in a relationship long enough to think about getting married," I say as I park in the empty circle-drive, "but I know I definitely wouldn't choose here."

"Where *would* you choose?" Bulan asks with interest.

"A registrar. Courthouse. Maybe a hotel package. Something ordinary."

"You're a terrible wedding planner," he says.

"Thank you."

But an *actually* terrible wedding planner would dump the décor and flowers and flee immediately upon seeing the state of the venue. I, on the other hand, pack up the rented dolly and lead it to the foyer in hopes of finding the venue coordinator. At least two TikTok wedding planners explained that venue coordinators exist to guide wedding planners around, unlocking rooms and feeding planners sparkling water and gossip. From my experience at the hotel, sometimes a random employee gets the short straw for the day or, as punishment for something else, gets pulled into the position.

No matter what, there's always, *always* a venue coordinator. A wedding planner would never get free rein. Without supervision, their transformation of a venue can do a lot of damage, down to the studs.

So I enter the foyer, wielding the décor-packed dolly ahead of me like a shield, and call out, "Hello? Anyone here?"

Beyond the black-and-white checkerboard tiled entryway, the building interior fades into darkness, with no reception area in sight. It's not my favorite, but it totally matches Mr. Dark Dave's vibe—the only indication so far I'm at the right place.

"Hello? Hell-ooo?"

Bulan joins from my arms. "Hell-o-nnff?" He's straining as if holding back a sneeze. Uncomfortable with the idea of his bodily fluid being ejected over me, I place him on the dolly.

"Are you naming me the navigator of this doomed ship?" he asks.

"No, I'm calling for the venue coordinator. Think they're using the bathroom?"

"Maybe they took the life raft," says Bulan.

Being that we're located in inland Massachusetts, not by the sea, I ignore him. We use my phone light to claw through the hallway, searching in vain for bathrooms. At long last we discover a ballroom. Flickering candle sconces dimly light the curtained space. I guess the coordinator arranged that before bailing. It seems they did little else: the four dusty long tables beg for linens; the curtains are stained with either mud, blood, or a severe misuse of jam; and the pattern of the historic wallpaper is interrupted with either black mold or something less sanitary.

It's . . . not great. Even for fashion-impaired, undead vampires. Maybe I should've discussed the room's layout a *little* more with Dave and Amanda before arriving for setup. And asked them when the catering would arrive with freshly laundered black linens for the tables. And maybe I should've required a guarantee I'm not breaking and entering an abandoned seasonal haunted house.

Oh well. At least our decorations will rock this aesthetic.

"Let's get dark," I say to Bulan. I go for a high five before I remember he can't really do that. "Whoops, my bad."

"It's okay," says Bulan. "I appreciate the effort."

He means it, too. Bulan has a creative, upbeat spirit. And he's surprisingly adept at pulling tape and cutting ribbons with his teeth. Unfortunately, there's a limit to the support he can offer. Each trip to and from the SUV sucks more than the last as I haul in heavy hurricane vases, buckets of brittle dead plants, activated charcoal water, and more. I'm starting to regret my choice to use a dolly and not a wagon. At least my vision comes together fast for the table arrangements. It takes mere moments to re-fluff and re-pose the little flower corpses. While I'm double-checking the number of place settings and chairs, a loud noise interrupts my focus. From the void of the hallway, a figure emerges, cradling his head as if he's hit it on a low overhang.

Instead of having a heart attack, somehow I recognize him.

"Hanry!"

There's a reason I didn't recognize him right away: unlike last time, my cemetery forager is all dressed up. His white button-down, paired with navy suspenders, accentuates the solid span of his chest. The hulk of his shoulders. The pressed chinos and unscuffed Chelsea boots. For a nocturnal lumberjack, he cleans up nice. *Real* nice. My heart's beating even faster now—and probably faster than it did when he first found me on Grandma Rose's grave. I feel as if I'm looking at Hanry for the first time. Except the sparks are even more intense than our first meeting, probably because I'm not distracted with committing a minor crime.

"Samantha!" he calls back. "Or is it Sabby?"

"Sabby," I confirm. He holds eye contact with me, approaching in an alarmingly short number of strides.

At once, I realize that I am wearing: a black apron, the sparkly Crocs I bought when I was thirteen, and a black turtleneck that covers a cross necklace I found in Grandma Rose's flamboyant costume jewelry jar. My hair is up in a basic claw clip. Bulan looks slightly more the part of a wedding guest. He insisted on another nice hat—this time a top hat—which I've tied firmly around his chin-butt. I never thought I'd be jealous of a head, but here we are.

"I'm leaving right after the ceremony," I inform Hanry, rather than greeting him like a normal person. "That's why I'm underdressed."

"Oh."

"The venue is supposed to take care of the send-off. Not me. So."

Hanry seems to accept that. Now that he isn't weighed down by his forager's knapsack, he stands at a more impressive height than I remembered. It's annoying. Rude, even. I was planning to chew him out for foisting this job on me and assuming I'm the type to casually interact with vampires. But the height and the suspenders are too damn distracting.

"A shame you won't be staying longer," Hanry says in a congenially towering fashion. "I was looking forward to you being here."

Again: how annoying.

"Well, I'm here now."

"As am I."

Wow. This is a great conversation, not the least bit awkward.

In a moment of unexpected empathy, Bulan rescues me. He asks, "What brought you here early, Hanry? Are you a groomsman?"

In order to see us, Bulan has rolled onto his ear at the expense of his hat. This reveals a strip of tape stuck to the wiry red hair on his upper lip. Neither the presence of a talking head nor its poor sense of hygiene fazes Hanry.

"I came here to check in on you," Hanry says to me. Then to Bulan: "Hello."

"Hello," Bulan says.

I return his top hat to its proper position, to preserve what little there is of Bulan's dignity. I also consider ripping the tape off his wiry red mustache, but no: I've got bigger fish to fry. Bigger ones, even, than the question of how seemingly human Hanry is wrapped up in the paranormal community, and why he was foraging in the graveyard, and how he got so damn tall. I'm here to get this wedding picture-perfect, so I must correct the wonky shape of this cobwebbed branch amid my shriveled fungus kebabs. It's not a centerpiece if it's off-center, right?

While I work, Hanry surveys the shabby, near-festive mess of the ballroom. I watch him from the corner of my eye.

"What do you think?" I ask. Because for some reason, I care about his opinion.

"Everything looks great," he says.

My chest gets unexpectedly warm and fuzzy. "Thanks."

"Can I help you put anything away?"

I puzzle at him. "We've only just started decorating. We need to do finishing touches on the other tables, put together the ceremony room, set out chairs and signage. Then I'll give the bridal party their bouquets and pin on some boutonnieres . . ."

"Huh," says Hanry. "Isn't everyone arriving in an hour?"

I don't appreciate that kind of joke, but I still fake-laugh, right until I realize he isn't teasing. I check my phone. It's already four.

"Where the hell did the time go?!" I mutter to myself.

Bulan answers from the floor. "Don't look at me, Sabby. I'm not your timekeeper!"

"Are you going to be okay?" Hanry asks.

Am I?

Filling one last hurricane vase with charcoal water, I say as lightly as possible, "Well, I definitely won't be able to complete the wedding arch. Which is the most important job of this whole wedding. I hope no one eats me alive for it. Ha ha."

"Wedding arch?"

That's such a boy move, not knowing what a wedding arch is, or why its inexistence seals my doom. I set a bloodred tea light inside the hurricane vase, sprinkle burgundy rose petals around it, and release a sigh.

"Theoretically, I'm supposed to make one for Amanda. As a backdrop for her nuptials."

"I don't know what a wedding arch is," Hanry says, confirming my suspicions, "but I'm a decent hand at woodworking, if you'd like some help."

He seems to be genuine. If only to spite him for drawing me into this mess in the first place, I say, "Sure, that would be great. You can help me escape with my life here."

Now, only *now*, Hanry laughs as if I were joking. And he lights up as much as anyone can in a room that's basically an ink stain. Rather than comment on it, I dump the remaining petals at the end of the table to form a flowery pool of blood. Then I leave Bulan to play fake-Roomba again, sucking stems and scraps from the floor, while I lead Hanry to my rental.

I've always had a thing for strong guys. I think it's like how people get a kick out of hugging redwood trees they can't reach their arms around. It's embarrassing, but what can you do? I slyly planned study sessions as close to the NYU fitness center as possible. Once, it resulted in romance—a guy named Marcus and I dated in the spring of junior year. It seemed like it was going somewhere, until it wasn't.

Hanry has better arms than Marcus anyway.

I try to keep up a normal conversation and not ogle too much as Hanry handily thrusts all five pieces of the wedding arch over his shoulder. This goal is helped, once we return inside, by the branching hallways' deep, disturbing darkness.

"Do you think the venue coordinator bailed?" I ask conversationally. "Or got drained?"

"Third option," Hanry says. "They never showed. Knowing Dave and Amanda, those two would've forgotten to put down money to secure the venue."

I nearly drop my phone. Considering that my phone flashlight is all that lights the hallway, that'd be a bad move.

"Shit, Hanry. We're trespassing?"

"Maybe. But what's it matter? We're surrounded by vampires."

"And that's supposed to make me feel *safe*? Why are you friends with vamps, again?"

Hanry jostles the wood on his shoulder. I think he's shrugging. "We met at a salsa class. They're nice, as vampires go."

Wow. I can't imagine a more banal explanation for befriending nonhuman beings. But I'm also curious about the dancing.

"I had you pegged as a woodsy person." Or a criminal. "Not a late-night-dancing person."

"The term I like is 'Renaissance man.' I'm full of surprises. To the point I surprise myself sometimes," says Hanry. "Hey, do you think this is the ceremony room?"

We pause, having arrived at a pair of monstrous double doors made of glass and iron and begging for rust cleaners and Windex.

"The greenhouse? Should be."

In spite of the dust, something's visible beyond the other side of the door. A few moving orbs of green light, reflecting in fractal patterns over the greenhouse's glassy walls. I work hard to ignore the pit opening in my stomach.

"The bride and groom haven't arrived yet, have they?" I ask.

"Don't think so. They're getting ready off-site before their grand entrance. Wanted to make sure it was dark out before they left for the wedding," Hanry says, his attention divided between our conversation and the scene beyond the glass. He frowns but otherwise doesn't move. Because there's no sense in standing here, dreading whatever I'm going to dread anyway, I push the doors open, scattering dust over our heads.

"Dave!" I call out. "Amanda?"

Coughing, Hanry says, "Sabby, no. Those folks don't look like Amanda or Dave."

No. They don't. Those folks—who are now visible in the center of the greenhouse—look nothing like our soon-to-be-wedded couple. In fact, they aren't the least bit vampiric.

Or opaque.

That's because said "folks" aren't living at all. They're ghosts . . . I think? The six beings hovering in the center of the room are distinctly wispier-looking than regular humans. With gloomy expressions, they're moving in circular patterns as if on a fixed track, à la Disney World's Haunted Mansion.

They are also significantly noisier.

"Is that . . . music?" I ask, pained.

Hanry winces with me. "I think so?"

Goddamn ghosts acting like they own the place. I don't have time for this. "I am *not* going to be blamed for tone-deaf ghosts ruining my wedding setup," I declare.

"Maybe we can ignore them and hold the ceremony on the other side of the room?"

I snort. "Do you think anyone could ignore those outfits?"

Because I couldn't. The ghosts' clothes redefine the term "ghastly." I'm talking puffed silk sleeves and flower crowns; flamboyant suits with untenable pant hems they'd trip on if they weren't hovering. One has a vintage silver microphone stand in their skeletal clutches like an Elvis impersonator in hippie busker drag.

Hanry shifts the giant beams on his shoulder. "I'm guessing this is your first time dealing with ghosts."

"It's not yours?"

"I've heard things," says Hanry. "Enough to know they can't hurt anyone. Ghosts are self-absorbed, focused on their unfinished business. Poltergeists are the ones you have to worry about."

I shiver a little, rubbing at my arms. "It's freezing in here. How can we warm this place up?"

"Before you suggest it, a bonfire would burn us down in a minute."

I side-eye him. "Who said anything about starting a fire?"

"You look like you could commit arson," Hanry says. "You've got an edgy vibe."

"Moving on," I say, because if I'm being called "edgy," then this wedding is bringing out the absolute worst in me. Something that might be bordering on a similarity to Grandma Rose. "We need to get these ghosts out. Can we make mousetraps? Use ghost pepper spray? Do you think this venue has vacuums?"

"The only guaranteed way to get rid of ghosts is resolving their unfinished business. But that could take weeks. It's not worth trying."

I scowl at this and try to manifest a plan. This room is where Amanda's supposed to join with Dave in actual-forever-love. To walk down the aisle—or fly down it in bat form? I don't know how this works.

As I fight not to hyperventilate, my phone buzzes in my apron pocket. *James*, the caller ID reads. James?! Why is he—oh, that's right, I hired him to come tonight.

Oh. *Oh*.

"Hey, how is 'unfinished business' defined, exactly?" I ask, fixing my gaze on a wannabe rockabilly ghost. "'Cause I'm betting we can give these ghosties some *new* business to worry about instead."

"Sabby! Look at you, so profesh!"

James barrels out of his vintage station wagon to wrap me in a hug. The last time I saw him, he had taken a break from interview prep to busk in Washington Square Park. He's now sporting a bright-pink fauxhawk, which seems at odds with New England's office culture. I'd comment on this, except there's literally no time.

"I'm super great," I say after he releases me. "Thanks for driving up last minute. Let's get you inside. Come on."

"There's so much to catch up on! Your new business, your grandmother. God, I'm sorry for your loss. It *was* a loss, right? You were so cryptic in your texts."

"Inside, inside," I say.

It's probably best to get him and the band out of the parking lot. Now that twilight has fallen, the mansion's pitched roof glows like a marijuana dispensary sign. James, as usual, has not noticed. He's not one of those "noticing" people. It took him almost a month working at his public accounting internship before he realized they were calling him the wrong name, so of course it's escaped him that this place is haunted. Moreover, he's unflappable in the face of my brisk tone. As is his equally fauxhawked boyfriend, Eric. Like attracts like and all that.

"It was so sweet of you to invite us to play," says Eric. When James steps back, he gives me a friendly squeeze. "You never know when the big break's coming. Maybe this is it! We can leave our day jobs behind!"

"Yeaaah," I say. James and his well-meaning, if slightly less-than-destined-for-stardom bandmates enthusiastically unpack the trunk. "It's a themed wedding. I told you that, right?"

"You did," chirps James. "We brought glittery eye shadow and pumpkin earrings."

"The best we could do on short notice," Eric laments.

"Look!" The third member of James's band, the bassist—James called him Remy? I think? It seems to change every other month or so—pulls out a sign. It looks like it was made for a car wash. "I made this so everyone can follow us on socials."

"That's so earnest," I say, because I don't know how else to compliment him. "Now, I know you've got to do a sound check before the reception—"

"Yeah, we should do one of those!" says Eric.

"—but I need you to handle something else first. The groom's family is making trouble."

This is a little bit of an exaggeration. A white lie. A white avalanche of a lie. I'm a bad person.

Then again, how bad could my plan be if I've gotten Hanry and Bulan on board with it, too?

"What kind of trouble?" asks James, whose giddy excitement remains unabated. I lean in conspiratorially.

"They want to play the wedding."

Back in the ballroom, Bulan has concealed himself in a garbage can with my phone. I suspect he's playing a farming game and mashing in commands with his nose. It's a disgusting but necessary sacrifice: while James's obliviousness sometimes seems limitless, I doubt he would overlook a talking head without a body.

Ghosts, weirdly enough, might get past him.

The Vampire Weekenders take over the ballroom stage, plugging in amps and pedals and crossing wires as they arrange themselves for sound check. Before long, a ghost floats into the reception room and streams up to the as-yet-unlit stage.

"Hey man," the filmy figure intones. "We can't hear ourselves reciting anymore."

"Well, you can't expect us to shut this down," says Eric. "We're paid to be here. It's a gig."

"Big gig," agrees Remy. "We're the Vampire Weekenders."

The ghost considers this. "I think I've heard of Vampire Weekend."

"Not the same," Hanry explains from beneath the wedding arch, which he decided to construct here and carry to the greenhouse later. "They're a cover band."

A second ghost appears in the doorway with a quiet *pop*. Eric and James shrug it off, but Remy jumps back, glancing around for confirmation that something unnatural just happened. I raise an eyebrow at him, which gets him back on task.

"You can't play Vampire Weekend's music," the second ghost says. "That's copyright infringement."

"You can't take this from us," says Eric, smiling firmly. "You're wedding guests, not professional artists. Besides, you're drunk. Look how you're walking."

James nods. "It's big weird."

"We turned off the smoke alarms once to enjoy some kush before our friend Jake's wedding." More ghosts swoop-wander upon the stage. Several have brought instruments. "But we also turned off the carbon monoxide monitors."

Is that how the ghosts died? Not that it's my business. Also, who calls weed "kush"?

"Are they back on?" asks Remy, eyeing the ceiling. "This venue doesn't look well-kept."

"Who can remember? We've been drunk for forty years," says the original ghost.

"Drunk math," puts in Eric. "Bad form. You should be ashamed of yourselves."

"You're not taking us seriously at all!" This complaint comes from the Elvis-like ghost. He must be the ringleader, because at his statement, the ghosts begin vibrating with anger. Yikes. Jokes aside, these are actual *ghosts*, and potentially dangerous. Someone could get hurt. Namely, James. Goddamn it.

I step forward. "Hey, guys, how about—"

Hanry lays a hand on my arm. I can't help noticing how nice it looks there. Not overly large, but a good size. And in spite of his calluses, he has trim knuckles. All evidence indicates he isn't a vampire. But also that he might be a misogynist.

"You have strong wrists," I say aloud. "Now, quit manhandling me. I need to save my friends from a haunting."

"Dave's arrived," Hanry says, redirecting me to the doorway and Dark Dave. The vampire groom is dressed in a tuxedo straight from a 1940s movie, with tails to the floor, and spectator shoes with the white parts blacked out by, presumably, Sharpie markers.

"So much light!" He braces himself against the wall. Then he collapses with a whimper. "Please, someone, end this suffering!"

Hanry sends me a pointed look, and I know with a sinking feeling that that someone is meant to be *me*.

8

WHAT I'D GIVE FOR A MOBILE BLOOD BANK RIGHT NOW

I MIGHT HAVE TAKEN BULAN'S AND HANRY'S ASSURANCES THAT a vampire's bark is worse than their bite a little too much to heart. My gallows walk across the ballroom to Dark Dave takes about five seconds, and to my dismay, it's rudely anticlimactic. I don't have a life-flashing-before-my-eyes montage the way you should with a harbinger of death. Dave's prostrate, pale form and twitching leg make me think less of wolves and dangerous doom and more of beached porpoises. In fact, the only scary thought bothering me now is what I'll do if the wedding fails so spectacularly that Dave and Amanda decide I won't get paid.

"Hi, Dave," I say, squatting to join the vampire groom where he lies despondently on the floor. "How are you doing? Excited for your big da—night? Your big night?"

He runs trembling hands through his jet-black bangs. "It's terrible!" he says. "Disastrous!"

"I hear you. Is there anything I can do to help?"

"The light!" Dark Dave curls into a fetal position. "It's too bright."

"I'll blow out some candles. Anything else?"

He gestures limply toward the ballroom.

"What's that noise?"

"I think our bands are having a showdown. A battle of the bands, if you will." After a brief show of interest, Dave moans and curls up tighter. This is going nowhere fast, and I don't have time. "Listen, Dave. Let's focus on why we're here. For your wedding. To Amanda. The love of your life! And when everyone celebrates you together tonight, it's going to be spectacular."

"Did you just say *spook-tacular*?"

"I—no?"

"Like your last name? Spük? It's very clever. *Spük-tacular.*"

Dave's expression clears. Rather than looking like he wishes for his second death, he now looks like he's wishing for a darker corner to sulk in. It's a marked improvement.

"There's something else," I say, nursing the onset of positive vibes. "Your friend Hanry has been helping us. He made the wedding arch look awesome."

"He's here already? I'm honored. What a prince."

There! That's the flamboyance I was aiming for.

"Yeah, he's in the ballroom, see him? He came early. Almost like . . . like . . ." I trail off, rather than say aloud what I'm thinking: that Hanry knew I'd need him here. "Never mind that. Let's get you to the room where you and your groomsmen will chill before the ceremony."

"What room is that?"

I shrug. "No idea. Wanna choose?"

It takes ten minutes for Dave to find a dusky room to his liking. By that point, I'm getting nerves. I don't have my phone, but I know the wedding ceremony's starting soon, and the ceremony room isn't ready. Plus, I don't know where Amanda is.

Speaking of, I don't even know where *I* am.

The chasmic mansion's pitch-black hallways obscure everything. Annoyed and lost, using the extended toe of my foot to keep track of the walls, I bump into something small and soft. It could be a giant rat, except the noise it makes is way too gleeful. Just going to ignore that.

Fortunately, the next thing I bump into is less bizarre: the wedding officiant. Thank god or whatever he believes in, he's got a phone. And he seems human?

"I've got to say, it seems hazardous to have low lighting to this degree," the officiant says, guiding us down the hall.

"Not my circus, not my monkeys. Though I convinced the groom to include *some* lighting for his non-vamp—his more light-inclined guests. See?"

Up ahead, a light emanates from a door. I think it's the ballroom.

"Good thinking," the man says. "Huh! What a nice-sounding band."

He's not wrong. The sound leaking into the hallway is unexpectedly harmonic. I'm not sure how that's possible. I didn't recommend James's band for their vocal abilities.

I crack the door open, discovering this *is* the ballroom. But Hanry and Bulan are nowhere in sight. More importantly, the ghosts haven't decamped. Instead, they've taken positions onstage around the Vampire Weekenders—some at microphones, several with guitars they've pretend-plugged into amps. One ghost has a bongo strapped to its chest. Surprisingly, James, Eric, and Remy sport wide-ass smiles on their faces.

James greets me in his typically bright-eyed fashion. "We've decided to play together," he says. "They bring a sort of—I don't know. *Dimension* to our sound."

"A je ne sais quoi," says Eric, styling James's fauxhawk distractedly.

"Great," I say. "Just don't touch them."

"What?" Remy rubs down his arms with a shiver.

Since there's no time to explain, and frankly, I doubt it would help anyway, I take James's phone, leave them to their practice, and whisk the officiant to the greenhouse.

It's a glorious sight: lit up by Bulan, who's holding a flashlight in his mouth, Hanry puts away power tools. Behind him is a towering, masterfully nailed-together Gothic black arch.

"What do you think?" Hanry calls out.

My gratitude hits so hard, I can't help being honest. "It looks great."

"Thanks!" say Hanry and Bulan in unison.

"I'm going to put up as many flowers as I can. Hanry, can you set up chairs? Rev, you can do your . . . priesty things."

"Got it!" says Hanry.

"I'm actually not religious," the officiant says. "Be that as it may, I'll search for Amanda and ensure she has her vows ready. If there are any problems, I'll return. Good luck, all!"

I stride into the room and begin decorating the arch. Standing on an upside-down bucket, I drape wilted and dry, brittle vines over the black-stained wood, attaching a spray of bloodred rose blooms on the left side. This is a nod to the only color Dark Dave can probably stand. Admittedly, I'm going for a less-dense design than I'd originally planned, since easily half my dried flowers shook off their petals in transit—but "light and airy" is totally a look. Also, it's a good thing I'm not overly invested, because while I carry out the last of the buckets of unused stems and Hanry places down the final row of chairs, the first wedding guests arrive.

They flood into the greenhouse, dragging feather boas, lacy parasols, and more questionably bad fashion decisions to their seats. How many of them are vampires, I can't say. At least one appears to be a lion. When the beast crushes two chairs in the process of settling into his row, Hanry cautiously re-seats himself farther away. Can't blame him.

"Sabby," Bulan whispers from beneath my arm. "I think you're supposed to go back outside."

"I like this little corner," I retort. It is, in fact, less of a corner and more of an open tool closet with a small seat. "Why do I need to go anywhere?"

"Because you're the wedding planner."

"In name only. And I've finished my planning."

"Suit yourself."

The ceremony begins with music outside my hearing range. Said music is provided courtesy of a flock of bats. I'm unclear on whether they're regular bats or vampire bats, but the guests' head-nods and rapturous sighs tell me it doesn't really matter and I'm missing out on some goddamned glorious Bat-hoven.

After that, the quiet continues. Long enough that the guests start muttering aloud. They seem to be wondering what's going on. At the end of the aisle, where he waits beneath the now-magnificent arch, the officiant raises his eyebrows in my direction—like he's prompting me to do something.

And now he's adding a little pleading into the crinkle of his eyes. Oh, come on.

"The groom's supposed to enter ahead of the bridal procession, right?" Bulan whispers at me, *again*. "I think Dave needs direction. One a wedding planner might provide."

What I'm realizing he needed was a rehearsal. And I hadn't pushed it, because I'm *not* an expert at this wedding business; I'm a human pretending to be a potted plant in a tool closet.

But since I'm on the hook, I allow myself one last resigned sigh before I dash for the hallway. Past the greenhouse's double doors, a few barely visible, hissing male vampires creep about. I catch some staring at the walls, some defying the laws of gravity by walking on said walls, and a few fluttering their hands uselessly. I don't distinguish Dave among them.

"Where's our groom?" I ask the closest, best-dressed figure.

With a flash of fangs and bubble gum, he hisses, "In the back."

"Back of where? I need him up front, stat."

At my command, an onyx-black coffin is moshed forward and nearly strikes me in the head. I'm not sure how exactly it's levitating. Or how it got to the venue. What's more important is, I'm positive it contains Dave. Meaning he's been with us in the hallway this whole damn time. I've no idea why his groom-vamps didn't bring him into the ceremony yet. Maybe they thought Dave crawled inside of his deathbed to escape the light? Poor Dark Dave! He's surrounded himself with the worst problem-solvers this side of the Berkshires.

"All right, groomsmen, let's get ready to carry Dave in!" I tell the group, waving James's phone above my head like an aircraft marshal with glowy orange sticks. "Gather up single file and stand next to Dave's coffin in a line. On the . . . right." I wiggle my arm to clarify which side "right" is. "You, in the moth-eaten cravat. Tell the bats to make more music."

"You smell good, but your voice is fearsome," the vampire says to me.

"No one put on our boutonnieres," another whines.

Since at this point I have no idea where my boutonnieres went, I scrounge up a few leftover roses from a bucket in the hallway, pull a pincushion from my apron pocket, and work quickly on a backup solution.

When I finish, Dave's coffin is jostled forward, and the groomsmen parade into the greenhouse, flaunting their little skewed roses on their lapels and hissing with delight.

The next to process in ought to be Amanda and her gang, but naturally they are nowhere to be found. Since the officiant never told me he'd had problems finding Amanda, I assume she's in the haunted house somewhere. Sure enough, I discover the undead bridesmaids in the bathroom, toying with a mousetrap, while a coffin lays abandoned in the adjacent powder room. Sensing these vamps need instruction too, I arm them with bouquets, push them over to the greenhouse, and in the end, they too send Amanda and her coffin down the aisle with only a minor delay.

At last, the big reveal: at the front of the room, beneath the surprisingly aesthetic black arch, the relieved officiant says a few words. The coffins wiggle and creak. Then the lids pop open. Dave and Amanda emerge, rising into the air through a shower of dust and feathers. Amanda's corseted, mildew-gray wedding dress hangs off her like an old lady's tablecloth. Her hands are clasped around her dead-and-dying bouquet. A swan-feather boa-noose trails ruthlessly down to the floor. As they meet midair, Amanda smiles. Dave gazes back into her pale-as-a-moon, necrotic face with a dour expression. He seems almost pleased. They both do. Because they're in love.

My god. I've done it—I've pulled off the wedding.

Once the couple returns earthside, their toes tapping down, the officiant intones blessings. I gather there won't be any praying, kneeling, or singing during the ceremony. Floored and flummoxed and out of breath, I watch the whole thing from the door. At last, Dave and Amanda are pronounced married, till second death do they part. Sharing kisses, the couple traipses back down the aisle, this time with their coffins following behind like obedient, floating dogs. As they pass me, the audience claps and hisses politely. Bulan rolls into my heels.

"What are you doing?" he asks.

"What are *you* doing?"

"Wondering why you're still standing here when there's work to be done."

I groan. Of course there's more. "Let me guess. I'm supposed to go to the reception hall?"

Bulan nods. And you know what, fine. It'd be good to check on James anyway.

I pop Bulan onto my shoulder and carry him to the ballroom. As if my entrance is the signal, James leaps into motion and kicks off his patchwork band.

Letting guests trickle in, I sink into the shadows and survey the scene. The ghosts jamming, the curtains drooping, the floral arrangements holding artful poses on the shabby-not-chic tablecloths. Yet, I think something's wrong. Something is . . . missing, only I can't put my finger on the problem as easily as I could during the wedding ceremony. I'm going to have to guess.

I glance at Bulan, my acting shoulder angel. Mostly I'm looking at his bright orange hair, but that's not the point. I need to surreptitiously draw his attention to the dance floor.

"Is it bad etiquette for couples to start dancing before the bride and groom enter?" I ask.

Bulan's reply comes uncertainly. "Maybe," he says. "Amanda and Dave didn't tell us when they wanted to have their first dance."

"True. So if you and I get blamed for breaking the wedding code, we have plausible deniability." At least one would hope. "Do you think the dancing's what's wrong, or something else?"

"What do you mean?"

"Sabby!"

The new voice belongs to Hanry. If James and his band have allowed a treacherous deviance from wedding etiquette, Hanry seems unaware. In fact, he's smiling so winsomely, I let him lift Bulan from my shoulder, put him on the ground, and take my hand.

"I need to show you something," he says, tugging me out of the shadows. "Quick!"

I brace myself. I knew it, I knew something was wrong. "What? Show me what?"

"That I'm a good dancer," he says, and drags my stiff, confused body in among the couples and breakdancing circles.

9

AND NOW I'M DANCING WITH DEVILS. I GUESS THIS IS MY LIFE NOW

MY AFOREMENTIONED STIFF, CONFUSED BODY IS NOT GOOD AT dancing on a regular occasion. And there's nothing regular about being pulled into a horde of paranormal beings. I would rather be anywhere else on the planet than this dance floor. Yet my traitorous, fluttery stomach also says I'd rather be nowhere else than with Hanry. The net of this is that I have indigestion.

"You're sneaky," I manage eventually. "And foolish. I'm a bad dancer."

"Let's see about that."

"Nope. It's nonnegotiable, and I don't appreciate your deceptive tactics."

Hanry laughs. "All you have to do is follow my steps."

Hmm. That's probably why I'm not talented at dancing: the whole "following" bit. No surprise that when Hanry tries to push me into a waltzy thing, I end up lurching.

"Don't worry about them," he says, pulling me close. His eyes flick to the creatures swarming around us, decked out in peacock plumage and ostrich feathers and worse. "We were invited to this wedding. That puts us under Dave and Amanda's protection. No matter how delicious-smelling our blood, we should be fine."

"I'm not worried about that. I have a crap diet," I say. "My blood smells mediocre, at best."

"I have a feeling there isn't anything mediocre about you," says Hanry.

I rearrange my hand around Hanry's bicep. He doesn't seem to mind my giving it a subtle squeeze. In spite of how he's befriended vampires and misjudged me as eccentric, I can't help noticing that Hanry is kind and hot and maybe flirting with me: a potentially flammable combination.

"I didn't have a chance to thank you earlier," I say. "So, thanks. There's no way I could've pulled off the florals without you."

"You seemed like you were in a bind." Hanry grins. Until I step on his foot. "Ouch."

"Sorry."

"For what it's worth, I thought your concept was solid. And in the end, the decorations got finished on time. The ceremony happened with minimal issues. I'd call that a win."

"You pieced the arch together well."

Hanry leads me in a swoopy, broccoli-armed move. "Why do you sound surprised? Ha. I have a thing for woodworking. And I like using foraged materials."

Does he, now? Am I really supposed to believe he was collecting pine cones in the graveyard that night? Breathlessly, I say: "Salsa. Foraging. Woodworking. You have too many hobbies."

"I do. But I don't own my own wedding planning company," he points out. Apparently, the next step in this broccoli dance entails me being dipped into ranch dressing. "That's impressive."

"Am I?" I ask the dark, mildew-stained ceiling. "Do I?"

"All right, Miss False Humility. Time for a loop-de-loop."

"A what?"

Hanry smiles down at me right before leading me in yet another cruciferous contortion. Miraculously, I don't smash into anyone. I've never lasted this long through a dance in my life. I failed PE in eighth grade because Coach Bradley thought I was intentionally trying to hurt people during our dance sessions. I bet that wouldn't have happened to

Hanry. He may be built like a tree, but he's more willow than oak. He was *trained* to dance from an early age; I'd bet someone else's money on it.

"Have you thought of taking on an assistant?" he asks. "For your wedding business?"

I snort. "Absolutely not."

"It could be a good idea. I might not be able to show up and save the day every time."

Oh, please, like he saved the day by standing there, holding a hammer. Well. I mean fine, he sort of did. It was a onetime thing, though, just like this—my first and only foray into the wedding industry. I don't belong here, in a haunted room full of extravagantly weird paranormal beings who might be tempted to eat me. But why does the otherwise wonderful Hanry?

"Question for you," I say as the song winds down. "How long did it take before you figured out Dave and Amanda were vampires, and why didn't it freak you out?"

"I, uh. Guess it didn't come as a surprise. Dave's pretty obvious. And unthreatening."

"Like . . . a vegan?" I ask.

"Excuse me," a voice wedges in from the side. It belongs to the officiant, carrying Bulan.

"We have a problem," says Bulan.

I hadn't realized how much Hanry had loosened me up. But looking at these two and their paired expressions of poorly reined-in worry, I feel like I'm smacking into a wall of bricks. If I were in a car, my airbags would have exploded, and I'd be batting the puff-bags vainly out of my face.

"What is it?" I ask.

When the officiant sucks in his breath, I stiffen more, my automatic threat response kicking in.

"The caterers haven't showed."

Shit! The lack of food on tables or service carts. That's what was giving me "off" vibes. I should've realized it right away. Worse, lacking sustenance, some of the guests are starting to act more . . . vampiric. At least, I assume that's what all the drool is about.

I release Hanry, turning my full attention to Bulan and the officiant.

"This isn't my fault, right? Dave and Amanda never asked me to do catering."

Hanry reaches out to place his hand lightly against my back. It's a big hand, which actually makes it reassuring. And inappropriately so, under the circumstances.

"I'm sure any hungry guests will go out and search for food on their own," he says.

"Like a scavenger hunt!" exclaims Bulan. "You may be right, Hanry."

I allow myself to briefly imagine the vampire horde trolling the unsuspecting countryside, sneaking into farmers' houses, helping themselves to the old ladies and their cows.

Poor cows.

"Are you sure there isn't something else we can do?" I ask the group. "Anyone see a blood bank on the way over here?"

"There may have been a chiropractor a few miles back . . ." says the officiant. At my glowering expression, he says, "What else do you want from me? Ma'am, this isn't a Wendy's."

Who is he calling *ma'am*? Also: "Why are you bringing up fast food?!"

"Because we have a fantastic blood-chili. Off-menu," the officiant explains. "I told you, I'm not religious. I'm just a manager at the Wendy's off Lafayette Street."

While I process this disturbing revelation, the instrumental section of the song ends with a flourish. James taps his mic.

"Thank you, thank you," he says, beaming at the gathered faces on the dance floor. "We're the Vampire Weekenders! We're so happy to be here, playing at the wedding of, uh, Amanda and Dark Dave!" I probably should've mentioned that Dark Dave was a private nickname. Oh well. "I'd like to welcome our happy new couple to the stage! In the meantime, allow me to introduce the full band!"

No, no, *no*.

Grimacing, I get on my tiptoes and perform a *cut it* motion, drawing my finger over my neck. The last thing James should do right now, in a room of hungry vampires, is call extra attention to his human self and his band. It just isn't worth the risk!

But before James gets the chance, a ghost takes his mic.

"Thank you for allowing us to perform for this event. It has been groovy and magical, man."

The semitranslucent figure throws back his head and sighs rapturously. On cue, he and the ghost bandmates pop out of existence, one after the other.

Remy screams, "I knew it!"

Backing up, he trips over an electrical cord. I'm not sure exactly how this leads to the next thing, but hardware starts dropping everywhere onstage. Maybe the ghosts were holding it up? Or has this old mansion started crumbling around us? It's hard to tell in this stupid, dark room. Remy isn't alone in his panic: the guests are wondering what's going on, clamoring in tones that are harsh and loud. But not so loud that we miss Eric's devastated cry:

"I think Remy's dead!"

10

CONSEQUENCES, SCHMONSEQUENCES

REMY IS NOT DEAD.

What he does have is a concussion. This might be for the best.

"Did I really see— I could've sworn I saw—".

"Shh, shh. You don't want to say something you'll regret," I tell Remy as the officiant uses a broken guitar neck to herd the band, sheeplike, through the reception hall and out the mansion's back exit. I've just gotten my phone back from Bulan, but I hesitate to return James's. Under the moonlight, James and Eric limp along, expressions devastated, but their bodies otherwise uninjured. At any moment I suspect they might abandon Remy and run back onstage to finish their set. So the instant they've packed themselves into the back seat of my rental, I click on Child Lock.

"Erp?" asks James.

I salute the officiant goodbye and kick the SUV into first gear. Then I quickly shift into automatic again, before I kill us.

"Don't worry," I say with more calm than I feel. "I'll come back tomorrow for your instruments."

"And my station wagon?"

"Sure. I'm coming back for Bu—for my bags of décor, anyway."

In the meantime, what I need to come up with *now* is a good lie that'll keep James, Eric, and Remy from realizing they were gigging a paranormal wedding. Including some direct interactions with ghosts.

As I drive the boys out of the parking lot, Eric collapses with a *thonk* against the passenger window. "We only played *one song*."

"Did we?" asks Remy. He sounds dazed. Encouragingly so.

"Yes. And then . . ." Eric, for his part, sounds like he's halfway asphyxiated himself. "I'm not sure what happened. I mean . . . that couldn't have happened, could it? They . . ."

I clench my teeth, readying a million excuses.

". . . *loved* us," finishes James.

The Vampire Weekenders hyperventilate the whole way to James's family home in Winchester. Remarkably, in spite of driving a fair distance from Salem, I don't turn into a human puddle along the way.

But then again, it's well after 9 p.m., meaning Grandma Rose's ascension is complete. For all I know, she's left behind a pile of confetti in her wake, somewhere on the streets of Salem, or possibly atop her ghoulish grave.

I drop the boys off, waving them goodbye with a giant smile. Who could blame me for being happy? In addition to no one dying, I just earned four thousand dollars, kept the wedding ceremony from spiraling, narrowly avoided my friends learning about ghosts *or* being served as vampire hors d'oeuvres, and flirted harmlessly with Hanry Burleson. All in all, an excellent night. And now I can go back to New York, where I belong.

I connect the Bluetooth to my Spotify *Cleaning with K-Pop* playlist. That's when it happens.

The SUV decides to explode.

By this I mean that electricity shorts out in the SUV, and when it comes back on, the navigation screen is fizzling, so it's a minor explosion. The GPS headings scramble, and I'm thrown back into my seat as the car takes off, on its own, forcing me onto a magical autopilot for—

For Salem.

But I can't be heading back there! You can't be controlling me through technical wizardry, Grandma: you're supposed to be dead, ascended, and at peace! And I'm supposed to be in the clear.

I *have* to be.

Once I hit the city limits, I jerk the steering wheel back into my possession and drive for Derby Street. I whizz past the docks and the vaping tourists, their puffs of smoke glowing red from streetlights and brake lights, because of course they're walking in the road instead of using sidewalks like normal people without a death wish. When I get to Winter Island, I force the SUV to a halt and run for the disappointingly named Waikiki Beach.

The water line is high, lapping against dry, rock-speckled sand.

Confirming that the tides are, in fact, doing what they're supposed to be doing.

It's Grandma who isn't with the program. Grandma, who is violating *her own magical will*.

Grandma, who is forcing me to stay here in Salem.

I pass out in my clothes, only stirring when my phone buzzes. It's seven o'clock on Sunday morning, and sunlight rakes my face like a pleased cat with its claws out, ripping right through the gauzy guest room curtains.

The person joining in that aggression is my mother, calling my phone.

I stare at the ceiling, listening to the blaring rings, trying to remember the last time Mom called me of her own accord. Is it bad that I wish it were Steve calling me instead, begging for forgiveness, asking if I want more time off? Or Baldy, with an explanation for why all seven tides have passed twice over, but Grandma hasn't kept up her end of the bargain?

But if I'm a bad daughter, Mom's a worse mom.

I pick up the phone just before it goes to voicemail.

"Buenos Aires!" Mom screams into my ear. I fumble to activate the speakerphone and drop the phone on my pillow.

"Buenos días," I correct Mom tiredly. "Buenos Aires is a city."

"Did you say you were still in Salem?" she asks. "That looks like your grandma's house."

I guess we're on a video call. Fun. I try to rearrange myself on my pillow, and frankly, it hurts. My stomach's killing me, and I can only chalk some of my ear-ringing up to Mom's voice. Are paranormal hangovers a thing? Or is this garden-variety exhaustion? Also, my arms are putty. Who knew handling wedding decorations could be so physically taxing?

Presumably, real wedding planners.

"If you'd read my texts, you'd know Grandma's lawyer won't let me leave," I tell Mom.

She gasps loudly, in a way that would be feigned for other people.

"Has he kidnapped you, Samantha!?"

"Yes," I say into my elbow. "I'm kidnapped. Inside Grandma's house. With my iPhone and everything. But don't worry, I'm using my phone to make TikTok videos about my captivity. I'll be famous by noon."

"Now I know you're joking. The last thing you want is to be famous."

It must be the fatigue, but for some reason I blurt out, "Wow, you got me. It's almost like you've paid attention to who I am since you fell down your herbal medicine whackadoo rabbit hole."

Mom is speechless. Whoops. I peel back my puttylike arm and sit upright in bed. I usually know better than to say anything too honest and unfiltered to her. Not because she'll take offense or use my words against me, but because being honest leaves me vulnerable. The one thing Mom's good at besides day drinking is shooting her arrows of apathy into my heart.

"Ha ha," she singsongs. "You're too funny. Anyway, when you get back home, can you send me a diffuser from that Japanese Moogi store?"

Yep. There she goes, ignoring me again. With effort, I say, "It's Muji, not Moogi. And what do you need a Muji diffuser for?"

"They're ultrasonic is why. *Ultra. Sonic.*"

"Can't you just order it online and ship to your hotel? Or come back yourself, to—"

"Ay-ay-ay, *mucho fuerte*!" Mom interrupts with a giggle. I know that giggle, unfortunately.

I pinch my nose bridge. "Who are you talking to, Mom?"

"The pool boy!"

"Please stop flirting with people half your age. And massacring Spanish. Mom?"

A long beep informs me that my advice has fallen on deaf ears.

Well, that's no surprise. I roll over. The mattress emits a flatulent creak, then leaves me to silence, which is weird after the last week of Bulan's chatty, endless monologues. I wouldn't say I miss him, but his voice sure beats out my life-bringer's. He has a surprisingly nice tenor, actually. I wonder if he's any good at karaoke.

Or if he could tell me why I'm stuck here, despite doing everything right.

After a shower, I dress in a carefully neutral plain white tee and jeans, grab a frozen, maybe-moldy cannoli from the freezer, and drive the rental back to the wedding venue. Crested by a wash of cool sunlight, the mansion looks different from yesterday. It's derelict, but cozily so. The ceiling seems intact in every room, including above the ballroom stage. And with the exception of Bulan, who greets me from a puddle of ragged curtains he's made into a bed, it seems all paranormal activity has left the building.

The lack of bloodstains on the ballroom floor is particularly encouraging.

"No bloodbaths in Essex County last night?" I ask Bulan as we shove décor and wilted floral arrangements into garbage bags.

"None we're responsible for," the head answers with a cheery grin. "A twenty-four-hour Shaw's had its butcher department cleaned out, however. And I think the local rabbit population may have been culled."

"Amazing. So . . ." Where do I even start? With the simple things, I guess. "Where'd Dave and Amanda leave my payment?"

Bulan wobbles uncertainly. "I might be mistaken, but I don't believe they left it anywhere, Sabby."

Worry strikes me like a blow to the back, but I try to hide it. I was so busy planning the wedding that it only now occurs to me I forgot to set up a payment plan with the couple.

What if this means I don't get paid?

But that wouldn't happen. Though my family's irresponsible, not everyone is. *Most* people follow through on their responsibilities. It's all part of being normal. Besides, Dave and Amanda know how important it is to me to be paid . . . or at least, they should.

"Perhaps the happy couple left it at the shop," Bulan consoles me.

They better have.

After I return the SUV, hoping the rental company doesn't notice the navigation system's new and improved fizzy personality, I walk silently to the apothecary with Grandma's pet head. I have Bulan in his increasingly well-established position of mimicking a puppet. It's sunny out, with puffy, marshmallow-like clouds polka-dotting the sky. It should be a good day, a hopeful day. The day I was planning to head back to Manhattan—*again*.

Nevertheless, here I am. Feeling the dreadful grip of . . . dread? Despair? Terror?

Either that, or I'm once again a victim of Grandma Rose's cooking.

Arriving at the shop begins with disappointment. I don't find a cash-filled envelope slipped underneath the door, in the mail slot, or taped onto the ceiling, dangling down like a bat. I'm left with no recourse but to text Amanda and Dave, sending a message or two. Or five. Maybe add another zero. Who's counting?

The answer, of course, is me, because *it's my job to keep track of money*! Especially the kind that vanishes in unseemly ways.

"What do you want to do next?" Bulan asks after I've moved on to more productive tasks than texting. "Besides taking out your feelings on poor Rosie's herbs."

"This works great for me," I reply. "The sound of smashing glass helps clear my mind."

"I see," says Bulan.

"You haven't asked me why I'm still here," I mention. "You knew I was planning to leave the moment Grandma Rose ascended to the heavens, didn't you? That I was going to get on a train this morning?"

"Ah, yes. What happened?"

I drop my arm, the violent impulse evaporating at the empathy in Bulan's voice.

"I'm still here. And that isn't acceptable. I need to go back to New York to work. To *live*. If I'm stuck in Salem, I'm going to go broke. I could *starve*."

"Oh no! That would be terrible," says Bulan. "I'm sure Rosie wouldn't have wished that."

"She clearly did."

"There must be some sort of misunderstanding. It was 'seven tides, twice passed' that you were waiting for, correct? Perhaps the wording of the will was more nebulous than you realized."

"Grandma was terrible at riddles, but she loved wordplay," I say, frowning. "Maybe I should look at the will myself. See if there's some kind of misunderstanding in what she said."

"That sounds like an excellent next step!" says Bulan.

And who would trust Baldy's interpretation, anyway? I should've asked this a long time ago.

As I sweep the last armful of broken herb jars to the trash, I catch sight of a strange figure darkening the doorway outside. He's a well-dressed man with a deeply unpleasant expression. The smolder of it makes me jump in place, like an agitated gazelle.

"Bulan," I say once I'm level-footed. "We have another creepy visitor."

"Getting into position!" he calls out.

Deftly avoiding the glass on the floor, Bulan rolls into an emptied box and hides. Why did he do that? The sight of this random stranger has wormed hope back into my heart.

"Get out of there! He could have my payment from the vampires."

Muffled by cardboard, the head replies, "I doubt it. He would've left it at the door, rather than staring at you for the past hour."

I don't know how to process this. "What?"

"From across the street. He was hiding behind that green Prius."

"No, I mean, 'what' as in 'why didn't you tell me sooner?'"

"Sorry, I thought you knew. You might reconsider that violent smashing practice of yours, Sabby; it doesn't seem to be helping."

Bulan has a point. I push away my thoughts of Grandma and the will to take another, harder look at my stalker. The hook-nosed man leans against the door and sips at his coffee, blocking anyone from entering. He isn't wearing a cape, dressed up, or otherwise doing anything suspicious beyond exuding a sexy air that could potentially melt the historic brick wall he's settling against. He's nowhere near my type—I'd take Hanry over him any day of the week—but whatever he's here for, he sure is causing a scene.

This is impressive because over the two miserable weeks I've been stuck here, Salem has stumbled ever deeper into the stupor of its Halloween season. You'd think the tourists would have something else to titter about than a moody Adam Driver look-alike who isn't even in costume. That they'd have jack-o'-lanterns to carve or Wiccan candles to melt onto the stoops of their Airbnbs.

I frown. This guy better not be here to complain about Dave and Amanda's wedding. Fighting back worry, I swing my garbage bag of old herbs and broken glass over my shoulder and walk them to the trash.

"If he's here for me," I say, resolved, "he should've come in already."

"Indeed. Unless, of course, he can't." Bulan peeks over the edge of the cardboard box, his bushy red eyebrows knitted. "Fay can't enter a room uninvited, you see, and that one has big fay energy. They can be such bitchy brats, I swear."

"Fay? As in fairy?"

"The very same."

Hmph. I don't know anything about fay, but with the mood I'm in, a bitch-off sounds great. I give the stranger another ten minutes before I stroll to the door and push away the fake spider and cobweb decorations dangling over it.

"Feel free to come in," I announce to the air. "Mr. Fairy Man."

Acting like he doesn't hear me, the dark and sexy character swigs back his (presumably black) coffee and glares at generally nothing and no one.

Oh god, he's *resentful* that he's been made to wait so long. I love this.

"Well, I'll be inside," I say.

More than five minutes later, he finally enters the shop. Ignoring the googly-eyed spider that drops onto his arm, he announces, "I've finished my coffee." His deep voice reminds me of caramel. But after it's returned to room temperature and gotten stiff and globby. "Where is your waste receptacle?"

"Corner, behind the antique broom collection."

He sullenly follows my directions, then spins on me with a sharp tap of his dress heel. I may have limited experience with Salem's paranormal underground, but how can this guy be fay? Mom filled more than half of her bookshelves with stories about fairy boyfriends and courtesans. Those fairies seemed capricious, violent, melodramatic, lascivious. This guy, on the other hand, seems as hard-boiled as a cop. Oh, shit—what if this semi-sexy guy is both a fay *and* some kind of detective from, I don't know, the Massachusetts Commonwealth Paranormal Bureau of Investigation? What if he's here to arrest me for the vampires' hungry antics last night? Worse—what if Grandma has magical debts in addition to normal, human ones?

"Samantha Spük," he rumbles.

Play it cool, Sabby. Play it cool. "Can I help you?" I ask.

"You may call me Rochester. And you know why I'm here."

"Because I invited you inside?"

The self-proclaimed Rochester doesn't respond to my joke. In fact, he directs an expression at me that's so cold and intense, it feels as if he's pressing down on my rib cage.

"Calm down," I say-wheeze. "Go ahead and tell me."

"On behalf of my client, I wish to procure a sample wedding planning package."

After I get over my surprise, I spare a glance at the box where Bulan is hiding. In spite of my sustained attention, he doesn't blurt out any helpful behavioral cues. Fine. I guess I'll power through this congealed butter-stick of maybe-fay, bitchy-sexy energy by myself.

"So," I say to Rochester. "What if I told you I wasn't taking more clients right now?"

Rochester, apparently not a fan of active listening, whips a bound book of parchment from his overcoat.

"These are my clients' requests," he says. "I will return upon the eve of the waning moon to accept your quote."

"Bad news, Roachster. You're going to return to an empty building. I'm leaving for New York tonight."

I'm surprised Bulan doesn't call me out on the obvious lie.

"If you are not here, I can retrieve your custom quote from the doorway," says the fay.

I shrug. "I could use more help with the recycling."

With us in terse agreement, the self-proclaimed Rochester drops his stack of nonsense parchment onto the table. Then he exits, slamming the door on a plush spider. Rude.

Once he's out of sight, I beeline for Bulan's hiding place.

With a slightly manic air, I say, "Get out. Come on. We're going to find Baldy and get to the bottom of this tide thing."

"Sabby, don't be hasty," says Bulan. "Are you truly not considering that job?"

"Of course I'm not!"

"While you two were talking, I was thinking about last night's wedding. Against great odds, you managed a fantastic event. It was a rip-roaring success!"

Time for a friendly reminder. "Remy nearly died."

"Sure. From behind the scenes, the wedding wasn't seamless," Bulan allows. "But by daybreak, the guests were raving about the party—"

"As they drained the blood from half the rabbits of Essex County. Or decimated that butcher shop. Either way."

"—and catering quirks aside, the guests truly enjoyed the intrigue and spectacle of your decorations! They had a great time. As did Dave and Amanda."

But not enough to pay me. I place him on the table and sling my bag over my shoulder. "What's your point?"

"I know you've noticed how many members of the Community have visited you, Sabby, including this most recent fay. Now that you have your first big success under your belt, your business could take off tremendously! And some clients might pay their deposits up front, if you asked! You said you were worried about starvation. Perhaps this could ease your fears."

Bulan waggles his eyebrows, as if that might be the final argument to convince me. It does not. I'm not particularly susceptible to facial hair.

Feeling the weight of stress bearing down on me like a pianoforte, I abandon Bulan with my bag on the table and pace my prison cell, aka Grandma's apothecary. I refocus on the room and my reality with a miserable and near-defeated sigh. The circumstances are against me: I'm trapped in Salem, I'm hungry, I need to pay rent to Jane, I have no idea what I'm going to tell EFG, and I have shudderingly begun to make a reputation for myself here.

"I need to make a phone call," I say begrudgingly.

"I don't think that fay left a number, but I can check," says Bulan. He uses his nose to rifle through the papers Rochester left behind. I force myself to inhale a shallow, pained breath. This room smells like dust and herbs and the cruelty of fate. It's funny how when your life burns down around you, it doesn't have the decency to leave a smell.

"I'm going to have to call Baldy. Then Steve, my supervisor in New York," I explain to the head, as well as to Grandma's doubtlessly listening-in spirit. "I think I'll try to claim FMLA. Even if my company fights it or tries harder to get that a doctor's note, that'll buy me time. It'll mean I still have a job to return to after . . . after I figure out how to get out of here. I'll take up one or two more jobs as a wedding planner in the meantime."

"Oh! All those words just to say you're having a change of heart."

"*No*," I say. "This is only temporary. I'm a faux wedding planner. A hungry one."

"Well, if you're accepting deposits, I believe your customers will expect you to stay in business and carry out their weddings. If you ran out on them, that would be stealing."

"I'm not stealing," I reassure Bulan as I bring out my phone.

The last thing I want to do is commit sketchy white-collar crimes that could land me in jail. Nope. I'm going to use this unique, unfortunate opportunity to supplement my financial education.

What could be more hands-on for an accountant than to learn how to run a small business? Monitoring expenses, finding avenues for growth and all that?

A lot of things, probably. But if I'm going to be stuck in Salem, I refuse to let the paranormal world suck me into its grimy vortex, swirling me like water down a toilet. Nope. I'm going to get work experience.

Take *that*, Grandma Rose. Take. That.

Baldy must be elated to bill more hours to Grandma's account, because in spite of it being the weekend, he calls me back immediately after I send my text. Then he leaves a *voicemail*, which lasts so long, my phone is tied up the entire walk from the shop to Grandma's house. According to the live transcript of the voicemail, he's gotten to the point of quoting Proust when I text him:

> that's all really cool, thx, but all I want are pictures of the will and that section talking about the tides, up close and in high-def, ok?

At Bulan's request, I set out a bucket of water for the head to soak in—whether this is a method of relaxation, hygiene, or (as he suggests) feeding is unclear—and pace the room while he sloshes water onto the carpet. Normal people have roommates who utilize bathrooms. Take Jane Doe, for example, who religiously showers at 11 p.m., rubs lotion on her legs, and stretches. If only last night had gone how it was supposed to, I could be joining in that routine too, while gossiping about literally nothing. If only . . .

No. I've got to stop thinking about how upset I am to be here instead of New York. What will angst do, anyway, except bring me down? Insulting Bulan, on the other hand, is a guaranteed mood lift.

"Hey, Bulan," I say. "You aren't peeing in the water, are you?"

"Absolutely not!" Bulan recoils. "That was uncalled for! A warlord has dignity."

I raise my eyebrow. "A warlord? You?"

"Indeed I was! Many centuries ago," says Bulan, his sorrow puddling around him. "Alas, I am now nationless. And armless. Would you grab me a towel?"

Pleased at his tacit acknowledgment of my superiority, I grin and duck out—but not to comply with his request. Instead, I take a shower of my own. While working my hands through a surplus of shampoo bubbles, I ponder Bulan's existence.

Following my freshman year of college, I'd been forced to spend a few weeks with Grandma. Obviously it wasn't ideal, but I hadn't figured out how to get on-campus summer housing, and James's bachelor pad reeked of poor male hygiene. Grandma was ecstatic I'd come to visit after more than five years' absence. Her friends got excited too. Which is why I spent most of my time hiding from them at the public library.

The way Bulan talks, it seems like he was as well-established a fixture in Grandma's house as her yard flamingos. How could I have missed that when I came to visit? Like, who ignores a severed talking head? I know I've been single-minded about getting my degree and qualifying for my CPA license and starting my job. Which might've meant I was triple-minded. In other words: too busy. I guess I was just too busy.

And now the tap's running cold.

Once I'm dressed, I use a kitchen towel to create a landing pad where Bulan can dry off. He may be a severed head, but once you look past that, he really is a model house pet.

"By the way, Sabby, you missed a visitor," he says as I pat his ears. "While you were singing moodily in the shower."

A tired hope flickers in my chest. Could Dave and Amanda have returned, after everything, to pay me for the wedding? I would do anything to avoid eating more frozen Italian illness-food tonight.

"Please tell me they were newlywed vampires," I say.

"Alas! I cannot."

Though I deflate slightly, I cover it with a scowl. "Then who? Baldy?" We both shudder. "A mourner for Grandma Rose? Remy, recovered from amnesia, demanding to know why ghosts were onstage last night? That fairy guy, Roach? Someone who can rescue me from tidal hell?"

"A person."

How dare Bulan be so coy. "You're really not going to tell me who it was."

"I'm not your butler, Sabby." For some reason, he blows a wet raspberry at me. "Besides, they left a note."

It's true. I find said note freshly tucked beneath the doormat. The text is short and to the point and written in absurdly polished penmanship. It reads:

Sabby,

I was glad to hear you arrived home safely last night. I'm sorry I missed you today. If you're free, I'd like to see you again soon. Maybe you can join me in a forage on Wednesday night? I suspect you're a night owl like me. If you want to come, here's my number.

Yours,
Hanry

"Yo," I call out to Bulan. "Hanry's asked me out on a date! Whoo!"

"Don't say 'yo,'" he replies from the other room. "You sound lame."

So what. I pocket the note, stunned to feel my lips tug upward in an unrestrained grin. I don't know how I'm managing to smile when my life is crumbling around me.

But then again, this is an invitation for a date. Not even some kind of casual hang, but a *date*. With *Hanry*. And he wrote, "Yours." *Yours!*

Last night I was ready to be done with Salem for good, and done with handsome foraging men too. But maybe being stuck here for a few more days won't be the worst thing imaginable after all.

Just the second-worst.

11

I'VE REALLY GOT TO START LOCKING THAT DOOR

ONCE AGAIN, I AM NOT IN MANHATTAN ON MONDAY MORNING. But today, I have *goals*.

To prepare for the grand opening of my sham business, I dress in a greige skirt, a button-down cardigan, and crisp white sneakers—basically, as far from "Salem attire" as I can find in my luggage—and stick Bulan deep in a canvas tote. Armored with a pet head and a laptop in my bag, I open Grandma's shop at 8 a.m. sharp.

Outside, the sidewalk teems with oddly dressed hordes, all doing their best to pillage Salem, robbing it of any historical Puritan temperate decency. Whether or not they're of the paranormal variety is unclear, but what's important is that none of them enter through the front door. After half an hour, Bulan gives up waiting and whines at me until I set him up with an iPad and a high chair we found in the back alley.

Following that, I slide my laptop from my bag. I don't want to waste any more time waiting on customers, or waiting to hear from the concerningly silent world of EFG, or daydreaming about an upcoming date with Hanry. Nope. Definitely not. Much better to focus on the one part of my life still fully in my control: my CPA exam prep.

By midafternoon, right as I've maxed out on the amount of information my brain can hold about tax compliance, Baldy attempts to hand-deliver me a copy of Grandma's will. Once more, I ignore him until he leaves, and only afterward retrieve the documents from the doorway. I flip through the pages, searching for answers. Grandma's will is handwritten, her penstrokes characterized by a swoopy and loopy mess. As far as I can tell, Baldy read that part of the will about her spirit ascending accurately. It's almost impossible to know for sure, because Grandma's writing looks more like bunnies and mice leaping over each other than actual words.

"Bulan," I call. The head rolls to my table obligingly. "Do you think this looks like 'twice'? Do you think it might say 'thrice'? If it's thrice, maybe all Grandma's spirit needs is another few days of moon observance. And then I'm off the hook."

He pops up on the table, scans the page.

"Oh, is this a visual will? That's unusual."

"Those are words, Bulan."

"I see. It appears Rosie was about as talented with writing as she was with numbers. It was, of course, her personality that kept her so well-resourced to the end."

Ignoring the misguided opinions of Grandma's personality, I sit back and speculate: "What if the spell put on the will overrode her words with what she *intended* to write, instead of what she *did* write? Is that a thing?"

"It could be. Magic can be delightfully zany!"

I roll my eyes. What could possibly be delightful about unclear guidelines with potentially disastrous consequences? It sounds like the only way I'll know for sure when Grandma has ascended is by making more attempts at leaving. And probably failing.

Great.

With hopes of a reasonable solution to my magical curse dashed, I resort to escapism. I'm scrolling wedding TikTok when someone pounds on the shop door. It's not Baldy, but a short blond woman.

I jump to my feet, the picture of customer service.

"Hi!" I say, unlocking the door. "I mean, welcome. To my shop. To my wedding planning . . . business."

The woman bursts inside. She doesn't notice my awkwardness, or the fuzzy purple spiders dangling over her head. She's too busy panting.

"Hi," she wheezes between exaggerated gasps. "Whew!"

She's in her early twenties, with a glazed-over expression and a tight, chin-length blond curl stuck to her bottom lip. Her skin's eggshell-pale. It emphasizes her cheeks, red as fire hydrants. She gives off Marilyn Monroe vintage-blond-bombshell vibes, but she's coquette too. She looks like she was born in her pastel-pink Mary Janes.

"Are you okay?" I ask.

The woman all but explodes with syrupy delight. "I'm Mandy!"

"No, I was asking if you're all right."

"I'm *fantastic*! Thanks for letting me in! I ran the whole way here." So much for the "running from trouble" theory. "Wow! What is that? Is that—THAT IS AMAZING."

She's fondling a dried lotus. Why, *why* is that plant so popular with weirdos? Finally remembering my customer service script, I shut my laptop with an exaggerated arm-sweep.

"How can I help you?" I ask.

"SO many ways," Mandy bursts out, beating at the ruffles of her pink skirt. I suspect this is her standard way of expressing herself: like Bubble Wrap, popping again and again. In the process of the fabric abuse, I can see that she's wearing a thick piece of silk ribbon on her wrist. Familiar magical shapes have been embroidered into the design, marking her as nonhuman. "You see, I had to come as fast as I could! Because I'm looking for a job. My landlord kicked the bucket, and I have to pay rent to this machine now. It's terrible. And working is *teeeerrible*."

The sunniness with which she says it nearly distracts me from her words.

"You're in here because you want to work? For me?"

"In your wedding business. Yes!"

"Even though you think working is terrible?"

"Exactly!"

I fix Bulan with my stink-eye. He wouldn't have been involved in this, would he? He knows I can't take on employees for my sham company. Much less nonhuman ones.

"Who put you up to this?" Bulan asks, in an obvious hurry to shift blame.

Mandy huffs. "I read about this on the job board, silly head!"

I pause, reeling. This is all happening quickly and it doesn't strictly make sense. I only decided to continue wedding planning yesterday. But on Saturday night, I had a conversation with a certain handsome guy who was convinced I needed an assistant. Could said someone have then mysteriously posted a listing on my behalf?

I doubt it.

"Did the listing say to get in touch with someone named Hanry Burleson?" I demand.

Mandy worries her lip. "I don't think so . . ."

"Are you sure?" I won't push it, but if Hanry's interceding that far on behalf of my fake business, that kind of swings him into psycho-stalker territory. For one paranoid second, I fight off the notion that he might've made some kind of deal with Grandma Rose to try to keep me here. I'd probably prefer a run-of-the-mill stalker.

"Some crows might have posted the job," Bulan reflects. "They're very helpful, crows."

"Oh, are they sentient?" asks Mandy.

"Yes indeed, mine are! And poetic."

Enough with the supercool crow friends Bulan hasn't introduced me to, and who may or may not exist. I need to know who's recruiting for me. It's creepy, yes. But I am reluctantly—a little, very small, tiny bit—grateful to them. If I end up having to work another wedding before going home to New York, I *will* need an assistant.

One with limbs.

"I might have a job," I say slowly, hedgingly, "but just so you know, working for me won't create money out of thin air. If you need to get paid today, I can't help you. So far, I haven't been given a dollar. Or a dime. Or a penny."

"Do you even carry change?" Bulan asks.

"The point is, Mandy, I might owe more money than when I started last week."

"That's all fine!" Mandy says with a giggle-beam. "I don't care where the money comes from, as long as you pay me eventually."

"If you take the job, you'll be paid under the table," I say.

"I can crawl under tables!"

"The other thing is—"

"Tell me, tell me! I can do it."

"Without knowing what I'm going to ask?"

"I can get anything done. Anything! I have my ways," says Mandy, exposing two rows of sharp teeth with her smile. They look like they belong in the mouth of a toy shark.

In spite of this, I consider Mandy's offer. Since I'm officially sick of Grandma Rose's defrosted, mushy pastas, I come up with a quick grocery shopping list. After I arm her with that, plus a request to market to customers of the non-creepy variety, she scurries off with glee.

Once she's gone, I perch on a table, facing Bulan in his high chair.

"Did I just hire someone?" I ask. "Someone nonhuman?"

Bulan nudges the iPad screen with his nose and pauses on a close-up of Regé-Jean Page's glamorous calves.

"Seems like it," he says. "She's a pixie, you know!"

"A . . . manic pixie. That's a movie trope, right?"

"I don't know about that, Sabby. But what I can tell you is that pixies are closest to hummingbirds, comparatively."

That throws me.

"Did Mandy have wings that I missed somehow?" I ask.

"I don't believe so. It's rare for a pixie to be born with wings these days! You see, pixies used to flock near flowers and sap-producing maple trees, and flight was more useful then. Since humans learned to refine sugar, pixies have become endemic to cities instead, and prefer to keep their fluttering near humankind. Also, they're colorful. And a delight to watch."

"So . . . the hummingbird thing is an analogy. Not a scientific categorization."

Bulan offers me a neutral look. "Perhaps."

"You weren't ever educated, were you?"

"I was not!" he says proudly. "Now, where was I? Ah, yes. Fortunately,

Sabby, as energetic and charming as pixies are, they have a sneaky side too. An ability to manipulate situations in their favor, much like—"

"A hummingbird?" I smirk.

"—a siren. All this to say, I bet Mandy will return with everything you requested. And likely at a bargain price!"

This sounds almost too good to be true. "Do you think she's as harmless as she looks?"

"Only because you're straight as a headboard," Bulan laughs heartily. "At least she isn't fay! They can be such brats, I swear."

"You've said that twice now."

"Precisely. I'm providing information," says Bulan. "That's the service I agreed to provide. That, and tape cutting."

"You're a fantastic tape cutter," I agree. I readjust his iPad and pat him generously on the head. "Not to mention the cheapest pet I've ever owned. Please don't ever tell me how you sustain yourself biologically."

That night, I visit the commuter rail platform again. Just in case Grandma ascended at high tide today, without being so kind as to let me know.

While I'm recovering from the process of becoming a human puddle, a seagull poops on my head.

Tuesday starts off about as miserably as Monday finished.

I am once again unable to board the commuter train leaving Salem—though I'm wise enough this time around to wear a hat, in case I'm visited by more seagulls. While I'm debating the pros and cons of reaching out to my manager, Desmond, about the fact that Steve's essentially ignoring me, a young couple walks inside Grandma's shop, a tale of plain woe on their faces.

Clients!

The bride-to-be introduces herself as Myra . . . Myrafififi . . . no, that's not it . . . Murphy? Okay, I can't remember her full name. The point is, *Fi* and her fiancé, Asher, are in trouble, and their peril is so serious they're willing to seek my help. Sweeping her showy red hair behind her back, Fi outlines her dilemma: for months, the couple meticulously planned their mostly DIY wedding—and apparently, Fi's mom kicked that off years before then—but as their wedding day drew closer, the couple grew concerned about Fi's ability to coordinate the ceremony while participating in it. Fi's mom disagreed. She said that Fi should be more than capable of being in two places at once. It is, apparently, part of Fi's druidic heritage.

Fi is relatably neutral on said heritage.

Once they'd heard about me, Fi and Asher realized they could avoid blackmailing a non-paranormally acquainted wedding coordinator into ignoring the "unusual" aspects of the wedding. They are very excited to have found the right person.

I am not that person. But I'm desperate. See: my bruises from yesterday's attempt to flee, my near-empty bank account, and the food stores in Grandma's house that give me far too few options for a safe-to-eat dinner.

Anyway, Fi and Asher's requests don't seem unreasonable. Unlike Dave and Amanda's wedding, their event has actual functional parts. Not to mention a full guest list! The complicating factor is that it's also going to be held *this weekend*. At sunrise, on Saturday. Meaning I have less than five days to figure out stuff like what a vendor actually does, how a wedding florist and coordinator should work with said vendors, and—oh yeah—how to be a boss.

I can barely remember to brush my teeth at night. How am I supposed to be a good boss, and not just a girl boss? To be ethical and manage at least a week's pay and benefits for my pixie employee?

Well, that's a later Sabby problem. Today Sabby needs to teach Mandy not to run with scissors blade-first. Between running errands for Fi's wedding, I ask the pixie to change out the front window of the shop so it looks slightly less "Grandma Rose." We reposition the dead-eyed, dreadlocked mannequin so that she gazes into the abyss beside a three-tiered layer cake.

If that's not a symbol of marriage, what is?

With Bulan and Mandy's encouragement, on Wednesday, I tack a handmade sign on the shop door. It reads SPÜKTACULAR WEDDINGS, LLC.

I still can't leave Salem, and I haven't heard back from anyone at EFG, but who knows, maybe my emails to Desmond and Steve were so banal and blandly written that they forgot about them. I do send a follow-up to HR in case they need me to file something more official.

Then I get to work. *Wedding* work.

As much as I hate admitting it, I know I can't wing Fi and Asher's wedding like I did for Dave and Amanda. As long as I'm stuck in Salem—which I'm starting to worry is going to be even longer than another week, with how little I've figured out—I'm going to play the part of a wedding planner more convincingly. I need to learn how actual event planners do their job, and what it means to be a "day-of coordinator." But why waste time building vendor relationships and drumming up event management strategies when I can just poach that info instead? Clearly, it would be less work for everyone.

Wedding TikTok tells me that most of the wedding industry is run out of secretive storefronts and people's homes and coffee shops. The only public-facing part is the venue itself.

Ergo: I'm going to crash some weddings.

So, equipped with my phone, my tote bag, and a basic oversize button-down shirt, I set out on my mission. I cruise down Front Street, and don't stop until I find a bougie hotel with a vibe as close as possible to the one where I worked in Midtown. Utilizing my powers of wallpaper-blendiness, I breeze through the glassy double doors and pass the concierge and lobby in search of the event area. Once I find a staff member folding tablecloths in the hallway, I approach him.

"Hey!" I say. The man spooks as if he hadn't noticed me. Or as if he thinks I've burst out from his pile of laundry. Either way, I've still got it. I am as boring-beige-recycled-socks-blendy as ever. "Where can I find the hotel's private event schedule?"

"I think I've got a copy somewhere," the guy says. "Why? Who are you, exactly?"

I smile appealingly. "A wedding planner."

This does not go over well.

Which honestly surprises me. It would've worked at my old hotel. I guess the waitstaff here have *standards* and *like* doing their jobs or whatever.

Since I can't travel back to that hotel in Midtown East to ask my old coworkers for wedding planning tips, I'll have to try somewhere local. This leads me to Hamilton Hall in Salem's historic district. While unhappily sharing air with an extended family of tourists from Orlando, I catch two clipboard-armed women in ballet slippers setting up for an off-weekend wedding, probably tomorrow. Rather than approach directly, I crouch in wait behind a bush for about forty-five minutes like a very boring, very stiff-legged sparrow. At last, the timing's perfect. I pounce on one of the event staff and, while she's still shrieking, run away with her clipboard. At least she can get a copy from her counterpart.

"An absolute treasure trove," I tell Bulan and Mandy that night as we flip through the planning team's printouts. "Look. A whole page listing out the décor they're bringing on-site. It's called 'Details and Décor.'"

"It's itemized!" says Bulan, impressed.

"And check out this spreadsheet." I point at names in green. "The different colors indicate different vendors' responsibilities."

"There are so many of them," says Mandy. As she talks, she pushes a giant peppermint against the inside of her cheek. "Do wedding planners know lots of people? Lots of 'vendors'?"

"I think so. Seems important for us too. Think about it, how would a random satyr or minotaur know who's the best florist in the area? They couldn't exactly walk in and ask around. They have hooves."

"A dead giveaway," says Bulan. "Though I'd be happy to have any sort of foot, myself."

"It doesn't matter if they have hooves," Mandy says around her mint. "As long as they have good attitudes! And smiles!"

The flash of her abnormally disarming dimples gives me an idea.

"Mandy," I say. "You and me. Let's hit a wholesale florist tomorrow morning. In person."

Bulan cottons on immediately. "Clever. One with male staff? Or anyone who prefers to be in the company of women, perhaps!"

The pixie flashes worried looks between us. "What's clever? And why's it matter that they like wom—OH. I see! You want me to seduce them into working with us."

"Just *pretend* to seduce them," I say gently. "Flirt a little, make them feel special. Unless that makes you uncomfortable. I don't want to—"

"It's no problem, Sabby, I can do that!" Mandy beams. "My mom always told me to use my powers for good, not evil. And what's more good than true love?!"

Completely beyond my control, my mind jumps to Hanry. Who is *not* my true love, and hopefully not a stalker, but a smooth-dancing, normal-ish guy taking me on a date tomorrow.

"Sabby, are you . . . *blushing*?" asks Bulan.

Absolutely not. I clap my hands together to draw my employees' attention back to me as a professional. Because that's what I'm pretending to be for the moment.

"Okay, on to the next thing. Using these lists, I'm going to build out some spreadsheets, and tomorrow I'll crash the wedding and compare their prep to their timelines. Then we'll meet back here . . ."

And that's when I realize it: I'm a goddamned paranormal wedding planner.

12

I RECEIVE A WEAPON, ROMANTICALLY

FINALLY, IT'S WEDNESDAY EVENING—TIME FOR MY DATE. I DARE to exchange my daily T-shirt and jeans combo for a matching boxy brown ribbed sweater-and-skirt set. I'm not sure if "sexy tree" is a look, but if so, I've nailed it.

Hanry greets me at the cemetery gates with a broad smile and an empty jute coffee sack thrown over his shoulder. Up close, he also carries, enticingly, the scent of pine wood shavings. This is an improvement over Old Spice, which is what my high school boyfriend smelled like. Granted, what *isn't* an improvement over a purloined fragrance from CVS?

Said boyfriend, Andrew Tsai, was a closet kleptomaniac. The fact that he wanted everyone to use his full first and last name should've been a red flag. In my defense, he was a defensive back on our high school varsity football team, so he probably stole those flags right out of midair when I wasn't looking. Maybe I should spend some time reflecting on why I keep finding myself attracted to quasi-criminals.

It's happened more than once. My first college boyfriend, Blake, got caught plagiarizing his English essay and was placed on academic suspension a few days after taking my virginity. As far as I know, the next, Marcus, never did anything unlawful—if anything, he was too good for me. Too good at making me feel appreciated and seen, both when we were in bed together and when we weren't. But *especially* in bed. And on rugs. And countertops. Which once led to missing class, and my one and only late arrival to a catering shift. When my manager chewed me out, I got defensive. And had a weird flashback to Mom losing her job after forgetting to call in while on another spontaneous trip with a boyfriend. I knew after that I'd have to cut Marcus from my life. Clearly, I couldn't juggle a boyfriend with work and school. Maybe I could reconsider once I graduated and got a steady job.

Maybe I'm reconsidering now.

The point of all this is, I'm not into bad boys. No, my type is this: someone who doesn't mind me taking the relationship slow if I need to. Who's big and strong and conscientious. Who seems nurturing and stable, like a house.

Not houses like Grandma's, but, you know, more functional ones.

"Ready to desecrate some graves?" I ask Hanry in greeting.

He seems confused as I approach. "Would you do that?"

"Would *you*?"

I'm genuinely asking, but Hanry's expression clears, and he laughs. I guess he's taking my weird greeting as a joke instead of a sign of nerves. Okay, cool. More than cool. The way Hanry smiles into his thick stubble is stomach-melting, and happiness wreaths his face like a goddamn autumn miracle. I really hope he isn't a stalker or a colluder with my grandmother. The vibes he gives me couldn't be further from that. But just in case I'm wrong about the former, I've packed Grandma's unwitch hazel spray in my chest-bag, locked and loaded.

"I thought this might be a familiar place to meet," says Hanry. "Then we can walk. Sound good?"

He draws my attention to the friendly-looking gravel path that runs alongside the cemetery. It's got red-orange leaves lolling beneath warm lamplight like a happy dog belly-up in front of a fireplace. Artfully fallen acorns ripe for crunching. Not a speck of trash or unseasonable gloom.

Suspicious.

"I'm not going anywhere yet," I say, rooting in place.

"Uh. Okay?"

"There are a couple things I need to know. Two of them. First, did you set up a job listing for me?"

Surprise shows on Hanry's well-illumined and high-cheekboned face, but not too much, which makes me want to trust him. Unlike this path, which is trying too hard with its rustly fall charm.

"No," he says. "Why would you think that?"

"Because you said I needed an assistant."

"It's your business," says Hanry. "You can run it however you like."

"Exactly."

"So . . . someone set up a listing for you? That sounds sketch," says Hanry, shifting to a concerned tone. "Where was the job advertised?"

"Doesn't matter." Hanry's off the hook, so I'll shove that concern aside to worry about tomorrow. Or never. I plan to find my way back to New York next week, after all. "Second question. Can this be a casual thing, not a date?"

"Can it be both? I was thinking apple picking."

"Ripping genitals off plants?"

"A classic," he agrees.

Sure, for some people. James's family made an annual tradition of marauding as far as Maine in search of a frankly mediocre doughnut. Last year I went with them. My key takeaway from the event is that picking fruit at a grocery store and on a farm aren't so different. You need to pay attention to what you're grabbing. Specifically: you need light.

"Any reason we're picking apples after dark?" I ask.

Hanry laughs instead of taking my grumpy belligerence at face value.

"I'm friends with some guys who own their own orchard. By coming at night, we can hang out without crowds. Or lines. It's better for talking."

Huh. "That sounds great, actually."

It's also nice to know Hanry has friends who aren't vampires.

We saunter down the Path of Fall Suspicion for a mile or so, ending up at a wooded plot of land off-limits to the public, if the New Hampshire–inspired NO TRESPASSING signs are anything to go by. I let Hanry walk slightly ahead of me so his brawny body can take any rogue bullets. Apparently, it's unnecessary. When we pass a side window of the colonial home on the property, two farmer-types wave from their dinner table, where they're getting wasted on some kind of homemade cider. I relax somewhat as Hanry greets them by name.

"Any chance you have some of that cider on you?" I ask as my date walks us to a small collection of apple trees in the backyard. "I wouldn't be opposed to drunkenly falling off a ladder and having you catch me."

"That's funny," says Hanry.

I side-eye him. "Who's joking? I might be into playing the damsel in distress."

"Then I should warn you," he says. "I might find it funny to fake out catching you and let you fall."

"Wow. You're an asshole," I say, undeterred.

"I'd regret it afterward," he laughs. "How about this—I'll go up the ladder first. That way you won't have to worry about me pranking you."

"Nuh-uh," I say. "You don't need a ladder. You're basically the height of a tree already. And if this is too easy, it won't be any fun. I nominate myself apple acquirer."

"All right, but don't say I didn't warn you."

Hanry hands me an apple picker and, with his freed left hand, casually lifts a metal ladder. Just like that, we're off, and we settle into a rhythm as smooth as the moonlight. I pluck an apple and toss it to Hanry, who catches it deftly, adding it to his jute bag. I begin throwing them at more difficult angles. Nine times out of ten, Hanry manages to catch them anyway. His bag fills up gradually, to the point where he looks like a lumberjack Santa, only hotter.

"So tell me about yourself," says Hanry.

I guess the silence was growing awkward. Crap. I hate being asked to talk about myself. I'd prefer a nice, obvious, basic question.

"What do you want to know?" I ask, pushing my hand back into the leaves of the apple tree.

"Sorry, didn't mean to offend you. I thought . . . Well, we agreed this is a date," Hanry says. "That's like the first thing you say on a date. Isn't it?"

"If that's what you think, then you should go first." Ha, take *that*. "Do you have family around here?"

"More or less. They're alive and kicking."

"They on that healthy-lifestyle train? Or are they on the kicking-their-legs-to-stay-afloat train?"

I toss a new apple to Hanry, who catches it with an easy smile. "More like 'kicking' as in strong-willed and aggressive toward . . . uh, people. They're unhinged and undisciplined."

Oh. *That* I can understand.

"I also have a brother," he adds. "Kind of."

I pause before plucking my next apple. Something in his tone makes me pay attention. "Half brother?" I ask.

"Yeah, something like that. He didn't grow up with me, though I see him sometimes. My parents kind of pretend he isn't . . . family. They've never treated me that way, so . . . I don't know. I guess I feel bad about it? It's complicated."

"I get it." Sensing his discomfort, I yank the fruit off and add, "My family's complicated too."

"Oh yeah?"

"Very. I never met my dad, my mom's been AWOL for years, and my grandma was deranged. You know what's worse? She's still trying to make me in her image from beyond the grave." I stare up at the sky pointedly. If you have anything to say to that, Grandma, now's your chance.

Nope? Didn't think so.

"Was she a wedding planner too?" asks Hanry.

"Not exactly." Well, there goes any chance of him having known her, thankfully.

Palming my apple, I run Hanry through the stories of Mom, Grandma, and the generations of mostly unwed Spüks who came before them. "Anyway," I say in closing, "the eccentricity has to max out at some point. It's my fate to land our family legacy safely on greener pastures. What runs in your family?"

"We like bossy women." He says it too casually for me to ignore.

"Are you calling me bossy? Hey, don't stop holding this ladder while I'm on it."

Hanry raises his eyebrows but doesn't answer my rhetorical question. Wise move.

"What's your weak point?" I ask, climbing down a few rungs until we're at the same level. "Seeing as you've picked up on my worst quality without trouble."

"Have you seen *Howl's Moving Castle*?"

I roll my eyes. "Duh."

"Okay, so the wizard Howl," Hanry says. "He's described as a slither-outer-er, right? I think I do that more than I should. Try to get out of things when I feel they're pinching at me."

Chilled, I rub the goose bumps down on my arms. I relate to what he's saying more than I'd like, to the point that I can feel it beneath my skin. "I don't think that's a weakness."

"You don't?"

"Nope. It's survival. Keeping yourself from getting nailed down is a good default move, so you don't get trapped living a life you hate."

"Wow. I guess that's it." Hanry moves his hand near mine on the ladder. "Is that spoken from experience?"

"Kind of," I admit. It's why I clawed my way into NYU and that internship at EFG. It's why I'm so desperate to get out of Salem, present moment aside. If I go down the paths Grandma and Mom went down before me, I might take on the worst parts of them too, and become neglectful and lonely and unpredictable in all the worst ways.

"You're not allowed to slither out on me," I say. "If we have a second date and you ghost me, I'll send Mandy after you. She's a manic pixie, you know. Very sharp teeth."

"Is that your new assistant? Congratulations."

"Yes, and she has arms."

"A pair of congratulations, then."

"Can I ask you something?" I lean back on the ladder, in spite of it digging into my back, trying not to look like what I'm about to say matters. "You're human, right? Like wholly, definitely, every moon of the month and with every drop of blood, human?"

Hanry smiles. It's a knowing look that also seems like it has secrets behind it. "Yeah."

"You promise?"

"Absolutely promise," he says.

"Don't change your answer on me," I say, which makes him laugh but not elaborate. Tempted as I am to poke at it, we've only known each other a little while. And we won't stay in each other's lives for much longer, anyway. So I let it go.

Once we've collected enough apples that even Hanry begins looking worn-out, or at least bored, we climb to the top of the hill behind the property. Up there, illuminated by a waxing and offensively poetic moon, Hanry has laid out a picnic blanket and cheese boards with crackers, grapes, and—of course—freshly baked cider doughnuts. But that's not what's so special.

My name is carved into one of the cheese boards. Not Samantha, either. *Sabby.*

"You made this?" I marvel, picking up the wooden plank and investigating its smooth surface. It feels . . . sanded. This is awesome. I now have a cool kitchen tool. Or a makeshift weapon. You never know when these things might come in handy.

"Woodworking's a pretty serious hobby of mine," says Hanry. He has a way of tucking in his chin, hiding behind his stubble like he's embarrassed, that I find really appealing. "Sometimes I use found objects too. You like it?"

Yeah. I do. In fact, it's making me teary-eyed.

"Thank you," I say to Hanry's slightly blurred shoulders. "I'll have to host some fancy cheese parties now."

"I wouldn't be opposed to an invitation."

I put the cheese board into my lap, pat the soft fabric covering my thighs, and wish I'd worn overalls. Sure, they're undignified, but they have pockets for storing fruit, and more importantly, my midriff would be less exposed than it is in this cropped sweater. It's not *my* fault everything is cropped these days, even when you're looking for something frumpy.

On second thought, maybe it isn't so bad. Hanry seems to appreciate my section of bared skin, if the direction of his gaze means anything. I don't mind that. In fact, I really want him to like the way I look. To be into me.

Afraid my eyes might give me away, I concentrate on slathering apple jam onto a piece of cheddar.

Our relationship thus far is built on mostly lies. Hanry doesn't know that my business started as a sham, or that I'm only here for a few more days. He doesn't know that yesterday, I shimmied out of a window in the back of Grandma's house in order to avoid her witch cabal chanting in the front yard.

And, at least for tonight, I want to pretend that Hanry and I could have something worth nurturing.

But if I told him he's not allowed to be a slither-outer-er to me, how can I do that to him? He's such a nice guy. He deserves more honesty from me. I can't let this go any longer—even if it means this is the moment where it ends.

"I'm not really a wedding planner," I say. "Or an event planner of any kind."

Hanry's silent for a moment. "Okay."

"Okay?" I suck in my breath. "That's it?"

"Yeah, I'm . . . just processing it. Why've you been pretending to be one?"

His tone isn't judgmental, just curious. Hanry is, all in all, taking the revelation better than I expected. It makes me feel both safe and bold enough to tell him more. "I fell into it because of you. *And*, before you say anything, I wasn't planning to take any more jobs after Dave and Amanda, but I've been trapped here in Salem by my grandmother's magical will."

Skeptically, Hanry asks, "How does that work?"

"I have no idea. She was eccentric."

"Aren't most people?"

I give him the stink-eye.

"Or not. So, what do you have to do to get out of it? I'm guessing you're still trying to."

"How do you know that?" I ask, unable to keep defensiveness out of my voice.

"You did say 'trapped.'"

Oh. Right.

Since Hanry has a point—and I've committed to telling him the truth—I take a deep breath and let it all out.

"A few weeks ago, I didn't live in Salem. I only came here after my grandmother died, to execute her will. I didn't realize there'd be a catch."

"Most magical things have a catch," says Hanry.

"I'm learning that," I sigh. "Anyway, Grandma needs my help for her spirit to ascend to god-knows-where, and it can only happen after seven tides are passed twice, high and low. In other words, a week, right? Unless it's thrice? But more than a week has passed, and I'm still stuck here. And I don't know why."

"Are you sure the seven tides thing refers to time?" asks Hanry.

"What else could it be?"

"Tide Pods."

I snort. If only.

"The truth is, I'm supposed to be in the middle of my second week at a new accounting job in Manhattan right now. Since I've been trapped here, I've had to call in bogus excuses, one after another. Worse excuses than the one I gave you for being in the cemetery at Grandma's grave."

After chewing on this, Hanry asks, "Gotcha. And what *were* you really doing there?"

"Trying to bury Bulan."

Although he's been admirably serious up to this point, Hanry laughs out loud. "Why? He's hilarious!"

"I know that now!" I retort, but that only makes him laugh more. Of course a guy like him wouldn't have to worry about finding a head without a body and being accused of murder. If the charm didn't work, all he'd have to do is turn it off, and his towering mass would terrify anyone into silence. I don't have that advantage.

"So you really made up that whole thing?" Hanry asks, wiping his eye while smiling. "About being a florist and an event planner? And you didn't correct me or try to back out after I mentioned my friends' wedding. Holy shit, Sabby. Is this why you were so weird about your duffel bag?"

"Yeah," I admit. "I didn't really expect you to follow up!"

Hanry whistles. "This is amazing," he says. "Sabby. I stand by what I said on Saturday—you did a great job. I'm even more impressed now that I know the circumstances."

I thought he'd be mad at me for lying. He's taken me by surprise, and I'm stunned at my own relief. How good it feels to be open, to trust someone with a secret like this. Flustered, I ask, "Really?"

Hanry has barely caught his breath. "Yeah! That was your first wedding? Unreal. Now I want to know what else you've been keeping from me."

"Well, I can promise you I was honest about one thing."

"What's that?"

"I wasn't lying about my dancing skills. Those moves were completely authentic."

"Yeah, we'll need to work on those. How can you be so bad at dancing and so good at faking that other stuff?" he asks.

"The only kind of dancing I like to do is in a place where people can't see me."

Hanry glances around. A smile sneaks onto his stubbly face, catching shadow. Marking mischief. "We could dance here," he says. "Right now."

"Hell no," I say before biting into an apple slice.

"Really? All right, suit yourself. I guess I'll just have to dance . . . by myself . . ."

"Have fun," I say as Hanry clambers to his feet. He can't be serious.

"I'm going to do the boy's part first . . ." And he does. He puts out his arms as if holding an invisible woman, presumably me, and starts to glide on the grass, humming. "Now for the girl's part . . ."

Once again, his footwork is nothing short of masterful. Head to toe, he's graceful, strong, coordinated. And all while being silly as hell.

"How do you know the girl's part?" I demand.

"My dance instructor made me learn both," says Hanry, somewhat breathlessly. "It's really hard doing some of these movements without someone holding on to you."

"It was awkward," I say, sympathetic, "even with you holding on to me."

"What's a loop-de-loop?" he says in a falsetto. "Oof! Ahh!"

I'm blushing, but thankfully it's so dark, I doubt he sees. "Shut up. I don't sound like that."

He just laughs. "Nah. But I like your voice."

Finally, Hanry gives up his single-man dancing and comes back to the picnic blanket. He does that annoyingly hot thing where he tumbles off his feet, landing in a perfect, model-esque slouch across from me. I've seen guys do this in movies. I didn't know real people were capable of it, much less on a first take. It's enough to make me feel like this isn't real.

And then I remember.

"So explain something to me," I say. "You're wrapped up in the whole paranormal world and its weirdness. In spite of being . . . not so weird. Why is that?" By which I mean, *Why would you do that to yourself?*

He shrugs.

"I don't know. The Community isn't all bad. At least not bad-weird. It has its pros and cons, same as the regular world."

"Yeah, I don't buy that. I need specifics," I say around a mouthful of cheese.

"Okay, Miss Bossy," Hanry laughs, settling closer to me. Wow—he smells good. I already knew this, but it bears repeating.

"Humans can get a little boring," Hanry says. "I like staying on my toes. Or at least, I'm used to it."

"Is that why you're so tall? All those toe stretches?"

He nods, feigning seriousness.

"Well, good for you, Sir Toe Fetish." On that note, it's time for my next question. "Were you really collecting pine cones that night?"

Hanry nods, reaching for one of my cheesy crackers. "I use them to make wreaths. And sell them."

"Ew," I say. "Those things grandmothers buy?"

"And great-aunts."

"At least you know your niche. Are you on Etsy?"

"Definitely not," Hanry says after swallowing a bite. "I'm bad with computers."

"I'm a spreadsheet champion," I brag. "Which is what makes me so great at my true calling."

"Auditing." Hanry nods.

For the rest of the date, Hanry and I talk about work—which sounds boring, but it's not. He tells me about traveling up and down the inland highways of the Northeast, playing nice with small-town strangers, selling foraged and wood-hewn wares at farmers' and handcraft markets. It's clear he's not the college type. This should mean he's not *my* type. How could pine cones pay for a blasé McMansion in the burbs? I shouldn't be so enraptured by him. But I am.

Hanry's playful nature makes it hard to be rational. The simplest things seem to give him joy—including being with me, for some reason.

Besides, there's something about his physicality that gets me. I really like Hanry's hands. They swallow mine up when he holds them. They're also slow enough to let me grab the last doughnut.

And they support my weight with gentleness when I lean forward to plant a kiss upon his lips.

At once, the chill in the air falls away. The warmth of Hanry's mouth, the sweep of his arms encircling me, it's like being wrapped in a wool blanket. I'm riddled with sensation—with heat. When Hanry's hand slips under my sweater hem and slides across the sliver of skin exposed below my ribs, my breath hitches. I push myself toward him gratefully. But Hanry moves back.

"Sabby—" he starts, but I interrupt.

"It's cold out, damn it. You've got a job to do," I say.

When I hook my hand on his neck and pull his face down again, I feel Hanry's laughter; how it shakes his chest, how his lips turn up at the edges against mine. His thick stubble grazes my cheeks and chin.

And as we kiss again, I answer his smile with one of my own.

13

I AM THE GIRL BOSS, COO COO CA CHOO

MY DATE WITH HANRY WAS, SIMPLY PUT, A ROUSING SUCCESS. So much so that before he says good night, we make tentative plans to hang out again on Friday. It gets even better: first thing in the morning, I finally hear from someone at EFG.

It's my HR admin contact. Apparently, Steve is in trouble for failing to reply to me within a seventy-two-hour window. Also, FMLA is a touchy subject with HR, and they've ensured me they'll fix things—and that I should have as much as twelve weeks, per company policy. This gives me rapturous relief. Twelve weeks is certainly a long enough time that I can figure out how to help Grandma's spirit ascend. I text Jane about the situation, promising to keep paying rent while I stay in Massachusetts for ambiguous family reasons. She speculates that Steve and the admin might have internal work drama I can use to my advantage. She says Desmond is nice.

Presumably, this is why the winds of fate—those cruel, stupid, Salem-y winds—fail to shift any more in my favor.

For one thing, when I get puddled while attempting to board the commuter rail at 7 a.m., the rail guard openly laughs at me. This has become a daily occurrence.

For another thing, while I'm trying to brew a pot of coffee in what may not actually be a coffee maker, I catch my grandmother's friend Matilda gathering the flamingos from the front lawn. She wanders away with them tucked beneath her arm, which I'm fairly sure is a criminal offense. Why is she doing this? Unwilling to engage further, I wave a solemn farewell.

For a third thing, the late afternoon wedding I'm crashing at Hamilton Hall is a thousand times duller than Dave and Amanda's. It's got some lovely points, though: for one, there are exactly zero vampires present. This major win aside, the bride's choice of fringe tulips as an accent flower is inspired. So is the silver-and-lilac color scheme, and the extra chairs she sets aside for unexpected plus-ones—or wedding crashers like me. This is about where the highlight reel ends. During the long-winded, boring speeches, I employ my powers of invisibility, standing near the various doorways of the venue like a well-dressed fly. I listen intently to the drink staff whine about the bride's desire for a champagne tower, forcing them to serve flat, warm champagne. And while I shovel dry, gray, blueberry-crusted cake off a chipped ceramic plate, I overhear the planners manage the unexpected presence of someone's pet rabbit and source a spare battery for the videographer.

Evidently, the devil's in the details when it comes to weddings. Which is good news for me. I love details! Finally, a transferable skill.

I don't get caught in my nefarious wedding crashing until I'm purloining samples of couple-themed goods. The wedding planner chases me halfheartedly down Chestnut Street, but I blend into a tour group and lose her. All in all, I'd call my spy mission a success. Mandy and Bulan, the recipients of two pilfered, overly herbal cake balls, agree.

It's late Friday afternoon when I catch Rochester glowering at the Spüktacular Weddings sign, his frame backlit like a sexy jack-o'-lantern in my shop doorway.

Honestly, I can't believe that bitchy fay is back.

"How long should we make him wait?" I call out to the interior of the shop. Mandy and I have filled the room with bohemian pillows that a vendor delivered for Fi and Asher's wedding. I don't like them.

They're more over the top than a camping tent made out of caftans and macramé. But the main issue is, I had to put down a deposit for them. Fi and Asher's vendor demanded I pay one before he left—which felt like something Fi should've done—and it absolutely devastated the funds I've been saving up from Fi's and another client's wedding deposits. Possibly, I've been scammed.

On a happier note, Mandy discovered that Grandma installed speakers in the ceiling, and now the shop is filled with the high-volume croonings of BTS. And the boys are so, *so* beautiful.

From where she's plucking dead leaves off a flower stem, the pixie cries over Jungkook's dreamy voice, "We should make Rochester stay there all day."

"I support that thoroughly," says Bulan.

"Oh good," says Mandy. "Because I need to STARE at him."

And not only stare, but drool. Well, it's time to cut the fun short. Mandy's saliva could ruin the delicate silver dollar eucalyptus she's clenching in her death grip. Getting those from the wholesale florist in Danvers took hard work. Apparently, he "needs florists to submit orders months in advance" and "doesn't have extra stems and greenery for nontraditional clients." Unless you bring along a disarmingly pretty pixie, in which case exceptions can be made.

I let Rochester in.

"Thanks for knocking," I say.

He enters the room, paradoxically fluid and stiff. I guess this answers the question I never had of what it's like to meet an animated block of ice.

"I did not knock," says the frigid fairy.

"Yep, that was the joke. How can I help you today?"

He ignores the plush spider that has landed on his shoulder and says coolly, "I'm here for your quote."

"I don't have it," I say.

He frowns. After a solid half minute of two-sided stonewalling, I say, "Just kidding. I wasn't *going* to give you one, but I've changed my mind."

Kind of.

Rochester's documents laid out a vision for an elaborate, gorgeous wedding. Clearly, the financial reward for accepting his clients' job would be ample—I suspect comparable to half a year's pay at EFG. But I have common sense in addition to financial sense. It's what tells me that accepting money from fairies is too damn dangerous.

According to Bulan, the fay are responsible for mischievously starting wars in the Community, and for plaguing humans with strange, unearned afflictions—from pimples to polka to full-blown insanity. They're rumored to steal children. Plus, *these* fay are choosing to communicate through an intermediary, likely making them extra dangerous. I can't risk taking their money and running out on the job.

Here's my dilemma: outright rejecting Rochester's clients might come off as suspicious to other potential clients. Salem is small, and based off what Bulan's told me, the Community's got to be even smaller. So my goal is to make Rochester's mysterious clients lose interest in me by putting together a dumpster fire of a proposal. And oh, what a foul-smelling, accelerant-laced dumpster fire it is. Grandma would be proud.

I signal my one paid employee. "Mandy?"

"Oh, right! On it!" Blushing, she dashes to the back of the store. With that matter taken care of, I brush the spider off the stilted fairy's shoulder.

"So, Roach. *Roachster*. Can you tell me more about your client?"

"Those whom I represent would prefer to share more details *after* confirming their interest in working with you."

"I take it they're important?"

"One might say that."

"I've got the folder!" Mandy returns, waving a pink portfolio, red-cheeked and adorable. She passes the folder with her bow-tied pink shoe popping off the ground, but tragically, Rochester fails to notice. His eyeballs clench onto mine like he's attempting to pierce my soul.

"I will inform you if we choose to proceed," he says.

"Cool cool," I say.

Deigning to give us a final, stoic nod, Rochester leaves. Once the front door shuts, Mandy presses herself against it with a dramatic sigh.

"I wish he would notice me," she says.

"The rest of the street has." I tap the glass in hopes she'll observe the awestruck tourists who have essentially walled up the sidewalk, plus the two dads who have caused incalculable anger in their wives. "Now come on. Stop pressing your boobs against the glass and get back to our garlands. They're not going to make themselves."

Around 11:30 on Friday night, my alarm punches into my dreams with the unfriendly sounds of electronica.

If I close my eyes, I can envision a backwards, happier version of this life, where I'm up at eleven thirty because I go out dancing in SoHo on the weekends, or I stay up late studying with music in my ears. But no. Nope. This accursed version of Sabby Spük goes to bed before sunset so she can wake up to perform nuptial assistance to druids.

That, and flirt with Hanry Burleson.

These two reasons combined explain why Hanry, Mandy, Bulan, and I congregate in the shadowed alley behind the shop at midnight. We're here extra early so that, unlike at Dave and Amanda's wedding, we have enough time to set up, plus leeway. Within the next six hours, we'll receive, deliver, and set up the vendors' supplies for Fi and Asher's 6:32 a.m. druidic wedding ceremony and reception. The nuptials are timed to the sunrise, of course.

Technically, Hanry isn't here to do anything but load the rented U-Haul truck; he's mostly here to be eye candy. That, and to perform duties as my emotional support animal.

Our plans to "hang out on Friday" became a three-part adventure. The first thing Hanry did the morning after our date was to visit the shop with a single white rose in a freshly hammered wooden vase. He came back at dinnertime with a coupon for two-for-one oysters near Pickering Wharf—and what's more romantic than a man who wants to save money? As loathsome as I find being downtown during Salem's holiday season, it turns out you can avoid most of its chief annoyances when accompanied by a man the height and girth of a medieval battering wall. As a bonus, Hanry's presence alone diverts any and all potential attention more than a foot and a half above my head.

Which earned him a make-out session after dinner, while we walked the waterfront. I guess Hanry wasn't put off by my scowling at the waves as they lapped against the pilings, rocked the docked boats, and mocked me in general for failing to understand the magical functioning of their tides. If anything, he seemed like he wanted to help me, and kissing was the best way he knew how.

"You sure you don't need me to come with you?" he asks now, having kindly piled the last of the pillows and pallets into the trailer for me. His eyes are doing that whimsical thing again, making it hard to answer in a reasonable way.

Fighting temptation, I ask, "What time is your craft fair in Maine, again?"

"Not too early."

"Uh-huh," I tsk. "You told me it was eight a.m. No driving without sleep."

"Is this another 'rules for thee, not for me' thing?" says Bulan from Mandy's arms.

"I got sleep!" I retort. "What did you think I was doing in bed after dinner?"

"I didn't want to ask," says Bulan, eyeing Hanry. "I assumed the same thing you'd been doing with the rest of your free time."

"All right, I think I'm going to leave you all to it. But only because you insist, Sabby." Hanry seems adorably sad he can't role-play the noble knight again. "Text me if you need me, okay?"

"We will!" says Mandy on my behalf.

After waving Hanry goodbye—and kissing him good night, to Mandy's squeak of delighted embarrassment—the three of us depart for Dunks, a warehouse, and the florist. Then I drive us to Harold Parker State Forest. Mandy devours half my doughnut holes and downs my iced matcha before I can take a sip. I'm discovering she isn't great with personal boundaries. But she keeps the conversation lively, so we're all in a good mood when we unpile into the woods at two thirty in the morning.

I walk around the side of the U-Haul, the forest air piney and fresh in my nostrils. As Bulan and Mandy chat giddily with each other, I take a moment to catch my breath. I do a round of calm yoga breathing like Jane did that one time her rotisserie chicken was shoveled onto her plate with herbs instead of being served plain.

I have a bad track record with being in the deep of the woods, just outside Salem, at night. But what's it matter?

Tonight will go differently. Because tonight, I'm not a naïve twelve-year-old.

Tonight, I'm the *boss*.

14

ENTER: MOMZILLA

"ALL RIGHT, BULAN," I SAY, ROLLING UP THE REAR TRAILER DOOR. "What's first on our agenda?"

Bulan, carrying a pen in his teeth, observes from atop a shiny new clipboard: "Paranormal review session! Druids today trace their descendance from a line of Celtic nymphs, possibly as many as ten generations back. Most of them are no longer capable of turning into trees at will—"

"Such a disadvantage," I deadpan.

"Really is," coos Mandy. "Palm trees seem so happy."

"—but they can communicate with most anything that has chlorophyll on a cellular level. They have a strong reverence for the cycles of nature, for the earth, and of course they are responsible for funding Greenpeace. Also, many Scottish Highland dramas."

"Ooh, I didn't know that!" Mandy says.

"Do druids have any magical abilities I should worry about?" I ask.

"Depends! I was friends with a druid once!" says Bulan. "Well, you could say he and I were . . . more than friends, actually . . . Oh, look what you've done. You've made me miss my body."

Mandy pats him on the head. "There, there."

"What's next on the list?" I say, because lamenting a centuries-past romantic tragedy is not a good ritual for a wedding.

"Right!" Bulan returns to form, all but cross-eyed as he evaluates the bullet-pointed items on the clipboard. "We need to create the wedding stage, then tackle the seating. And bring over the flowers, the catering—"

"Weren't you supposed to be illiterate?" I ask.

"I have a highly detailed memory!"

"Great. Anyway, let's get the pallets out first."

"To the secret island!" Bulan shouts with a two-foot-high bounce.

Mandy claps her hands together. "Yay, secrets!"

According to Google Street View, the only thing in the middle of Frye Pond should be lily pads and frogs. Maybe mosquitoes carrying West Nile and malaria. But Fi told us to expect an oddly luminous island in the center of Frye Pond, and sure enough, that's the spectacle we discover. It's so mesmerizing, it initially keeps us from looking at the shoreline—and our feet. Which is how I end up banging my shin into the first of five canoes with firefly-lit lanterns affixed to their hulls.

"At least that solves how we're getting to the magic island," I mutter, rubbing my leg. "Let's load up, team."

"Check!" calls out Mandy after biting into a chocolate bar.

"We can only say check after we've gotten the pallets ready," I remind her.

"Uncheck!" Mandy pretends to roll up her sleeves, then jumps into action, alternating between chewing and chattily unloading pallets to me. The two of us pack the first canoe, only belatedly realizing we'll need to be inside them to cross the pond. As a result of our oversight, I'm forced to sit hunched, with my head twisted so far left it's like I'm auditioning for *The Exorcist*. Which is how I happen to spot the hazy form of something in the woods, ten feet deep into the trees.

Pretty much the moment I see it, the indefinable, whitish thing pops out of sight. Like, it actually *pops*. What the hell?

"Did you see that?" I ask.

Mandy cranes her neck. "What, the moon?"

I shake my head. "It could've been a plastic bag . . ."

Though those don't randomly move or pop. A ghost, maybe? Only, it didn't remind me of the ghosts at Dave and Amanda's wedding. I cling hard to the oars, feeling weirdly vulnerable, when salvation appears in the form of a light over the water.

"'Ello," calls out a voice emanating from the glimmering light. The person who the voice belongs to seems to be—

I'm sorry, it's not a person.

Okay, that's rude. People can be hairy. That doesn't make them lose their personhood. But this person is ungroomed to the point of approximating a friendless primate, without a companion to pick bugs from their hair. I squint.

And, shit. It really isn't a person. It's Sasquatch.

So, apparently, Fi failed to mention that her venue coordinator is America's #1 Most Wanted Cryptid.

"'Ello," the Sasquatch booms again. "Are you Sabby?"

"Yeah, hi," I call back. "Are you my venue contact? Robert?"

"That's right," says Robert the Sasquatch, balancing a lantern on his head as he swims toward us. "Lovely to meet you, Sabby and friends."

I check behind me once again, confirming the plastic bag hasn't returned for an encore performance. Then I sweep my arm toward my staff in introduction. "This is Mandy and Bulan."

"Hello!" they say.

"How nice, and hello!" says Robert. He emerges from the water, all eight to nine feet of him, and in a very experienced way, shucks off his head lantern and shakes away pond water like a gleeful golden retriever. Grainy footage always depicts the Sasquatch as being lopey and dopey, but Robert is impressively slick, with a great sense of balance.

"We need to get across the pond," I say. "Can you push these canoes for us?"

"Absolutely," he says. "Not."

Pained, I ask, "Which one is it: yes or no?"

"That was a joke!"

"Sorry?"

"I'm a stand-up Sasquatch," Robert says. "The joke was when I said 'not.'"

Unfortunately for Robert, comedic timing matters. I stare at his overwrought, fuzzy forehead until I get the feeling he might run off awkwardly in shame. Sasquatches are notorious for this.

In the end, Mandy's the one to rescue us from not laughing. Balling her hands into fists, she cries, "I'M SO EXCITED! This is my first wedding! EVER!"

Either appeased by Mandy or enraptured by her, Robert agrees to do his job. And so Mandy, Bulan, and I release the oars and let a man-ape ferry us across the pond to Fi and Asher's extremely makeshift venue in a worrisomely porous canoe.

In retrospect, maybe I *should* have worked through lunch to earn a longer nap. Because looking past the pallets and my companions, at the glowing island ahead, I feel a sense of . . . I don't want to say that I'm overwhelmed.

It's just a lot.

I shut my eyes, imagining I'm far away from this boat of grim passage—specifically, that I'm back in New York with Jane. That I'm well-rested and unruffled, with my taupe, pilled cotton comforter tucked up under my armpits. A blah and characterless apartment wall in front of me, and a dry, drab-covered book about tax history askew in my lap. That would be great. So great that I meditate on this image for the entire crossing until the canoe lands on the island's shores with a sloshy, wet bump.

The island, it turns out, is also a bit leaky.

When I clamber off the now-dampened pallets and jump onshore, mud floods the toe box of my Crocs. This is a just punishment for wearing them to a wedding again. One must reap what they sow and all that. But does it have to be this . . . mushy?

Mandy hops into the slop beside me, apparently unworried about her rainbow-striped tights being swallowed to the ankles. Then she shrieks.

"Chihuahua tongues!" Her shriek becomes a laugh. "It feels like tiny dogs licking me!"

"The island does that," calls out Robert from the shore. "He's just saying hello."

"*He?*" I demand.

"We call him Dexter."

"What kind of name for an island is Dexter?"

"Oh, let me guess!" answers Bulan. "He goes by Terry for short!"

Because the world is unfair, Bulan doesn't sink into Dexter, the overly friendly island that also goes by the nickname "Terry Firma." Instead, Bulan finds himself bouncier on this surface than usual. He's practically an astronaut, freshly landed on the moon. He jumps like it's his job.

Which reminds me. We have a *job* to do here. I forcibly wrest my attention from Dexter/Terry and focus on the circle of boulders at the island's center. It's lit dramatically by floodlights, which explains the glowing from the shore.

"Robert, is everything ready at fake Stonehenge?" I ask. "Can we set up?"

"It's a historical replica," sniffs Robert. "Not 'fake.'"

"Sure it is. I'm going to start off with the ceremony area, setting out pillows and pallets. Mandy will go to the reception. If you could point her to where she should store the catered food, then . . ."

"A head? Right here!" Robert points at Bulan defying gravity and laughs.

"Or right *hair*," says Mandy, grabbing onto Robert's dangly arm hairs.

"Har-har!" Robert is now bent over laughing. "Har-har-har!"

Bulan jumps up and down to emphasize the hilarity of these puns.

Since everyone around me is useless, I act as if it does not, in fact, feel like my feet are being perpetually greeted by Chihuahuas and unpack the pallets by myself.

Armed with a venue coordinator and an able-bodied assistant, I should have no trouble setting up for a wedding—even if said wedding is hosted on a not-entirely-inanimate island. And that seems to be true initially:

by the time Robert pushes the last of our supply-bearing canoes across the pond, Mandy and I have finished creating the base of the stage-cum-wedding-altar in the center of the stone circle. We've covered the pallets with carpets, emptied twelve trash bags of leaves on top, and laid out the freshly woven garlands of silver dollar eucalyptus, threaded with dahlias, daisies, and white phlox. I artfully pluck a few blooms out and strew them across the ground, which . . . eats them.

And burps.

Thankfully, Dexter doesn't have a taste for stones, the stage, or the seating. I appreciate this, because the tasseled floor pillows are rentals. Robert helps Mandy and me position them meaningfully around the stone circle; then we walk the venue, ticking through items on the checklist. Our wedding setup seems to be going off without a hitch. The venue looks almost boho-cool instead of just weird and random.

I hold up a hand.

"High five?" I ask Robert. He eagerly lopes to meet me, and gears up to slap my palm with satisfaction, when we're interrupted by a huff.

A disapproving, ominous one.

I turn my head and am met with the most terrifying middle-aged woman ever. She's a redhead, clocking in at over six feet and easily two hundred pounds of pure muscle. She has aggressively pointed eyebrows and biceps that would make a gym rat weep. Her outfit doesn't tone things down either: she's dressed in a silky knee-length skirt, and held in place at her neck by a twisty silver brooch is a deer pelt cape. With the head still intact. The deer's eyes are bugged out. Its tongue lolls to the left. I think this was homemade. As in, last night.

"Are you the photographer?" I ask hopefully. But Robert takes a soggy knee to the woman, dashing my hopes. Mandy, politely noting the cue, curtsies in her strawberry-embroidered skirt. Bulan bows nose-first into his clipboard.

"Good morning, Becuille mac Nuadat!" Robert says. His reverence merely prompts another huff. I swear Dexter starts trembling a tiny bit beneath us.

"Knock it off," I grouse, stamping pointedly.

"It is not yet morning," announces the she-monster, Becuille. She then shifts her ire to me. "I, Becuille mac Nuadat, am the mother of the bride. Master of ceremonies. Chief Druidess of the Northeastern Shore. And I *did not* approve of . . . those."

I attempt to follow her gaze. It seems she's referring to the pillows. Which aren't laid out in a seating arrangement anymore, but instead are forming a pyramid. It gives the energy of ancient Egypt mated with the Woodstock concert of 1969. What the hell? Is Dexter expressing an aesthetic preference? Or was he preparing to turn them into a midnight snack?

"We'll be putting the pillows into the arrangement Fi wanted," I say soothingly. Or at least what I want to be soothing. It clearly isn't the right tone, because the druidess clenches her teeth so hard, a vein sticks out of her neck.

"Who is Fi?" she demands.

"Your . . . daughter?"

"I see you refer to the sole child of my womb, Mryyaofionnadynn mac Nuadat," says Becuille, who I now choose to think of as Hell-Mother. Only a creature of darkness would terrify an animated chunk of dirt. Or worse, give their daughter a name too long to fit on a Scantron. "I told her your services would not be needed today."

"Okay. Well, we signed a contract. You'll have to take it up with her."

"I will." Before stalking away from me, she adds, "No pillows. Disgusting. Robert!"

Relieved to be off the hook, I slink away in search of Bulan.

I find him hiding, understandably, behind the cake stand. I'm glad he's avoiding the Hell-Mother's all-knowing sight. Compared to Robert and me, he has the disadvantage of being the shape and size of a soccer ball. And Becuille has the physique and vibe of a good kicker.

"Bulan," I hiss. "Someone moved the pillows."

"Well, I suppose you should move them back, then."

Oh, like it's easy. "The bride's mom wants me to get rid of them. If I put them back how they were, I know she'll be pissed. But I have to; it's what Fi wants. What could Becuille do to me, Bulan? Can she curse me?"

"Stab you," Bulan corrects. "Oh, I have *not* missed interacting with druids. So pretentious! You know they're crunchy too. The pillows probably have polyester woven into the—"

"I don't care if they're made from orphaned babies' hair and threaded with octopus tears. This wedding is for Fi and Asher, not Fi's mom. What am I going to do?"

"Avoid creative punishment?" Bulan guesses.

Hmm. Judging by her deer-pelting skills, Becuille does seem like the creative type, not to mention the domineering kind. In #weddingtok terms, she's a Momzilla for sure.

Now that the Hell-Mother's landed on Dexter's banks, almost all the work I've been performing to meet Fi's requests gets derailed. She doesn't let me take a breath without disagreeing with how I'm doing my job. Crumpling my layout sketch, she tells me the salad bar needs to be positioned in line with the sun. On stable ground? Absolutely not! Oh, and what's with the tables? There shouldn't be forks. Why are there forks? What else are hands for? There go the forks, tossed into a makeshift fire she chanted into existence.

Becuille is such a terror, it takes me over fifteen minutes to realize that she's not only indicating bizarre changes she wants me to make, but correcting problems too. Specifically, she's noticing things I did that have been . . . undone.

Like the fact that all the knives somehow ended up in a punch bowl. And that the napkins, which we laid out facing right, are now facing left, out of alignment with the sun. It sounds like a small thing, but it's annoyingly time-consuming to fix, especially when I discover the placards with the seating assignments have been shuffled and placed randomly on the tables. Mandy and I didn't make this mistake; we checked.

This isn't us. It isn't Becuille, either.

Is it Dexter?

Maybe, but I don't have time to figure out how he could be managing this. Supervising Momzilla requires my total focus. While Bulan mostly spends the next hour hiding, and Robert takes an absurdly, maybe intentionally long time ferrying the canoes back across the pond, Mandy sticks bravely to my side.

During one particularly stressful rant, a glance at my phone informs me I've missed the scheduled arrival of Fi and her wedding party. Or, more accurately, *they* missed it.

Are they running behind schedule? And if so, how badly? I don't see Fi anywhere, in spite of the lavender tint creeping into the sky.

There is, however, a suspicious splashing coming from the water.

Fi crawls onto Dexter's bank wearing a white, satiny bridal dress with a sweetheart neckline, a lily pad stuck to her shoulder, and a completely blank expression. Presumably she knows her mother will have enough expression for them both.

"How could you let yourself fall in?" demands Becuille, dragging her wet daughter to her feet.

"The canoe had holes in it."

Hold up. Our canoe was leaky, but even with a ton of pallets, it didn't seem like it was going to imminently sink. I send Mandy a covert gesture she doesn't comprehend. Okay, fine: it's on me to go investigate, then. Because I can't let this go. It's my *job* not to let this go.

"Holes are nothing!" Becuille fumes at Fi, while I sneak over to the upside-down canoe that Robert is just dragging ashore. "You didn't beseech the water for safe crossing, did you?"

Fi answers sullenly. "No, Mom, I didn't. Let go of me."

"At least it removed that awful potion from your face."

"It's called makeup. And it wasn't awful."

Up close, I have no trouble making out the holes pockmarking the salvaged canoe. Some of them are easily one inch wide. Most seem clumped together. I would've noticed them for sure when we did our last crossing.

Meaning this is new. It's happened behind my back—like the pillow fort and the missing cutlery.

This is *sabotage*.

"Robert," I hiss quietly. "Something nefarious is afoot."

"Oh no! Do you think so?"

"I do," I say. At once, Robert throws his hairy arms onto his head in a stage-worthy display of fear. "It's almost like we're being targeted for—"

"ONCE AGAIN," snarls the Hell-Mother, scaring away a flock of shorebirds and causing Dexter to quake beneath us. "I disagree to disagree. What are you wearing? This isn't the dress we agreed upon!"

"Unfortunately, I fed that one to a bear," says Fi.

I look at Fi, absorbing everything about her situation in a way I haven't done before: the unfriendly presence of her Hell-Mother, the sabotage, the soaking-wet wedding dress and messy hair. An unstoppable wave of sympathy courses through me. I'm no wedding expert, but I'm pretty sure this isn't a great start to your wedding day. Fi deserves the day she's dreamed of, not the unhinged one being unexpectedly sprung on her.

In the shadow of Stonehenge Fake.0, I round up Bulan and Mandy.

"Any idea how we can help Fi?" I ask them. "Mandy, you first."

"We can set her mom on fire!" Lit by the floodlight, Mandy's shadow is actually, momentarily, more terrifying than Becuille's.

"No. Next," I say, filing that Grandma-like tendency away.

"Look, Sabby!" Bulan says, bouncing prodigiously. "The guests!"

On the opposite bank, indistinct figures are gathering. Several cars have parked along the break in the conifers near our van, and in the pale light of approaching dawn, I make out two saddled horses and what appears to be a moose. To be fair, the moose might be a coincidence.

All of this, however, reminds me of something important.

"You know how at Dave and Amanda's wedding, all that stage equipment fell on top of us?" I ask.

"Of course!" says Bulan.

Mandy shakes her head. "Was it wedding confetti?"

"It was not! And before that happened, I thought I saw something creepy in the hallway. I don't know what it was, but it wasn't a vampire or a rockabilly ghost. And remember I saw something tonight, before

Robert showed up? That I thought was a plastic bag?" Mandy and Bulan make noises of agreement. "I think it's followed us here. And it's sabotaging us."

"No!" says Bulan. "Not an evil plastic bag!"

"I think it's *been* sabotaging us," I continue, hoping that I've communicated my gravitas appropriately. It's hard to say. Though Mandy murmurs, "How terrible!" in spite of this pronouncement, she seems as pretty and cheerful as ever. Maybe that's because of the white dahlia tucked behind her ear, stolen off the garland or plucked from the maws of Dexter.

Hmm. Actually, that gives me an idea. There isn't much I can do if this wedding venue is being sabotaged, but maybe I can still help Fi feel—and look—bridal.

"Mandy, hand me that flower," I demand. After a little janky work with spare floral tape and the barrette I've clipped to my pant loop, I have the start of a flower crown. "Bulan, why don't you go to the ceremony site—Stonehenge *has* to stay intact, keep your eyes on it!—and wait for me. I'll be there in a few minutes. Come with me, Mandy."

Tugging a plaid tablecloth off a reception table, I slide into the middle of the rapidly escalating conflict between Hell-Mother and daughter with Mandy in tow.

"Hi, Fi!" I say brightly. "You're gorgeous! Wow. All you need is your hairpiece!"

"What are you—" The Hell-Mother pauses, mid-storm, to glance at the offering in my palm. "That 'hairpiece' is hideous."

"I love it," says Fi.

Beneath us, Dexter rumbles in either agreement or indigestion. To my mild delight, he burps up three more dahlias.

"Want to make it a flower *crown*?" I ask. "Seems like that would fit with the venue's, uh . . . vibe."

"You can't argue with the earth, Mom," says Fi. "Not your beloved earth."

Apparently, nature is the Hell-Mother's singular weakness. Capitalizing on this moment, I say, "Agreed, Fi! We better move fast and do what Dexter wants. How about we use this tablecloth to dry off? Amazing. Now let's come this way to get your hair finished and your meditation on. We can make sure you're out of sight when the guests arrive. Bec, how about you stay here to greet the guests? Mandy, keep a lookout for the bridal party."

"I'll send them your way!" Mandy says. "Becuille, oh my *trees*, your calf muscles are so BIG."

With the Hell-Mother distracted by Mandy's pixie-dusted ego-stroking, I rustle Fi to the safety of the ceremony site. As I get her situated on her meditation platform—aka pillow fort—I mentally run through a final, harried checklist. Bridal party, check. Bride and bride's family, check. But bride's future family and her fiancé, Asher? Nowhere in sight.

Oh no. This couldn't be more sabotage—could it?

"I was really hoping to look beautiful today," says Fi, her voice dejected.

My thought-spiral slams to a halt. Bending down, I look her in the eye.

"You *are* beautiful," I tell Fi earnestly. "That dress clings to you where it's wet, and it's hugging your curves, like, *wow*. Your skin is so well-hydrated, it's glistening. And your hair is taking on a dark, moody glow as it dries. You look incredible."

"I wanted to look like—like I did during my makeup and hair trial."

Of course she would. Wouldn't anyone?

"Didn't you come into my shop right after doing bridal portrait photos?" I ask, the memory returning to me. "The way I see it is, it's up to *you* to choose how you want to remember your dress. You can frame the photos you took while dressed up on Tuesday. As for this morning, I'll ask the photographer to take lots of distant shots and silhouettes. That way, you'll have lots of options."

"Oh," says Fi. "What about my makeup? I don't look awful, do I?"

"Hmm. You've got a soulful doe-eye thing going. Here, let me . . ." Digging a tissue out of my pocket, I wipe the more-raccoony-than-soulful eyeliner away. "There. I think it looks fine. Besides, Asher loves you for *you*. He'd marry you even if you wore your mom's dead deer as a tutu."

"Bet," says Fi. "You know, Mom would love that."

"Which is why we'll let sleeping deer lie. Do you want some time to dry off? Do you think your mom can hold back the sun?"

Though I'm halfway serious, Fi laughs. I'll take that as a win.

"It's fine with me if we start late," she says, tucking hair behind her ear. "Thanks, Sabby."

Leaving Fi embracing a Stonehenge replica rock, I seek Robert out. It comes as no surprise that in classic Sasquatch fashion, he's hiding behind an elm.

"Hey! Robert. Any chance you have a stand-up routine ready to go?" I ask, catching his arm before he lopes away. "We're going to push the wedding out a bit. And while our guests are waiting, I'm sure they could use a laugh."

"So could I," says Robert. "Badum-chaaaah. See? That was the sound of a mic drop."

"Not a drum snare," I agree.

"Correct! Snares are terrifying," says Robert as I herd him toward our arriving guests. "I lost a toe to one once. See?"

If Robert weren't a Sasquatch, I'd go out on a hairy limb to suggest he'd still have trouble finding work on the comedy circuit. The good news for everyone is that a low line of clouds keeps the sunrise at bay until the moment Fi's fiancé arrives. And when she walks down the aisle, the sun catching on her fiery curls, Fi looks beautiful. Really. Her golden-limned figure glows as warm as candlelight. Asher can't keep his eyes off her—to the extent that he trips over his feet, face-planting into Dexter. This makes for a great photograph, and it also allows everyone relief from forced laughter.

And yet, our drive back to Salem is mostly somber.

Actually, no: I'd like it to be somber, but Mandy and Bulan are working through the leftover wedding cake Fi wasn't allowed to bring back to her freezer.

They've also insisted on tuning in to classic radio.

"I thought it went well," Mandy says from the back seat, between outsize, crumbly bites and verses from Cyndi Lauper's "Girls Just Want to Have Fun." "I mean, besides, you know—"

"Fi falling out of her canoe," says Bulan.

"And her mother interrupting the ceremony."

"Multiple times."

"And Dexter vomiting during the handfasting."

"I guess it was an allergy."

"He's flower-intolerant," says Mandy. "So sad!"

I clear my throat to get the pair's attention.

"I think it went okay, too. Did you see how Fi smiled when she and Asher were pronounced husband and wife? It was brilliant." As I say it, I realize this was the first time I'd seen Fi's face break free of any tension. In spite of my exhaustion—maybe because of it—the thought makes me do the same. "Fi seemed happy, didn't she? In spite of everything. She even laughed when Robert tried to dance with her mom."

"I think she loved it. And we helped make it happen!" Mandy exclaims. "Yay!"

"Hooray!" Bulan echoes. "We didn't sink the party!"

And there goes my smile. The whole canoe debacle continues to disturb me. "What do you two think about the weird stuff that kept happening today? During setup?"

"I don't know. Was it Becuille?" Mandy asks.

Bulan effortfully turns in his seat, fighting to speak around the shoulder strap. "Hmmph. If anything, I suspect the bride was responsible. Fi could've been using you to go behind her mother's back, Sabby. She could've sunk her canoe into the lake on purpose."

"No way," I say, thinking back to her dejection about her makeup. "What woman doesn't want to look her best on her wedding day?"

"You're unusually obsessed with your appearance, you know," says Bulan.

"That's not true. I don't want people to notice me."

"Yeah, and you work *really* hard at it," says Mandy. "It makes you stand out."

"Indeed," Bulan pitches in.

Because they're callously colluding against me, I change the topic. "Fine, then. How do you explain that strange whining during the ceremony? The napkins getting an origami treatment? The food on the buffet tables jostled everywhere, like someone had tried to make scrambled eggs?"

"I thought it was romantic," says Mandy.

"No!" I interrupt, swerving the van unintentionally. "It wasn't romantic, and it wasn't just this wedding. We are the victims of sabotage. *Sabotage*, I say!"

Unconvinced, Mandy stuffs the remainder of the cake in her mouth.

"You really think so?" asks Bulan.

"I do," I say. "And I think it's . . . ghosts. The saboteurs are ghosts."

I think on this. Presumably Mandy does too, as she attempts to chew her massive helping of cake. Bulan just laughs at me, because he's a jerky, pompous know-it-all.

"Now, Sabby. That can't be it!" Bulan says with a knowing, puntable air. "Certainly, ghosts affected your last wedding. But they would've shown themselves, had they been present this morning. Ghosts are uncannily vain."

Ignoring him, I ask the back of the cabin, "What if it was Grandma Rose? What if it was her unascended spirit?"

Mandy hasn't successfully swallowed her cake, so she chews furiously instead of answering.

"Rosie?" I hear the frown in Bulan's voice. "I very much doubt that. She would never sabotage you."

"But she was weird. And unpredictable," I say. *And hurtful*, I nearly add but don't.

"She loved you," says Bulan.

I grimace. Yes, I know she did. And I should've loved her better, and I couldn't.

Maybe that's what this is all about—is this Grandma's revenge for me ignoring her for years? It's hard to imagine. Like Bulan said, she wasn't the vengeful type. She did want me to stay in Salem, though, enough to keep me here with her magical will. Besides, who else would be so invested in my success or failure?

Because I'm not. Not invested in these weddings in the least.

My only goal is to get back to my New York life: my bland and gray-walled apartment with its perfectly acceptable bedsheets and my reasonably enviable but not-interesting-to-talk-about-in-conversation job. When I'm not so busy, I'll do a better job of remembering that.

I stare grimly out at the road.

"Don't overthink this, Sabby. Sometimes things go wrong without a reason," Bulan says to console me. "In spite of it, time marches forward. Always! So we might as well make the best of it."

I switch off the radio, pivoting to my K-pop playlist. Sure, it's easy to believe whatever you want when all you have is a head. But I don't say that aloud, because Bulan acting pouty is no fun on a car trip.

15

WEREWOLVES AND GRANNIES AND GNOMES! OH, MY.

"SO YOU THINK YOUR GRANDMOTHER IS HAUNTING YOU," HANRY surmises. "Wow."

He's come to visit me at the shop on Monday, and he's brought work with him in the form of a half-carved wooden pumpkin. It's a cute thing to do. Adorable. As was the way he draped his shacket on my shoulders when I shivered in the cool draft from the front door.

And none of it matters. I'm too deep in self-pity. And mild annoyance at the fact that Bulan's more interested in life-altering romantic pursuits than my personal danger, based on how he's avidly watching the 1995 BBC production of *Pride and Prejudice* from his high chair, rather than joining our conversation.

"Not anymore. I did wonder briefly if it might be Grandma," I say to Hanry, my lone supporter in this world. "But I was sleep-deprived and running on fumes at the time."

"And now what do you think?"

"I'm still convinced she's laughing at me. But maybe not haunting me directly. She's more subtle than that. And while she may have had questionable food hygiene, she would never, ever, mess with someone else's food. Food was sacred to her. It's why she refused to wash anything before cooking. She wanted it pure, with all bacteria intact."

Hanry nods as he shaves a slender piece off his pumpkin. "From what you've said, your grandma doesn't seem like the subtle type."

"Nope. If anything, she was lazy. Grandma never liked doing things herself. I mean, without my assistance, she can't even—you know what? Never mind."

"Sabby," says Hanry.

It's so kind, it takes almost everything I have not to bury my face in my hands. Hanry squeezes my hand with his warm, strong, and distracting fingers.

"Whatever or whoever's causing all these problems, Sabby, I'm sorry."

"Thank you," I say.

"It sounds rough. Though I have to admit, my parents would've probably found it funny."

Ugh, men. Always turning it back to themselves.

"But what do *you* think?" I ask. "Do you think I can rule out Grandma Rose's ghost?"

Hanry releases my hand—just as I'm starting to really enjoy the touch—and picks up his steaming mug of nettle tea. After a sip, he says, "Yeah. For one, ghost hauntings are uncommon. Ghosts are self-absorbed. Focused on their own unfinished business."

"I told you!" crows Bulan from across the room.

"Go back to your Regency trash," I instruct him, which he does.

"You get poltergeists more often than ghosts," says Hanry. From his offhanded tone, he doesn't seem to realize he's pointing me to a paranormal danger I hadn't realized existed. "I doubt your grandma became one of those. Poltergeists have a hollowed-out sense of self, and they'd be happy to burn the world down if they could. Your grandmother doesn't seem like she had enough resentment for that. I'm assuming she put those up?"

His gaze indicates the spider stuffies dangling over the front door.

"What, you don't think I did that? Do I not seem like the plush, cuddly type?"

Hanry laughs. I mean, he's right, but still. I *could* have a whole ten-by-ten storage container filled with Beanie Babies and Labubus that I like to jump into and swim around in. How would he know?

"Remind me how you know all this ghoulish stuff," I feel led to say. "You *do* swear you're human, don't you?"

Grinning behind his mug, Hanry says, "Swear it."

I unsubtly check in with Bulan. Unfortunately, he's slurping Cheerios from his plastic tray, reverted to Roomba mode again.

All right, I get the message. It's time to set this aside and return to wedding work. It's the only thing I can do to earn money right now, and for some reason that doesn't make me feel sad or remind me of all the dreams I'm missing out on. When I pull out my laptop, Hanry begins to stack his sandpaper sheets and return his tiny chiseling knives into his leather-bound carrying case.

"No, don't leave. You won't distract me. I'm not studying." At his curious expression, I explain, "I'm about to send a survey to my clients about their close relationships."

"You have more weddings lined up?"

"In two weeks' time," I reply. Hanry seems pleased. He smiles into his light beard in that shy, secretive way I'm starting to like too much. "I haven't heard anything from work, but as long as I'm here, I might as well make cash. It's the financially responsible thing to do."

"And what are the surveys for?"

"To help me be as prepared as possible. I don't want to be caught wrong-footed by family drama again. Or surprise Momzillas."

Or saboteurs—though I'm less certain about how to plan for those.

"I would happily wear a mech suit to fight Momzillas," Bulan calls out. His voice and beard are equally thick with Cheerios.

I cast him a grin. "I'll see what I can arrange."

I don't really mean that, same as I don't really mean to be a wedding planner, wedding florist, or wedding anything. But as I expand my in-process spreadsheet, I can't help feeling like I'm faking it too well.

Over the course of the week, I continue to be foiled at the train platform by Grandma's nefarious will, and communication from New York remains eerily silent. This might be the first time in my life that not being sought out has stressed me out. Silence is supposed to be a sign that everything's okay, that the world is calm and good. But I'm unconvinced a metaphorical piano isn't about to fall on top of me somehow. That this is the downbeat before a laugh track sets off.

I've been in Salem almost a month, and I can't help getting concerned about my team's progress on the MicroOrange account, how hard it'll be to catch up. It's been ages since I've talked, much less texted with Jane, and my CPA exam is looming and dooming on me from a mere two months away. I should be forcing much, much more of my attention toward all of that.

Instead of on Hanry. Or my sham business.

But work beckons. I bang out two new wedding concept boards and email them to more potential clients who might give me deposits before the end of the month. I set Mandy on a search for a pigeon to communicate with a pair of elves who don't use email and possibly live in a tree. For the hell of it, I schedule an appointment to meet with the baker who made Fi's cake, in case they'd be willing to work with me in the future. I leave texts and voicemails for catering and décor specialists so I can source more than just linens, chairs, and tables for the discerning paranormal bride. Courtesy of Joe the scuba instructor, I schedule a meeting with two Finnish mermaids preparing for an American-themed elopement. I'm thinking they'll need tiki torches, tipis, a bushel of pampas grass, and at least three inflatable flotillas.

The biggest thing is my newest clients, Sidney and Brett.

Sidney Barroway is only a few years older than me. She's the great-granddaughter of an industrialist, possibly a Boston Brahmin, all up in her yacht club, yadda yadda. At least she was, until her interest in BDSM led to her getting bit by the wrong hairy person. Why she felt I needed this information is as mysterious as her reasoning, mid-consultation, for pulling her feet from her Jimmy Choo mules and filing down her toenails with a sheet of sandpaper.

When Sidney was turned into a lycanthrope, I think she changed in more ways than a full moon can account for. Which, I suspect, is why she kept losing wedding planners. The one who dropped out last week literally *paid Sidney money* to get out of doing their job.

Anyway, Sidney's wedding to Brett will take place—as I said to Hanry—two weekends from now in downtown Boston. Since it'll be a Catholic mass in a historic cathedral, per family tradition, the priests are restricting her input, so she's only requesting my help with the reception. That'll be held at a luxury hotel where I'll pick up the wedding planner's reins to coordinate seventeen vendors. In addition to creating the group text to rule all group texts, I'll perform a few physical jobs too, like delivering her catering and ensuring the safe arrival of her custom wedding cake, which is almost more expensive than a full year of NYU tuition.

The scale and costs of this wedding didn't boggle my eyes in the slightest. Nope. Watered them, maybe. But Sidney seems—in spite of the trust fund and unfortunately doggish characteristics—like she could be a friend. If I didn't know better.

Now and again, I find myself thinking about Fi, arriving wet onshore before the crack of dawn. I don't know what might've happened if I hadn't been there. It wouldn't have been good.

She would've felt alone. Lost. Desperate. And I know that feeling. I felt it when Mom didn't come home, and that first bill arrived, and I realized she'd never come back to pay it. When Grandma Rose's friends laughed at me, snaggle-toothed, while I held my vomit-covered apple.

Point is, I need to know all I can about Sidney and Brett and their families. To ensure their big special day doesn't become their worst. So I clack away at my keyboard, Hanry sips tea, and Bulan occasionally bursts out with accusatory language toward Elizabeth Bennet.

Generally, the great vibe continues until one morning, Hanry enters the shop with such an air of significance, he basically swarms half the room.

"I know what to do," he says.

"With what?" I ask. "Your pumpkin art?"

"My mech suit?" asks Bulan hopefully.

"You're still on that?" I ask Bulan.

"Better," says Hanry. He accosts me with a dashing smile. "I'm going to help you with your saboteurs."

To my disappointment, Hanry's solution isn't violence.

"You need something more hands-off," says Hanry as we dodge

the ruffians of Salem. "Besides, you don't know who your target is. It's dangerous—and rude—to presume."

"True," I allow begrudgingly.

It's a beautiful fall day, irritatingly sunny and cinematic. As Halloween approaches, the number of witches in this place is growing more alarming, and more diverse, by the minute. You've got your influencer witches, your gauzy-veil-wearing witches, your brujas, your steampunk-librarian-with-feather-tufted-eyeglasses witches, your pit-bull-terrier witches, and your Japanese schoolgirl non-witches. Everywhere I look is a feast for Grandma's eyes. Even the Dunkin' is spooky.

Why, Grandma. Why did you have to die at the cusp of Salem's most rabid season? Why couldn't you have passed away at a more innocuous time, like Christmas?

"Just to check, you said the white blur you saw in the woods was hiding, right?" asks Hanry.

"Hiding or floating. It reminded me of a plastic bag. Can a witch disguise themselves as a plastic bag?"

"That sounds like a lot of work."

I shrug. "Grandma's friends are retirees. What else do they have to do except cosplay?"

"I don't know. I guess I'm asking because . . . well, it matters whether the source of your sabotage is living or not." At my curious expression, he explains, "If you were being sabotaged by a plastic bag *or* by someone living, a psychic couldn't help. For one thing, if your grandmother's friends were behind this, they wouldn't appear at a séance. Séances are for the dead."

Wait. I can't believe I'm saying this, but—

"We could reach out to Grandma Rose," I say. Why didn't I think of this before? "She's been watching me this whole time, right? Forget the weddings. She could tell me what she was trying to get out of me in her will! She'd let me know exactly what the tide thing's about."

"I haven't recommended that for a reason," says Hanry, his voice kind. "Sabby, séances can go wrong. They can lead to spirit possession.

The longer your grandma lingers in the in-between, the greater the odds of her wanting to hang on to this world. Most legit psychics wouldn't consider doing it for you, no matter the price."

"So visiting a psychic is a last, worst-case, nuclear winter-y scenario."

"You still have other options. One *good* option." Hanry's voice is painfully encouraging. A pedestrian light changes, stopping us at the curb. I wait as Hanry chews on his lip and sticks his hands into his pockets. He seems unwilling to say what he's about to say. "Gnomes."

The pedestrian light flickers on again, musically, obnoxiously. Before Hanry and I can move, before I can ask why Hanry suggested we purchase lawn gnomes for Grandma Rose's front yard, a random cowboy two-steps between us, breaking apart our clasped hands. "Yeehaw!" he says.

I cover my eyes. Everything in my life has to be a goddamn spectacle, doesn't it?

Hanry rescues me with a solid push to my back.

"I . . . don't know what that was," he says, guiding me past. "Let's just go this way."

In spite of Hanry's odd reluctance to be up-front about the gnomes, I suspect they were the thrust of his plan all along, because minutes later, we arrive at a Home Depot with a garden center. I take his hand in mine, squeeze, and release some of my fizzling indignation at the universe. Yes, I'm still living in Salem the Madhouse. No, I'm not in New York. But at least I have Hanry, and Hanry is bringing me to a box retail store, a normal place. Because he's a nice, normal person.

Yet I'm suspicious. And cranky.

"How will redecorating Grandma Rose's yard help, exactly?" I ask. I haven't told him yet about the kidnapped yard flamingos or the earthen craters lingering tragically in their absence. Already a couple of tourists have started throwing coins into the largest hole in my Grandma's lawn, thinking it's some kind of bleak, decorative Halloween-themed wishing well.

Gently disregarding my mood, Hanry points us past the garden center entrance and to the Home Depot's back wall. He casts a few longing glances down the aisles with drill bits and power tools but perseveres until we near the bathrooms. He stops at an unmarked swing door.

Of course we'll be going through that door. Of course.

"This way to wonderland," I mutter.

"Nah," says Hanry. He gives my shoulders a reassuring squeeze. "Wonderland is only accessible by tunnels. And with PBI clearance only."

"Who?"

"The Paranormal Bureau of Investigation."

Pleased, I say, "I knew that had to be a thing! Can I hire them to help me?"

"Probably not. Their main job is to erase human memories about the paranormal community," he says, to my disappointment. "Anyway, this room leads to Special Services. They're the ones who can send out gnomes for you, to do whatever you need."

On that unsettling note, Hanry pushes the door open. A single buzzing fluorescent bulb lights a sterile room, featureless but for a long counter with a hanging sign that reads SPECIAL SERVICES. Behind the counter, a bored woman with a pierced nose and a buzz haircut flicks to the next page in her book. Hanry places a forearm casually on the countertop, smiling. This behavior should come off as unbearably gross, but his smile is somehow un-smarmy and un-creepy. I cross my arms so he knows how little I appreciate his display of effortless charm.

Hanry doesn't pay attention. He is a man on a mission.

"Socks," he says.

"One moment."

The woman dog-ears a yellowed page in her paperback. She places it face down and leaves. Which is odd, because I note that this room has no windows. Or doors. Or air vents.

I look around. Where the hell did she go? Where did the door we entered through go? And what's with the secret password?

"Did you know," Hanry says out of the blue, "that you can fix your phone by turning it off and on again? No matter what's going wrong?"

I shoot him a disbelieving look.

"Really. You can," he says, misinterpreting me entirely. "I visited an Apple store recently. Have you been to their Genius Bar? They've got some great tips."

"Hanry," I say, "they aren't geniuses. They're dweebs with peak TikTok keyword skills."

The representative returns with an off-brand iPad. Hanry has it turned upside down as he passes it to me. He nearly drops it.

"Sorry. I, uh, forgot where the buttons are."

I know that Hanry more or less called himself a Luddite, but this enters anachronistic time-traveler territory. If I didn't know better, I'd think he was raised by a lost Amazonian tribe. But then again, he's from New Hampshire.

"Tablets don't have buttons," I say as I take over, tapping through the single icon on the main screen. When the app loads, I scroll down a list of services. "What am I looking for?"

Somewhat distressed at the speed of my window-opening and swiping, Hanry points to the bulleted option between *TALK TO CATS* and *RAPSCALLIONERY* that reads *GNOMES*.

Interdimensional Buzz-Cut Lady chimes in from her book. "Suggest the specific mayhem you prefer. Then fill in the address of where you'd like a visit."

"Thanks," says Hanry. "What she said. Petty linen theft is the lowest tier, but it gets all the way up to lawn and sod trampling, persistent plumbing issues, pest infestations, and 'other.' Gnomes thrive under creativity."

"Wow," I say. "Gnomes are like, the jack-of-all-jacking-up-trades."

"The MVPs. Especially when it comes to subtle, hard-to-trace chaos. You can't get any better." Hanry rubs his one-inch-shy-of-bearded chin. It looks very scruffy and scratchable from here. "The first time I used the gnomes' services, I was ten. I had some cousins visiting for the first time, and they started bullying me the moment our parents left the room."

"Ah. Classic. It's hard to imagine *you* getting bullied, though. How badly were you outnumbered?"

"By four," says Hanry. "They were older and stronger than me. I didn't know how to get back at them and needed extra help."

"You could've told your parents." Not that this would've worked for me, but I remembered that James's parents would do anything for him. Same for the parents of my high school friends, who had strong opinions about fighting houselessness in Portland and let me sleep on their springy mid-century sofas.

"My mom knew I was getting bullied," Hanry says. "She wanted me to toughen up, I think."

"Yikes," I say, returning to the present. "That's brutal."

"Yeah. My dad might've intervened, but he was away on a business trip."

"Now I see why you moved away. Plus, the head damage from bullying explains your weird hobbies."

"Touché," laughs Hanry. "I love my parents, but yeah. Getting away is nice."

"No kidding. With the way you talk about your family, I'm amazed you turned out so decent. It must've come about in spite of their best efforts. Happens sometimes."

This drops me into unwelcome thoughts of my own parentage—the similarity between Hanry and me doesn't escape me—and I'm so deep in thoughts of Baja California, I almost miss it when Hanry says, "Well, that's, uh . . . the funny thing. I'm adopted."

I look up from the iPad screen. Hanry is pressing his lips together, like he's wishing he hadn't spoken. He's tensing his jaw too. Maybe setting it against the hurt shadowing his words.

"Really?" I ask. "So on our date, when you told me things were complicated . . ."

"Yeah," Hanry says. "My parents—my adopted parents—aren't perfect. But they do their best. I want to make them proud of me, and happy with me, if I can. It's the least I can do. They're better than my, uh, birth parents."

"You don't have to tell me about them," I say, sensing we're entering private territory. But Hanry keeps going.

"They always kept me inside. They were chronically online, get-groceries-ordered-to-the-door people. We never went anywhere, never did anything. Even when we were together, we weren't. I'd tell them things, and it would go in one ear and out the other. I mean it. One time I broke this finger. They told me to google how to reset it instead of taking me to a doctor. You can see how well that ended up." Hanry lifts his left hand, revealing his subtly crooked index finger. For all the times it's touched me this past week, I never noticed. "They didn't seem to even know what I looked like. I'm serious."

"Damn," I say uncleverly.

"My adopted parents—I like to think of them as my real parents. My real family. We actually mean something to each other, you know?"

I nod, understanding. I definitely do know what it's like to have a parent who isn't present. That's one thing about Grandma I liked: when she spent time with me, I could tell, in that moment, that I was the center of her zany, black-hole-riddled universe.

Hanry continues, "They already had a son my age named Seb. We're not close. That's probably my fault. I think he felt like I was replacing him, and I get that. I was trying so hard to be good enough for my family, I was always trying to match up. It's stupid, because we're such different people. I wish I could go back and undo it. Or at least apologize, but at this point it feels like too much. So, I don't feel like a decent person, but I'm trying to be one."

I can't help the tightness in my throat. Shit. I figured Hanry had baggage, like anyone, but I hadn't realized life dealt him such a difficult hand, or that he blamed himself for it. The sense of understanding I had earlier remains—only now I'm feeling a twinge of gratitude to Mom, who at least never compared me to other children. Who was willing to keep a distance from Grandma when she heard what happened to me on Halloween night. Even now, she makes the effort to call every once in a while, even if she's drinking tequila more often than not.

I can't imagine how Hanry must have felt, being forfeited by his parents. Complete abandonment. I want to ask, but more than that, I want him to feel okay. If it were me being vulnerable, I know what I'd want him to do: ignore it. Or make a joke. So in the end, I smile awkwardly at Hanry and say, "If you ever get a lethal injury in my presence, I promise to call an ambulance. And do all the googling for you."

"Thanks."

With that settled between us, I tap the iPad screen and reopen the list of gnomic tomfoolery. “Aha! This, here. Found the ‘gnome detail’ option.”

“Yeah, that’s the one,” says Hanry. He sounds relieved to be back on safer footing.

“Good. I’m going to type in the description, ‘stay vigilant for potential schemes of sabotage, then report back to me.’”

“Smart,” Hanry says. “Don’t forget to add ‘violent retribution, optional.’”

Hanry’s gaze drops down on me. I was right: he looks like he’s more comfortable again. Maybe sharing his secrets with me has made him feel lighter too. His blue eyes are shining with mischief, and in spite of his technological incompetence, I could kiss him. Maybe do more than that.

“I shouldn’t be surprised you have a devious side,” I say. “I did catch you sneaking into that graveyard, after all.”

“My motives were pure,” Hanry argues. “I was creating art, sustainably.”

“Art isn’t pure. Have you *seen* the Venus de Milo?”

“Have you seen yourself in the mirror?”

“Oh, flirty again. I like it.”

The rep doesn’t, based on her annoyed huff. Who cares what she thinks? I’m in a better mood now that I have a working plan to hire nefarious beings of nonviolence. We can sabotage the saboteur, fight the paranormal with the paranormal. I like the justice of it.

“Why do gnomes take jobs like this?” I ask, returning the iPad to Buzz-Cut Lady.

“Because,” she answers, “gnomes are little assholes.”

Harry nods in hearty agreement. “It’s due to fracking, probably. Some members of the Community lost their homes to the fossil fuel industry. The gnomes, the fay—”

“That’s right! Fay live underground.” I read that in one of Mom’s favorite books. I think it was called *The Court of Sexy Times*. I blush, remembering one particularly spicy scene and trying not to look at Hanry’s arms. Confusingly, the sexiest thing about him might not be his biceps, but the way he understands my sense of humor. I never thought that was a priority before. Well, I guess he's raised the height of my romantic bar. I can't believe he lets me rib him as much as he does. And I don't mind the way he counters back, not in the least. "So, Hanry, do fairies hang out in caves, like bats? Are they secret vampires?"

"The fay don't suck blood, and they don't have wings," he ticks off. "They don't live underground anymore either. Sometimes near cave entrances, but not always."

I think back to Rochester. He was definitely wingless, unless you counted his eyelashes.

"How do you differentiate them from humans?" I ask. "Secret little claw feet? Telltale moles?"

Struggling to keep a straight face, Hanry answers, "Personality defects."

"You mean like—"

The rep clears her throat.

"Can you please complete your payment? My book is becoming impatient." She's not joking. Her copy of *A Complete History of Chocolate Making* has started growling at a low level. Maybe it's not a book but a chocolate-themed, historical cat. "And sign here?"

When she taps the number on the screen, my eyebrows shoot up my forehead. They nearly crawl into my hair before I chide them back.

Hanry whistles. "Whoa, that's expensive."

I shush him. "It's fine."

Hanry isn't wrong; these gnomes cost a lot of dough. I'd be worried if I didn't know for a fact enough money's coming in with Sidney's wedding to cover my half of the rent in that Midtown East apartment, the Home Depot's gnomic army, *and* Mandy's undefined wages.

Buzz-Cut Lady offers me a receipt, seemingly materialized from the air. I take it, prepared to ball the paper up and toss it over my shoulder, when I'm stopped: on the back of the receipt are coupons for Home Depot's various business partners. And one of them has a name I could never, ever miss:

DA SEVEN TIDES SCUBA SHOP.

16

WEREWOLVES CAN BE CLASSY, TOO

HANRY, BULAN, AND I BEHOLD THE FRONT OF DA SEVEN TIDES Scuba Shop with differing degrees of wonder.

"I feel like it's had a rebranding," I say finally.

"That's one way to put it," says Hanry.

In the window, the painted driftwood sign revealing the shop's name is lost beneath a burden of barnacles. And by "barnacles" I mean witch junk: crystals backdropped by tie-dye sarongs. Odd statues with vaguely spiritual vibes. Lava lamps. A sincerely painted canvas of a werewolf riding a surfboard.

"Joe's had something of an identity crisis since discovering he was one-eighth mermaid," says Bulan. "Best not to mention his snorkel."

"You're talking about Scuba Joe?" I say, stunned. "Our mermaid-client liaison! This is his place?"

"Well, yes. Weren't you planning to pretend that you were coming here with questions about the mermaid wedding?" Bulan blinks at me questioningly.

"No. I was planning to be honest."

"That doesn't sound like you!"

It's not, but sometimes, one must compromise their values. I don't want to hear any rambling that isn't Grandma-related.

"I'm trying the door," says Hanry, ever helpful. Grateful as I am for his diversion, unfortunately, the door doesn't budge—and if Hanry's heft can't do the trick, what can? And I may be new to entrepreneurship, but I can't imagine closing my shop in the middle of the afternoon during peak season.

"Bulan, can you get in through the pet door?" I ask. "See if anyone's inside?"

"Much obliged to try!" Bulan pops out of my arms.

A passing tourist points as my pet head vanishes behind the plastic flap. "Cute cat," she says.

"Thanks," answers Hanry. "I trained him to be off leash."

I roll my eyes, evenly irritated at both conversing parties. Hanry has a habit of rolling with the oddities of Salem, rather than finding them grating. My current theory is that New Hampshire isn't too far from Stephen King's Maine, so he must've witnessed some paranormal horrors in his time, beyond what even Salem can cough up. I have a whole zombie-hunting logger fantasy that Hanry has neither confirmed nor denied.

The door swings open, revealing a familiar whiff of chlorine and a scuba-clad owner. Sure enough, it's Scuba Joe.

"Hello, Sabby," he says after removing his mouth from his snorkel. It looks slightly algaeic: both the snorkel and his mouth. "What a nice surprise, seeing you with your coworker! And your noble companion! As I told Bulan here, I'm in the middle of feeding, so my attention might be divided. But come on in!"

"Watch your step!" says Bulan, not quite fast enough to escape the edge of Scuba Joe's flipper. Poor head.

Predictably, Hanry holds the door for me. I can't help mouthing "my noble companion" at him. It triggers an adorable blush.

Scuba Joe floppily leads us past the crystals and two walls of diving equipment, backlit by a few empty aquariums, colored LED lighting, and a hint of tropical wallpaper. Through the back door into his office, we find . . . much weirder aquariums. These are inhabited, but I don't know by what. Is that a starfish? It has far-too-prominent lips.

And *that* is definitely some kind of a bear with fins, but it's the size of a gummy bear. It growls menacingly when we make eye contact and flings itself at the aquarium wall.

"I'm getting some weird Ursula energy in here," I whisper to Hanry. He shrugs.

"I hear you. I associate glowing lights with evil," he admits. "At least most of the lights seem electric-powered."

"So, how can I help you three?" asks Joe, lifting his mask onto the top of his head. Looking into his dark eyes, unmediated by a reflective layer of plastic for the first time, I gather that he came by his shop's Caribbean theme honestly. The Jamaican flag pinned to the wall is also a decent indicator.

"I'm curious what you know of my Grandma Rose. Did your shop mean anything to her?"

He thinks. "She helped me source my kelpie kelp," he says, gesturing to a slime-filled bucket with a concerning stench. "It was a great tragedy she passed. My new supplier overcharges. She wants nail clippings along with my payment."

"Unacceptable!" cries Bulan, followed by a splash.

This is because he has leapt into the sea bear's aquarium.

"Whoops, sorry!" says Hanry. He fishes out Bulan, who seemed happy to bob around as the tiny bear-monster beat its claw-fins against his ears.

"How'd Bulan get in there?" asks Joe, concerned. "That shelf is five feet up."

We are *not* going to talk about the physical impossibility that is my pet head. "Please, never mind that."

Joe allows his attention to be drawn back to me.

"Did Grandma come visit here often?" I ask. "Did she rent out this building before you, maybe?"

"No and no. Are you trying to learn more about her life? I've gotten skilled at compiling genealogies, should you be interested. I've got friends at the Maritime Museum. Salem was once renowned as a maritime town, you know, and my great-great-grandfather—a whaler, in fact—had the strangest experience in the Bermuda Triangle. It's quite the tale."

"I'm sure it is."

Behind Scuba Joe, Hanry surreptitiously reaches into another aquarium and fishes Bulan out again. Damn it, Bulan! Must all bodies of water be a siren song to you, but with no siren required?

Whatever. I'm just going to have to cut to the chase.

"My grandmother mentioned *seven tides passing* in her will," I tell Joe, then recite the words back to him. "I'm wondering what it meant, and if it might have something to do with your shop. Any ideas?"

"Seven tides meant something to you, evidently," Bulan tells Scuba Joe, dripping onto Hanry's shirt and arm. I take back all the sympathetic feelings I had for Bulan's bodilessness and pass them to my freshly waterlogged Hanry.

"Seven Tides Lane was the address of my old shop in Seaport," says Joe. "In Boston."

"It was?" I ask weakly. "That's where the name came from?"

"Correct! I doubt it meant anything to your grandmother. But seven seas—if she had written about seven *seas*, that would be noteworthy! There's seven oceans across the globe. The Atlantic, Pacific, Mediterranean, Indian . . . Maybe Rosamund wanted you to visit all seven seas and feel the tides on each of those foreign beaches, twice over?"

This lead has turned out to be a bucket of slop. How could I globetrot while being trapped in Salem? Grandma was zany, but she wasn't completely impractical.

"Wrong," I say.

"Probably," Hanry agrees.

"Sorry," apologizes Joe. "The only solution I have for you is to wait around until whatever she meant becomes clear. The tides bring up all sorts of interesting things in their time. Oh, on that note! A note. Would you like to see this message in a bottle I found yesterday? It's mysterious. Remarkable!"

We lean in, mildly interested, as Joe uncaps a plastic bottle of 7 Up.

"I think that's a receipt from Whole Foods," says Bulan, then shakes himself all over us like a musty, wet sea dog.

Over the next week, I wait for the gnomes to pop in and inform me they've rounded up my saboteur, all while doing my best to ignore my despair-inducing failures at interpreting Grandma Rose's will—and of course, my failure at escaping its clutches. Every morning, I wake up, slog to the train tracks, and test the limits of magical physics at Salem Station. It only reconfirms what I know: that I'm the captain of a personal, paranormal *Titanic* weaving through a malignant iceberg armada, waiting for my hull to get ripped open and for a wailing love song to bear witness to my life of tragedy.

In other words, both Grandma's spirit and I are firmly stuck in Salem.

But most days, I'm able to push the disaster from my mind. I have a lot to do between getting back to wedding vendors and attempting to study for my CPA exam. And of course, hanging out with Hanry. We've kind of become unofficially-officially a thing.

Leading up to Sidney's wedding, Hanry and I are together almost constantly. He brings me coffee in the mornings—black, so Mandy won't steal it when I'm distracted—and he takes me on dates after finishing up at his craft fairs and farmers' markets. Salem has a surprisingly romantic infrastructure, once you get past the witchery. We visit a pizza shop that claims to fill their orders in hell, steal the largest pumpkin from the courthouse, walk the rocky beaches of Fort Pickering, and talk.

A lot.

Right now, we're in his apartment while I wait for the electricity to come back on at Grandma's place. Turns out she stopped paying her utilities about a year ago, and now that she's gone—and no other elderly people live in her home—the state of Massachusetts has permitted the local utility to stop providing service. Salem's such a small town, so *quaint*, that the electricity won't be turned back on until morning. On the upside: that means tonight, Bulan's nesting in a tree with his questionable crow friends, and I get to stay at Hanry's.

And Hanry doesn't have a spare bedroom. Or a spare mattress.

Or, for that matter, spare floor space.

The old lady who rents her garden apartment to Hanry is half-senile, and that's a good thing, with how he's modified the place. In addition to installing rosebushes at the entryway, he's affixed wooden wind chimes along the staircase downstairs. He hung one of his dried seed, red berry, and pine-cone wreaths on his door. And presently, at least twenty more half-constructed pine-cone wreaths are strewn across his living room floor like circular land mines. This would be bearable, except that while I sit with him on the couch, I occasionally feel the brush of a passing bushy-tailed red squirrel.

"Remind me why you have a squirrel again?" I ask, drawing up my feet with a shudder.

"Oh. He was caught in the rain two nights ago, so I rescued him," says Hanry.

"But why did you keep him instead of forfeiting him to animal control? Are you offering wreaths and rodents as a package deal?" I ask. "Buy one wreath, get one bubonic plague free? Or do you have to pay extra for the rabies?"

Hanry laughs. "Want some tea?" he says, clearly to distract me from the squirrel. "I'm about to make a new pot."

Usually I'd say no, but Hanry has regaled me with foraging tales for weeks now. I guess now's as good a time as any to indulge my curiosity and see what the big deal is.

We scuttle through the autumnal scene of war into his kitchen. Hanry is the kind of person who has a tea cabinet. It's filled with rolled-up paper bags so fragrant I can smell them from across the room. I watch from a stool as he goes through the motions of brewing tea, which is oddly sexy. Dressed in loose pajama bottoms and a T-shirt, Hanry's arms are fully exposed for once, tensing flatteringly when he reaches for an artisanal ceramic mug. He's so . . . good-looking. And as the red squirrel dashes away to hide behind Hanry's sofa, it strikes me Hanry is also just *good*. He could hands-down win this year's title as Newest Disney Princess.

All right. That's it. It's decided. Tonight's the night when we don't just Netflix, but escalate to the "chill" part of the equation. With nervous excitement fluttering in my stomach, I take the mug from him and carry it with me to the sofa.

"How's the tea?" he asks.

I take a sip—and nearly spit it back out. Hanry's alleged "tea" tastes like dirt. I'd rather mow someone's lawn with my teeth than drink this abomination.

"It's great," I say with a Duchenne smile.

Then I nestle against Hanry's side. He starts the movie, and I abandon the tea for the cozy warmth beside him.

Uninterested in his Halloween-inspired choice of horror film, I slide my hand from Hanry's arm to his broad shoulder, squeezing meaningfully. Making subtle little noises of interest. I trail my fingertips to his chest, waiting for him to respond. His shadowed blue eyes remain fixed on the screen of his Roku TV—on a badly CGI'd mutant beehive exploding.

It's kind of insulting, frankly.

Making less subtle noises, I push my leg against Hanry's. When he doesn't respond, I slide my leg all the way across, hooking my heel around his well-muscled calf. I'm sending out irresistible clingy energy, like a sexy octopus.

"Sabby," he laughs as he picks up the remote. "You sound like a race car."

"A sexy race car, right?"

Pausing on the swarm, Hanry turns to me with a knowing look. Eyes crinkling, he says, "You're not enjoying the movie, are you?"

"There's something I want to enjoy more."

"Oh yeah?" asks Hanry.

Maybe Hanry was just pretending to be dense. Now that I've gotten his attention, he cups the back of my head with his hand and sweeps his tongue over my lips, parting them. Kissing me, long and slow. Finally. I hum with satisfaction when his arms draw me closer. His fingers slide up under my shirt hem, to the clasps of my bra. Finally. Wanting to encourage him, I kiss harder. I splay my hands on his stomach, basking in the smooth heat against my palms.

Hanry's breath catches.

"I promise I find you more interesting than bees," he says, so close that the words fall warm and heavy against my face.

"Good," I whisper back.

Then his hand travels to my hip—and lower. I shift, rising so that his hand cradles my butt—a jolt like electricity travels between us—and suddenly the apartment floods with the sound of angry buzzing.

"What the hell!" I shout over the cacophony. As I jerk, the image on-screen jumps from a swarming alien bee army to a flatly animated man chasing a goose.

"Honk!" ejects the avian rogue.

"Sorry, sorry!" Hanry laughs, his hand groping around under my thigh. "You must've rolled over the button. Scooch over."

"Are you calling me fat?!"

"No, I—it's a goose game . . . like a video game with a goose . . ."

What is it with everyone's obsession with birds around here? First Bulan, now Hanry! "Why can't you just turn it—agghh!"

I'm drowned out by buzzing so loud, I have to cover my ears. Finally, Hanry pushes me *right off the sofa*, so I land in a blankety pile of devastation on the floor. Spilled tea makes itself known, soaking through my pants. "What the hell!" I grouse again as Hanry reaches between the sofa cushions and untucks a remote control. Clicks it.

Finally, the TV ceases screaming at us.

In the once-again quiet, cozy living room, Hanry draws his eyebrows together in his typical whimsical apology.

"Sorry," he repeats, extending a hand to me. "I . . . like the size of your butt?" he says with an uncertain smile. Which I appreciate, but ugh. Just . . . *ugh*. I am tea-muddy and my ears are ringing and the mood is definitely over. At least I won't have to drink the mud-tea.

"Whatever," I say. And after I change into a pair of Hanry's ridiculous, oversize sweatpants and come back into the room, Hanry has put out a set out of linens and wool blankets for the sofa. He pulls me back up beside him—this time, settling a few inches farther away. He seems as bummed out as I am about the way the evening has gone, but he's not trying to fix it, either.

Again: ugh. I can't believe this. My de facto boyfriend may be the best, but this slow-burn, lady-blue-balls bullshit? It's the worst.

And if I didn't know better, I'd think Grandma's magical will or saboteurs or some other unknowable force was responsible for it too.

The night before Sidney the werewolf's wedding, I stay up until midnight.

There are more than a few reasons for this late-night debacle. The primary reason is that I'm toggling between twenty-four-hour-ahead confirmation emails for Sidney's seventeen vendors and an email chain with her venue's event coordinator. It's been a lot of work, a lot of stress—but it isn't what's keeping me up. No. The source of my insomnia are the two emails from EFG with the subject lines:

Checking In About Samantha's Monday Arrival

And:

Samantha's Reassignment

Within the latter, I discover a long email chain—evidence of what's been going on for several weeks behind the scenes—that outlines my immense corporate peril.

Steve and Desmond have mutually determined I don't have enough hours to qualify for FMLA, and losing pizza privileges is insufficient retribution for leaving my MicroOrange audit team underresourced on their project. This leads to the HR admin's rebuttal: As a woman, surely I wouldn't be penalized for societal expectations to take care of family? That would be sexist, right? *Surely* EFG would not let itself be accused of sexism. Again. For which Steve was partially responsible, last time, in a public exposé.

So it has been taken up the chain. To the *partner*.

Who has reassigned me to a new team with a less flashy client, with the additional encouragement that I find a way to wrap up my family matters by the start of next week.

It's worse than a bad rating. It's the first step toward being fired.

This house is so worryingly quiet. All I can hear are distracting, annoying questions whirling around like pinwheels in my head. I'd been planning to shoehorn in exam reading and problem sets before bed, but I've put those aside, replacing them with blind panic. I wish I wasn't so alone right now; that I had someone to talk to. I tried texting Hanry, but he's on a short trip to visit his parents and pretty much AWOL. At least he's promised to be back by Sunday in order to take me to a Halloween party for which he's already bought us couples costumes.

Despite that sounding like the pinnacle of my worst phobias, for some reason, I said yes. Possibly because Hanry gift wrapped my costume and left it on the porch for me, which seemed so romantic I couldn't say no.

So here I am. All alone, suffering from some kind of bizarre, unending insomnia, spooking at every thud, and—

Maybe I should just give up. Watch something on TV.

"Bulan!" I call out. "Bulan, let's binge something!"

When he fails to answer, I go hunting for him. For once, the head doesn't turn up immediately in the places I've come to expect him. I look in the sink, in case he's lounging in a sink puddle; on the recliner, in case he's snoozing on a TV remote; at the ceiling, in case he's planning to drop from the rafters to scare me. Grandma's place doesn't have exposed beams, but I wouldn't put trying that past him. Maybe I should take down the ceiling fans.

In the guest bedroom, at last, I find a sign: a partially opened window. But what's it mean?

Could it be the saboteurs? Or could he have . . . jumped?

"Bulan!" I shout, worry spiking. I stick my head out the window and search the ground below. "Bulan!?"

Only when I cast my gaze upward do I see it: crested by moonlight, ten enterprising crows caw and honk while suspending a black trash bag midair.

"Sabby!" Bulan's voice calls out—from the trash bag. Of course. "My friends just picked me up. We're off on a little adventure!"

"In the middle of the night?" I shout back.

"Halloween's only two days away! I need a costuuuume!"

The window drops a little on my head. Goddamn it, that's going to bruise. Rubbing my scalp, I say, "Fine, whatever. Stop making a scene!"

"Okayyyyy! To the dump, friends!"

The crows flap off, briefly catching Bulan against a telephone pole, before bravely soldiering on into the inky night.

Godspeed, Bulan. Godspeed.

"He's not a pet," I explain to Mandy the next morning as we wait behind a local butcher shop. "There's no need to be mad about it."

I'm certainly not upset. I've pushed it out of my mind, along with all thoughts of Grandma's malicious will and my reassignment at EFG. So successfully, in fact, I'm not thinking about it this very moment.

A fair distance down the alley, the butchers stuff a half-dozen blood-besmirched Igloos into our rented van. I'd have us stand closer, but the smell of frozen raw meat upsets Mandy's stomach. Impressively, nausea isn't stopping her from attempting to finish a five-pound Halloween bag of Laffy Taffys before noon. I'm not judging, really. It's good to have goals.

"I just wish Bulan had told me he wasn't coming," Mandy sniffles between rabid rips of candy.

"He was never going to join us anyway. Think about it. Most humans would be terrified of a bouncing head at their wedding. No one wants a party interrupted by John the Baptist."

"Is that his costume?" asks Mandy.

"Who knows?"

"You know," says Mandy, "I think the way Bulan moves is SO impressive. My head can't move like that! Neither can yours!"

I draw my hand to my neck, feeling very self-aware. "I'm grateful mine is still attached to my body."

"Right?! That's why I wonder, is he . . . I mean . . ." Mandy turns contemplative. "What is he?"

Now that's surprising. As a paranormal being herself, I assumed she knew. I twist fully to look Mandy in the eyes.

"You don't know?"

"No, not a clue! Gosh. From your expression, I'm guessing he never told you either?"

"I never asked. I figured there were loads of disembodied heads wobbling around the planet. It would explain all of those headless horsemen myths."

Mandy doesn't seem taken with my theory. I guess I haven't thought about it much since the first few days he and I started cohabitating at Grandma's. I figured it wasn't important. I maintain that, actually.

But it *is* interesting how quickly this mysterious being has become integrated into my life and my routines. This morning, I caught myself readying Bulan's bucket of fresh water before realizing he wasn't home. And wondering idly when exactly he started spending so much time with those crows. Maybe he's always been a crow-head? Was he just waiting for me to become comfortable in Salem, to prove I could handle myself in the Community without him, before going back to his normal routine of crow hangouts?

How *did* I become so comfortable around him, anyway? And living here in Salem—how has this routine become so easy that it seems all but instinctive? When did I start wanting to know more about the paranormal community instead of working off a strict need-to-know basis?

I've been here too long. I'm sure that's all it is.

Oblivious to my thoughts, Mandy gives me a fat-lipped pout and says, "I tried asking him."

"Yeah?" I ask, refocusing on the present. "What'd he say?"

"NOTHING! He wouldn't tell me, no matter how much I begged. He was completely immune to my wiles! Even when I did this."

Mandy twists a curl around a finger and cocks her head, the expression guileless and doe-eyed. I have a feeling this is supposed to be more than simply cute, as she waits a few moments for me to respond. When I don't, she throws herself against the grubby alley wall in dejection.

"It didn't work again! Why? Am I not as good-looking as I used to be?" she cries. "Is working wearing me down, Sabby?"

I offer her a consoling pat on the shoulder. This also gives me the opportunity to brush off dirt. "It's only been two weeks. Give it a year, maybe?"

"I should ask Bulan. See if working is why he lost his legs? If they just . . . wore away."

"He claims to be a couple centuries old, at least. And that he was once a warlord of some kind. I think he's tougher than he lets on."

Which is why Bulan should be fine today, wherever he is on his costume-hunting mission. I'm glad he has something to do while we handle Sidney and Brett's wedding reception. Like I said to Mandy, Bulan's presence would disrupt the guests' otherwise sentimental experience.

And I have a dark feeling that my saboteurs will cause enough disruption on their own.

After the butcher's, we make a pit stop at the cake caterer, then set out for North Marblehead—only to be blockaded by a truly evil swarm of cars. It pains me that Sidney chose to be married the night before Halloween, the holiday better known to Salem's paranormal community as All Hallows' Eve. This holiday is, unequivocally, the reason Salem traffic has taken on such an on-theme, nightmarish cast. We inch forward, recirculated air engulfing the interior of the van with the smell of raw meat and cake. I'd prefer to be sniffing Bulan's used bathwater. Hell, I might even prefer drinking it.

All right: if I'm ever in charge of planning a whole wedding or doing another day-of coordination again, I should require caterers to handle their own catering. I bet it's possible to request on-site delivery. While at a standstill, I'm typing this note into my phone when my attention catches on the fizzing navigation panel of my most recent rented SUV.

Fighting off a weird embarrassment, I tuck my phone away and refocus on the road. I won't be stuck doing this job much longer. There's no need to get better at it.

Especially when this highway wants to kill us.

By some miracle, we arrive almost on schedule at the reception venue. Sidney and Brett, unlike us plebes, will travel here by helicopter, landing on the roof an hour ahead of their guests. Yes, that's right: this luxury hotel has a *helicopter pad*. Among other bougie features. Mandy whistles in appreciation as I park beneath the vaulted porte cochere. Soon these marble columns will be lit with accent lights, the urns loaded with flowers in Sidney's wedding colors. Already the venue is more than gorgeous. The hotel lobby has wall-to-wall windows, so I can see right inside through the entryway, bar, and lounge straight to the sea. Everything's bright and subtly sparkling—the crashing waves, the custom-looking chandeliers. It's all high-end without seeming like it's trying to be a palace in France.

No sooner have I opened the door than I'm greeted by a valet in crisp, modern black.

"Excuse me," he says, pushing aside his earpiece. "Do you mind wiping your shoes?"

I glance down, past my subtle, black, and wedding-vendor-appropriate attire, to my Crocs. They have a sheen of blood on them, courtesy of the butcher delivery. Eww.

"My bad." I shrug. "Some of the meat must've leaked. Anyway, I'm here for the wed—"

"The vendor entrance is around the back," the valet says with a look that doesn't have to be snooty. It's *beyond* that, like I don't even deserve snooting.

Fine by me. I'm all about keeping a low profile. Dutifully, I follow the valet's directions. Once my shoes and feet are rinsed in a bottle of Evian, Mandy and I divide and conquer.

Like the good pixie she is, Mandy swishes off to deliver raw meat to the kitchen and to remind the hotel's catering staff not to light the grills. I check in on the team of florists. They're moving flower-covered foam squares into the venue entryway, where they're affixing the panels from floor to ceiling. The idea is to create a ten-foot-long, arched flower tunnel out of enough baby's breath, hydrangea, and roses to smother a four-alarm forest fire. I leave Mandy to supervise that beautiful debacle while I double-check the tables, chairs, place settings, and flower arrangements against the printouts on my clipboard. I've got to ensure Sidney's vision comes to pass. Every linen must be the correct shade, well-ironed, and pressed. Not one candle can go unlit—or be positioned too close to any arrangement, potentially setting it and the table ablaze. Midway through setup, I meet up with the first of the four photographers, a youngish guy named Levi. While he jabbers on, I eyeball the room again. A critical part of my work tonight—both as a Spük and as a wedding planner—is to ensure no one figures out Sidney's a werewolf.

So far, everything seems to be going normally. Completely unsabotagey.

I don't trust it.

Yet, by the time the staff tells me Sidney and Brett's helicopter has landed, the venue appears ready. With the flower wall complete, the florists have dispersed to do final touch-ups to their arrangements and the décor exterior to the ballroom. A vaguely famous-looking jazz crooner and band have arrived, along with the ballerina troupe and the mirrored surface where they'll perform a reprise of their en pointe wedding march. Drapery is pinned to the vaulted ceiling; the electricians are testing the accent lighting. Everything's beautiful and opulent. And more importantly, on the surface, paranormal-free.

Could the gnomes be keeping the saboteurs occupied? That's got to be it.

With a quick flash of gratitude to Hanry's foresight in hiring the little critters, I head to the penthouse suite. When I waltz into the open-plan living area, Sidney is seated at a marble high-top counter on a silk-cushioned stool, getting her blush touched up by a makeup artist, or MUA. Having avoided the traffic by gift of helicopter, she looks like the picture-perfect New England bride. She's wearing the first of her two reception dresses. It's more than incredible: the corseted white dress is high-necked, long-sleeved, and sheathed in a layer of romantic

3D floral motifs and botanical lace. Full coverage was a wise move, though Sidney doesn't seem the least bit furry. That said, the hair on her head is particularly luscious and thick. It's being re-pinned up in a classy bun-thing, revealing diamond earrings that probably cost as much as her helicopter.

"Congratulations!" I say over the pop music pulsing from the room's hidden speakers.

"Thank you!" Sidney's earrings shimmer as she shakes her head delightedly. "This is the best day of my life."

"Yay!" cheer her bridesmaids, showering the room with equally unrestrained enthusiasm.

Surveying the suite for signs of sabotage, witches, or plastic bags, I catch a blond bridesmaid in the process of lifting her friend's dress. She sniffs her friend's butt, then gives a thumbs-up.

"Looks like you're all having fun," I say.

"We are! Samantha, please—have a macaroon!"

I consider the elegant but vaguely disturbing dessert and raw meat charcuterie spread artfully laid out on the counter.

"Thanks, but I'm good," I say. I've got a niggling worry starting that in spite of all I've done downstairs, these werewolves may—by nature of their canine behavior—fail to blend in with the rest of the guests as well as I'd initially hoped.

"You're all still wearing your little wristbands, right?" I ask. "The ones with the magic runes or whatever on them, to keep yourselves from . . . becoming too noticeably wolfish?"

"Of course we are!" laughs a bridesmaid. "But ours are *jeweled* bracelets. Only the best!"

"Is everything okay, Samantha?" Sidney asks. "Wait. Please don't tell me if anything *isn't* working out, okay? Oh, and can you check on Brett? I miss him already!"

"Awww," chime more of the bridesmaids. "She's so loyal!"

"Aww," I echo, and plaster on a smile. "I'll go visit him now. You just enjoy your day. I'll take care of everything. By the way, you look gorgeous."

"Okay! Thank you, yay! And let me know how he likes the drinks I sent!"

Theoretically, Sidney could text her new husband to ask. But I'm being paid handsomely for this, so I muster up the strength to match her enthusiasm and give a peppy "Sure!"

As I exit the room, I nearly trip over a person.

"Merry Christ—I mean—ahh," the person says. "Sorry about that."

Expression dazed, Levi the photographer rightens himself. He lifts his camera and struggles to focus his lens. I step aside, meaning to let him into the suite. But he hasn't recovered his footing. He stumbles into a glass bar cart, splashing his face with vodka, making the bridesmaids bark with laughter. Meanwhile, my heart thuds hard in my chest. Because even the most awkward person should still be able to enter a room successfully.

Something's off with Levi.

Could the saboteur be behind this? Is this their new strategy—not sabotaging *things* but *people*? An ominous wash of dread scuttles down my back.

I call the concierge to bring coffee to the room, stat. Then I call Mandy, summoning her upstairs. She must've been on her way over already, because no sooner have I arrived at the elevators than I run straight into her. She clutches onto my arms, gasping for air.

"Sabby, were we supposed to leave gifts in the guests' rooms?" she asks.

That throws me momentarily off-track.

"Who asked you that?"

"The staff! They told me that—that Sidney's mom said—"

I shush her. "It's fine. Sidney, Brett, and I signed a contract. And our paper trail doesn't mention anything about random gifties. We can worry about that later. Don't tell Sidney. Now, let's leave that for the moment, Mandy. I need to know—did you see any suspicious signs of sabotage downstairs? A white thing lurking near Levi, maybe?"

The pixie withdraws, biting her lip uncertainly.

"Uh, I don't think so? Though I might've been distracted by his face."

I sigh.

"I know, I know," says Mandy. "You're off the market and only have eyes for Hanry. But Levi really is cute!"

At this she giggles shamelessly, and my worries about sabotage give way to exasperation. I don't know what pixie powers Mandy has, exactly—if it's pheromones she uses to make humans smitten or something else—but either way, I suspect she's been up to no good.

"Did something happen between you two?" I ask, rubbing the bridge of my nose.

Mandy completely misses the warning in my tone. She explains cheerily: "Levi was taking photos of the dessert table and he asked me if I liked thrift store shopping. I said yes! Apparently, he collects vintage cameras and likes scrapbooking. We're so well-matched!"

Yikes.

"Control yourself," I say.

She throws back her head in distress. "What, *whyyy*? He isn't a groomsman! Or a guest!"

"No. Stop." I lead her to the elevators. "We're working, Mandy, and you're on details duty. No more making boys crazy."

"You're no fun." She pouts.

"We can have fun later. For now, we need to be serious. Remember, we can't let any of the human guests realize you're a pixie. Or that Sidney's a werewolf. Same with her friends."

"I guess you're right. It's probably better for me not to get caught up with the PBI again," she agrees.

"Again?" I ask. Do I really want to know? I decide I don't.

As we turn the corner, I think I see something in the hallway flicker for just a second. But it's just a chandelier—I hope.

I really, really hope.

In the groom's suite, I find Brett and his groomsmen in good spirits, watching college football and taking shots with all the gusto of a synchronized swimming routine. Mandy controls herself admirably. After one quick photo for Sidney and a reminder about the wedding timetable, I leave the boys to their masculine delights.

But by the time guests are leisurely rolling in from their midafternoon cocktails to the reception hall, I realize I might have been too sanguine.

"You sent too much booze," Brett is complaining to Sidney as I approach them inside the floral tunnel.

"Oh, come on, Brett!" Sidney throws her whole effort into cajoling him. "It's gotten everyone friendly! And here you thought my girls wouldn't get along with your boys."

"Yeah. Your friends are kinda . . . weird."

"What do you mean?" Sidney asks.

And that's my cue. Brett's answers can wait for the next full moon, or potentially a post-honeymoon visit to the dog park. Tonight is *not* the night for Sidney's big reveal. We have witnesses—and happy memories to make, sure—but mainly witnesses. Three hundred and fifty of them.

"Hey, lovebirds," I interrupt. "Time for dinner to start. Everyone's excited for toasts!"

At the word "toasts," Brett's expression returns to resting dumb face. It's exactly what I'd expect from someone with repeated head trauma from college football. In his defense—from his stature, I assume he played defense—the guests don't seem overly excited about dinner and toasts, either. The room's ample number of formally dressed and wealthy-beautiful attendees reluctantly take their seats when the band welcomes Brett and Sidney to the head table. Preparing to return appetizers to the kitchen, the catering servers draw back. The photography team's cameras flash terroristically throughout the room. With afterimages of the lights unjustly gripping my eyes, I notice that table 3, the groomsmen's table, is all but empty.

Which I'd consider a minor issue, except for the waitstaff attempting to induce the lone groomsman to stop using the table as a footstool. Belligerent, in addition to unhygienic, the groomsman furiously shakes a full-length beard and three feet of shiny black hair. This guy didn't have half this much follicular mass twenty minutes ago; I would've noticed.

Meaning, horrifically, that this frat bro is Rapunzeling right before my eyes.

"Sabotage," I say under my breath. Which means our gnome plan didn't work.

I check on the bridesmaids at table 2. Their scalps seem mercifully unaffected, though several of them are casually plucking flowers from the arrangements and popping them into their mouths. It's drawing attention from the other tables.

Sidney seems blissfully oblivious.

"And I love my pack," she weeps into her mic. "You girls are all the best. Thank you for supporting me in my choice of alpha!"

"Pi Kappa Alpha, whoo!" shouts the lone groomsman at table 3. He stands on his chair, raising his champagne glass with all the grace of a four-legged dog balancing on two hind legs. To be clear, he's the last person in the room who should be having this problem. Sweeping his record-breaking hair and beard behind his shoulder, he shouts, "Whoo!"

"Chi-O for life!" cry the bridesmaids.

They howl in unison with Sidney for a solid minute. At table 1, Sidney's mom, the esteemed Mrs. Barroway, looks like she wishes a hole would open up and swallow her.

At least she doesn't seem to realize that this wedding is being attended by any paranormal guests—or that it's being plagued by unknown magical forces.

I've got to make sure it stays that way.

As soon as the toasts end, I send Mandy straight to Brett's room to herd the missing groomsmen down for dinner—and if necessary, to put her newly acquired scissor skills to the test by acting as emergency barber. While I hurriedly discuss the issue of excess champagne during the toasts with Maryam, the hotel's head of catering, Sidney's mom swishes up to me in a beaded halter gown and a sheer, floor-length cape.

Masking my worry, I turn from Maryam to greet the elegant, and evidently agitated, woman. "Hello, Mrs. Barroway. Can I help with anything?"

"Yes." Elizabeth Barroway's voice rolls out low and languid. But the tightness of her Botoxed-away jowls makes my own smile freeze in empathy. "I suspect the bridesmaids are . . . well . . ."

I brace myself.

"*Furries*," she whispers.

"Oh no," I say.

"Indeed. Could you encourage them to be more . . . discreet?"

"Absolutely," I tell Mrs. Barroway, relieved I won't have to be the bearer of bad and hairy news. "I'll go over now. I'm sure they'll be understanding."

"Thank you. Oh, and Samantha, I think some of the groomsmen might be missing."

Remembering Sidney's notes in the survey about her mom's anxiety, I figure it might be time for redirection.

"The staff is preparing a vintage bottle of Moët to be sent in a gift basket to each of your guests' rooms. They're including a courtesy note about the option to enjoy the hotel's specialty soufflé, which they can order through room service tonight or tomorrow morning. I'd love you to make an announcement for your guests before the dessert course."

"That sounds . . . understated," Mrs. Barroway says, but then she makes a purposeful eye at table 4, where Brett's less-absurdly-rich family is seated, and I know I'm off the hook. As she sweeps away, I'm surprised to think of my own mom, wondering how she'd treat my future in-laws.

Mom hasn't talked to me for a few weeks, and she didn't ask about Hanry after I texted her about our first date. If they were to meet, would she be nice to him? To his adopted parents? Or would she forget my wedding, the same way she's missed my last two graduations? I can't believe I have to wonder that. Also, why am I thinking about *marrying* Hanry? We've only dated a few weeks. I'm going to have to leave him for New York soon.

It must be all these weddings. Still, it's definitely creepy. Stop being creepy, Sab—

Oh god. Am I imagining things?

Did I wish this into existence?

Because in the midst of this room of barely constrained chaos, my eyes have landed on an absolutely un-wolfy, un-drunk, and truly gorgeous man—my very own Hanry Burleson. Here, seated among, and also a head and shoulders above, the guests.

How did I miss him on the guest list? When did he get back from visiting his parents? How does he know Sidney, or Brett, or . . . ?

Doesn't matter. He looks *incredible*.

When I used that same word to describe Sidney today, I meant it in an unbiased, objective way. There isn't anything objective about the rush of blood coursing through me now as I look at my unofficial boyfriend. He's wearing a gorgeously fitted tuxedo with a loosened black bow tie resting around his neck and laughing with unconscious abandon at something his tablemate said. He must've arrived late; I would've known if he'd been here since the beginning. I need to ask him how he knows Sidney and where in the world he gets his outrageously beautiful, bespoke dress outfits.

I step toward him.

Catching my eye across the room, Hanry brightens. Then he winks. And, whoa. I think that smolder just melted my ovaries. I'm absolutely molten.

How am I going to bear leaving him when the time comes?

I don't know. But first, I've got to find Mandy. Shaking myself, I give Hanry a little smile, then spin on my heel and leave the ballroom.

Okay, Sabby. If you were a pixie on a mission who'd gotten off-mission, where would you go? Sugar. I'd search for sugar.

On the way to the end of the hall, where there's a nook filled with vending machines, I call out Mandy's name.

Something pokes into the back of my shoulder.

"Man—? Ahh!" I say, turning to a toned woman with long, sparkly red acrylic nails. It is very much not Mandy, but one of the bridesmaids. "Can I help you?"

"What sorority were you in?" she asks me.

I do a double take. "What?"

“I’m Alpha Kappa Alpha.” She edges closer. “Not Chi *Omega*. Or a *Beta* Phi. That would be gross.”

“Uh-huh.”

“Because I’m an alpha,” she growls directly into my ear. “What are you?”

“Not interested in your auto-insert Omegaverse fanfiction,” I reply, pushing the were-woman away and retreating at a brisk jog. She calls after me, “You smell really nice!”

It’s the traces of blood left on my Crocs, that’s all. I need to find a hose. But first Mandy, and—

Passing the entrance to the kitchen, I stop short.

Because through an opening in the fabric door, I find myself eye-to-eye with something that isn’t Mandy. It jiggles a sinister aluminum can in its fuzzy white paws. Its body has a vague flimsiness, like a plastic grocery bag.

But of course, that’s not what it is.

It’s my saboteur.

17

A MYSTERY IS UN-MYSTERED

ON THE WHOLE, THE SABOTEUR LOOKS LIKE A SMALL RABBIT. Which is not a descriptor I've used for any of Grandma Rose's friends, or for Grandma herself, so there go those theories.

"You!" the white and fuzzy creature says.

I push through the curtains, boggling as pieces fall into place. "Me? No, *you*! You're the one who's been stalking me! I recognize you from the forest! And—were you at Hamilton Hall!?"

The saboteur twitches its pink nose once, then darts for the depths of the kitchen, squealing like a pig. Ergo: it is not Grandma Rose, a rabbit, or a pig, but some strange fourth thing.

This would also explain why it's carrying lighter fluid.

"Stop right there!" I pounce for the speedy not-rabbit and miss.

Freed of me, the creature tests the lighter while bouncing down a crowded galley. Waitstaff, servers, and catering chefs curse and bark in confusion as the pest springboards through gaps between their legs, followed by me shoving furiously past.

"I said stop!" I shout after my enemy. "This isn't *Ratatouille*!"

The creature is fast. Insanely, supernaturally fast. By the time I've advanced past the first row of prep tables, the rabbit-thing has made it to the kitchen's far end. Near the cake. Oh god. The *cake*. Finding the fracas hysterical, the creature flings spatulas, ladles, and pastry cutters in my direction, making a noise like a teakettle that's run out of water. "Tee hee ter ho terr herr."

A caterer claws onto my shoulder. "Raw meat is one thing, but bringing in live animals is another!"

"Is it a monkey?" someone yells in confusion.

Oh god. I can't let them figure out what this creature really is.

Whatever it is.

Ripping the caterer's fingers off me, I shout: "Everyone get out, and we'll tip you each a hundred extra bucks!"

Dodging flying paper towel rolls and measuring spoons, the staff hightails it. Having been a poorly paid caterer myself, I understand completely. But my knowledge of hotel kitchens fails to prepare me for the creature yelling, "Food delivery!" and sending a steel pan whizzing past my head. Sizzling caramel splashes off the side—it's the most threatening squiggle of melted sugar I've ever seen—I shout "Holy shit!" and duck behind a steel table.

"SUGAR!" cries Mandy, because *of course* she's in here. "HOW SAD!"

"Mandy!"

I stand up, locating her on top of a worktable. Waving a ten-inch-long butcher knife.

"Sabby!" she cries. "I think I know who's ruining your weddings!"

"Why are you holding a—never mind, protect the cake, Mandy!"

Mandy hops from her perch to block the pestilence before it can launch itself at Sidney and Brett's glorious ten-story masterpiece. Either that or escape through the back exit. Whatever the diabolical, white-furred thing was planning to do, it skids to a stop, registering Mandy's manic, sharp-toothed smile and knife with appropriate concern.

"Foiled!" it squeaks. "Oh. That's what I'll do. Foil!"

Expertly quick, the lighter's snapped open and the battery taken out into its little paw. I don't like the look of this, the rapid planning and capacity for destruction. Without question, this is the creature who has been ruining my weddings. I don't understand its reasoning for assaulting me with such evil intent, but whatever: the sabotage stops here. Today.

"You are *not* going to set this hotel on fire!" I shout.

"Oh, but I can! And I will!" the fuzzy cretin proclaims. "Behold, the stoves!"

Shit! The saucepans that weren't hurled at me are rapidly converting salted caramel into fire hazards.

"Do I stab it?" asks Mandy as I lunge for the central range.

"NO!"

"No indeed! We are nonviolent!" agree a dozen voices near my feet. Furiously cutting off the gas to the burners, I notice glints of light and moving shadows among the scattered pots and pans at my feet.

The gnomes. They're here! *YES!*

"It's about time!" I shout.

"What would you like us to do, miss?!" pipes up a particularly heavy pot.

"Get the fire extinguisher! And build a perimeter—blockade that thing in!"

"On it!" cry the gnomes. "Catch the pooka, gnome-men!"

"That won't help, ter her!" My saboteur—apparently called a "pooka"?—giggles characteristically as a jangling clatter announces the gnomes' call to battle. A parade of upturned steel cookware encircles the room, carried there by visibly dirty, leather-booted feet. From a tall shelf, a line of measuring spoons flies off, flung by unseen hands. One by one, they bop the pooka on the head.

"Grr herrr!" squeaks the creature, pulling down its ears. "That's annoying!"

I've just turned off the last of the burners when the fire extinguisher activates, flooding the range and room with white, hissing gas—and abruptly rocketing into the air.

"Ahhhh!" cries a troll-like silhouette, clutching to the device as it bounces off the ceiling repeatedly. "I'm too wee to control it!"

"I can't see anything," cries Mandy, slashing at white fog with her knife. "Where'd it go?"

"Oh no! To the perimeter, lads," squeaks a gnomic voice. "Take defensive measures!"

The pooka laughs triumphantly. "How the tee-ter-tables have ter-turned!"

That's *my* line, damn it!

Gritting my teeth, I heave a hot frying pan over my shoulder, prepared to go in for the kill. Because while that pooka may be rendered temporarily invisible to everyone else, I know everything there is to know about blending in, and I don't miss a thing. A thin line of fluorescent light illumines the diabolically fluffy edges of the pooka's silhouette as it waits stock-still in the galley. With its body mostly—but not completely—covering the foil ball and a tiny, flickering flame.

It's eyeballing the gas lines connecting the wall to the range with a dangerous, beady eye.

"Go ahead," I say. "Do it. You can burn it all down. But you won't be happy if you do!"

The pooka grunts. "Whyever not?"

"Because the guests will think it was a spectacle paid for by the bride's family. They'll love it. They'll all clap."

"Oh," says the creature sadly. As the CO_2 from the fire extinguisher clears away, the pooka's form grows more obvious. It crinkles up its ball of foil, tossing it over a furry shoulder. Then its ears perk up. Oh no: it has an idea. It bounces in three massive springs, straight at me. Too fast for the gnomes to tackle it, or for me to do anything but brace for impact. Except the pooka diverts at the last moment for a toppled catering cart. At that moment, Levi the photographer rolls out from behind the food-service equipment.

"What the . . ." I say. "Why is he here?!"

"Eep!" says the pooka.

"Umm," says Mandy.

"Hoo hoo hoo! That man will do!"

The gnomes pick Levi up and hurl him straight at the startled pooka—and right into Sidney's thirty-thousand-dollar wedding cake.

18

SO LONG, AND PLEASE DON'T FALL INTO THE MOP BUCKET

OH NO. NO, NO, NO, NO, NO.

"Tee hee terr herr," the pooka says as Levi rolls out of the ruined top tier of the cake. Sensing her moment, Mandy drops the knife and swoops in, snatching the creature from behind.

"Cuddle attack!" she shrieks, squeezing it joyously.

"No! My weakness!" the pooka sobs.

Mandy cries too, apparently overwhelmed by its evil-cute vibes. I can barely contain my own tears. All that work, and the saboteur has won. The wedding cake is lost—an absolute, irredeemable, thirty-thousand-dollar mess. Also, is Levi okay? He's gone unconscious—I hope he won't need a hospital trip?

Once I confirm Levi is breathing, I grab a loose apron and get Mandy's help to roll the pooka in it longwise, like I'm constructing a giant, savory croissant.

"Nooooo!" the pooka wails. It paws its icing-covered mitts desperately against the apron. "I've been trapped!"

"Tee hee her herrrrr," I tell it.

The pooka doesn't find this amusing. Kicking futilely, it cries, "Let me free, let me free! And I will answer your questions three."

Satisfying as it might be to spend the next five minutes watching the pooka squirm, finding out what it's doing here would be better. I squat, up close and personal. But not so close it could kick me in the neck.

"All right." I catch my breath. "I'll let you go if you answer my questions and leave this wedding alone. Why are you here?"

The wiggling of the impromptu-croissant stills. "I'm here to test you."

Aghast, Mandy throws a hand to her forehead. "Oh, it was *you*! You started throwing whiskey around when I was kissing Levi!"

I—nope. I can't deal with that now. A chortle emanates from the pooka's dark, dark heart.

"Yes! It was me!" brags the pooka. "I fed glamoured wine to the groomsmen, from the land of Fai-*ry*. Misdirected a caterer with bags of blood. Poked holes in those boats. Have you two enjoyed my sowing of oats? Oats of *chaos*?"

I stick a finger right into the plush fur of its belly, causing it to yowl. "Have you done anything else to mess up this wedding? Are there more disasters waiting for me?"

"How could you!" cries Mandy.

Before Mandy's question can wreck my chances at stopping it, I interrupt: "That question doesn't count!"

"Oh, fear not!" The creature squirms sassily. "I am pleased to answer. Miss Pixie, Miss Planner, I dare for it's my nature, but be not too upset with me! I'll bring no more trouble unto thee. I'll bring thee no more tests! My work is done in threes! I am filled with woe and wan, for I could not make this room explode."

I glance at Mandy, concerned.

"Do you think he's telling the truth?" I ask.

She shrugs. "I don't know, but let's please not keep him afterward. I don't think he'd make as nice a pet as Bulan."

Mandy and I are in agreement.

"Last question, pooka, then I'll free you," I say, my attention returned to the spiteful being. "Did you do this for my grandmother, or her friends, or someone else?"

"I do not know of which woman you speak, so I cannot say if it was she!" The pooka kicks at me through the apron. I hold fast.

"That wasn't an answer!" I growl. "Who sent you?"

"Alas, your questions are complete! Release me from this foul and floury sheet!"

What an asshole. Bravely, I reach forward and unpeel enough apron to stare into the white, wiggling creature's beady eyes. It's maybe a little terrifying.

"Fine," I say. "I'll let you go. But if you attack again, know that we'll retaliate. Horribly. I have friends in high places."

"That you do! That you do! Tee herr herr herr," laughs the pooka in a disturbingly knowing way. "Now unhand me! UNHAND ME!"

I give Mandy a signal. Together, we take the pooka out through the back kitchen door and unwrap it. The tiny monster bursts from the apron like a Ping-Pong ball with jet-packs.

"Goodbye, chaos!" cries Mandy as we watch its hind legs scurry away. "And good riddance!"

Back in the kitchen, the gnomes cheer. Levi moans and smacks his icing-encrusted lips together uncertainly. "Delicious," he manages.

And me? I feel a weight drop from my shoulders.

I've done it. I've caught my saboteur and kicked it to the curb. It can't cause any more trouble. What's more is, if that pooka hadn't gotten involved, Sidney and Brett's wedding reception would have proceeded up to this point without a single hitch.

Who'd have thought I might actually be good at wedding planning and coordination? And not just that, but that I'd *feel* good about being good at it?

I should probably leave that thought for later.

"Do you know how much that cost?!" I gesture at Sidney and Brett's ruined six-tier once-masterpiece. "That cake sold at a higher price than my wedding planning package. It's like, the same cost as a mortgage for a house."

"Not in this economy," drawls Levi from the floor.

"There, there." Mandy pats his cheek.

"Mandy." I draw her attention back to me. "You shouldn't have let this happen. Seriously. Do you really think your pheromones or whatever will erase this guy's memory?"

"I don't know. I think they will?"

"I hope you're right. Because if the PBI comes knocking, I legitimately will not know how to help you."

The pixie sniffles with unmistakable guilt as she hauls Levi upright and helps him find kitchen towels to freshen up with. I use the time to investigate the damage to the cake. By the time Mandy's returned, I'm not optimistic.

"So. The top two tiers of the cake are definitely ruined. The bottom ones are surprisingly . . . intact, but the detailing and sugar flowers look like smashed Play-Doh you'd find in a pre-K classroom."

"I don't think it looks so bad," Mandy says hopefully.

"I'm not done with my negatives. The biggest one is this: food can't be eaten after touching the ground. This cake is finished. It's done for. Like us."

"Is that really true? Because I've seen you eat—"

"The five-second rule doesn't apply in a business context," I explain.

"Oh," says Mandy, eyes downcast. "I guess it's been more than five seconds."

"The point is, even if we cover up the damage, we can't let people eat this." I cast a look at Mandy. "Not any people."

"Ohhhh," she says.

Ohhh is right. I snap my fingers, drawing the gnomes' attention. "You guys owe me big after that pooka-catching disaster. So. How about some gardening?"

Borrowing the kitchen knives, I command the gnome army to rebuild our cake. The multitalented little men scrape away smooshed fondant, giving the cake a "semi-naked" look. With unexpected artfulness, they affix loose leaves and blooms into the crumbled dents and crannies of the damaged cake, so it becomes more forest than disaster. I mean, really: the wedding cake has taken on the appearance of an ecologically intact forest, replete with tiny roly-polies peeking out of sugar-spun clover. While pretty, the result is more than a bit whimsical, a bit too ready for a nature documentary, and it resembles nothing of Sidney's vision. Also, while dogs and other canines may not mind eating food off the floor, this cake will be inedible for the vast majority of our guests—which is why I approach the head table with distinct unease.

"Sabby!" calls out a familiar voice.

I should've guessed Hanry would find me. A good half hour has passed since he spotted me, and the memory of his wink alone makes my toes curl—which would be more pleasant if it weren't for the stickiness of blood and sugar inside my Crocs. And on my face. And in the insides of my ear canals.

"Where've you been?" Hanry asks. "You look—"

"Frazzled?" I ask. "Overwhelmed? Like I'm losing my shit?"

"Beautiful."

Hanry reaches down to wipe icing from my cheek, drawing his index finger slowly across my skin. Only after I suck in a breath do I realize he just complimented me, and my instinct wasn't to immediately sink back and hide. This is novel. This means I'm changing; he's changing me.

Or maybe I've inhaled too many oven fumes.

"Not now, Hanry," I say, detaching his hand from my face. "I'm one mistake away from this whole party imploding."

"Can I help?"

"I already took care of it." Kind of. Sort of.

Though visibly disappointed, Hanry doesn't push. "Yeah, I bet you did," he says. "You've gotten good at this." He untucks his handkerchief as if to wipe icing onto it. But then he changes his mind. He draws his finger to his lips and sucks off the icing, smiling at the taste.

Dear god. A hot jolt of desire blazes down into my belly.

"How about," I say without thinking, "you meet me in the catering closet in five minutes? The one near the kitchen?"

Hanry's eyebrows jump in surprise. "Okay."

Oh, hell yeah.

"See you there," I promise.

As the band plays a jazz cover of "Hungry Like the Wolf," the caterers begin passing out the first of the four raw meat courses. Seizing the opportunity, I escape from the reception hall, my thoughts all Hanry. That mouth. That touch. Once I'm past the flower archway and confident the coast is clear, I throw open the door to the catering closet—

To find it empty. Of handsome, broad-shouldered types, anyway. There's a dinky yellow mop bucket filled with gray, sudsy water, and the attached metal pole appears precariously close to bashing my head. Clearly, this is a mislabeled maintenance closet. I wonder if that was the pooka's doing? If so, I'm grateful. I can't imagine making out with Hanry in here. I'm glad he had the same idea.

Doing my best to stay unnoticed, I shut the door and walk casually around the flower arch, where I find an unlabeled closet. More encouragingly than last time, it isn't surrounded by a scent-moat of lemony cleaning product. I try the handle, which takes a bit of jiggling to open, but—

There. There Hanry is, in his tuxedo, seated on top of a white-cloth-covered catering cart, his phone in hand, the top of his jacket and bow tie undone. He's waiting for me. And, dear god. He's as hot as ever. He's *hotter* than ever.

I've dreamed about this. Making out with him, sure—but specifically, the catering closet. Having spent so many years in catering, it's like my own personal Mile High Club fantasy.

"That other closet," Hanry starts, "was kind of cramped—"

Whatever he has to say doesn't matter. I slip in behind the door, and no sooner has it clicked shut than I tackle Hanry, hard enough to send the catering cart a foot backward.

In the dark, snug room, Hanry kisses me. His hands run over my neck, my back, my arms. I return the favor enthusiastically. I tug off his bow tie. I sweep my hands over his chest. I want to feel the place where his hip bone dimples, the line of toned muscle at the base of his abs that leads down to further heat. I want to feel all of him. I need his pants *off*.

"Stop," says Hanry, taking hold of me with passion. I grin against the warmth of his neck.

"Oh, you like that, do you?"

He fishes for me in the darkness. Takes my other wrist in his.

"Sabby. *Stop*," he says again. This time I hear the shift in his tone of voice, and it chases away the heat in my belly. Confused, I slide off Hanry's lap to stand.

"If it's this room that's the problem, Sidney promised I'd have a hotel room upstairs so I can crash after the party. You could come too. Would you?"

Hanry has frozen in place. Like I've shell-shocked him with my offer, and—oh god. I've made the wrong call. It horrifies me, and I feel my shoulders tightening, because yeah, I'm taking the rejection personally, of course I am—but you know what? No. Hanry is attracted to me, I *know* he is.

"Hanry, say something."

Rather than looking at me or telling me what's happening inside his mind, Hanry chooses to focus on the closet wall. Oh no. He's searching for a light switch. What better way to kill the mood than to flick on the fluorescent ceiling light?

It's brutally bright.

I can't stand feeling this exposed a second longer.

"All right, I'll say it for you," I joke. "You're a virgin. You're saving yourself for marriage. You tried the raw meat, and you're having a weird gastrointestinal reaction to it."

Hanry doesn't chuckle. Instead, he runs his hands over his face and squeezes his eyes shut. Then opens them again. His blue eyes are lit from within, crisp and bright like an icy winter sky. They're vivid. Alive. Full of desire. For *me*.

"I'm not reacting to the meat," he says, his gaze on my lips. And falling lower.

I knew it. That I'm not imagining it: he wants me too. Maybe everything's okay. I respond, pliant in Hanry's arms as he pulls me slowly to him, his face nearing mine.

My heart rate accelerates, and I catch my breath.

He parts his lips. I can feel the warmth of his mouth a few inches away. When the hem of his jacket falls across my hand, my eyes drift shut, and I wait. At last, Hanry's mouth touches mine, covering it, and for a moment the world is soft, warm, and perfect.

"I want this more than you know," Hanry whispers against me. "But I don't think continuing would be fair to you."

My eyes fly open.

Hanry leans back on his hands, moving his face slightly back too, and it's my turn to be shell-shocked. I swear I see stars around the edges of my sight.

"Hanry," I say, my heart sinking; my eyes squinting in the starkness of the closet.

"I can't kiss you like this and keep it light between us, Sabby. And I can't go upstairs with you."

"Okay," I say, more unsure than I've ever sounded around him. "We don't—we don't *have* to go anywhere."

"I know."

"So what's this about?"

"I just . . . don't make this harder, Sabby. Today already sucked," he says, putting more space between us. "I had a hard talk with my mom this morning. Before I left."

Like me, Hanry doesn't usually bring up his family without provocation. The fact that he's doing it now, to avoid talking about *us*? Not my favorite.

"Cool," I say, in an attempt to be the queen of sympathy.

"I told you I have a brother, right? Seb. He's about the same age as me. The way Mom was going on, I don't know. It made me worry about him. I think she might try to fuck up his life more than she already has. That's what she's good at—causing situations to spin out of control—so I know I shouldn't be surprised."

Hanry must've been hiding these feelings behind his sexy tuxedo mask all night. Maybe it was good I pulled him into this closet before he publicly had the stuffing squeezed out of his feelings-burrito. I'm unsure whether or not I'm helping him, though. He's still not quite meeting my gaze.

He also remains unspeakably hot. I reach across what feels like a thousand miles to squeeze his thigh, but Hanry moves my hand away. Damn him.

Without looking at me, he speaks so fast, I almost don't catch the words.

"I can't keep dating you," he says.

I go still.

"You *what*?!" I burst out. "You can't kiss me like that, then break up with me seconds later!"

"I'm sorry," Hanry says—a total nonanswer. And total crap.

"What's your deal? Is this because you're too serious for me? You don't want to waste time dating someone you can't be with forever, and you can't see yourself in a suburban, single-family home someday?"

Hanry shifts as he resettles on the cart.

"I can't see myself doing that with you, Sabby. No."

I want to scream.

Of course he doesn't. Who was I kidding? Woodsy, artsy Hanry has no interest in the banality of the American dream. I knew that, and yet my lungs feel like they've been crushed by a giant, rolling boulder chucked out of a temple of doom.

I feel utterly crushed.

I think I might not survive the hurt of it, not to mention the humiliation.

And, what makes it worse? It's not Hanry, or his dreams, that are so painful. It's *me*. I'm the problem. I knew he was just a fling, something that would end the moment I figured out how to leave Salem—but I kept spending more time with Hanry than I should've. I let myself think of him before falling asleep at night, wanted his opinion anytime I finished a wedding proposal or envisioned a new décor idea.

I let him see *me*.

And that's who he's rejecting. He's rejecting the real me and the idea of an "us."

I know this is the last moment I should be vulnerable, but he has to know how I feel. It's my last chance to stop this, to show him there might be another way.

"I don't want to lose you," I say, the words burning as they escape my throat. Hanry swallows, evidence he *is* conflicted, in spite of everything. "We could do long distance?"

"You told me this was always going to end at some point," he says.

"I . . . did," I admit.

"What if you don't go back to New York?" Hanry suggests out of nowhere. I'm not sure what *that* is supposed to mean, and since I'm lost for words, of course he thinks he should keep talking. "I'm not saying you need to quit your job for me. I'm just saying you don't have to go back if you don't want to."

"But—but I do want to." I lick my dry lips. "You know I've been faking this wedding planning schtick for weeks so I could leave."

"I hear you. I've heard you. I just, I don't know. Seeing you out there tonight, you were in your element. There's no shame in walking away from something that doesn't serve you anymore," Hanry says.

Intensely irked, I catch my voice going low.

"I *like* accounting, Hanry. The neat little rows on my spreadsheets, the color-coordinated headers. The predictable formulas that tell you what will happen in all the little boxes. And I like Manhattan and my roommate, and I like that all of it gives me a life that's predictable and safe and unchaotic and awesome."

"Then you understand why I'm doing this. You're as afraid of getting hurt as I am."

I squeeze my eyes shut.

I should've done all of this differently. If I'd been vulnerable and honest from the beginning, if I'd let Hanry know how much he mattered to me, maybe he would have considered coming with me to New York, or at least trying to make a relationship work in spite of living a couple hundred miles apart. Maybe then he'd have considered that this didn't have to end in heartbreak for both of us.

Now it's too late, and I can't stand it. I can't stand the fact that he matters so much to me. We're a pair of romantic cowards.

For some reason, though? I can't stand the thought of calling him out. And he doesn't demand more from me either. As the wedding music trickles under the door, we sit there wordlessly, too close to each other, and also too far, a thousand things hovering in the gap between us, neither of us wanting the moment to end.

Until finally, time's up.

"I've got to get back in there," I say, dry-mouthed. "You know. Before it's time for dessert, and cake cutting."

Hanry's eyebrows draw together in apology. "I get it," he says. "Goodbye, Sabby."

My heart thuds. This can't really be goodbye, can it? For so little reason?

I don't want this. I couldn't want anything less. But I force my breathing to normalize and mirror him.

"See ya," I say.

It doesn't sound half as smooth as it did in my head.

Cool cool cool cool cool.

19

THE AI AUTOCORRECT OF GREAT AND UNNECESSARY SUFFERING

I MAKE IT THROUGH THE LAST FEW HOURS OF SIDNEY AND BRETT'S wedding on autopilot. I drive Mandy and I back to Salem, completely forgetting about the lush accommodations available to me at the hotel. Only after passing out on the living room recliner and waking up to unfiltered sunlight from the unkindly unadorned window does reality set in: last night, I pulled off another wedding. I unmasked the saboteur. And I lost Hanry.

I'm about to lose my dream job too, but my imminent firing doesn't sting as bad, for some reason. Probably because it's been such a long time coming.

I check my phone. Start reading through my last texts with Hanry before I can stop myself. I'm going to need a lot of ice cream to get through today. I think Mandy has a secret stash with helpful spells worked into the cream. *Hexlato*, she called it. Maybe one of them contains an emotional-numbing spell? A paranormal brain freeze wouldn't be remiss.

A banging sound coming from the front lawn forces me to roll over in bed and get up. I'm mostly certain the noise belongs to a horde of go-getter revelers. No surprise the holidaying Salem pilgrims are starting festivities early, and with a questionable understanding of private versus public space. After all, today is the worst day of the calendar year: the one that memorializes my trauma.

Halloween.

I can't believe I'm back here for this.

Grumbling, I make my way to the window, arms wrapped around my waist to close up my not-nearly-cozy-enough cardigan. Lean out to view the trespassers, prepared to shout at them to stop confusing my yard with a tourist stop.

It's not tourists, though. It's Matilda and the rest of Grandma's witch cabal.

Somehow, that's worse.

"Go away!" I shout at them. "You've already taken the flamingos, you can't take the landscaping! I'm going to sell that eventually!"

In spite of her hunchback, Matilda waves back at me, but otherwise ignores me to join her friends in doing the conga. That's it. Loud noises and petty theft are one thing, but Boomer dancing is where I draw the line.

I rumble downstairs, ready to tell that crew what's what. Swing open the front door.

"Hi, Samantha," Matilda creaks at me. "Care to join us? Kawbaha-haha."

"Absolutely not. Who's the Oompa-Loompa?" I demand, pointing to the person at the end of the line. The witch's skin has the hue and texture of an orange, so I'm sure I would've noticed her before.

"I'm Carol," the witch says.

"You're a warning advertisement for tanning beds," I say.

"She just came back from Tampa," Matilda explains. "She lives there now. Part-time."

"There's a nice community of brujas down there," adds Carol. "Except for when Mercury goes retrograde on a full moon."

One of the witches on the lawn, wearing bedazzled butterfly clips in her silky white hair, messes with the dials on a boom box. She is wearing white tiger-paw gloves.

"Why are you all here?" I ask the group—bravely, I might add. "Isn't your thing to meet up in the woods at night on Halloween? Not waking up innocent twentysomethings at the crack of dawn, digging up the yard like a herd of wild hogs?"

"It's a special occasion!" Matilda sucks in her breath, coughs, then lifts her arms dramatically to intone: "We blessed sisters seven, tied together by eternal bonds—"

The others chime in, monotone: "—seven tied together by eternal bonds—"

"STOP!"

They do, thankfully. My heart is going wild in my chest. I can't believe what I just heard. Actually, I must've misheard it. It sounded—

It sounded like they said *seven tides*.

"Say that again," I demand.

"We didn't finish it," says the tiger-pawed one. "We didn't talk about the highs and lows yet."

"I still prefer saying 'thorns' and 'roses,'" says another.

"I thought it was eight, not seven?" asks Carol.

"I don't know about any of that, but I heard you all just say," I repeat, breathless, "that you were seven sisters, tied together by special bonds."

"*Eternal* bonds," confirms Matilda, her neck cracking. "That is true."

"See, that's why I think it should still be eight sisters," says Carol. "Including Rose."

The witches look at each other, nodding and shaking their heads like a dashboard of bobbleheads. Their confusion aside, I'm more confident than ever with what I've heard. And what I think it means. These seven still-living witches are best friends, tied together by their cabal. Seven, *tied together* . . . the "tides" that Grandma must've been referring to in her will. But Grandma was using that grammar-checking app that Bulan talked about, with its nefarious and inaccurate AI! Which means all this time, the words in her will had nothing to do with the ocean, lunar time, or a scuba shop.

Grandma Rose was trying to say that she needed her friends to say goodbye.

Why didn't I realize it before?

I zoom in on Carol, the Florida Orange and the seventh member of the cabal. She's the reason I must've discounted them. Because before, there'd only been *six* witches.

"You weren't at Grandma's funeral," I accuse. "Were you?"

"Well, I tried to make it!" protests the witch. "But I couldn't very well let myself be hexed by—"

"Carol, we all know it's because you hate the Halloween traffic," someone interrupts.

"It doesn't matter now," I say. Streams of hope are springing in me unexpectedly. Like a leak in a water main. I have a vision: an idea. A feeling that I finally know what to do to settle Grandma's spirit once and for all. "Come on, witches. Come with me. Not because I'm me, obviously. But for Grandma Rose. She needs her sisters. And that boom box."

I all but skip to the cemetery with Grandma's witch cabal in tow. It's more crowded than ever, but I easily ignore the pilgrims and their cameras as I lead us to the grave site. This time, I have to admit, the trip goes much more easily. This is the advantage of not needing to cut security wires and jump fences and lie to attractive pine-cone gatherers named Hanry.

I'm fluttering with excitement and nerves as I arrange the witch cabal atop the grave, like I did the flowers.

Here you go, Grandma Rose. I hope this does the trick for you. I hope you feel better and can do your whole ascending schtick now, knowing that you're not alone. That your community, the Community, always had your back.

"Now what?" croaks Matilda.

"Line up from tallest to shortest," I say. Just in case the "high" and "low" bits also refer to their heights.

They oblige me, amazingly enough.

"Now, together, cross over Grandma's grave twice," I instruct.

"And the boom box?"

"I assumed you'd prefer to do this to music," I say dryly.

"Yes, we *were* going to learn this wonderful new dance Carol discovered in Tampa." They put on "the Conga." I shake my head, watching the witches as they figure out how to arrange their hands on each other's shoulders and wiggle their feet under the robes in a dance-suggestive manner. "Let's go, merry ladies!"

"No one says *merry* anymore, Joanna," chides the tiger-paw witch.

"Shh, shh!"

I rest my hand on Grandma's headstone.

This is what she wanted, I think. It makes sense. These were her people.

"Goodbye, Grandma," I say.

Something happens. A breeze picks up, first catching in the bare-branched ash tree beside us, stirring the dead leaves at its roots. Then it moves, carrying over me, drawing with it leaves and black silk flowers and a phantom touch of human warmth.

The wind feels like a frail but wiry hug. Clinging to me with all its strength, just for a moment, as my nostrils fill with that combination of catnip and thorny rose lotion. I feel love—a love I'd forgotten. Not a perfect one, but a real one. It was *there*.

It was *her*.

The witches dance on, cackling as they trip over each other's hems. And I don't need to wipe my eyes or anything as the breeze dies down, and the leaves and flowers settle, and I sense Grandma Rose serenely drift away.

In Salem, Halloween requires forging the rivers of postapocalyptic humanity in order to perform basic survival functions. The downtown has more or less run out of food, same as it's run out of space. Yet holidaying pilgrims only keep spilling out from trains and buses like sewage. It's impossible to tell who's wearing costumes or regular clothes. All is black. All is dire. Gone from the air is the tang of fall and pumpkin spice. The smell of rotten pumpkins, marijuana, tobacco, and dollar-store incense permeates all.

In spite of that, the skipping continues, as I cross block after block of redbrick roads to Salem Station. My miserable, Grandma Rose–induced sham-life is over. Obviously, I'm happy about it. My inner being is *radiant*. It doesn't matter if anyone else here understands how joyful it is to say goodbye to this place. I can lean into it. I've earned that much, damn it.

"Good effing bye," I mutter at every crosswalk, dragging my things behind me one final time. "I hate you, stupid crossing light. You're never long enough. Oh, and you, tree root. I see you there, trying to trip everyone. Not having that anymore. Nope. Ow. I'll get you next time, second tree root."

While I'm lugging my overstuffed suitcase and my sorely abused duffel to the front of the station, I find myself faced with another feature of Salem I dislike: Baldy.

Baldy?!

There's no question he's here waiting for me. His throat-clearing is insufferably loud, and among the hordes, his head shines like a beacon. He really missed his calling as a lighthouse.

"Samantha," he announces, attempting to flag me down. "Samantha Spük!"

"You're putting it all behind you," I tell myself. "All behind. Way behind. You're throwing it from the caboose."

Though I admit that if it weren't Baldy but Hanry here—armed with a grand gesture and romantic overtures—I might be willing to stop walking. As it is, Hanry doesn't want me. So I have to focus on what matters: *finally* catching my train.

"Samantha! Would you stop walking?"

"Grandma's ascended, and I'm out of here," I gloat as I pass the lawyer by. "Sic a new spell on me, and I will personally attack you with knives."

"I wouldn't dream of it," Baldy says. He strides to meet my gait with unexpected speed, though I guess that's necessary in order to push through the station's crowds. "I do not expect you'll want to return anytime soon."

"Nope," I say, my hackles rising. How dare he peg me so well? "Why are you here?"

"If you would allow it, I thought we might take this opportunity to do some final paperwork. For the next court hearing, in which we will be required to apply for the estate debt to be . . . Ahem, allow me to cut to the chase. I need your permission to make future hearings virtual."

I squint, amazed at the restraint. The brevity. The fact that behind Baldy crouches a little shadow amid the station's landscaped pocket garden, its twitchy shoulders ruffling the dead leaves of a browning hedge. A twig is being poked, repeatedly, into the leg of Baldy's too-tight trouser pants.

I probably should've remembered to call those gnomes off. Oh well.

"Please sign here, here, and here," says Baldy.

"Not so fast," I say, pocketing his pen. "I'll need time to read these first. I've learned a thing or two about contracts."

He sighs with annoyance, as if he's the one with a train coming, not me. But when I flip through the contract, confirming the name of this government form with an internet search, it becomes clear Baldy isn't pulling a fast one. I sign every blank. And at the end, Baldy puts out his hand as if to shake mine.

"Samantha—"

I recoil. "Eww."

"Keys," he says, the skin of his forehead pinching between the eyes. "For the Realtor."

Oh. Right.

I dig into my pocket, wishing I didn't suddenly feel churned up, like I've misguidedly finished off Grandma's frozen ziti. They're just keys. I *came to Salem* to do this—to put everything to rest for Grandma Rose. I should be ecstatic: this is the final step to get me back where I need to be. I can be normal and happy anywhere—absolutely anywhere!—else.

But especially in New York, where Jane and I can go to bars and not meet guys while scrolling dating apps on our phones. I can take steps toward a career that will be meaningful and stable and never the least bit unhinged.

And yet, as I deposit the keys in Baldy's soft and torpid palm, I can't help regretting that I didn't pay a visit to the shop one last time to say goodbye to its half-finished wedding décor and our lopsided window display. To the ridiculous ghost chairs. To the baubles and the burnt mirror and the plush spiders.

Well, maybe not the spiders. Those googly eyes always creeped me out.

On the platform, brisk October wind whips my hair into my face. Even so, among the crowds of costumed heathens and witches and Frankenstein impersonators and paranormal folk who seem to be cheekily not wearing their magic-disguising bracelets, my eyes catch upon a sign painted on burlap.

GOOGBYE SABREE

It's being held by Mandy, red-faced and blubbering. For some reason, she's wearing glasses and a tweed blazer. Beside her is a bassinet stroller with a baby blanket arranged over its canopy.

"W-w-we're going to m-miss you," sobs Mandy.

From within the bassinet, I hear a sniffle. This could be because the inhabitant is sad; more likely, it's because the pink wool blanket has fallen so that it itches the tip of his nose.

"What a terrible thing has transpired," says Bulan, sounding nothing like a baby.

He starts moving around. I hide my emotions by correcting the blanket. "That's sweet, Mandy. Bulan, you're full of it."

"Please don't leave," Mandy cries. "It's too sudden."

I know what she means. She's only had a few hours to process the news of my departure. Secretly, I'm impressed that Mandy and Bulan were able to meet me here to say goodbye, and with a sign, no less. It's almost touching.

"I have to. Mandy, please don't cry. It's Halloween. Your favorite holiday!"

"Happy Halloween," she says dispassionately.

Her tone surprises me. "Mandy, do you not like Halloween?"

"Not at all," she says. "It's so cheesy. It's great if you love time with family, but what if you're alone in the world? Who's going to give *you* presents?"

I see what's going on now. "You're talking about Christmas."

"No," sniffs Mandy. "Halloween. It's the worst. The music is SO stupid."

"That's true. And it's starting earlier and earlier every year!" adds Bulan from within the bassinet. "Jingle hells bells, Batman capes, Jokers full of dread—"

Mandy thrusts her hands over her ears. "I can't take any more!"

Okay, time to intervene. I fish an envelope out from my pocket and extend it. "Here, Mandy. This is for you."

Sniffling, my ex-employee takes the envelope and shakes it. "Is there candy inside?" she asks, her tone hopeful.

"It's your payment, Mandy. You can use the cash to pay rent or buy a month's supply of chocolate. I recommend paying rent first. It's easier to seduce meals from a guy than to get him to lodge you for free."

Mandy's bottom lip puffs out, showcasing her disagreement. I realize I may have underestimated how much chocolate she needs per meal.

"How about this," I try again. "Keep treading water until I get access to the money in Grandma's estate. Then I can send you more money, plus instructions for returning the other deposits to customers."

"Where am I supposed to tread water?" asks Mandy. "The bay is freezing."

For her sake, I hope Mandy someday learns the business of metaphors. I smile at the pixie. I'm going to miss her. And Bulan too. It's a good thing I'll have Jane—all the companion a normal girl like me needs.

Besides, our apartment has a "No Pets" policy. I assume that extends to severed heads.

"Sabby," Bulan says from behind his knit curtain, "do you really think it's a good idea to leave Mandy with so much responsibility?"

"She's a smart pixie. She can do this. Look, she's wearing glasses now."

"Thanks, Sabby." Said pixie bursts into tears anew. "I'll always treasure your kind words."

"I'm sorry your life has led you to believe I'm kind," I say comfortingly.

"Don't be fooled, Sabby. That pair of fused-together monocles is just part of Mandy's librarian costume—" Bulan is saying when his voice is interrupted by a loudly arriving train.

It doesn't whistle, exactly. But all the same, it hails me. I give Mandy and Bulan one final, tight-lipped smile and a farewell salute, then close my eyes and inhale the train station's sweet, sweet scent of burnt oil and grime. This time, when I move forward and toe the yellow line, I don't melt into a puddle. Or falter. Or think about how nice it might've been if I were still able to attend that Halloween party with Hanry, wearing the yet-unopened couples costume he'd purchased for the occasion. Why would I do any of that? I'm free now, a free bird. But not an eagle or a phoenix or anything noteworthy. I'm more like . . . a pigeon.

And the moment I'm back in New York, I'll be back to living my best pigeon-y life. The best life anyone could live—100 percent paranormal-free. No drama, no excitement, no surprises.

Nothing but freedom.

20

FREEDOM, SWEET FREEDOM

NIGHT HAS FALLEN BY THE TIME I MAKE IT TO THE QUIET(ISH) and safe(ish) neighborhood of Turtle Bay. Of course, this being New York City, the beautiful humanity here is gearing up to party instead of winding down. Like an awkward salmon unwilling to push upstream, I hang back at the entrance to the Lexington Avenue station and observe them: gray and beige sweaters and black blazers and neutral hair colors, solids and designers and knockoff designers. Sure, here and there, people wear bright-colored and eye-offending clothes, like parrots. What matters is this: not a single person appears to be a witch, or like they're trying to be one. Halloween means little to anyone here but a party trick. A couple of people are overconfident with the cologne, but on the whole, the masses smell showered. And not like they cleansed themselves in a mugwort bath filled with rune stones and crystals, either. Like they used tap water. And generic, store-bought shampoos.

I release the breath I've been holding for weeks.

Armored by a frankly unsettling calm, I head to the apartment. More familiar glories meet me there. Behold! A Target lamp on the entry table. A mass-produced canvas of abstract "modern art" above a gray, pilling sofa. In my bedroom, I draw my hands lovingly over my prepackaged bedding set, not even 100 percent cotton fill, because nothing needs to be *too* nice. The normalcy is the luxury. The sweet, delicious taste of vanilla.

"Sammy?"

I pan from our half kitchen and living room to the open door leading to the bedroom opposite mine. A room that is technically a large closet. Visible within is the most wonderful creature I've ever met, Jane Doe, sitting cross-legged on her single bed. A claw clip holds back her off-blond hair. She's in matching cotton sweats. Her phone is propped against a pillow, the screen turned to a video call. A man is on the other end. She waves at me.

I let out a longer sigh of relief than I did at the station. Then I shout, "Jane!" and run forward to greet her with a hug.

She hugs me loosely. "I've missed you, Sammy!"

I draw back, unable to stop smiling in spite of her repeated mistake.

"It's actually Sabby, remember? With a *b*. I had a cold when I started using the nickname. I wanted to go by 'Sammy,' but my nose was clogged, so everyone heard it wrong."

"That's a little weird," says Jane.

"Which is why Sammy's fine too," I say really fast, hugging her again. Because this is everything I've ever wanted. My life. My normal normal *normal* life.

And yet, as I unpack my bags and we catch up, and she reintroduces me to her boyfriend as Sammy on the video chat, my chest gets uncomfortably tight. And no, it's not my sports bra. It's something else, some unnamable thing that makes me feel like I'm being squeezed between two fingers. Like a pimple.

After I'm done unpacking, and I've showered, I lie at last on my medium-firm mattress with the lights turned out. I try to fall asleep.

I don't know why, but it takes quite a long time.

My first day reclaiming my big-city life opens with a frenzied whirlwind. Being busy is on-brand in New York, a thought that lifts my mood in spite of waking up briefly terrified that I've been turned into a down-alternative-filled burrito. Compared to Grandma Rose's drafty pink house, this apartment unsettles me with its hyperactive radiators.

Since the wind will soon rob me of my unexpected warmth, I shrug on my tan faux-wool coat and four shades of beige beneath that and swelter my way down the city sidewalks. This outfit is good for more than the warmth; I pass ten people in this exact combination en route to Starbucks.

And that. Is. Glorious.

My neighborhood is not generally thought of as a neighborhood. That's why I wanted to live here. Because people say, "Oh? Do people *live* in Turtle Bay?" That's how little of a vibe it has.

I pass a hundred businesspeople, several unhoused people, a punk grandpa leashed to a shih tzu, and possibly a celebrity influencer. Among such unique people, I'm more than invisible. They are, strangely enough, *also* invisible. Catching no one else's eyes, as far as I can tell, but mine.

As much as weirdness has become normalized in Salem, I think I'd forgotten how weirdness goes unnoticed in New York too. Like it doesn't bother anyone. Like people don't see any slipup of being weird as a *big deal*.

Previously, this comforted me.

This morning, I'm not so sure.

Once I have my most basic of basic coffees in hand, I arrive at the EFG headquarters a safe twenty minutes early. I tuck my clipboard with my printed schedule beneath my arm and lift my eyes to the skyscraper's soaring glass windows, reflecting a narrow strip of sky and the buildings mostly blocking it. Doubtlessly, the sight of this towering building confuses small, migratory birds. But I'm not confused. I just feel awestruck by what I'm beholding.

My future, unfolding before my eyes.

I hurry inside before a pigeon can poop on me or worse.

After informing reception of my arrival, I perch on a stiff Nordic chair and alternate between reviewing flash cards for my upcoming CPA exam and trying to look as inconspicuous and poised as a well-placed coffee table. At last, Deborah from HR arrives and whisks me to a conference room on the fifth floor. She makes small talk about the rat that was trapped in the elevator last week, which sounds painful for all involved. Particularly for the security guard who now has three broken bones. The rat, thankfully, escaped unscathed.

"Anyway, the first thing we need to do is get you badged in," says Deborah.

"We've modified the workspace since you interned last spring," she explains as I stare transfixed at my badge. It's finally resting in my palm, like a precious, long-lost treasure. This must be how Indiana Jones felt after fording continents and fighting off his enemies. "It's open plan. We did it as a cost-control measure—ha, ha, see what I did there? Ah, good times—so we don't give staff their own desks. After all, they so often go on-site for their projects . . ."

Since it now seems clear that Deborah won't be mentioning any of my recent HR-related hijinks, I don't pay her any more attention. Instead I slip the badge into a protective sheath, focusing on the light brunette with hazel eyes and warm beige skin smiling soullessly out from the four-by-four badge. Mascara perfectly separates each of her eyelashes. She has a light spattering of freckles on her bump-ridged nose, but with the practiced angle of her chin, and her foundation, you'd barely notice. With her low ponytail, beige blouse, and gray blazer, she looks more put-together and functional than pretty. She's manifesting synthetic-rug chic. Which is great, and as it should be, but . . . I don't know. It doesn't look right.

And I would know, because it's me.

Anyway, Deborah has moved on, rolling straight into her IT spiel. I nod encouragingly, but the longer she speaks, the more her gigantic eyebrows draw together with suspicion. What's her deal? Can she tell I'm not listening? Or that I haven't had a single sip of my burnt-smelling coffee? I should probably bring the lip of the cup to my mouth.

No. It does nothing.

"Is something wrong?" I ask, finally unable to keep the loose thread of anxiety in.

"I haven't seen a clipboard in *years*. Most new hires use apps to take notes," she says bigly. "Are you over twenty-five?"

Okay, at least it's not my appearance making me stand out. Blood trickling back into my fingers, and my nail beds recovering their feeling with unpleasant tingling, I smile.

"Nope. I found this in my grandma's closet. It's a cost-control measure. Ha, ha."

On the way out of the conference room, I toss the clipboard in the trash. Who needs that old thing? I'm free and confident. And a very typical member of my generation, thanks.

In fact, as I turn on my shiny and perfect new laptop, waiting for the screen to load with a triumphant *ding*, I look around at my new coworkers and the functional lines of this modern gray office. And I feel utterly empowered.

Because beyond Deborah's potato-like face and the open-floor plan of floor six, I see the road ahead, pushing me toward the future: the gleaming suburban streets of freshly poured concrete and the green, low-cut grass of treeless front yards, the rows of houses packed together with mere feet in between, the double-wide garage doors swarming their homes' facades. The women in Ray-Ban sunglasses, walking dogs to the melody of Bluetooth meetings. Their hours whiled away in minivans, at Chick-fil-A drive-throughs, and in school pickup lines winding into cul-de-sacs. Ferrying around soft, runny-nosed children who never have to defend their home against debt creditors with the use of lead pipes or cleverly faked adult voices. Whose biggest battles involve video game bosses, not microwaving dinner.

That's going to be me. I'm going to be one of those women. I *am*.

At least, that's how I feel right up until the end of my first day of work, when I return to my apartment with Jane.

While slinging my Hunan chicken takeout onto the counter and toeing off my sneakers, it strikes me that my bedroom door isn't locked. In fact, it's cracked open. Also, two voices are leaking out from behind it. I'm guessing they belong to Jane and her boyfriend.

But why are they hanging out in my room?

Since I'm a respectful roommate and friend, I pause out of sight to listen. I don't want to walk in while they're doing something intimate. Or worse—fighting. I nearly take a chicken wing with me, but at the last second think better of it. I'm trying to be subtle, and there's nothing subtle about hot honey.

"—this whole time?" Jane is asking her companion.

"Yes, precisely!"

Oh no. That other voice . . . *No.* It doesn't belong to Jane's boyfriend. Absolutely not. The speaker's way of speaking is decidedly old-fashioned. Not to mention Welsh-accented—and ridiculous. And welcome.

I squelch the shot of happiness that runs through me. Because I can't be glad to hear his voice; this is obviously very, very bad. I allow myself to slump against the wall, wondering if I can imagine this away. The answer appears to be no, I can't—so I bang the bedroom door all the way open, choosing the path of righteous anger.

"How!" I cry, announcing my presence. "And *why*!"

Jane Doe sits in the velvet chair beside my bed, her shapeless chin cupped in a French-manicured hand. She stares with fascination at the top of my bed, where a head with a luxuriant, auburn-red hipster beard lies face up on my pillow, the bedsheets and blankets tucked right up to the chin. Said head doesn't rest there, silently feigning sleep. Oh no. It's chatty.

It is—he is—always excruciatingly chatty.

"Bulan!" I hiss.

It should be obvious I'm horrified and angry. Yet Bulan grins over at me with unchecked jubilee. Only Jane, for her part, looks embarrassed. Great. Now, layered on top of my anger sundae is a dollop of guilt for being a bad roommate.

"Sammy, I hadn't realized your boyfriend was staying over," Jane says. "I must've missed your text."

My *boyfriend*? He's not my . . . no. Bulan wouldn't tell her we were dating.

Unless he did.

I point at him as angrily as my finger will allow. "Since when were you my boyfriend?"

"Since forever, Sabby!" he answers. Bulan's smile is bright as sunlight, and I glare in its ultraviolet, cancer-inducing warmth. That lying, trespassing head. With Hanry's and my breakup less than forty-eight hours old, it's nothing short of cruel.

And the fact that he's here, invading my precious, paranormal-free space?

If Jane weren't present, I'd punt him all the way to the Brooklyn Bridge.

But since she *is* here, I have to come up with something quick. It's bad enough Jane thinks Bulan is naked or something. The last thing I want is for her to discover his ruse and end our friendship permanently; to spread an office rumor I'm dating a headless ghoul.

"A juvenile, immature prank," I say aloud. "That's why you're not wearing any clothes, isn't it?"

"Indeed, yes! That's it!" crows my grandmother's stupid head.

Jane gives him a second confused look and stands. "Well, anyway, I, uh, guess I'll go to the kitchen now. Got to refill my Stanley. I look forward to hearing about your first day later, Sammy."

"Yep, sounds good," I say. "Bye!"

Once the door to my room clicks shut, I rip the blankets off. Piles of unfamiliar dirty clothes—presumably Jane's—have been formed to create the lumpy appearance of a six-foot man's body. It's honestly a feat of engineering. Bulan must have dragged the clothes in his mouth and jumped onto the bed with them in his teeth. But I refuse to applaud his ingenuity. How did he even get in here?

"I was telling Jane that I meant this as a fun surprise!" says Bulan, presumably in explanation. "You didn't warn me she'd come home ahead of you."

"You aren't supposed to be here at all," I remind him. "Now get out."

Bulan rolls his face into my pillow. He takes on a mournful air.

"I went to all this trouble to visit, and this is how you treat me?"

"You can't just come visit me."

"Well, technically I'm not visiting. I moved in with you. In fact, I *moved with you*. My crows were hard-pressed to carry me the whole distance, following those trains of yours. They're fast, aren't they? Did you know dragons were once that fast? They were. It's true."

This is a lot to take in. "I thought you were going to stay with Mandy."

"Mandy's apartment is extremely sketchy," Bulan says, mostly muffled by the pillowcase. "You should pay her better."

"She's no longer on my payroll. I've refunded everyone whose deposits I didn't need to give to Baldy, and I made plans to refund the rest. That's what it means when you close a business."

"So you say."

"Yes. It is what I say."

And that should be the end of it, but there's something to his expression I don't like. I fold my arms. "What don't I know, Bulan?"

"She's still planning to put on all your weddings."

I balk.

Mandy can't do that. She is—was—a talented assistant, sure. But she needs someone to give her directions. To keep her from eating the cake ahead of the bride. These commonsense things, they don't come to her naturally, desire for seriousness notwithstanding.

"Why?" I ask. "Just—why?"

"She wants to prove she's a serious sort of pixie," Bulan explains proudly. "That she's much more than just a seductress and a charmer! And I couldn't be happier for her, Sabby. This is a big step. Surely you can see that. Can't you?"

It's a fair question.

I mean, the first thing that pops into my head is that this probably won't work out well for Mandy. Or me, whose brand name she's presumably doing this under. But if she ruins my reputation, what does it matter? I'm not going back to Salem. If anything, maybe this is good: no one can accuse me of failing to follow through in providing the services they placed deposits for. They can blame Mandy instead. Unless, more happily, Mandy proves me wrong and turns out to be a success.

"Fine," I say at last. I throw up my hands because that seems like what people do in these situations. "Mandy can do what she wants."

"And so can I," says Bulan, face rotating back into the pillow. "Which is why I'm staying here with you."

No. Absolutely not. The last thing I need is to be haunted a second longer than necessary by Grandma Rose's paranormal world.

But I can't quite bring myself to turn him out, despite all this. I'm a little bit—just the tiniest bit—happy to see him. And I'm sure Bulan will get bored of staying here eventually. Once he runs off with his crow friends again, everything will be fine.

And normal.

So very, very normal.

Please.

21

THE GRITTY SANDWICHES OF NEW YORK CITY

MY FIRST WEEK AT EFG IS BOTH EASIER AND MORE DIFFICULT than I expect.

It's easy because Jane and I share matching, rigid schedules. She likes working in a twenty-minute yoga routine before her morning coffee. Because what Jane does, I must do also, I join her every morning at five thirty, to the protest of my recalcitrant spine.

Generally speaking, the true difficulties of my days kick in when Jane and I part ways at the elevator lobby. She heads for the fifth floor, and I go to the sixth, where I meet up with the tech auditing group. For accountants, being able to work with companies like Oracle and MicroOrange in the AI space is the pinnacle of slick and sexy. In that sense, being reassigned has no downsides. None.

Any discomfort I'm having can be attributed to how bad I am at brewing caffeinated drinks, even compared to Hanry, whose company I can't help missing. Working quietly beside me, he was always ready to meet my eyes with a smile, with confidence in my abilities. Whereas, as a new staff hire—the newest one on the floor—I can't yet be trusted with reconciling accounts or working directly with clients. I get kicked out of a ten o'clock meeting by a senior accountant who clearly hasn't kept up with the Slack channel and is convinced I'm some random street urchin who stole a pass card. He doesn't say that, but I can tell. I've thrown that look at numerous nameless members of the Community.

It's . . . unpleasant being on the other side of it.

Jane says this is normal. That all new hires have to surmount such indignities before they can jump rank and confront new indignities, like listening to the client explain how AI is going to render bookkeepers irrelevant. Although we've yet to see an AI understand it isn't fraud if MicroOrange increases the price of its subscriptions.

As the days pass, I find myself sleeping poorly. Part of this is because I'm working late, and on Saturdays. Most of my insomnia I attribute to the apartment's hyperactive radiator. I struggle to keep my eyes open at my desk. Occasionally, when I stop typing and let my hands rest too long on my keyboard, Bulan will bang into my leg from inside the duffel bag.

"I'm waiting for you to get bored and leave," I tell him one day at lunch hour.

"I'm waiting for *you* to get bored and leave," he says.

"Stop imitating me."

"Stop imitating—oof!" We're in my new hire class's favored deli on Park Avenue. It's highly visible, and crowded, meaning I can't have extended conversations with my duffel bag and escape with my reputation intact. Especially not when Jane approaches, a workmate in tow.

Jane's friend is the pinnacle of color matching. She wears a blazer and flared pants in exactly the same ash brown shade as her eyes and hair. Her manicured nails and her milky coffee appear to be in sync. Altogether, she seems like great friendship material. She could be a true source of solidarity. Like hardwood flooring.

"Hi," I say, tossing my bag on the floor, making space at Bulan's expense.

"Are you Sammy?" Jane's friend sits. "I heard that you snore."

Damn it, Bulan.

"I've ordered special nasal strips, but the shipping company lost them," I lie. "Last I heard, they were in Toronto."

"Oh." The girl unwraps her sandwich. Turkey. Cheese. Multigrain bread. A banana, because she's trying to be healthy, but not trying too hard. This is what I'll order tomorrow. "That's far."

"It is," I say.

"I think Kansas City is farther," says Jane. That's where her family lives, and I can see her doing the mental math. "By a thousand miles?"

"I can google it," says Jane's friend. She doesn't go for her phone, though. I guess none of us care enough to. "Didn't Desmond say we have an account in KC?"

"Huh, maybe," says Jane.

Hoping to smooth over the ensuing awkward silence, I say, "I've always wanted to visit the Plains. They sound nice. Or at least, nice enough."

"They're all right," Jane agrees. "Really open. Wide and stuff."

"The jet stream makes it perfect for tornadoes." Jane's friend shudders. "I hate that. It sounds so dangerous."

"Yes!" I exclaim, finally finding my footing in this conversation. "Tornadoes are the worst of all natural disasters, right? They come out of absolutely nowhere and ruin everything!"

Jane laughs noncommittally.

"Most storm systems aren't strong enough to yield tornadoes. The ones that do touch down are usually no more than F-1 or F-2. Plus, they hit in cornfields more than cities. And we have tornado shelters, so. It's not a big deal."

"Oh, I guess it isn't bad, then," says Jane's nameless friend, who still hasn't introduced herself, and probably at this point never will. She looks down at her phone and wipes her chin with a napkin.

"Did you see this meme? Oh my god," she says. I wait for her to flip her phone and show me what she's watching, but she doesn't. Shifting on her seat, Jane silently joins in watching the screen. At one point, she sends a vague frown at her dip-powdered nails. Nothing's wrong with them. They're fine.

When I finish my own gritty sandwich, I pack up and return to my work desk. But instead of logging back in, I stare up at the ceiling, counting the cracks in it until Bulan rolls out of my bag and bites my ankle.

I let out a sharp yip, but no one on the sixth floor pays me any attention. Behold, the power of noise-canceling headphones.

"What are you doing?" Bulan asks.

"Thinking," I whisper back.

"Well, that seems boring."

"No more boring than our lunch conversation."

"Yeah, what was that?" barks Bulan. "Didn't you tell me it was fun to be a young twentysomething in New York?"

"Be quiet. And yes," I hiss. I was promised, repeatedly, that EFG was fun by a half-dozen recruiters and coworkers during interview season. They said work would be spectacular. That we'd have pizza parties in-office, complete with Kool-Aid, and make meaningful impacts for our clients. But, like most of the other non-nepo-baby newly hired staff, I've only been trusted with reconciling A/R. Though satisfying, it's certainly not spectacular. The better word I'd use for it is "repetitive." And "lots." Because it's usually late when I finish work. The best part of my day is coming home to Jane. And it's almost like . . . Jane isn't enough.

She's just . . . when we hang out, there are a lot of screens involved.

On the weekends, my study sessions for the CPA exam don't fill as much time as I'm used to having filled. I wonder if I should get on a dating app to stop daydreaming about Hanry. To keep *busy*. To feel less itchy, less unsettled all the time.

During meetings, I keep catching myself sketching *table settings* without meaning to. Sometimes I even imagine coworkers falling in love, and I wonder if I can guess what type of wedding they might have. Bohemian? Beach? *Bridgerton*-inspired? No. It's always something traditional. I bet they'd search no farther for venues than directly across the street.

Not that I should judge: I'm struggling to daydream anything romantic for myself. There aren't cute boys to stare at here at work. Sure, a few of them might be slender enough to compete with Jungkook, but I haven't met any single men of the handsome, lumberjack-esque variety. They all seem . . . crisp and square. They remind me of stale white bread. Tasteless and forgettable. They barely hold substance in my mind.

Hanry and I only dated for a few weeks. I should be able to shake off the way I'm missing him, but I can't do it. I *can't*.

Why did he have to be part of Salem's paranormal community? If only he could've been a guy with regular ambitions who would've considered moving with me to New York. I know it was just a handful of weeks, but . . . maybe we could've compromised, with him keeping dogs instead of squirrels. Would he have ever considered replacing his love of salsa dancing with an interest in Broadway shows?

I wonder what he's doing right now. I imagine him curled up on the sofa, cozy under his wool blanket, a mug of once-hot cider tipped over on the floor. The top buttons of denim shirt undone, exposing his collarbone, a sliver of his chest . . .

It's a nice image. It would be nicer if I could see it up close, if he were dozing here with me. If I were wrapped in his arms, sated and warm.

I wonder why he hasn't texted me yet. Has he met someone else at his salsa class? I hope not. I want him to miss me. To be wistfully knitting his brows as he works on yet another wreath, eating cold pizza by himself.

And Mandy. Is all the wedding prep going okay? Is she struggling to do the work by herself in the shop? Does she ever feel like the space is cavernous without me and Bulan?

If it weren't for Bulan and the endless client returns I'm stuck reviewing, I wonder if I'd be lonely too.

I don't get the chance to wonder for long.

About two weeks after I've started at EFG, I wake up and find a very strangely worded note on an empty takeout bag near my bed:

MY nemezis has track t me
Im of f wi th the b I r dz
Hab f u n!

It can't be from Jane. Her handwritten script is blocky, neat, and lacks Bulan's undercurrent of hasty enthusiasm. Also, as far as I know, Jane doesn't have birds in her friend group. Or a nemesis. Since when did Bulan? I think maybe he's lying to soften the blow.

I stare out the window and the brick wall it faces, wistful. I hear no telltale crow squawks, just traffic and distant sirens. If I strain, I can hear the idea of pigeons.

Obviously, Bulan fit in as terribly in New York as I'd thought he would. But he decided to leave his life in Salem to join me here, and I can't think of a good reason he would've jumped ship, unless he'd grown unhappy. And not just regular unhappy, but *deeply* unhappy.

Miserable, even.

He would've written a longer note if he'd really planned to leave for good, though. Right? This life may not be up to par with his usual sense of adventure, but I'm not in a suburb—yet. New York has plenty of weird people in it; I've seen them on the streets, in the patchwork fabric of the city's throngs. Can't we talk this out? Give it another go?

I fight back waves of disappointment when Bulan isn't back by the evening.

Or the next.

On the Friday night before Thanksgiving week—more than a week after Bulan left to hang out with the crows, who are more fun and interesting than me—I'm packing away my exam notes when Jane knocks on the door to my room. She's pulled on a pair of polished derbies instead of her typical sneakers. This is a sign she's going somewhere cool. But not *too* cool. In New York, this is a critical distinction.

"I'm heading out," she says predictably.

"Where to?"

"Drinks with Erin and some of the others in our class," says Jane. "Sammy, you should come!"

Yes. *YES*. My whole being sings at the idea of it. At the thought of noise, of energy, of people. Friendship. Friendship with *work people*. The opportunity to meet a fellow accountant who'll help me achieve my dream of suburban bliss, and make me forget Hanry—who I really maintain should have checked in on me by now.

I slam my laptop shut.

"Let me get ready," I say.

As I dress, I prod Jane for details about the party. She doesn't say much except that we're going to an apartment, rather than a bar. Apparently, some of our coworkers are trying to go FIRE, meaning that they're on a stringent, money-saving early-retirement plan. I'd probably be doing that too, if I weren't throwing my money into paying back Grandma's debts in order to cover house-selling legal fees. Anyway, the party at Erin's apartment is just a few blocks away. Which is fine—I wouldn't want to go somewhere too fancy or noteworthy, anyway.

It turns out that Erin's apartment is fancy in its own way. It has epic skyline views. Sure, it's a crowded studio of about the same size as Grandma Rose's living room, including the kitchenette and bathroom, and it's clearly not meant to host the thirty twentysomethings who have gathered in it. Not to mention all the booze. The *ample* quantities of booze. In the corner, there's a kegger; somewhat paradoxically, the counter has been commandeered by a spectacle of bottled wine. Pretty much everyone seems to be arriving with a bottle in their right hand, then replacing said bottle with poured wine in a stemless cup. A few embarrassing people hold their cups in their left hands. Obviously, I am not among them.

In the dense throng, I lose track of Jane almost immediately. Part of this is because the room's female contingent have unanimously decided to wear black halter tops and light-blue-washed, wide-legged cargo pants, and I can't tell anyone apart from behind. The nonbinary and male percentages are all wearing a blend of patterned dress shirts and slacks and starter-pack beer guts. The effect would make even a *Where's Waldo?* tournament-winner quail.

"—it's a simple formula," I overhear a guy near me saying. "*D* times *A* equals *X* divided by one hundred. *D* for dependability, *A* for amiability."

"Oh, gotcha," says his not-athletic-looking friend. "So the more dependable and amiable—"

"—the higher the likability quotient, yeah. I suspect you need at least an eighty percent to make partner."

"That explains so much!"

Okay, I'm not jumping into that conversation. But I should jump into *someone's*. Whose? And how? I twitch, anxious with the need to do something. I start arranging pillows on the couch, neatening them up before I remember I'm the guest and not the person throwing the party.

"Is this the wrong apartment?" I ask Jane once I find her. "You didn't bring me to a meet-up for math majors, did you?"

"No, no." She screws up her face. "Didn't you see the nice wine? This party is classy."

It may be classy, kind of, but also, it's . . .

Well, I'm sure *someone* here will be more interested in friendship than in deconstructing it into a formula. Determined to try harder, I weave through my colleagues over to the wine-laden counter. A few people stand there, chatting. I wait for one to separate from the herd so I can pick them off like an injured wildebeest. To keep myself occupied, I down a glass of chardonnay. The next thing I know, I find myself rearranging the wine bottles by region and varietal, repurposing two emptied cheese boards to use as a stage. I find and refold some paper napkins. Having nailed a much classier, if slightly boho-chic aesthetic, I perch on the edge of the wet counter and wait to be complimented. It takes a while, so I pull out my phone and reread texts from Hanry. I scroll through them, all of them, until stopping at the last one Hanry ever sent, on the day of Sidney and Brett's were-human wedding.

Let me know when you get home safe.

I didn't answer.

But I should've! My fingertip hovers over the speech window. Should I text Hanry? If I did, what would I say? Obviously I could mention that I returned safely to New York. But now the floodgates open. What else could I say? How about: *I miss your not-quite-bearded face*? *I think you're fun*? *Work parties aren't as great as everyone says*? *I know we decided to break up, but isn't this like, a little* too *broken-up, actually*?

Sure, we're worlds apart and it's probably irreconcilable, but what if, I don't know, what if maybe—

Before I can press send and deliver my stream-of-consciousness novel, someone bumps into my side. Their arm flails, and fizzy beer spills over my shoulder and down into my bra.

"Whoa, sorry!" laughs the nonathletic guy from before. "I didn't see you!"

I pluck at my shirt. "I'm sticky!"

"Sorry!"

"Do you need a Tide Pen?" asks the guy's companion. Both of them are equipped with central-casting face. I feel almost too bored to look between them.

"Tide Pens only help with stains," I snap. "What I need is a hair dryer. Do you have one of those?"

"Uh, no," says the guy with skinny, useless spaghetti arms. Both of them walk off. Fine. Good riddance. Why ask if you're not going to be helpful? I pull an emergency Kleenex from my crossbody bag, grumbling.

"You need me to grab a towel from the bathroom or anything?" asks someone else with a drink. I take a better look at him: a brunette with a nice outfit. Not the kind to stand out in a crowd. His Afro temple fade is immaculate. In a way, it's perfect.

"Hey," I say. "No thanks."

He replies with a chin nod. Which is subtle. This interaction is getting better every moment. "I don't think we've met."

"No," I say, sipping from my stemless abomination of a cup. "I just started at EFG, in the tech audits group. We haven't met."

"That's because I've been on-site at MicroOrange," he says.

And then it strikes me. This is my enemy.

"Oh, cool. You must be Desmond," I say.

The alleged Desmond gives me the briefest once-over.

"You don't look like an auditor," he says.

I jerk so hard, some of my white wine sloshes across my fingers.

"I don't? How come?"

"I don't know. A vibe, I guess." Taking a calm sip, Desmond asks me what Netflix shows I'm watching. Yikes. Since the start of October, I've watched nothing but old romantic dramas set at least two hundred years ago. As for social media, I average easily three hundred wedding TikToks a day.

Not quite despairing, I down another gulp of chardonnay and say, "The popular ones."

"I love the popular ones."

Wait. Is he . . . is he *flirting*? I think so. It sounds like flirting. But why don't I feel anything? Probably because Desmond tried to get me fired. Does that make this negging?

A touch on my shoulder causes me to turn around.

"Hey," says Jane, unaware that she's interrupting a possible moment. "I was heading outside to smoke. Wanna join?"

Huh. I wouldn't have guessed that from Jane. A spark of interest, finally, flames to life inside my dulled and bored-sick brain. Better still: smoking seems like a normal thing to do, and Classic New York. Saying goodbye to Desmond—then once I've turned away, stuffing a couple cocktail napkins into my bra—I step outside after her. On the shallow balcony, a bone-chilling gust drives straight through my wet shirt. I shiver, detecting snowflakes.

Of course the sky is dueling the apartment for the prize of cold-hearted unfriendliness.

How rude of you, New York Sky.

"—on the weekend," Jane is saying. I wonder how long she's been talking and why I wasn't listening. I mean, she never really says anything interesting, but she's my roommate. And the only friend I have at this party. And potentially in this entire city.

"Uh-huh," I say, trying for politeness. "I hear you."

"Yeah? So we can start tomorrow. What do you think?"

What *do* I think?

I tip my head back, aware of the elevator jazz and voices trickling out behind us. The buildings surrounding me; the hundreds of them. They stay bright whether it's daytime or nighttime or fall or winter.

This whole city's bloated with rooms full of people who don't care about me—and who I don't care about either.

"Does it get better than this?" I ask. "Or is life always this predictable? And lame?"

Jane unpockets a vape pen. "What's lame about coming up with house-cleaning schedules? I like schedules."

Smoke covers my view of the buildings as Jane takes a hit. Of course she doesn't smoke cigs or something; that would be too edgy. And this is the girl I've spent months idolizing. The person I've tried to emulate. I can't help the shuddering revulsion that threatens to overtake me.

"Oh, Ann!" Jane flags down a woman in a gray cardigan that perfectly matches her expression. "Welcome back! How was Atlantic City?"

My phone buzzes against my chest, pulling me from their conversation. It's weird. I was sure I turned off Slack for the party, and besides that, no one should be reaching out except for . . .

Wait. Did I send Hanry that lovestruck text, after all?

Horror drying out my guts, but tragically not the space between my breasts and bra, I reach into my crossbody bag and lift out my phone, holding the screen up to my eyes.

I. Did. Send it.

But Hanry hasn't replied—or read it. The reason my phone vibrated was to send me a spam message from an unknown number. A message that reads:

What the hell is this?

And why is this the most interesting thing that has happened to me all night?

I stare down at the avenue eight floors below. At the lights, the cars, and the people, the busy scrambling on their hedonic treadmills. I blame my right-handed wine for what I do next.

I call the random number.

"AHH, SABBY!" screams Mandy's voice in my ear. "I DIDN'T KNOW YOU COULD READ PIXIE! I'M SO GLAD!"

"I—what?!" I ask, rubbing my temples. Casting a quick glance at Jane and the others, who might have also temporarily lost their hearing, I whisper, sotto voce: "I didn't know you had a phone."

"I DON'T, this is the cricket's!" Hold on. Did she say cricket? Since when did crickets have phones, and since when have they been large enough for a full-size person to *type* on? "I just wanted to DOUBLE-CHECK, so DON'T worry about anything! But you know on the wedding schedule, well, I was thinking . . . what if the photographers were enchanted? Do you think that'd be a problem? It's not a problem, right?"

It takes a beat before I remember what Bulan said: that Mandy was going to plan and coordinate the weddings I'd bailed on. But I'd never thought of the broader implications. If I'm remembering correctly, this weekend is the one that Rochester's clients had selected for their event.

So she's decided to pick up the wedding for Rochester's clients? The *fairies*? Oh no, Mandy. Oh no.

"Mandy," I say, determined to be calm. "Are you telling me that some of the vendors for Rochester's mysterious wedding have been hypnotized? Paranormally?"

"Yes, but in a friendly way!"

"That isn't friendly! That's coercion."

"Oh! Like you said about hugs?"

"Sometimes, Mandy." I pull in a steadying breath. "Why is this coming up now?"

"Well, the wedding's tomorrow, and the cricket's picking me up and he said— OH! I think I have to go! Well, I'll tell our clients to un-enchant them if they can! THANKS, SABBY!"

The line goes dead.

Holy. Shit.

With all my research, effort, and luck, I barely succeeded in pulling off the weddings for Dave and Amanda, Fi and Asher, and Sidney and Brett. Planning such a huge, lavish event with less than a month's experience? No matter how badly Mandy wants to impress Rochester, there's no way she can do it. For one thing, she won't get the fairies to change their minds about enchantments. When people—or creatures, or monsters, or whatever—plan their weddings, they're pretty reluctant to let go of their vision. Even if said vision includes violations of the Geneva Convention.

Too easily, I visualize the calamity of Mandy's failure: the flames, the howling, the possible injury. Mandy's stress-born consumption of a beluga whale's weight in chocolates.

No. I can't let that happen to her. Not to my friend.

"I've got to get out of here," I find myself saying aloud.

I have to go, to help. To make sure Mandy gets the linens right, and the flowers, and the timing. To help the enchanted photographers nail their jobs. It's not like I have anything better to do this weekend. Like, making a cleaning schedule? No thanks.

"Sammy, are you afraid of heights?" Jane asks. "We can go inside."

"What? No. I mean for the weekend. I have to visit someone." To reassure my roommate, I add, "I'll be back at the apartment before work on Monday."

Jane says, "Oh. Okay."

Putting her dubious tone aside, it *is* okay. I'm more than ready to leave this balcony and this party. To take a break from these people.

Problem: I don't know where the secret wedding venue is or how far away it might be. And I don't know who, exactly, is getting married. Only that they're probably fay.

Since it's evening, the wedding rehearsal should already be underway. I don't want to miss anything else. And one thing I know for sure? Getting there will be significantly more complicated than jumping onto a late-night commuter train.

22

DESPERATE TIMES, DESPERATE VEGETABLES

I RACE BACK TO MY APARTMENT, HOPING I'M NOT TOO LATE. IN my room, I throw my laptop open on the bed and shimmy out of my sticky top and bra. I pull out my duffel bag and riffle through the immaculately folded clothes in my drawers, searching for dark-hued dresswear that would be formal enough to meet the Roachster's standards. No luck. I snag a black pantsuit from Jane's closet. It's not like she'll miss it over the weekend.

While hastily brushing knots out of my hair, I review the folder in My Documents titled *Spüktacular Weddings' Proposed Large-Scale Event for Rochester's Allegedly Influential and Rich Power Couple Who Still Aren't Disclosing Any Information That'd Be Helpful*.

If Mandy is following the wedding prep timeline we quoted Rochester, the rehearsal dinner should already be in full swing. Barring a meeting with a future time-traveling Sabby, I doubt I'll arrive before midnight. But there's no reason I can't try.

The closest Home Depot is only a few blocks north of here, at Fifty-Eighth and Third. Walking at a New Yorker's pace—largely to stay warm, since wearing a pantsuit with no coat in November is an unpleasant consequence of drinking too much alcohol and forgetting to chase it with food—I arrive in a quick twenty minutes. The storefront's closed up, obviously. Since I haven't come to buy a hammer or return a crate of plywood, I whip around the side of the building in search of an employee entrance. At the building's rear, I find a private, brick-laid circle-drive cutting through the center of the city block. It leads to a gourmet Japanese restaurant, the lobby of a luxury condo complex, and a largely unnoteworthy—and unlabeled—pair of white double doors.

"Here goes nothing," I mutter. Then, with a surging, dramatic impulse, I knock on them. "Abra-cada-bra-lo-hamora Special Services."

The right-side door cracks open.

"Hold up. That was seriously the password?" I ask. The doors don't answer except to shimmer with annoyance, revealing shiny glass windows for a split second. Sensing my entrance may be in peril, I try the door handle and enter a fluorescent-lit back room.

The room is utterly sterile. Also, it's familiar. As in, potentially the same place I've already been. How else does one explain how it's staffed by the same lady I met back in Salem?

Like before, she has her nose deep in a book, dark eyes enraptured by the words. This time, it's a chocolate-themed romance set in Bulgaria.

"Hello," I call out, hoping I sound at least half as winsome as a Bulgarian chocolatier. "I'd like to request service."

She turns a page in her book, ignoring me. What was it Hanry did to get her help last time?

"SOCKS!" I shout, remembering. "SOCKS."

At last she deigns to offer me her notice. "You again. The gnomes not working out?"

"No, they've been great," I say, tapping the counter. "Although I probably need to call them off. Maybe tomorrow. Higher priority: I want to pick up additional services."

"There'll be a late-night surcharge, I'm afraid."

As if that matters.

"I can work with that," I say. "I mean to say—my client can."

Thirty minutes later, I'm at the corner of Tramway Plaza, my toes sticking out a few inches past the edge of the curb. I've just set up the most unlikely group text ever, including Dave the deadbeat vampire who *still* hasn't paid me and other spooky folks I met while running Spük-tacular Weddings. As I wait for them to confirm that they're prepared to render last-minute, epic-scale wedding assistance, I do my best to look like the person in need of a paranormal pickup while also remaining inconspicuous to the rest of NYC. That said, my usual desire to be unnoticed is losing out to bouncing. It's a light bounce, granted, but it's definitely happening.

What's also happening: a bright-yellow smear making its way across the gray-paved horizon. It's the color of a taxi.

But it is not a taxi.

It's longer, taller, and technically some kind of oblong sphere with cutout windows. Also, it's being led by a team of unnecessarily regal white horses. When it stops in front of me, my senses confirm:

It's a pumpkin.

A giant, horse-powered pumpkin.

"Technically, a gourd," says the coachman, settled on a platform abutting the winter squash. He has absurdly long and spindly legs, so his knees reach his chin. Reins to the horses rest somewhere in his lap. He's wearing a vest that looks like it was stolen from a Victorian-era traffic guard. Affixed to it is a lapel with a pin that reads, to my delight, SPECIAL SERVICES.

"And you?" I ask. "You're . . . a person?"

I probably shouldn't question him so publicly, but I think the ship of normalcy has sailed tonight.

"Of course," the coachman huffs unconvincingly. Also, his eyes are bugging out. "Do come in. And keep the curtains closed."

I ascend the steps into the hollowed-out carriage, well aware I'm catching the attention of passersby.

"What?" I call out. "You've never seen an art car before? Art. Car."

When this fails to make an impact, I follow the coachman's advice to slide the curtains across the pumpkin's pulpy windows.

The carriage smells like Trader Joe's in October. Having made a jack-o'-lantern with Hanry on one of our many impromptu dates, I can appreciate the carving of the vehicle's vegetably interior. Precision cutting. The seats aren't the least bit stringy. Though pumpkin juice is seeping through my pantsuit and into my fresh pair of underwear. Oh well, better this than beer.

We bump and rattle our way across the Queensboro Bridge. I close my eyes, resting until the horses whinny with a touch of harmonic drama. When they bring us to a stop, I crack open the thick-fleshed pumpkin coach door to catch a glimpse of our progress. By which I mean I brace myself to witness—inevitably—the land of Fairy.

We're in a forest. Mostly conifers. There's an old Wegman's bag on the side of the road.

"Hey, Jiminy Cricket," I call to the driver, opening the door farther. "Where are we?"

"Hello, Miss Samantha! We're outside of Albany."

"What, like Albany, *New York*?"

The driver nods so hard, I feel sympathy whiplash. "Yes! Our destination is but a few dozen miles from here."

Damn. I always heard Upstate New York was weird.

"I should've guessed"—I laugh in spite of myself—"that Fairy wasn't far at all."

"Indeed! Now, please step out, for the party we're meant to intercept should be right—aha! Right along!"

We're intercepting a whole party? Well, I guess that explains the glowing orange light I'm just able to make out, advancing toward us on this country highway.

Surprise, surprise: it is another giant vegetable.

To my pleasure, though? *This* pumpkin rolls up beside mine, and a small, pretty hand throws back its ornate, gauzy curtains.

"SABBY!" cries the hand's owner, who is no other than Mandy. "You're here! You're coming to the wedding! I'm so HAPPY!"

My pixie assistant, and the interim lead planner for Spüktacular Weddings, is dressed in a frilly black ensemble with a gathered skirt and a giant ruffled trim. I love it. And I love her. My heart absolutely gushes with affection, and it's kind of gross.

"Of course I'm here," I say, rolling my eyes to emphasize how chill I am about seeing her. "We have a job to do, don't we? Now, make room for me in your pumpkin."

"I would, but it's a spaghetti squash," says Mandy. "The sugars caramelize differently. Anyway, get in!"

"Will do," I say. I wave in thanks to my own personal Jiminy Cricket and glance at the second, taller of the two coachmen guiding Mandy's contraption. He meets my eye, his familiar brow poised in arched disdain.

"Rochester!" I exclaim. "Hey, you're a sight for sore eyes."

He continues to disdain me with such great power that I feel it's best to dip into the squash, lest I become a roasted vegetable myself.

"What's he doing here?" I ask as I slip around into my seat.

"Rochester is a fairy godmother," Mandy informs me, toweling off her hands with a dainty kerchief. "All fairy godmothers have to study carriagecraft."

"A fairy, I get, but a godmother? Why . . . a mother . . . Rochester is a . . . You know what, no. I'm not asking. Where's Bulan?"

Mandy's expression swiftly shifts from giddy and lovestruck to slightly panicked. "I thought he was with you!"

My stomach sinks. If Bulan didn't go back to Salem, what *did* his crows do with him? Maybe they've made him a full member of the gang now, and he's sporting a new raven tattoo on his nose or something.

"I'm sure he's fine, wherever he is," I say uneasily. I bang on the squash's fleshy wall.

"All right, Roachster," I call out. "Time to take us to the ball. Chop-chop!"

Mandy pouts. "It's not a ball, remember? Tonight's the rehearsal dinner."

"Oh, Mandy," I say. "It was a joke. You have so much left to learn."

"I do!" she cries, and tackles me with such a hard hug, I nearly fall back through the carriage door and onto the earth of Mid-Nonsense, New York. But thankfully, these squash vehicles are made of strong, if stringier, stuffing, and soon we're just another giant plant flying down the road. In fact, as far as I can tell, the only thing going faster than us is Mandy's mouth. She has a month's worth of hijinks to catch me up on, and only a short time to do so.

"... and after that, Rochester brought me the deposit and signed the contract for us, you see? And I was too googly-eyed to say no and on top of that, there were all these Community folks calling and checking in about their weddings and new weddings and talking about their invitations and the fonts and the printers and consultations, and I just had to keep it going. And it was so hard, but through it all, I knew you'd come back!"

I ignore the last comment, interjecting with effort: "When Bulan told me you were doing this, I thought about stopping you."

"You should've!" Mandy cries. "I'm able to hold almost anyone's attention! And I can hold SO MUCH candy at the same time! But I can't hold together much else."

"I'm sure you've done your best." I pat her shoulder.

"Getting things organized is *your* superpower." She hiccups. "I want to be serious, Sabby, but I don't know if I can. What if my only superpower is seduction?"

"I don't think you get to call something a superpower if it's your species' innate ability."

Mandy dabs at her eyes with a lacy sleeve.

"In any case," she says, "your instructions were so clear, all the scheduling you did for this wedding and the other weddings, I just kept following them as if you were there, and if I fell behind on anything, I imagined you were really angry!"

"Glad that helped," I say. My phone pings, and immediately I scramble to remove it from the bag on my chest. Are we back in cell area? *Did Hanry finally reply to me?* But no. My phone is just announcing that my battery's about to die. And I left my charger in the apartment. Shit.

"I had no idea what else to do," Mandy continues. "I still needed to pay rent."

I return my useless phone back into my chest bag and refocus on Mandy. She seems genuinely upset.

"Mandy. You've done a lot these last few weeks. You deserve more from me. And better."

"It's okay!"

"Wage theft isn't."

She cocks her head to the side. "What is *that*?"

"Something I learned about in college. But seriously, why didn't you try to find a new job when you ran out of money?"

"Oh, umm. I didn't want to leave Salem, and, well . . . Remember how happy Fi was? And Sidney? If I could make that happen again, I knew I would. No matter how hard it was." After a moment's pause, she bursts out, "Wow, didn't that sound weighty?"

"It did," I agree. Reaching into my duffel, searching for my laptop case, I say, "Let's lean into that energy. I've heard that faking it till you make it works. So from now on, your new name is Serious Mandy."

"Yay!"

"But I'm going to keep calling you Mandy."

"Okay!"

"That's probably all the time we have to catch up," I say. Pulling out my laptop and opening it, I ask, "What do we need to do to make this wedding happen tomorrow? Where are we on details? I remember the couple originally wanted to use a local vendor for the flowers, but have you been able to follow up with them to talk about responsibilities for setup?"

Mandy passes me a folder of her own, and together, we enter a familiar discussion. Which feels nice, until I realize none of the answers to my questions are precise enough to offer peace of mind. Each one forces me to write, inevitably, *Discuss on arrival*. Worst of all?

"The bride and groom didn't fill out their family background surveys. In fact, Mandy, there's no information in here about them at all."

"It's probably because the mother of the bride is another Becuille mac Nuadat type. You know, what's that word you used?"

"Momzilla," I say.

"Yeah! She probably wanted to make sure you didn't talk to the REAL bride and groom to find out what THEY wanted. I bet she thinks she's being sneaky. Oh, what chaos!"

No kidding. If we have this right, then the cunning and callousness I've experienced so far bodes poorly for tomorrow's wedding. And it explains why I'm struck by a moment of terror as Rochester calls on the horses to halt, and Mandy crawls across the seat to the curtains, pulling the fabric back to reveal our final destination.

A goddamned fairy castle.

23

THE GODDAMNED FAIRY CASTLE

LET ME EXPLAIN WHAT THAT LOOKS LIKE.

You take the Disney World template and squeeze it around the middle like a tube of toothpaste, so the bottom and top bulge to bursting. Then you throw in a little extra leafery and accidental trees sticking out of windows. And maybe drop in walls with angles that aren't strictly correct. Example: a second-floor greenhouse lingering without support underneath (though it's connected to the castle by an arched stone bridge, obviously). A roof composed of tulips instead of tiles. On top of all that, you add an extremely intimidating verticality. Like since when did you need more than one, or at most, two turrets in a building? Why twenty? Does *everyone* need their own winding staircase? What about ADA access? The more I look at it, the more my discomfort grows. Then eases. Then grows. Then completely, utterly dissipates.

Yeah, all right. It's a fairy castle. So, presumably, I am here to help throw a royal fairy wedding. This explains the preposterous budget. And the spectacular Momzilla-levels of entitlement. And the secrecy. But you know what?

These fairies have *no taste*.

And I know how to work with that.

As much as I can't wait to hate-view the castle entry hall, it's probably for the best that Rochester deposits our spaghetti squash coach at the rear-facing servants' entrance. The moment we step out, we're met with a security screening procedure rivaling TSA's.

"Please pass over your bag," drones a fairy in combat boots. She taps at a sign covered with gibberish. "Any under-wing items will be confiscated if found upon inspection."

"None of us have wings," I nearly say, but stop myself. Beneath my classy couture pantsuit, I reek of alcohol and pumpkin sweat. My previously trustworthy pet head isn't here to guide me in courtly fairy manners. If I'm going to help Mandy pull this wedding off, I need to offend as little as possible. So I hold my tongue.

Which is truly difficult to do when, past the security checkpoint, we enter a scene stolen straight from a middle-schooler's D&D game. Tall, obscenely attractive workers swarm us. They take my duffel and Mandy's luggage, staring openly at me. One photographs me with his phone, and I see he's got Snapchat open. Cringing under their attention, I can't help wondering if these fairies have lived their whole lives on this property and I'm the first human they've encountered. Is that possible, or do I just stink worse than I realized?

Maybe it's not just the pantsuit. Maybe they smell the city on me, the stuffy *eau de EFG*. The whiff of ink on freshly printed spreadsheets. They must be thinking: What's a dull and washed-out girl like that doing here? They can't see what I am. What I'm capable of. I *almost* want them to notice. Just, for the right reasons this time.

Unlike me, Mandy seems to be in her element.

"Being invited to royal grounds is such a treat!" she says as Rochester instructs the staff to take us deeper within the castle. "What an honor! I can't believe this."

With effort, she restrains a squeal, then squeals in delight that she's managed it.

I pat her arm. "Good work."

"I will show you to your rooms," says Rochester. His expression is such a cross of staid irritation and detached, statuesque joylessness, I can't imagine a single bippity-boppity-boo in him. We follow the worst fairy godmother ever into a hallway with vines encircling a series of low, exposed wooden beams. Compared to the castle's facade, the décor here is more cottagecore than confusing. Personally, I prefer a ceiling with more than a four-foot clearance, but that's just me. As we proceed through the hallway, mimicking hunchbacked zombies, Mandy grabs onto a vine, plucks off a pink honeysuckle, and sucks on it with a creepy, full-body giggle.

"Oh my sugar starfish, this gets better and better, Sabby! Ahhhh!"

"Please do not eat our house," Rochester says, stonily turning to lead us into a more functionally heighted hallway. The wooden beams with their flowering vines ascend beyond Mandy's reach. That said, as we pass through the doorway and straighten our backs, I get the weirdest sense that I recognize the patterns carved into the wood. Should I be concerned? Maybe, but who'd be surprised if Grandma Rose somehow stole fairy art and forgot it in a cupboard?

"So, Roachster," I say. "Any chance our rooms have a printer? Phone chargers? Also, wet wipes?"

"I can arrange for towels while you make yourself comfortable."

"Great. So, is the rehearsal dinner still happening?" I ask. "Any chance we can pop in?"

"*Sabby*," whispers Mandy with unnecessary confidentiality, "our clients don't want us at the wedding banquet tonight."

I don't bother to whisper back. "Why not?"

"Well . . . it's a banquet, not a rehearsal dinner."

I push away the honeysuckle she's trying to hide behind.

"Mandy," I say, worry spiking. "How much of the proposal did our clients actually accept? What changes did they make that you haven't told me about?"

"We have clothes for you in your quarters," Rochester interrupts. "You may also bathe if you wish. Though I must inform you, you two will share facilities tonight. Guests have taken the other rooms."

I stare at him. It almost seems like he's intervening with an olive branch. Either that, or he hasn't heard a single word Mandy and I have said to each other.

All right. Here's my new plan: I'll shower tonight, then catch up on the revised wedding schedule with Mandy, niggling out any details she may need my help uncovering. Maybe we'll manage a few hours of sleep afterward.

Our room in the servants' quarters, when Rochester leads us inside, instantly reminds me of Bulan's beloved period dramas. It's fussy, ornate, and armed with enough unique patterns to keep an MLM leggings company in business forever. Is there a reason, though, why the wood-paneled room has outlets, but not a single clock on the wall? Or a flat-screen? I search in vain for a helpful poster acknowledging the Wi-Fi password.

"I will let our hosts know you have arrived. They will be pleased to greet you in their Plangent Chamber," announces Rochester. Then, stationing a fairy to wait outside our door, he exits.

"God, he's so mysterious," Mandy says, collapsing onto the closer of two canopy beds. Feathers escape and drift around her, cooing in disturbing agreement.

"Yes, Mandy. That is one way to describe a void of personality."

I cross the room to the large armoire and do my best to spit-wipe my bra line while I search for a phone charger. Discovering only a USB-A charger in the back, I give up and peruse the mostly barren hangers in search of my promised new outfit. The pair of checkered pantaloons and the zebra rug—with head included—couldn't be the clothes meant for me, could they? No. But I refuse to consider the one option that remains.

"So," I say once I'm sure I haven't overlooked anything obvious, like a secret portal to Narnia, "there's nothing black in here."

"Of course not. Fairies don't wear black to weddings," Mandy answers. She's kicking her legs into the air dramatically to play with the fairy feathers.

"Then why are you in black?" I ask. "The staff we've met so far were wearing dark colors."

"Ooh, ha ha. What a cutie!"

She's ignoring me. I guess after a month, she's out of practice following my leadership. More authoritatively, I say: "Mandy. Stop playing with those goddamn ghost geese feathers and help. There is nothing *marginally* appropriate in here for a wedding planner."

"Just put a nice dress on!" Mandy shouts, frustration brimming over. "It's not so bad if you look good for once, is it? Let yourself stand out. You might actually like it."

I gape. I actually gape. Where is this coming from?

"That's like . . . not even it."

"I'm waiting outside," says Mandy. She half crawls, half tumbles off the bed on her way out.

"Fine, thanks for doing your job of *helping me*," I shout after her.

Mandy slams the door. With a deep sense of pain and injustice, I unstick myself from Jane's black pantsuit and douse myself with the chilled water pitcher on the bedside table. Then I shimmy into the only dress in the armoire. It's horrible. Terrible. It feels like yet another accusation. A condescending statement in fabric form. *You think you're some kind of an expert wedding planner? Really?* asks the dress, all rude and swishy. *Ha ha ha ha.*

Sure, fine. You're right, dress: I swore to leave that part of my life behind, and yet, here I am. No, it doesn't really make sense. So what? I'll do what I want. And I want—for reasons I can't handle dwelling on right now—to be here. Doing *this*.

At least the dress doesn't have petticoats or a train, or a line of buttons reaching to infinity and beyond.

In fact, it fits so perfectly, I suspect Rochester snuck my measurements to a tailor. I'm not sure how he got those, actually; I should ask him what they are. You never know when that info might come in handy.

I'm staring at myself in a floor-length mirror when a knock comes at the door.

"Mandy?" I call out. "If that's you, come in. Apologize and witness my shame."

"I'm a photographer," a voice says from the other side.

Photographer?

Seeing my eyes widen in the mirror, I hurriedly mask my surprise. In my original wedding outline, I had the photographers coming on the wedding day, not the night before. I suppose our clients could've modified this with Mandy's approval. What other changes could she have made? I've got to get my hands on our clipboard outlining the details.

"Come in," I say, moving toward Mandy's luggage.

I haven't fully crossed the room before the door opens, and the wedding photographer shambles in. I stare at him and his strong, chiseled jaw. The expensive camera around his neck. His appearance of being in stork-patterned pajamas.

"You're . . . Jurgis Boggus," I say aloud. "They really hired you? Really?"

"I'm a photographer," he repeats.

"I know. You're practically the top wedding photographer in the world. You completely revolutionized night portraits."

"Night," says Jurgis. "Beautiful. Yes."

The smile on Jurgis's face remains fixed. Feeling unnerved, I wave a hand in front of his face. His smile remains white and straight-toothed, with only the slightest exposed gum. Jurgis Boggus does not apologize for the bird-themed holiday pajamas. Jurgis Boggus doesn't move, and he doesn't know what's going on. But I do, and although I knew it was coming, I'm still dimly horrified by it.

"Are you aware they enchanted you?" I ask.

"Excuse me?" Jurgis says in a thick accent. It's Lithuanian, right? I think he's Lithuanian royalty. Oh, perfect. That makes this an international incident.

"I wrote your name as a joke. Sorry," I say. "In a court of law, that's what I'll maintain."

"Excuse me?"

I pat his shoulder. "Come with me," I say. "Can you do that?"

Though Jurgis neither nods nor verbalizes any confirmation, he appears able to take direction. If anything, he seems pleased to have something to do. This is great news, overall. Jurgis can follow orders. And if the other vendors are similarly enchanted, that means I've been made the commander of a tiny zombie wedding army. Ahem. Not that I approve of brainwashing.

Reveling in my power, I find the clipboard in Mandy's bag. Then I guide Jurgis to the hallway. The green-haired fairy who Rochester stationed at the door perks up, though Mandy is nowhere in sight. That is . . . troubling. Also troubling: how he's ogling me with obscene delight.

"So *you* are Samantha Spük," he says. "Hmm, interesting."

That's it.

"Are humans fascinating in some disturbing way to you? Or do you think a wedding planner is supposed to have a big neon sign flashing over their head or something?"

"Are you ready?" the door-fairy asks, annoyingly unperturbed. "If so, I will take you and your photographer to visit our hosts."

I straighten. This is the first bit of good news I've had since arriving.

"Is that where my assistant went?" I ask, self-consciously touching my claw clip, then my dress.

"Potentially. Shall we?"

"Not yet." This servant may be low-ranked, and he may dislike me, but I've got to try and fix my wardrobe problems while I can. "You may not have noticed, but the dress I'm in . . . it's white."

"Correct," says the fairy servant.

"With a tulle skirt. And hand-beading."

"Correct."

"So, it's a wedding dress."

The door-fairy looks affronted. "Absolutely not."

I stare at him until he looks bored.

"You know," he says, "I expected a little more from you. Visually speaking."

Fine. Goddamn fine whatever. "Jurgis? Let's go."

Light sparks in Jurgis's eyes, like he's equipped with his own internal flash button. "Photos now?"

"No, no. Save your batteries, bub."

"You, bride?" he asks.

I have a feeling this will get old, fast.

The servant fairy guides us down long, winding corridors into a new section of the castle. Here, the walls morph from cozy and torchlit to ornate and magical, decorated with old tapestries lit by candle sconces. Said sconces hold floating balls of light. The honeysuckle is orange, interspersed with purpling ivy. And there's more carvings overhead than ever.

Ugh. The colors and patterns are just *not* working. Only a professional designer could pull off this techno-magic and traditional décor, and clearly, such a designer was not involved in ornamenting this castle.

"Tell me this area won't be part of the wedding," I say to the fairy.

"It won't be! We're in the Green Wing, for visiting nobility."

I mentally take note. After all, I'll need acting knowledge of the castle's layout for tomorrow.

"Ahh, there's your assistant."

Sure enough, Mandy lingers at the end of the hallway, speaking to none other than Rochester. Seeing me, she flounces over in a newly acquired balloon-bottomed dress. It is not white, which feels both like a relief and an insult.

"Mandy," I say. "What's going on? This schedule doesn't match the quote I gave the Roachster."

"Some things have changed," she chirps. "Hi, Jurgis!"

So the appearance of this royal photographer doesn't surprise her. I rub my temples, making no effort to hide my annoyance. Unexpected changes to the wedding timeline, a weird dress in my closet—it all points in a troubling direction. I already knew that fairies were unhinged. Who's to say they wouldn't throw a wrench in their own wedding, just for funsies?

And then throw the blame on us somehow?

Rochester interrupts my silent contemplation with manly throat-clearing. I'm impressed when Mandy only melts incrementally against me.

"Sorry," she says. "Do we need to keep moving?"

"Indeed. My clients await you both."

Dismissing his servant, Rochester takes over leading our odd triumvirate through the hallways. Mandy alternates between randomly complimenting all of us.

"You look nice," she says, choosing me for the moment.

"I look like a bride."

"No! She'll be prettier than you tomorrow," Mandy observes bluntly. "Wow, I would just LOVE to know who she is!"

Licking my wounds, I mutter, "I'm guessing the princess of Fairy."

"No, no." Shaking her head, Mandy says, "Their *prince* is the one marrying."

Huh. Typically, with humans, the bride's family hosts the wedding in their hometown. I should've known by this point not to make assumptions.

"So what's the deal?" I ask. "Are we working for the groom's mother, then? A fairy queen?" From Mandy's blank expression, I can tell she hasn't thought to ask these questions. She probably thought of little except accosting Rochester each time he visited the shop.

On the bright side? I can tell I'll be getting my answers soon, because the hallway is opening up and giving increasingly royal energy. Ahead, the green walls give way to a lushly garlanded balcony and reveal the top of a grand, ostentatious staircase. Of course, it's no straightforward staircase. Why would anyone want steps or railings or anything remotely functional? Instead of carpentry, the castle's fairy designers have employed a gigantic bonsai tree to act as a staircase, stretching from the lower floor to this one. Wafting up from the base of the grievous botanical addition, I hear a chorus of flutes and string instruments and laughter. Also braying.

According to the agreed-upon quote Rochester delivered some six weeks ago, the wedding is meant to take place in a castle area he'd listed as "T Room." I suspect that stands for Throne Room, not Toilet Room, as Bulan had repeatedly suggested. The area downstairs of the grand, sentient staircase—which had been dubbed "TS" for Tree Staircase—must be the State Room.

This does not explain the donkey.

"I'm getting Jane Austen meets *FernGully* vibes," I say to Jurgis, grinning. "What about you?"

"I'm a photographer," he reminds me.

Rochester, in his stiff and obtuse way, interjects, "The banquet appears to have finished. I will proceed to the Royal Wing and confirm our hosts are prepared to greet you. You will discuss the event timeline for tomorrow morning."

"Sounds good, Roachster," I say.

He stalks off down the hall, presumably taking a servants' staircase to the party. There's no way to tell: there aren't candles in that section of the hallway, making it absolutely pitch-black. A void. A *decision*, I tell you.

This leaves Mandy, Jurgis, and I with no choice but to peek over the railing and eyeball the revelers from above. Long tables familiar from our planning documents are covered in tray after tray of lavish food and floral arrangements and a disturbing amount of sparkle. The food's being cleared by green-haired servants. Past the banquet, I make out the castle entryway. It's as gloriously horrible as I'd hoped. In fact, it's worse. I never thought a tree would interrupt the royal aesthetic. But prints of modern art? In neon? Yikes. I have a feeling my past months' diverted note-taking from wedding TikTok, Instagram Reels, and blog reading will come in handy.

"Do you see the bride or groom anywhere?" Mandy asks me.

"No, I don't. How would I know who they are? If brides don't wear white, what do they wear? And what about the grooms?"

"I don't know," says Mandy, leaving me to discern that the crowd is primarily wearing embroidered tunics, complicated dresses, and fur capes. They also appear to be fanning out from the tables like they're about to mob us with a flash-dance routine.

The music stops. I guess not.

"Step back," says Mandy, grabbing me and Jurgis. She draws us back, her voice shriller. "Sabby!"

No sooner have we been tugged from the balcony than I hear a collective shout.

"WILD CHASE!"

"MANDY," I whisper-scream. I know next to nothing about fairies, but a wild *anything* can't be good. Especially when pronounced in unison. Sure enough, Mandy dives for an alcove, her ruffled skirt ballooning behind her. I follow, bringing Jurgis down with us—he cradles his camera protectively—and the three of us tumble into a heap, not a moment too soon: a slew of arrows cuts through the air, arcing over the balcony railing.

"Holy shit!" I shout, scrambling to get untangled and upright.

More arrows come. They go wide and low or whatever it is arrows do, gouging into the floorboards on our every side. Somehow I'm not struck. Just squashed. I think we're all okay. A demented cheer rings out from *the worst guests ever*, followed by barking and scuttling and shouts. I crane my neck to see past Mandy's curls. An antelope, a fox, and a hawk dash up the tree staircase. We survived the arrows, but we're about to be stampeded, like tragic westward settlers on the Oregon Trail. But no—the animals witness our pitiful state and take off down the hallway opposite us. The crowd below lets out an *awww* of extreme disappointment.

When it's clear no more arrows are coming—at least not imminently—I dislodge Jurgis's camera strap from where it's wrapped around my elbow and get to my feet.

"Whew!" Mandy pants. "That was close!"

That is an insane understatement. "Mandy," I say with difficulty, "were you aware that fairies confuse warfare and weddings?"

Mandy blinks at me, pure and innocent. "Oh, is this what human war is like?"

I've never wished so hard for Bulan to be back. But in his absence, I take a deep breath and try again. "Do you think more weapons are in our future? Yes or no."

"I don't know, maybe?"

As the music resumes, we hear a deep groaning from the staircase tree. It has begun writhing in displeasure, dislodging its branches from the walls in order to pluck out arrows. Apparently, the tree can't be satisfied with cosplaying a piece of architecture; it also has to be an Ent.

"Stop being extra," I tell it. "You don't hear the walls and floors complaining about the arrows that hit *them*."

"Mrrungghghghgh," says the staircase tree.

Jurgis, grin cemented to his face, breaks from my hold. He picks an arrow up with blithe fascination. Reaches for his camera. "War photography. Journalism."

"Yeah, this is normal," I say, as if we aren't facing our likely deaths. "Mandy, let's go. I'm not waiting here for Rochester a second longer."

She shrinks back. "But we're supposed to stay here. If I go, will I seem flaky?"

"Better flaky than dead."

Thankfully understanding the strength of this argument, Mandy tugs at Jurgis's arm to get him to retreat. "I sure hope they haven't repealed that statute against hunting pixies."

Oh, great. Now we have to worry about that too?

We haven't gotten four steps toward the safe, encircling arms of the hallway leading to the Royal Wing before the music screeches to a halt.

"WILD CHASE!" the crowd shouts again.

Aghghhhhh, this can't be necessary. "Duck!" I yell.

Mandy and I launch ourselves at the pitch-black hallway. I'm aiming for a potentially protective column, but we don't make it and crash down onto a floor rug. I cover my head. Jurgis jumps around, giggling about the beauty of the night. I hear whizzing through the air. Something strikes me, but it's Jurgis's camera as he trips on Mandy's foot. An arrow slices through the marshmallow skirt of my wedding dress, gouging into the floor mere inches from my unsuspecting ankle.

Then, thank the violent fairy gods, the onslaught ends.

This time the tree's groans are louder, more immediate. What animals are the fairies sending up now, elephants? Dromedary camels?

"Groom, groom, groom!" the crowd chants.

Mandy rolls off me and gasps.

"He's running naked!" she cries.

I uncover my head. Judge me. If I'm going to die, I deserve to see this hilarity, at least. I search the staircase tree as it convulses and reaches with long, barky limbs to unpluck arrows from itself.

"They can't seriously be making the groom dodge an attack the night before his wedding, can they?" I ask the air. Not to mention: Would they really make him do it naked?

"Well, maybe, but wait, no!" announces Mandy. "It looks like . . . oh my sugar starfish."

Oh my—?

Oh.

Oh.

I catch Mandy's eye, sharing my horror with her for a split second. Then I return my focus to the groom. The groom whose identity has been kept from me for weeks. The naked groom who stares at me, his blue eyes opened wide beneath a pair of expressive, whimsical eyebrows.

"You've got to be kidding me," I say.

"Help," Hanry says, right before the tree pushes him back down the stairs.

24

IS THIS REAL LIFE OR IS IT A (REALLY WEIRD) FANTASY?

HERE, AS FAR AS I CAN SEE IT, ARE MY PROBLEMS:

1. I am in Fairy. Which is, apparently, in Upstate New York.
2. I am in a fairy castle.
3. I am in a wedding dress, in a fairy castle, in Fairy.
4. But I am not getting married. Oh no. My ex-boyfriend is.
5. My ex-boyfriend who was nearly murdered at his own wedding party.
6. I think it was meant to be a joke?
7. I now think I'm also here, hired as his wedding planner, as a joke.
8. To add insult to injury, the wooden floor in this royal en suite seems to burp a little with each of my pacing steps. Not creak, not hiccup. Burp.
9. And it's only happening to me.

"She'll be fine," Mandy is saying on my behalf. The pixie sits primly on one of two oak chairs, across from the raised, velvet-upholstered divan beds where our royal fairy clients sprawl out with bejeweled chalices in hand. Behold: the king and queen of Fairy. The most bizarrely spiral-antlered, yet gorgeous people—or beings—I've ever seen. Also, they're Hanry's parents.

Also also? They're drunk.

Mandy says with a shaking voice, "This is what Sabby always does at the start of consultations. She, she paces in silence. It helps her summon her, umm, inspiration."

This is absolutely not the case. Do they all not hear the floor burping? Who can think through all this burping?

I've got to try and clear my head. Okay. Sure. You could argue this whole situation is my fault, because I never demanded Rochester tell me who his clients were before moving forward. I never made Hanry explain his full connection to the Community. I might have, in fact, discouraged him from talking about it, because I've avoided the paranormal myself for so long. I took the references his paranormal friends made to his "nobility" and "princeliness" as an inside joke, not at face value.

Clearly, this was my mistake. But wait, no more victim-blaming here: Hanry promised he was *human*, which means he outright lied to me. I thought I could trust him. And he did *that*?

"I see," the queen says to Mandy, sloshing her drink artfully. "Hello. Hello, Salmon-tha. It is a pleasure to finally meet you. My pooka told us so much about you. My son, too, but also my pooka."

Hold it. Her *what*?

"Oh!" cries Mandy. "Sabby, did you hear that?"

Of course I did. My weeks of torment flash back to mind. I dealt with at least a dozen tiny, chaotic sabotage attempts while I tried to coordinate my weddings, and they all came courtesy of a pooka whose sender remained mysterious.

Of course that chaos was sent by a fairy. A goddamned fairy! I can't believe I didn't guess it right away. The only question is: Why?

No. I know why. The pooka said it was messing with the weddings as tests. Which means this royal fairy Momzilla inflicted sabotage on me to confirm I could handle anything. She was willing to ruin several other weddings to feel confident I'd be a top-notch wedding planner for her son.

Either that, or she did it as a joke. Because I was dating her son.

Hanry said his parents loved jokes. He also said they were "not perfect" and situations with them tended to spiral out of control. This more than checks out.

And now I'm realizing: when we broke up in the catering closet, Hanry told me he'd been fighting with his parents. Moreover? Hanry just asked for my help, giving me the impression he's not entirely on board with this situation.

So what if Hanry made a few omissions while we dated? Evidently, it wasn't *all* lies.

Hopefully.

In any case, I'm here. I may not be at the wedding I was expecting, but it's time to take back control. Why? Because I may be Hanry's ex-girlfriend and the butt of at least three jokes I can count, but I'm also a goddamned wedding professional.

And now, it's my job to prove it.

Feeling the blood flowing back into my extremities, I return to my chair. Yes, I do so in a frothy cloud of tulle and a burping Hallelujah chorus, but I'm able to paste on my thousand-watt wedding planner smile and curtsy before I take my seat.

"It's a pleasure to meet you too," I say, imbuing my voice with dripping-honey warmth. "Queen . . . ?"

"Mab," she drawls into her wine.

"Tits," says Hanry's dad. He's not fully straight-faced, the bastard. I bet that's a fake name.

"Pleasure to meet you, Your Highnesses, Queen Mab, King Tits."

"I'm a photographer," says Jurgis from where he's been made to sit cross-legged in the corner of the room. Gustavo, the Academy Award–winning Spanish director whom Rochester has brought to join us, adds with a similarly enchanted air, "I am a videographer."

"Have you enjoyed our hospitality so far?" Mab asks me and Mandy, as if we weren't pelted with arrows five minutes ago. Oh, look at that: King Tits is giggling behind his hand.

Fuck it. I'm not giving Hanry's parents an ounce more of my respect than I've already given.

The sarcasm-off is officially on.

"It's been great," I say. Plucking at my skirt, I add, "Thanks for getting my measurements right. To be fair, the length was slightly off, but your tailor noticed right away."

Mab frowns. "He did?"

"Mmm, yeah. One of his arrows sliced off a bit of hem. It now fits perfectly."

Mandy, not following, interrupts. "Why *is* she wearing a wedding dress?"

The king has been waiting for this.

"Because it's funny," he chortles. "Isn't it funny?"

"It's very funny," agrees Mab.

A dark cloud gloms onto me, but I bat it aside. "We have a lot to discuss for tomorrow," I say. "Mandy let me know you ran out of time to complete our surveys. Could you quickly tell us about the bride? Is she here at the castle and able to join us, by any chance?"

"She doesn't need to join!" Tits says. But I disagree: I need to know my enemy. The woman who would dare marry Hanry right beneath my slightly bumpy nose.

"If we could be introduced, it'll help me get a sense of how to instruct our photographer and videographer—"

"Princess May is our guest. She has traveled from Japan and has made her needs clear to us. We will handle everything on her behalf," says Mab, so firmly I know it won't be useful to push further. I let it go. In spite of my dread, I ask: "How about the groom?"

Tits replies with eager, sparklingly evil eyes. "Our son, Hanry—"

"Whom you've met," says Mab.

"—is the groom."

"Whom you've met," says Mab again, louder this time. "I believe you've gotten very close. I'm sure you'll know just how to make the day perfect for him."

I refuse to blanch and play into their hands.

"Of course, Your Fairy Majesties," I say sweetly. "Though I have to say the wedding details are . . . surprising, considering what I know about him."

"We had to make the day more befitting of a prince," says Mab. "He's too simple sometimes. Too rugged, too rough-edged."

"Too manly," agrees Tits.

Huh. They're just listing synonyms for "sexy." This is weird.

"Uh-huh," I say.

"He takes after his natural parents," says Tits. "They're from New Hampshire."

I nod, fighting hard to keep my expression neutral. So Hanry was honest about being human—that's a relief. Since he was adopted, that makes him a—what's the term? Changeling? No wonder the apple fell far from the tree. I consult my imaginary notes. "Is his bride human too?"

"Goodness, no!" Mab says. "She has lovely straight black hair. Unlike yours."

That was uncalled for. I mutter, "I dye it, anyway. I'm a natural blond." Seeing as this doesn't win me any points, I move on. "Would there be time tonight I can speak to him?"

"He's all tied up," says Tits. "No visitors allowed!"

All *tied up*? "I understand that, but we have a list of questions—"

"I have them here!" Mandy pulls the relationship survey from our planning folder. "Here's number one! 'How would you describe the groom and bride's relationship, and how do you know they're in love?'"

I glare at my employee, who doesn't have a single situationally aware bone in her pixie body. Unaware of the pain this conversation is causing me, or possibly just cruel, Mab waves her chalice-free hand in the air like a confused bird.

"Oh, you know how it is. Their relationship's tumultuous! But Hanry has to marry *someone*."

"And Princess May only likes humans," Tits adds. "It was the easiest match!"

Something goes *thunk* inside my chest. At the same time, another feeling uncrinkles, like a ball of foil being opened back up. This wasn't—isn't—a love match. Hanry hasn't fallen hard for May, the Japanese fairy princess. His parents arranged the marriage. This isn't his choice. She isn't who he wants.

Maybe—underneath all of it, I feel a whisper of hope—he still wants *me*.

Mab continues, "It's true; she does have a penchant for the antlerless. I see her wisdom, of course. Humans grow much better beards. Don't you think, Sam-a-bantha?"

"Hanry has a great shot at a beard," I hear myself answer. "He should go for it."

"*Prince* Hanry," Mandy corrects me quietly. "You have to call him His Highness."

Thankfully, Mab doesn't notice my error. And Tits is busily rubbing his chin and looking at the floor as if embarrassed by his follicular scarcity.

This whole thing is almost impossible to wrap my head around. I'm overwhelmed with questions. Like, how long has Hanry been set up to marry this fairy princess? Was he cheating on her? On me? And how does he feel about it, really? He sure didn't look happy running up the stairwell butt naked. Call me a bad person, but the idea that he might be fighting for his life makes me feel *slightly* better about him keeping his engagement under wraps.

As much as it sucks, all these questions and hurt feelings have got to temporarily take a back seat. I've got a job to do. Turning on my internal autopilot, I demand Rochester find the clipboard I'm just realizing I must have dropped in the hall. Then I turn our conversation to a discussion of logistics. I confirm the vendors' names, the new timelines Mandy came up with, the locations where prep will be taking place, and the support staff the castle will provide. I even jot down the castle's Wi-Fi password. Beneath it all, I can only think one thing:

That I've got to save Hanry. After I kill him.

I've got until morning to figure this out.

Considering that it's Hanry's wedding, it's beyond frustrating that I have no idea where he is or what he's doing. But for the moment, I need to center my concerns somewhere else.

Having introduced us to our clients, Rochester's next task is to lead Mandy, Jurgis, Gustavo, and me back to the servants' quarters. He shuttles us down a tight, winding staircase into a natural cavern with soaring ceilings, stalagmite-covered floors, and three dozen fairy servants dressed in velvet overalls. Only after eyeing a window at the end of the room do I realize this is a warehouse, not a cave. And those aren't stalagmites. They're Chiavari chairs thrown atop carpets of moss, surrounded by buckets of white anemones, boxes of candlesticks, and folded linens. I get it now: this must be the basement where wedding décor goes to die.

"What do I do with all this junk?" I ask Rochester.

"Is that not your job?" He smirks. "The servants have been commanded by Mab to work to your instruction."

"Really?" I ask, mollified somewhat. "I've got the power?"

"Yes. You've got the power."

"You look giddy," says Mandy.

"Of course I am! I have both a zombie and an Oompa-Loompa army, Mandy. This is my childhood dream." Before I swore off the paranormal world, I had a minor obsession with Roald Dahl books. So what? It doesn't *mean* anything, except that I'm power-hungry. Clapping my hands together, I draw the attention of my fairy hordes. "Listen up, team! I'm in charge now, while Rochester escorts Mandy to Princess May's room. They're going to discuss the princess's last-minute requests."

Though he seems suspicious, Rochester doesn't argue. I wave Mandy goodbye—she gives me a big wink that would blow our cover if she weren't so *Mandy*. Once she's gone, I set the Fairy-Loompas to reorganizing the room and determining what décor can be salvaged. I single one out, instructing: "Bring me your three most responsible fairies. Each of them will need to lead a team of . . . uh, six, to transfer our décor into the Throne Room for staging. And get my door-fairy to bring me the fishing tackle box in Mandy's luggage, would you?"

"Fine. Can I go back to bed after that?"

What a work ethic. "Absolutely," I say.

When my door-fairy does—grumpily—arrive with the emergency kit, I delve into the fishing tackle box and uncover a pack of saltines and a handful of glow sticks. I stuff the saltines into my mouth, then turn to my team, ready to investigate their progress.

Or at least that's what I intend, but instead come face-to-face with Jurgis's and Gustavo's empty, far-too-proximal grins. Making a guess, I say, "You want more information about the wedding site, don't you? To know how to position your shots? Get the best angles on your video?" I read into their empty smiles a befuddled acknowledgment. "Perfect. Follow me to adventure."

"Adventure?" asks Jurgis. "I thought this was a wedding."

"An adventure wedding?" cries Gustavo. "Will there be rock climbing?"

I roll my eyes and get to work, hoping I can keep my sanity until tomorrow.

Gustavo and Jurgis's desire to plan out their shots couldn't give me a better excuse for breaking away to search the castle. Bowing out from the wedding preparations, I retrace Rochester's steps and return us to what seems to be the castle's primary residential floor—mindful of potential hazards like hoofing antelopes and wedding guests in search of seconds.

"Dark?" asks Gustavo as we approach the Royal Wing.

"Bad lighting," I agree. "No good for video."

"Bad traps," says Gustavo. His tone of voice indicates more hopefulness than concern—which is a bit odd, until I remember how fond he is of putting booby traps in his movies.

"All right," I accede. "You two should stay back. I'll go down the hall alone. Get help if I don't return, all right?"

"Wish," says Jurgis. "See in dark. Whooo."

"What?" I ask, confused, but Gustavo laughs.

"Wish much," he seems to agree. "Monsters! Monsters, dark!"

The last thing I see before surrendering to darkness is Gustavo with his arms flapping as if in an attempt to fly. Jurgis gives a solemn nod beside him.

Remind me to never get enchanted by fairies.

Feeling my way along the wall, I walk about two minutes before I reach my first door. I run the back of my hand over the wood carvings, wondering where it leads. As far as I can tell, there's no door-fairy nearby, encumbering my entrance. Or booby traps. My biggest concern so far is that I might tug open the wrong door and run into Hanry's brother or his awful, bullying cousins—who will almost certainly not help. And will tell on me. Immediately.

Luck is on my side, though. Because the door unlatches at my touch, opening straight into a candlelit suite.

Right away, I can tell I'm in Hanry's quarters. It's subject to a familiar chaos of odds and ends and keepsakes. Like a bear pelt on the floor. A gallery of plant rubbings tacked to a far wall. A wreath hung over the bed. The bed itself has a bonus, two-foot extension to accommodate a sleeper with added height.

The chief problem is that Hanry isn't in this room, and it seems like he hasn't used it for a long time, either.

I swish inside, hoping I'm wrong. Artifacts of Hanry abound: I find a small collection of books, a childhood slingshot straight out of Mark Twain. A framed photograph—the first one I've seen in this whole castle—of a young Hanry and a lanky kid with a well-practiced scowl and mysterious, hooded eyes. Between the two of them towers the alleged King Tits, wearing a plaid flannel shacket over a Patriots jersey. And a muffler wrapped, turbanlike, around his antlers.

Could the kid be Seb, Hanry's brother? Maybe. But the photo's useless to me—it doesn't hint to where Hanry might be. Why he isn't in his own room.

"Come on," I say, frustration welling up. I ball my hands into fists in my tulle skirt. "Come on, something's got to—"

"I believe Their Royal Highnesses indicated Hanry was not to be interrupted this evening," says a deep voice behind me.

I pivot on my foot, only to face the imposing, shadow-born sight of Rochester. I've been caught, Hanry-room-handed.

Shit.

Rochester seems fed up as he deposits me, Gustavo, Jurgis, and Mandy in the servants' quarters. It so happens that the Royal Wing's rooms are equipped with silent spell-alarms to detect intruders. A further line of questioning reveals that these are actually just nanny cams. Either way, it puts the kibosh on any more Hanry-searching activities.

By this point, it's well past midnight. I've had a full workday, gotten drunk, traveled to Fairyland, been shot at by fay, discovered my ex is getting married, snuck into random rooms of a castle, and taken pains to get a wedding I really don't want to happen underway. I'm exhausted—and if Hanry's fairy godmother is trying to hide his fatigue, he's failing at it too. A single forehead-hair has fallen out of place.

"Well, Roachster, I hope you're planning to get some sleep. That hair of yours isn't doing so hot. You seem ravished," I say, elbowing his side.

"I wish," Mandy mumbles to a wall. Her longing for Rochester is entangled with some kind of desire to escape him—an interesting development I'm not too tired to notice. Hmm. She and Rochester were together kind of a while, weren't they, when he escorted her to visit Princess May? And they must've communicated often over the past month while I was in New York.

I wonder if Mandy tried something. Did it end badly? Poor thing.

"I will return to accompany you personally tomorrow," Rochester says, characteristically staring at me a little too hard.

I wait, ready to be subjected to more insinuations that I'm an untrustworthy deviant—but no. Rochester steps robotically over the sprawled-out, snoring door-fairy and leaves. Only after Hanry's fairy godmother rounds the corner do I crack the door open.

"Don't freak out," I tell Mandy.

She pales. "Why?"

"Because I went to Hanry's rooms. He wasn't there. Also, because of this."

Inside our guest suite awaits an entire flock of crows. Plus one vampire bat, emerging from a gloomy corner of the room. And—this part actually makes me smile—on top of an old-timey bag of leather luggage bounces a buoyant, red-haired, bearded head.

Bulan. Dark Dave. And the crows, even. I can't believe they all came, like I'd asked.

"Bulan!" Mandy exclaims. She sprints past me and hugs him, grip fierce and frightening. While they're busy, I usher Jurgis and Gustavo in behind me and pass the two of them a fairy tarot card deck I pocketed from the warehouse cavern. I don't know if the unenchanted versions of the men are woo-woo enough for tarot, but card games reliably keep empty minds occupied.

"Hello, Mandy!" Bulan grins into the pixie's chest. "I have missed your bodily assault! And Sabby. Nice to see you too."

I fold my arms. Sure, I'm ecstatic to see him, but Bulan left on terms that do *not* merit hugs.

"Oh, I'm just 'nice,' am I?"

"It's a euphemism!" he says warmly.

Mandy releases him. Still exuberant, she cries, "I found your body!"

What?

"What?" asks Bulan. The color drains from his face. "Oh no. Oh dear. That's terrible news."

"Whoa," I say. Fighting overwhelm, I pick my way across Bulan's murder of ruffled birds. "Bulan, what's this? You have a body?"

"Naturally! However, I fear that someone else has been carrying it with them for a substantial length of time," says Bulan. "Mandy, is she in the castle?"

"She is!" says Mandy, startling two crows near her feet.

I cannot think with all this flapping. Frustrated, I cry out, "Where is *who*?"

"Princess May," says Mandy, not understanding as usual.

With effort, Bulan lifts his eyes to the ceiling above my regal four-poster bed and answers.

"My ex."

25

I AM NOT A MEMBER OF THE BROKEN HEARTS CLUB. WHO'S GOT TIME FOR THAT?

"EXPLAIN," I DEMAND OF BULAN, WHO HAS TAKEN ON A SELF-pitying expression. Several crows caw with unnecessary sympathy, but I don't have sympathy. I have an ex, and he didn't tell me he was engaged, and do you see me pitying myself? Feeling upset and poorly used by someone I'd thought was a safe space for one of the first and only times in my life? No way.

"How is this possible?" I ask Bulan.

Preening, Bulan draws himself up an extra half inch.

"I once had a body," he says. "When I was a young kingling, a willow sapling of a child. One day, I was out in a field near Llandovery picking daffodils—"

"How lovely," says Mandy.

"Llandovery."

"Isn't that a place in Wales? Princess May is Japanese, so how could she have—" I shake my head. "No, no. Nix the story time, Bulan. We can talk about this later. First things first: we've got to save Hanry."

"Oh, your lover boy." Bulan's brows knit as I pick him up and resettle him atop my hand-embroidered silk duvet. "That's fine, Sabby. I don't need a body, anyway. It's highly overrated. What's Hanry doing here?"

"To put it simply, he was adopted by fairy royalty. Making him a fairy prince."

"Obviously. But what's he doing home?"

I stare at Bulan; he stares back. This is so goddamn unbelievable; I throw up my hands. "Did everyone know he was a fairy prince except me?"

"He was pretty open about it," says Mandy.

Bulan nods himself at her. "Yes, yes. His wood carvings were of well-known fairy tales. Sabby, did you truly not notice the whole Community referring to him as a prince? At any point?"

I choose to ignore their insults. "Bulan, if you knew that Hanry was goddamn royalty, why did you say he shouldn't be in the castle? Isn't this his home?"

"Changelings who come of age always spend a year in the human world. To test it out, in case they like it more than their home. Hanry seemed satisfied in Salem. I thought he might not return."

I tap my foot thoughtfully. "So why'd he end his fay Rumspringa?"

"Maybe he *was* satisfied in the human world until you left?" Mandy suggests. A few crows caw in either agreement, hunger, or a longing for plastic baubles.

"Unlikely," I say. "Hanry wouldn't even sleep with me."

Bulan coughs into his beard. "No wonder you've been so prickly."

"Stuff it, Bulan. This isn't about me. This is about Hanry. And our rescue mission."

"How are we supposed to rescue him from his own wedding?" asks Mandy.

I take a deep breath. Here goes nothing. "By taking a page out of his adopted mother's playbook," I say. "And the pooka's. We're going to sabotage it."

Bulan's gasp comes out like a croak. Mandy throws her head back with a wail.

"No, no! Sabby, all this work for nothing!?"

"Yeah, I know it's a shame, but—"

"Think what it will do to your reputation," Bulan adds. "A wedding planner who becomes a wedding disaster planner. It would be a travesty!"

I huff. Am I the only one here who finds it problematic to force people into matrimony? Apparently so. Am I alone in being pummeled, against my will, with worries about Hanry? I've got to figure out where he is. We've got to help him. And he better be conscious when we find him, because there's no way I'll be able to drag his six-five, two-hundred-whatever-pound body out of this castle on my own.

The lone bat of our gathered crew of would-be heisters picks itself off the floor, and taking wing, flaps around my head aggressively.

"Stop that," I say, batting the flying mammal away. "Transform already if you want to speak."

The bat lands, and with a *pop*, Dark Dave sprawls into existence, his hands covering his eyes.

"I hate transforming after a feeding," he moans. "Also, the candles! There are too many candles in here!"

Mandy, sniffling, assists me in helping him off the floor. "There, there," she says. "We can blow some out."

"No blowing out the candles. And sorry, Dave," I say, "But humans don't understand echolocation. I need you in not-bat form if I'm going to hear your point of view."

He moans feebly.

"Also, thanks for pausing your honeymoon to help out."

"It was the least I could do after forgetting your payment," he says. "Amanda will arrive after her blood spa, by the way. Shouldn't be long now."

"Great. You know you still owe me money, right?"

"Ah," says Dave, taking excessive interest in the carpet. Like so many things, I'll have to let that rest for now. Returning the room's attention to the matter at hand, I pull my computer from my duffel bag and set Mandy's folder on the floor.

Painstakingly, I transfer information onto a stack of sticky notes. Over the course of fifteen minutes, during which Gustavo and Jurgis shower the room with tarot cards and prod Dave, I lay out the wedding schedule—and our plan.

"Gather, minions!" I point to six sticky notes at the top of the diagram, labeled *VENDORS*. "Here are our forces. Based off what I've seen, all our vendors will arrive enchanted and lacking on the problem-solving front. Now, in addition to our vendors, we have a small army of overalls-clad fairy servants ready at our command." I place another sticky note down. It reads *MINIONS*. "The castle's minions are in charge of catering, serving whatever fairies drink for alcohol, handling the wedding cake and dessert table, and assisting in guest transportation."

"I look forward to seeing who arrives in a zucchini," Mandy says.

"If we run out of time and you miss it, I'm sorry. When all of this is over, I promise to introduce you to the Oscar Mayer Wienermobile."

"Wow," she says, confused but impressed.

"The minions and the vendors will be responsible for performing our sabotage," I say. "I'm going to give them ruinous plans. Now, look here." I gesture at the purple square at the heart of my floor diagram. It reads *HANRY*. "The rest of us—Dave, Bulan, Mandy, and I—are on groom-finding duty."

I bring the group's attention to a purple square labeled *CROWS*.

"If a crow gets your attention, follow them. Since some of you don't have cell phones, they'll be in charge of sharing information between us. Think of them as flying walkie-talkies."

"Caw," say the crows in either affirmation or mutiny. Hopefully not the latter.

"And lastly, glow sticks. Everyone will snap these onto their wrists in the morning. They're visual reminders to stay on schedule. Each stick has a four-hour light-life. This way, we'll know when it's eight, noon, and four."

"Aha. Because the wedding's at four," says Mandy.

"Exactly. Plus, if we need to enter the Royal Wing, they'll be invaluable light sources . . . and if Mab and Tits try to trick us by playing games with time, they'll help us keep our footing. Any more questions?" I rub my hands together. "No? Okay, on to the most important plan yet: our secret escape plan."

The word "secret" results in a chorus of impressed *oohs*.

"Very good! Most murderers get caught because they fail to stick the landing," says Bulan knowingly. He rolls across the *HANRY* sticky note and spends the next few minutes listening thoughtfully with the square attached to his forehead.

"What happens," he asks when I'm done, "if all else fails and we can't wrench Hanry away until the wedding itself?"

"We won't let it come to that," I say. "I trust you guys."

Mandy raises the water pitcher high. "Hear, hear. To us, and to the worst wedding ever!"

We all cheer, "Hear, hear!" and pass the pitcher around like we're preparing for some sort of baptism. As long as it's a trial by water and not fire, that's fine by me. I'd like for Hanry to make it out of this with as few burn scars as possible.

Mandy wakes me with a half-eaten piece of caramel sticking to the edge of her eager crescent smile. "The hairstylist and makeup artist are here!" she cries past her candy.

"For us?" I ask, hope swelling. Only then, reality breaks through, shattering my momentarily positive vibe. Here is the truth about my life: I've never had a hairstylist, ever. I am not in my Midtown apartment, or in Salem. Nope. I am in a fairy castle. And of all days and all mornings, it's the morning of the no-longer-supersecret Rochester wedding.

The wedding where Hanry is getting married. To someone else. Against his will. Unless I save him.

Now that I'm awake, Mandy casts me aside like an empty bag of chips. She skips over the bed, crossing the room with more zip than you'd get on a pogo stick. The scent of high-end patchouli replaces the scent of burnt sugar.

I'm glad to see that she's bounced back after being so beaten down last night. Between her Rochester-induced woes and my callous plans to bulldoze the wedding that was her pet project for a month, I actually expected a bit more rage.

It would be more than justified.

Maybe she's just rechanneled it into hyperactivity. She opens the door to our room so emphatically, she bangs it against the hallway's stony wall and only barely misses a trio of waiting figures.

"You have guests," says our door-fairy, introducing two disheveled, vinyl-bag-laden humans.

"HELLO!" shouts Mandy. The people shuffle into the room and drop their bags conveniently atop our sticky-note diagram. The blond guy wears a crop-top tank, athletic shorts with thermal leggings, and ribbed crew socks. The woman is in pj's. An intricate weave peeks from beneath a silk scarf. Unlike Gustavo and Jurgis, these two—Matthew and Shaki, respectively—are famous, in a not-dangerously-high-profile kind of way. Celebrity stylists and MUAs rarely get accosted in the street. But they're obviously professionals: in spite of being enchanted and whisked here from the midst of their morning routines, they both seem to have dutifully grabbed their equipment while being fairynapped.

"I said *he-llo*! Now you're supposed to say it back," Mandy tries again.

Enjoying her determination, I light my bedside candle with a butane candle lighter.

"I'm a photographer," says Jurgis, predictably. Then, pointing at Gustavo: "He is a *videographer*."

As the room lights up, Dark Dave screeches in obvious pain.

I grin at my friends and vendors. With a spike of disturbing optimism, I slither-tumble off my high bed and shut the door.

"What time is it, Mandy?"

"About seven," she chirps back.

"All right. Let's get going, people and pixies and heads. Mandy, destroy the evidence of our nefarious plans. Everyone else, grab your glow sticks. Are we ready to find Hanry and kick off our heist party?"

Jurgis and Gustavo, overnight BFFs, obediently click on their glowing bracelets while eyeing the newest vendors with mild suspicion. Jurgis lifts his camera. "Photography?"

"Not yet. For now, go where Bulan's crows tell you. Follow their instructions. They are your gods now."

"Caw," says a bird atop the desk.

Mandy laces her fingers together and grimaces. "Sabby, don't you need to get ready?"

That pours a bucket of water over my positivity.

How can I focus on my own appearance while Hanry could be suffering in a dark, dank, and mushroom-ridden dungeon? What if he's so hungry that's all he has to eat? Wall fungus?

"Mandy," I say tightly. "No."

"But, um . . . I was thinking you'd maybe want to change?"

I grab the hem of my wedding dress and shake it. "What do you think will happen if I take this off?"

"Our hosts will probably get angry."

"Naked. Bad," says Matthew the stylist. A desperate sweat has broken out over his forehead, belying his placid expression. Poor guy. If the enchantment can't fully override his sense of aesthetics, this castle must be doing numbers on him.

"Don't worry," I promise everyone. "Hanry has been naked enough for all of us. This dress is staying on. But Matthew, if you have any ideas, I'm all ears. Also, what are the odds you've got a portable phone charger?"

At 7:15 precisely, Mandy and I parade our MUA and stylist to Princess May's bridal suite in the aptly named Green Wing.

"It's Spüktacular Weddings," I announce with false cheer. You would never know I'd managed a mere two hours of sleep. That half the night I stayed up worrying about Hanry. Or that I'm preparing to cause more mayhem than is normative among the *least* normative members of the Community.

As an honored guest of Fairyland, New York, Princess May was placed in a suite that exceeds ours in lavishness. The seating area brims with activity: there's a harpist, a flutist, and a would-be sumo wrestler in a tutu performing interpretive dance. I'm not sure who these people are. Is it an entourage? Are they bridesmaids? Then I notice an awkwardly dressed male mannequin chilling in a recliner, a rug tossed over its head. And then I decide it's not my business.

"Announcing Samantha and Mandy," May's door-fairy says, pitchy-squeaky like a train on poorly maintained tracks. "Matthew and Shaki."

"I told you. Stop. Talking," says a low woman's voice. "You grate on my ears."

I seek out and find the imperious voice's source: a petite Asian girl with a chin-length bob, wildly untamed eyebrows, and a chic, modern gold crown held in place by bonsai antlers. The girl—princess, I should say—looks like she's barely eighteen. Her skin is crazy-perfect; not a trace of acne. Has it been magically removed? All I know for sure is that this is 100 percent Hanry's future wife—based off her antlers, *crown*, and the bored expression, which fails to conceal the personality of a block of cheese.

Also, I hate her. I hate how pretty she is, in spite of her rude expression.

"Did you bring your team to get me ready?" Princess May smirks. "By the way, nice dress."

I stick out my hand. "Samantha Spük. Nice to meet you, Princess May."

My rival flutters her eyelashes but stays regally still.

"My name is not May."

My smile doesn't break. It's Rule #1 of the wedding industry, right? Roll with everything. Even when you are facing up against someone who thinks they're better than you, and they might be right. I mean, seriously, what does an accountant-pretending-to-be-a-wedding-planner have on a fairy princess?

"Okay," I say. "What should I call you, then?"

"May is short for *hime-sama*. Of course, that isn't my name either. In the same way Sabby isn't your name. Except your name doesn't signify royalty, of course."

Got it. This princess is no block of anything. She's the kind of person who plays at cute while busily unsheathing mascara from the tube in order to stab you with it. This makes her somewhat more interesting, but *so* not Hanry's type. He'd be more likely to end up with that sumo-dancer. At least they seem straightforward.

"My name signifies witches," I say nonchalantly, not asking what her real name is. "And bad decisions."

May raises an eyebrow. "Whose?"

"Great question. How about we discuss it while you get ready for your big day? Mandy here—who you met last night—will help Matthew and Shaki with their work."

"Do I really need them?" May asks, waving dismissively at two of the best visual artists in the world. "I can cast my own glamour."

"Mm-hmm! So, I'll be back in about five hours with your lunch."

"Five hours? Why so long?"

I could swear Shaki flinches at the princess's imperious and annoyed tone, but Matthew merely smiles at his hair dryer. I unhand it from him and pat him on the shoulder. He deserves encouragement. After all, he helped get some charge back into my phone and did a bang-up job removing a foot of fabric from the hem of my wedding dress, making it easier for me to walk. Or run. Hopefully, when we escape from the castle, there will be a minimum of cardiac exertion.

An added bonus: it looks significantly less bridal now. I almost like it.

"This is a human wedding," I explain to the princess. "Traditionally, human brides take hours to get ready. But we'll go as fast as we can. Shaki, Matthew, find the power outlets and get on with it. Chop-chop!"

"I'll do the chopping," May tells Shaki as I leave.

Mandy stares after me with a kenneled-puppy expression. "Goodbye, Sabby," she whisper-cries.

That poor pixie. I know she's distraught at being forced to spend the morning in the bridal suite—the last place a male fairy named Rochester would be caught visiting. But I need Mandy here, using her oodles of charm to discover May's motive for marrying Hanry. To ferret out any doubts. Then she can launch a devious attack, asking coy and innocent-seeming questions, spurning May to question her decision-making. Maybe we can convince the princess to call the wedding off.

Granted, the odds of that happening are astronomically low. But is it wrong that I'd prefer to rescue Hanry in a way that doesn't beget a lifetime of fairy wrath?

After all, May's isn't the only anger I have to worry about.

When I arrive at the State Room, I am witness, first and foremost, to Mab, the queen of Fairyland. A twenty-foot length of eucalyptus garland drapes her arms and shoulders. It looks like she's carrying the love child she created with the tree staircase. Is she still drunk? Is this just the way she is?

No. They are my decorations for the State Room. How dare she!

"Good morning!" she calls out, fluttering the garland. "It's very green."

"Sure is," I say. I smile at her as I walk to the head table, where a crow has perched, clamping a tuft of red hair in its beak: either a signal from Bulan or the result of an accident. Possibly both.

"Does Bulan want to see me?" I ask the bird. "If so, can it wait?"

"It's greener than I wa-a-ant!" drawls Mab.

The crow spits out Bulan's hair and jumps, painfully, from the table to my shoulder. I face the queen and say with hopefully veiled confusion, "I see."

"Do you!?"

"Your Highness, the proposal suggested a largely green palette. Could you tell me what isn't working for you?"

"We need more purple." Mab drops the garland off one of her shoulders like she's Marilyn Monroe. I half expect her to call me "darling" or something, but instead, she says, "Salmon-ella-bee, I just feel purple would be nice. PURPLE, DO YOU HEAR ME?!"

"I'll take care of it," I say, in hopes I sound appeasing.

"Lovely, dear, thank you!"

Mab flits off, anger abruptly vanquished. The garland trails after her like a loyal hedgehog. Emphasis on the hedge.

"Do you want me to help you take that off?" I call out as she strides away.

She doesn't seem to hear.

Cool. Cool cool cool.

I survey the State Room, now cleared of distraction. I know that in the scheme of things, it doesn't matter if table 6 lacks decorations, since we're planning to kidnap Hanry before he takes his vows. And Mab's pleasure in adorning the room in purple flowers is unlikely to outweigh her anger at my criminal mischief.

Especially when all my ruinous, wedding-sabotaging machinations begin at 1 p.m., sharp. Beginning with the release of an impala. It's going to be a double black diamond downhill slide.

But when an overalls-clad fairy servant minion crosses my path, I grab him by his shoulder straps and ask, in spite of everything: "You! Any chance there's a flower market around here?"

The fairy casts me a Rochester-y non-look. "The closest market is in Albany."

"Is it a flower market or a supermarket?"

He offers a shrug in reply. Fine: it's up to me, then. I whip out my phone and text my Salem wholesaler to see if he knows someone local who can do a last-minute favor. Sure, it'll be great if I can appease Mab by getting her flowers. More importantly, though: when the carriage returns from its errand in Albany, it'll be empty and ready for us to use in our escape. That's why I'm doing this. Obviously.

Bulan's crow tugs unhelpfully at my earlobe. "Crraww?"

"Stop. I've got to finish this text," I hiss, protecting my unfairly abused head.

"Craww crawww," the bird-demon says.

"Fine! I'll go where you want. Minion, give me your phone number."

The fairy's mask of indifference falters, but he obeys. I send him a text so we have each other's contact information, then say, "Get a carriage ready and have your best-dressed, most aesthetically sensible fairy go to Albany and pick up our order at the address I'll send you. Tell your other minions to fill the vases a third of the way up with cold water and set up the garlands and candles following my outline. Leave a finger's width of space in the vases for additional stems. Got it? Keep those arrangements *loose*."

"I will allow them to run as they please," the fairy says hesitantly.

"No, there should be no running. Do I have to do everythin—WAGH!" The crow is ripping out my hair. From the goddamned root! "Fine! We'll go now, you fiend!"

A few chunks of hair poorer, I stalk out of the State Room. This better be quick. I have a feeling Mab isn't done with pitching last-minute ideas, and next time she might move forward without discussing them with me first. I've got to find a way to keep her busy. The last thing I need is for Momzilla cottoning on that I'm ruining her son's wedding.

Besides, I've just been violently depilated by a bird. There's only so much a girl can take.

26

BUT THEN AGAIN, CROWS ARE THE LEAST OF MY PROBLEMS

SATISFIED WITH ITS FEAST OF KERATIN AND STYLING PRODUCT, the crow settles into its new home above my shoulder blades, alternating nipping me right and left. It directs me up the grand tree trunk staircase and through winding hallways lit with glowing orbs until at last we arrive in an art gallery. Maybe the word "art" is too generous. The room contains row after useless row of sculpted heads and busts, all chiseled with kooky expressions and ill-advised facial features.

"Bulan!?" I call out. "Stop playing hide-and-seek."

One of the heads turns on his marble stool, grinning. Then guffawing.

"For once," I say, "you seem like the most normal part of the room. Why are you laughing?"

"What happened to your hair?" asks Bulan. "Are those bangs?"

"How many times have I had to tell you? Your gangster bird-friends aren't to be trusted." With an offended caw, the crow takes off from my shoulder. I take the opportunity to rearrange what's left of my front locks. "Have you found out where they're keeping Hanry?"

"Not yet!"

I glare. "Then why am I here?"

"Dave discovered oubliettes in the floor of the castle's super-dark Royal Wing."

"Ooblee-etts?" I repeat. "Is that a type of fancy tile?"

"I'm afraid they're holes, Sabby. Final resting places for prisoners." Bulan shudders, destabilizing his marble pedestal. I catch it, and him, in the nick of time. "The present king and queen must have determined that dirt cannot be relied upon for burials. I suspect they may also function as holding cells."

Damn. So, Gustavo turns out to have been right about the booby traps.

"I see. We'll need to investigate. You, infernal crow—"

"His name is Stefan," says Bulan.

"—can you inform Mandy about this? Pass it on to Dave too. Subtly, if you're capable."

Stefan the crow checks with Bulan before winging off to this vital task. As for me, I scoop Bulan up and carry him through the servants' quarters to the castle's rear. I'll return to the State Room in a jiff, but first, I need to be seen as doing my duty coordinating guest arrivals.

Besides, this offers the perfect opportunity to perform escape-plan reconnaissance.

Hanry will be happy to see me. No, euphoric. I can see it in my mind's eye: I'll release him from his jail and wipe away the dried blood on his tortured wrists. "We've got to go now," I'll say, but he'll stop me, wide-eyed and lovestruck, to mash his lips against mine in a fervent, dizzying kiss.

"Sabby," he'll say. "You look like a goddess. Such wild, tousled hair. I love the crow feathers. The new bangs."

"You are correct," I'll reply. "Worship me."

And Hanry will fall to his knees, pressing his forehead into my stomach, clutching me and trembling in awe. Or maybe not. Maybe he'll just throw his head back and laugh, relieved he only has to put up with my sense of humor instead of a lifetime supply of an arrogant fairy princess's whims. He'll rip a wooden beam from the wall and use it as a battering ram against the fairy minions blocking our path to the carriage. Nothing will stand in the way of our happiness.

Yep. That's how it'll go.

Something like that, anyway.

Bulan and I return to the State Room just shy of 10 a.m.—in other words, six mere hours before the start of Hanry and May's wedding ceremony. I'm doing my best to crumble said ceremony into bits, like a pastry in a plastic bag.

I try to push away the thought that what I'm doing is a shame; a waste of a perfectly good cookie. But obviously, Hanry must be saved.

The carriage returns from Albany with suspicious and likely magical speed, bearing a bounty of ranunculus, violet sweet peas, blue freesia, and anemones. As nerves prickle the back of my head, I watch the Fairy-Loompas integrate newly picked flowers into the candle-and-moss arrangements. Mab may be a Momzilla, but the inclusion of warm purple hues, particularly magenta, was a great idea: it ties in the neon of the entryway artwork, making the chamber feel almost cohesive. Alongside the Florist-Loompas, most of the catering fairies work diligently to lay out platters, serving ware, and glasses. The rest of them play *Farmville* surreptitiously on their phones.

Is that why I can't find phone chargers anywhere? Jerks.

With nothing left to do until Stefan and the crows return with the results of their oubliette explorations, I straighten the angle of the head table. Noticing the centerpiece is off-center, I fix that too. And rearrange a toothpick so it doesn't stick visibly from a mushroom's stem. Also, I recruit a fairy to add an anemone to the left side of the arrangement while I adjust the vines trailing to the floor. I put my hands on my hips, considering the arrangement from several angles. Then I loosen two last stems.

"Yes," I say to myself. "It does look better, doesn't it."

"You have a strange way of ruining weddings, Sabby," says Bulan.

Of course he would be harassing me now. But for once, it's welcome. I'm starting to feel like something must be going awry—something besides my own ruinating machinations. Something that has to do with my covert plan to save Hanry.

"All right, Bulan," I say. "Since nothing ever seems to bring you down, I'm open to your suggestions about how to not be consumed with anxiety."

"Hmm," says Bulan unhelpfully. "Maybe add more freesia?"

I make a point of *not* looking at my phone and checking the time. Which is now, according to my last check, a few minutes before noon.

"Yeah," I say. "Let's do that."

When a bat finally swoops into the State Room and circles my head, I nearly break down with relief. A transformation later, and Dark Dave collapses at my feet, exerting more than enough dramatic energy for both of us.

"What's going on?" I demand.

"I lost Gustavo and Jurgis," he moans into my shoes.

I pinch my nose. "Knew it. What else?"

Dave sprawls out, further prostrating himself in his angst.

"I was leading them by the hand through the halls. Until they fell through a hidden trapdoor—"

"An oubliette!" cries Bulan.

Goddamn it. Death traps are, officially, my least favorite home design concept.

"Why didn't you keep better hold of them?"

Kicking the floor with his Oxford heels, Dave whines, "I *tried*, I did. But I kept gravitating to that hole. It seemed so much better down there, so much darker. And I just let go-o-o."

Bulan crows with delight. "See, Sabby? What did I say about vampires? Weak. Wristed."

"Never mind that. Dave, I need you to fly down and see where that trapdoor leads. Maybe all the oubliettes dump the castle's prisoners in the same place."

"I see! And perhaps, there, we'll find Hanry!" Bulan exclaims.

"Exactly."

Done kicking, Dave says, "It's so much *work* to do all this reconnaissance. Why not just ask the groomsmen?"

The world seems to shift beneath my feet. The wedding day schedule I'd submitted in the Rochester Wedding Proposal suggested that a round of groomsmen photos be taken at 3 p.m. It seems like Mandy never crossed that item off the final schedule. So I guess it's still on. But who are Hanry's groomsmen, anyway? He doesn't have a lot of guy friends—besides Dave, I've not met a single one.

"Dave," I say, flipping through my clipboard. "Did you see groomsmen anywhere?"

The vampire covers his eyes, moaning.

"Yes, yes! They opened the doors, repeatedly! Lighting up this very hall! They were big men, Samantha, dressed as fancy as you or I, with horrible, shiny swords on their belts. Supremely intimidating."

Everything falls into place. These people Dave's describing aren't Hanry's groomsmen.

They're his jailers.

After sending Dave to free Gustavo and Jurgis, Bulan and I set out for a set of formal royal rooms. A rushed conversation with a minion has revealed that fay royalty fashionably have two bedrooms. It's the second one where, supposedly, Hanry's groomsmen are congregating now. In addition to the frustration that I got faked out last night, I'm bringing a wine bottle in hand, Stefan the crow on my shoulder, an unhappy head under my arm, and a newly snapped glow stick in my pocket. It is a *lot*.

While climbing the tree staircase and turning us into the dark abyss of the Royal Wing, Bulan says for the umpteenth time, "I don't like this, Sabby."

"We won't fall into the oubliettes," I assure him. "Dave said they're all on the right-hand side. Ergo, we'll keep left."

"Perhaps you should go alone," Bulan says. "I'm a no-good, useless head, after all."

Where is this sudden humility coming from? "You are a fantastic head."

"Fantastically useless, if I enter the quarters with you. How, then, can I mount a rescue in case anything goes wrong? Moreover! Should things go right, I suspect you and Hanry will be grandly reunited. No one likes a third wheel, Sabby."

Uh-huh. I'm starting to suspect something else is bothering Bulan.

Something having to do with how he avoided Rochester's gaze. Something connected to Mandy finding his body in the possession of his fairy ex, Princess May. The body which I now suspect I've seen myself—and may or may not have misidentified as a mannequin with a rug on its head.

I probably should've let Bulan have his story time last night. My bad.

"Fine," I say, seeing no way around his reasoning. "Get out of here. Scram."

"Thank you, Sabby! My dear friend Stefan: Could you lend me your beak?"

Stefan the crow lifts off my shoulder and swoops over to Bulan. Grabbing him by his bristly red sideburns, the creature manages to lift the head midair, albeit with some swinging. Apparently impervious to scalp pain, Bulan achieves a grin.

"Good luck, Sabby," he says.

"Yeah, yeah. Don't get into trouble. And no going after your body without my permission."

"What? I would never!"

Sure.

"I'll see you in an hour or so downstairs," I call.

Once he's lost to shadows, I follow the wall closely until I arrive at Hanry's formal royal suite. At least, that's where I hope I've arrived: like last night, I meet no door-fairy, and there aren't noises seeping out of the rooms. I don't know if it's a good or bad sign. But I want it to mean that Hanry's in as miserable straits as I imagine: that he's imprisoned. Waiting for my rescue. Held against his will, awaiting marital enslavement to an unkind and beautiful human trafficker princess fairy.

Any alternative is unimaginable.

He shouted for help, after all. He stared into my eyes and said, "*Help!*"

Ignoring the rapid beating of my heart, I lift my fist and knock.

The person who answers isn't a groomsman or a fairy servant.

It's Hanry's mom. Who is also Fairyland's queen, but I have to emphasize: Queen Mab has retreated from the State Room to hang out in her son's suite on the morning of his wedding. If that's not a red flag the size of Italy, what is?

"Sam-a-manta!" Queen Mab beams. "Perfect timing. I was just thinking. Nix the purple. We need yellow flowers instead. To glow like sunlight."

"Or pee," contributes a treble voice inside the room.

"Yes," Mab agrees. "Or pollen. Flower pee."

Another voice chimes in. "Actually, I believe that pollen is flower—"

"Your Highness, we have a problem," I interject before the group of Hanry's captors and friends can embarrass themselves further. These tacky fay need to get it together. "We have a capital-*P Problem*."

"Go on," says Mab.

"I've discovered that Princess May's ex is here. Inside the castle." I stare at Mab, imbuing my warning with all the solemnity I can. "And he's trying to steal his body back from her."

"His *body*?" Mab asks. It figures she'd be intrigued.

"Yes, she's been holding on to it for a few centuries," I explain, well aware this is borderline incomprehensible behavior. "Maybe you should look into it."

"I should say so!"

"Heads-up, though—you might need some of the groomsmen along to investigate. Word is, May's ex is extremely strong. A warrior king. And if he's back, body and all . . . he could do quite a bit of damage."

I know Bulan doesn't want his body back. As far as I know, he has no continuing interest romantically in its captor. And for all I know, centuries of atrophy have given him a dad bod.

But Mab doesn't know that.

The queen snaps her fingers. "You're talking about Bran!" she says. "I remember Bran! That rascal. Rochester, come here. Boys, we've got to intervene."

The name "Bran" feels like a close miss for Bulan, so I figure we're on the same page as Mab calls the groomsmen/jailors to her by name. I suspect she's the world's only mother-in-law of the bride-to-be who's excited about chaos on her son's wedding day. Oh well, works for me. While she commands the room's attention and barks orders, I do what I know how to do best: become invisible.

Slipping back against a wall, I aesthetically become one with a lampshade as the whole pack sets off, armed with worrisome, dangerous-looking medieval weapons. At least my hard-practiced skill of seeming bland to the point of invisibility is working. No one seems interested in me any longer.

Until the very last second, when a fairy groomsman brushes against my treacherous tulle while adjusting the sword on his belt.

"Don't mind me. I'm setting wine out for photos," I say, shooing him along. "You guys go on ahead. I'll be right behind you."

Once the fay departs, I abandon the lampshade and my wine bottle prop.

"Hanry?" I call out into the silence. "Hanry, are you in here somewhere?"

It's so still in here, so quiet, I'm nearly convinced he isn't.

But Hanry could be gagged. He could be unconscious! One of these doors could lead to a dungeon. Fueled by a morally dubious hope that Hanry is facing as much, if not more, tragedy than I've imagined for him, I poke my head into one room, then another. I dip into a closet. I lift a carpet, checking for oubliette entrances. At last, I find a room filled with desserts, aperitifs, and—and five extra-buff, weight-lifting-competition-winner-type male fairies holding hands in a circle around Hanry.

I shouldn't be surprised. Really.

And yet I am.

And so is he.

"Sabby?" Hanry exclaims.

The fairies divert from hand-holding to building an invisible wall with their hands. Like . . . mimes, miming a wall. Behind this hastily constructed barrier that should not be able to hold back a small rabbit, much less a prince, Hanry wears a gold-trimmed suit of ivory linen. He's got a very impressive sash. And manacles. Who could forget the golden manacles?

"This is . . . kinky," I say.

Hanry looks ashamed. "I can explain."

That'd be great. Also: Would it?

When I left Salem, I was getting to the point where I could recognize Hanry from behind. With his size, it wasn't exactly challenging. But looking at him now, head-on, he's both familiar and unfamiliar. Mostly the same. This Hanry looks better groomed, I'll confess. His hands aren't dirty. I think he's been moisturizing. Mostly, the difference revolves around his chin: his stubble has made admirable progress toward a beard. It almost hides his mouth. I try not to gaze too long at that mouth, remembering the feel of it on mine. My hands twitch to touch him.

But the only kind of touching they should do is whatever's necessary to lead him away from here. I swallow, finding my mouth unexpectedly dry. We broke up before I left for New York; he doesn't have any idea what I've been doing all these weeks. He doesn't know how horrible it was, how lonely.

How different the last twelve hours have been. How—how wonderful.

Minus the whole part where I found out Hanry was marrying a gorgeous fairy princess.

"My diversion won't keep your mom busy long," I say, biting down my weaker impulses. Namely, the ones that make me want to scramble to Hanry's side, begging him to declare his love and tell me he would *never* consider marrying May. "We've got five minutes, tops."

"Sabby, I know you have questions," says Hanry. "I owe you answers."

Ah, fuck it. If I can't get declarations of undying love, I'll take answers.

"You know what?" I say. "You're right."

I settle onto an upholstered settee in front of Hanry and his animate cage. I do my best to ignore the vigorously miming muscle and focus only on my ex-boyfriend's mortified blue eyes.

"Where do you want to start?"

27

BEHOLD, THE WUSS OF FAIRYLAND

"YOU'VE PROBABLY FIGURED OUT WHO MY PARENTS ARE," HANRY says to begin.

"Adopted parents," I say, waving him on. We're on a time crunch, after all.

"Yeah, well. The technical term is probably 'abductive parents.' I told you I was adopted, but the truth is, it was a sort of . . . quasi-legal process. I remember being in the human world as a kid, living in the middle of nowhere. I was bored a lot. Until I met my dad. Tits. I'd snuck out of the house to play outside, and I found Dad blowing up a car with a forked stick he'd pulled from a maple tree. So I was like, this guy is awesome. I wanted him to show me how he did it. I offered him my own stick, which apparently had a pretty nifty mushroom growing on it. Dad took it as a sign."

"I can't tell from your tone if this encounter was good or bad."

"Good," says Hanry, eyebrows rising emphatically. "My human dad wanted me to learn to code."

"Horrible," I say. But only because Hanry seems to be expecting it.

"Right? You've seen me with computers," Hanry says. "Anyway, Dad swore I'd see more interesting things if I went with him. Since he wasn't offering candy or anything, I figured it couldn't get me in too much trouble. And . . . sure enough, it didn't. I never missed my old life. When it was time to have my—you know—when I met you, I was exploring the world beyond Fairy. It's a tradition for changelings like me."

"Right. And when the Amish do it, they tell people. 'Hi, I'm Amish. I don't know what a dishwasher is, aren't I adorable? Would you like a fresh rutabaga from my garden?'"

I don't actually know if this is how Amish people behave. Under their circumstances, it seems reasonable, unlike whatever the hell it was Hanry thought he was pulling. He must realize this too, because the color in his cheeks flares.

"I didn't want you to think differently of me."

Oh my god. "Hanry, *I have a pet head*. Did you seriously think that being royal fairy spawn was a dealbreaker?"

"You hate the paranormal community."

The mime-fairies gasp silently. At least, most of them do; one of the five breaks his miming duties to scratch his aquiline nose.

"Hate's a strong word," I say. Although he has a point.

"I guess it doesn't matter," Hanry says at length. "You were always talking about leaving Salem, anyway. Weirdly, our time together made me more interested in Salem than I would've been without you. So thanks for showing me around. Introducing me to the night market, the wharf . . ."

"You're welcome. And now that we've cleared everything up, it's time to get you out of here." I point at my wrist, making the *tick-tick-tick* noise. I'm not sure Hanry can read time from glow sticks, but you never know. "We've got two, three minutes left at best."

Hanry glances at his guard-mimes. On cue, they begin hum-growling with emphatic menace. At least to me, it's intimidating, though Hanry's broad-shouldered enough that he could probably snap one of those fairy dudes in half.

"Back at Sidney's wedding," says Hanry, "I told you my mom and I'd had an argument."

I nod, remembering. "I'm guessing it was about getting hitched. Was she pissed when you told her no?"

"Not exactly."

"Ah. Sad, then?"

Hanry hesitates. And—oh god. Hanry, for all his burly manliness and kindness, has one flaw. One even he described as a flaw, on our first date: a tendency to slip out and avoid uncomfortable things.

"Hanry? You . . . you *did* tell her you didn't want to get married, right?"

The miming fairies, agitated, increase the speed of their rapid wall-building.

"Knock it off," I snap at them. "Tell me I'm right, Hanry. Tell me."

"I was trying to tell her!" says Hanry weakly.

Trying?

Heat rising in my head, I look at Hanry again. *Really* look this time. For a prisoner, he's well-rested. And he *is* dressed up, without mussed hair or bruising or scratches. I glance down at his handcuffs. His wrists are pale, with no signs of chafing or blood from attempts to claw them off.

In fact, the manacles look like bracelets.

Royal bracelets. Beautiful royal bracelets, without sharp, serrated edges, or any flecks of dried blood. The only thing they have are insignias carved into the gold.

This . . . this absolute trash human. This lumberjackass. Hanry hasn't attempted to escape; he doesn't *want* to escape. While I spent all night making plans, all morning tearing out my hair, somewhat literally, trying to keep my cool while I found out where he was being kept prisoner, he hasn't done a *thing* to stop this?

Down to this very moment, when he's letting himself be imprisoned by off-brand mimes?

"Hanry." I feel my nails digging into my palms. Apparently, I'm curling my fists. *Apparently*, I am 10/10 pissed. "How do you 'try' to tell someone you don't want to get married?"

"Well—"

I bounce from the settee to my feet. "Last night, I saw you running at arrow-point. Arrows, Hanry. Pointy death sticks. You were naked. You asked me to help you."

"Yes," he sighs. "I never liked that after-dinner party game."

I throw an egg tart from the dessert tray at him.

"Hey!"

"I stayed up all night *plotting a heist* for you!"

"And for that, I thank—"

The next tart smacks him satisfyingly in the face.

"Please don't do that," says one of the fairies. "It makes our wall look ineffectual."

"You *are* all ineffectual!" I burst out. "This is bullshit!"

"Sabby, I still need your help," Hanry pleads. "I don't want to marry May! She only wants me for my beard. And she's terrifying. She could literally take me apart."

"I could take you apart."

"But you wouldn't!"

I laugh maniacally, squeezing the filling out from the middle of a pastry. "You don't know what I would and wouldn't do right now."

"You like me!"

"I *did*!" I retort. "Before you proved you're totally spineless."

"You don't understand. My mom's terrifying!"

"Oh, whatever! I've said no to her twice today! And can you make your fairy manservants knock off with the French clown act already? I know they're not actually trapping or protecting you."

The fairies break apart from their circle, heads down as if ashamed.

"It's true," says the nose-scratcher. "He told us to do this when he heard you coming."

"Oh, for fuck's sake, Hanry. You're not worried about getting married, not really, or else we'd be leaving right now! You're just a coward."

"I am not!" he counters, finally starting to look as angry as I feel. "You're making this about you! But I have to stay here, to protect Seb!"

"Seb?!" I sputter. "He isn't even here—"

"Yes, Sabby, *exactly*!" Hanry says with heat. "If I don't marry May, Mom is going to make Seb do it!"

I only need a half second to process this. "Okay. So if *neither* of you can say no, then you're *both* spineless! Seriously, Hanry. I get that you want to play the noble hero, but why can't you back out and save both of your skins? What is wrong with you? I mean it. What is *wrong* with you?"

At this—at last—Hanry doesn't have an answer. He becomes fascinated with the opposite wall. He runs a hand through his hair.

"I—I don't know," he says.

Damn it. They're such strong, nicely shaped hands. They should be holding on to mine as we escape the castle together, or raised in triumph after he stands up to his parents like *an actual adult*. A freaking waste is what it is. It's . . . it's . . .

"Excuse me," pipes up a fairy-mime. "Are you finished yet?"

I stiffen. "What?"

"We really need to . . ." Two fairies break away from the rest, simulating the action of booting me out on my butt. And damn, that's annoying. Annoying enough that I can push my heartbreak to the side, and say, "Fine. I'm out. Have a good life, Hanry."

I have no idea what expression Hanry makes, because I've already turned away. Not just turned away, either: I'm moving, like I'm drawn by a magnet, against my control, out of the room. Out of his suite and into the pitch-black hallway. All I know is, I've got to get away. To be anywhere else but standing before my ex-boyfriend, who isn't who I thought he was. Who can't be the person I need him to be.

The door thudding behind me, I shuck off my glow-stick bracelet and toss it. In the darkness, I hear it clatter into a hole. Fine. Bye. It's not like I'll be relying on its light anymore.

I don't know what I'm going to do.

I've spent the last twelve hours risking my safety—and the Spüktacular wedding brand—to sabotage Hanry's wedding. To save a guy who has the noble-mindedness to help his brother but doesn't have the guts to try and save himself. I could probably still drag Hanry from the castle, but what good would that do? We'd get back together, and then what? Be on the run from fairy minions forever? Rochester would find him, or a pooka would, or even King Tits himself. As far as I can tell, Bulan has been on the run from his nemesis—Princess May—for centuries, and lately it's become his full-time job. At the end of the day, we'd get caught. And Hanry couldn't protect me from anything. He doesn't have the balls.

And that's the real issue. If Hanry isn't willing to fight for me, then there's no future for us.

None.

And my future without him?

I close my eyes, visualizing floor six at EFG with its predictable, gray, ninety-degree-angle lines. That stupid, boring office, where I'm forced to stare at spreadsheets and sit through meetings I can barely endure with my eyes open and make small talk with colleagues about the weather and what we did over the weekend. Where I'm exhausted by the constant, endless work of making myself unnoticeable and plain. I can't do it anymore. I can't.

There's nothing for me if I go back to New York. No chance my stable accounting job will lead to a nice, well-settled suburb that makes me any happier than EFG has. It's not going to be enough to own a cute rescue dog. Not even 2.5 *children* or a boring, sports-jersey-wearing husband will do it.

A future with Hanry, a future without him, it's . . . no different.

I see now what I'm made of, and what it is that I want.

And it's. Too. Damned. Late.

28

THE PUPPETS OF DARKNESS

I'M CRYING.

That's fine. It seems appropriate.

I throw out my hands, wandering the pitch-black Royal Wing, a trail of snot and tears littering the floor behind me. I have no idea where I'm going or where I am. Most likely, I will fall into an oubliette. Okay. That's okay. It's not much change from my present dark imprisonment—the one of my own making.

I've no other option but to go back to New York tomorrow. To resume living with Jane in my boring, cramped apartment. To typing out meaningless numbers on a computer under the harsh glare of fluorescent lights. To be an auditor forever. I put everything on the line to save Hanry, for naught. And now, the sabotage I've coordinated for this wedding will ruin the Spüktacular wedding brand forever. Even if I did want to go back to Salem and restart my business, no bride will want to work with me ever again.

So, this is it. I've made my beige, medium-firm, hospital-cornered bed. And I have no choice but to sleep in it.

Or at least wither away restlessly on it.

Grandma Rose, if you hadn't had the audacity to leave earth for your heavenly Italian buffet, I bet you'd know how to guide me out of this mess. But you're not here. So, I'm sorry. I'm sorry I didn't give you a chance after that Halloween night when I was twelve. I'm sorry for avoiding you that summer you gave me a place to sleep. I'm not super great about externalizing my feelings. You probably thought I'd had food poisoning instead of an existential crisis. As you can see, I've had my share of misunderstandings too. Look at all we have in common.

I liked your yard flamingos, actually. I admit it. They were an absolute vibe. I even like Salem, if we don't count Matilda and your other witchy, bodily-autonomy-disrespecting friends.

It doesn't matter now. Maybe all that matters is finding a trapdoor that would be too creepy for the October Halloween edition of an HGTV home renovation show, and jumping in. Maybe, for once, that'll take me to a place I can belong: somewhere I can lick my wounds in peace.

No, no. I don't want to die in this tacky dress. I can't let Mab and Tits and all those stupid fairies win. Oh god. If the wedding is this bad, imagine their *funerals*. I want to die with dignity. Or better yet, mope with dignity. Hidden away in the powder room of a ladies' toilet.

But what I want is irrelevant, because any hope of finding an alabaster throne is cruelly snatched from me in the form of a harsh tug to my hair. And to my dress. And ankle. It takes a moment to realize what's happening. Why I'm not allowed to wallow endlessly in my despair.

The reason is that I'm being pummeled by crows.

"You can't do this!" I flail, striking in vain at the birds' feathery bodies. "Dark fiends! I knew you were against me!"

"Sabby!" cries Bulan's voice. "There's a hole there! Watch out!"

"I *was* watching!" I shout into the black. How dare Bulan witness my tragedy? "Did anything I was doing look accidental to you? I—I . . . Hnngghhhkkk. I can't even find a bathroom."

The crows deposit me on the floor, cawing in a way that indicates they're reveling in victory. Oh, I hate them. *I hate them.* I really wish they weren't solid black, so I could see them and strangle one to prove it.

"Surely you know this is an inappropriate place to relieve yourself, Sabby," Bulan says.

"I'm going to pluck out every feather from your friends' wings," I say darkly.

"CAW-aw-KKK," a crow says in answer to my threat.

Bulan sighs. "No, no! I can't have you doing that—these birds are my friends! Think of it, Sabby! Their centuries of loyalty, their intelligence. Why, this corvid here is the twenty-seventh generation of my first and bestest friend, who I made as a wee child. Back when I still had possession of my body. Which I would've explained if you'd given me the opportunity. Oh. This is strange. Why aren't you stopping me from regaling you with my life stories? Sabby, truly, what's wrong?"

"Isn't it obvious?" I mean to growl, but the sound that comes out instead is hiccups. "I have no future."

"Hmm. That's dramatic."

Dear god. If Bulan thinks I'm being a drama queen, there really isn't hope. I sink deeper into the puddle of my dejection. I'm forming an actual puddle again, and this time, it's not the fault of a magical binding on Grandma's will. It's my own damned fault. Maybe my tears will create an ocean to lift me up someday. Or maybe not.

"Come on, Sabby!" Bulan nudges me with his nose. "Chin up! Your grandmother would hate to see you like this."

I moan-sniffle. "Nrghhrrrughhh guhh guhhkk."

"This is very unlike you, Sabby. You must tell me what's wrong! It's a matter of urgency. I have made a vow I can't turn back on, you see."

With effort, I manage, "I don't. Black halls. Remember?"

"I promised your grandmother I would look after you."

What?

Effortfully, I claw back to the memory of when I first discovered Bulan; of opening the closet door to find him—grinning ebulliently atop a dusty shelf of unfolded linens. He wasn't surprised by my presence. No; he couldn't have been. I'd been blaring BTS from my phone; stomping from room to room and muttering about Grandma's dubious friends and equally dubious housekeeping. Bulan must've known I'd find him.

He'd been waiting for me.

"She put you up to it," I realize, wiping my upper lip. "This whole time you've been Grandma Rose's puppet!"

"It's true," Bulan confirms. "I was determined to honor your grandmother, in spite of your cruel maltreatment. The attempted murder, the punting, the jokes."

"You love the jokes," I sniffle. "You're all about jokes."

"So are you. And so was Rosie! And both of you, whether you'd like to hear this or not, can be quite careless in how you treat those whom you love. But, deep down, your grandmother was a warm, fluffy pair of knitted socks. As are you."

What kind of metaphor is that? "Do you even remember why people wear socks?"

"Stop interrupting! Even Mandy knows when to be serious." That shuts me up. I huddle more tightly against myself, braced against the bitterly cold stone floor as Bulan rambles on. "Your grandmother regretted falling out with you. Oh yes, I was there—I heard everything that happened when you were a child! Terrible, that whole dagger business. In case you were wondering, I was living in the cupboard. Well, sometimes the bathroom cabinet. The point remains. Rosie pleaded with your mother to give her a second chance, to have you stay over during summers at least. She worried about you, and she wished nothing more than to ensure your well-being."

"She had a weird way of showing it," I mutter.

"Did she? In the months before she passed, Rosie changed her will and wrote you in. As a last attempt to help you, to keep you from abandoning your destiny. From throwing the head out with the bathwater, so to speak."

Maybe that's true. If so, Grandma had way too much faith in me. Elsewise she would have known I'm not cut out for the paranormal world, or any world. Not even oubliette world.

"I don't have a destiny," I say to the floor.

"You do too, Sabby," Bulan argues back. "Which is why Rosie made me swear that if I had the chance, I'd pick up the torch and help you."

"But there was no torch," I say. "Just a woo-woo stipulation in her obnoxious, nefarious will."

"Yes, that was a clever thing, wasn't it?"

"A horrible thing," I argue. "Not clever—oh."

I roll onto my side and stare into the darkness.

The implications had been lost on me until now, but if Bulan was used to being Grandma Rose's puppet, could he have taken on her postmortem mantle of being *puppeteer*? Is it possible his playacting ventriloquy with me when we walked around Salem was meant to lull me into a false sense of safety, when in fact he was aware of Grandma's plans for me? And he was even *helping to accomplish them*?

I beat away my scratchy wedding skirt, crawl onto my forearms, and somehow push myself upright.

"Don't tell me you were involved in trapping me in Salem," I say.

"Goodness, no," Bulan says. "But it wasn't *so* awful, was it?! You liked it in Salem! You enjoyed setting up the shop, the wedding planning—"

"So what if I did?" I shout, admitting it aloud at last. "I could've enjoyed the path I was already on if it weren't for you! And for Grandma Rose! Instead, I realized I hated it! My accounting job was hard, and it wasn't fun, and everyone I met sucked, and I hated living in New York, and now . . . now . . ."

"Now what?" Bulan huffs. "It sounds to me that nothing about your situation has changed. Merely your understanding of it."

I can't think of a rebuttal to this. Could Bulan be right?

Maybe this mischievous, Machiavellian, magnificent head—could be right.

The last few months, I was sure I was longing to start at EFG, but what if I wasn't? Maybe I was just longing for the idea of what I thought it'd be like. For what I thought my life could be.

Then, to hide my pain and disappointment, I got obsessed with missing Hanry. But that was only half of it. Hanry was the link to my Salem life I felt safe holding on to. I didn't want to admit that I'd been afraid to hold on to anyone or anything else. That I've spent years pushing away my family, even some of my friends, in order to achieve what I thought were my dreams.

That I've been lonely.

And since last night, while I've been theoretically focused on saving Hanry—that is, Prince Hanry, Changeling Abductee and the Wuss of

Fairyland—the truth is that as much as I've wanted him, he hasn't been the thing I've wanted most of all.

I've been in denial for who-knows-how-long. Only now, finally, the truth shines bright in front of me, like a trash fire.

I ran away from New York and came to Fairyland to throw a wedding. *That's* why I'm here—not for Hanry. Because I knew it would be fun, planning this lavish, outlandish event. I couldn't wait to be laughing with my friends and handling their hijinks and quirks and building something wonderful. My deep unhappiness in New York and at EFG ended the moment I left it behind. I don't mind the weird monsters and zaniness and unpredictability of the paranormal world. Not in the least.

The truth is, I have loved—I *do* love this stupid job.

Are you up there, Grandma? Are you watching all of this now, looking down on me and Bulan? Maybe you're choking on your ziti. You should start paying better attention; there are "I told you sos" to be said. I get it now, okay? I know.

There's something I like more than Hanry's face. And it's not threatening people with finger sandwiches. It's weddings. These damn amazing weddings.

And if it's not too late to turn this disaster around, then here's a promise for you, Grandma: Hanry's wedding will be the best one I've ever done.

29

AND NOW FOR SOMETHING COMPLETELY DIFFERENT

I PARADE OUT OF THE DARKNESS OF THE ROYAL WING WITH A confused but mollified Bulan under my arm. A weird and novel feeling swirls in my stomach. Could it be regret? A sense I'm making a terrible mistake, launching me onto a path I'm too late to navigate successfully to the end?

No. It's probably just hunger.

Throwing the entire tray of desserts at Hanry before I left the suite was likely unnecessary. Maybe Bulan's right and I should consider anger management. But that will have to wait. Pivoting from planning a heist to a counter-heist is going to require reeling in a hefty quantity of chaos. It'll take a miracle to undo my wedding-ruining machinations and make Hanry and May's nuptials worthy of the Spüktacular wedding brand. So, first things first: I've got to divert Queen Mab and her entourage from May's bridal suite.

I look left, right. Rub away snot dried onto my cheek. Aha. The Green Wing may be ineffably *green*, but the bridal suite will be around the corner and a few doors to the left. I remember the minty-toothpaste tinge of the wallpaper, and I remain unimpressed.

"Sabby, do you mind me interrupting your frightening determination to finish what I started here?" Bulan asks near my armpit.

Glancing down, I observe his pleading eyes. He could be intimating a thousand things, and I've no time for guesswork.

"What do you mean? Grandma Rose didn't have specific plans for Fairyland, did she?"

"Not that I'm aware," answers Bulan. "However—"

"Caww CAWW."

A frazzled crow emerges from the shadowy eaves, a red sticky note attached to its beak.

"Ahoy there, Stefan! Sabby, look!" As if I'm going to miss this harbinger of madness circling overhead. Since when did we have red sticky notes, anyway? Whatever. I reach up to take the note from Stefan.

It's sticky with *fresh blood*. Satisfied at causing horror, Stefan the doom-bird takes off, all casual-like, in the opposite direction of May's bridal suite.

"Ah, yes," says Bulan. "Dave's chosen mode of communication, blood! Stefan and I were looking into that sullen vampire's rather nonspecific dilemma, right before I saved you from yet another poorly concocted life decision. You're welcome, by the way."

I swat him. There's no need to rub it in.

"Listen, I'll follow Stefan and figure out what Dave wants. Then I'll visit May and Mandy. In the meantime, you go round up the rest of our troops and tell them about the change in plans. We're canceling the heist and sabotage. Got it?"

I put Bulan on the floor. He waggles his eyebrows cheekily.

"Yes, ma'am! We're still friends, right?"

"Shut up," I say, but Bulan is already roll-bouncing away. Stefan flaps ahead of me, leading me around the corner. Immediately, I stumble into some minions.

"You three!" I shout. "We've had a major change of plans. I need you to communicate this to the rest of the crew. Got it?"

"Got it," they say, but I'm already speaking over them: "First, we need to pen the antelope and the fox from last night, ASAP. Round up the ushers for me too. I want to go over their duties again, but they need to be clear that they *cannot be naked*. And when it comes time for the bridal entry, I know I said human women like to be showered in shoveled dirt and earthworms, but let's go with something lighter . . ."

"Helloooo, is that Sabby I hear?"

I'm not totally surprised Dave is still inside his oubliette.

What surprises me is that he sounds far more energetic than usual. At least until he adds mournfully: "Sorry about the blood. I forgot a pen."

Mollified by this return to his typical way of being, I get to my knees and peer over the edge. About ten feet down, Dave stands with his arms extended to the ceiling, his wrists illuminated by glow-stick bracelets. Also, his mouth drips with blood.

"Dave, I need you out of there. I'm trying to unwind some of the chaos I've set up for the wedding, and we don't have much time to do it."

"Oh, interesting! Well, good news, bad news, Sabby . . ." Really? This looks like all bad news. "I found a way to get Gustavo and Jurgis out."

"They're not with you?" I call down.

"Of course not!"

"Then what's the bad news?"

Dave doesn't answer immediately. Which is how, behind me, I hear flapping. And it doesn't sound like the feathery, soft, chaotic crow wings I've grown accustomed to of late. I think about turning around, but why bother? I have a feeling I know what I'll see. I close my eyes and take a steadying breath.

"Goddamn vampires," I mutter.

"What's that?" Dave asks.

Nothing. Just that I hope Jurgis and Gustavo really love the darkness of night and flying as much as they let on last night. Recovering, I call out, "I asked, 'Why are you still down there, Dave?'"

"Because it's very comforting." I can't see it, but Dave sniffs so loudly, it echoes up the chamber. "Sabby, my *apologies* for breaking their enchantments."

"Thanks. Though I'm not the one who deserves your apology."

After returning to my feet, I back away from the oubliette and turn to face the bats behind me—Gustavo and Jurgis, the newest members of the Community.

"Well, bats. If you're unenchanted, then I'll be honest: you have a choice. You could leave now, if you want, but I could still *really* use your help with this wedding. You don't want to start off on the wrong foot in the paranormal world, do you? No. Now, come on. Let's go downstairs. Stefan, you going to stay with me, or go to Bulan?"

Stefan caw-laughs at me and tosses a crumpled sticky note against my head. Having had its fun, the crow cuts across the corridor and vanishes. With Jurgis, Gustavo, and Dave gliding behind me, I step in the opposite direction, thinking nothing of Stefan's oddness—

Until, from way down the hall, I hear Mandy's voice, and Rochester's.

They're not talking. They're doing something . . . else. Something that would cause a barrage of burps to emanate—and echo—from an enchanted wooden floor. And that might cause moaning. So much loud, unnecessary *moaning*.

No wonder Stefan fled so fast.

"Spüktacular Weddings!" I announce as I burst into the royal bridal suite. "Hello, everyone! How are we doing?!"

Shaki is calmly, enchantedly mixing blush beside Queen Mab, primly perched on her settee. Matthew is removing hair balls from his brush. It's bewilderingly calm. You would never know Mab had just set out with an armed guard to commit murder.

"Oh, Sammy-mandible!" Queen Mab stands, a glass of fairy wine faithfully returned to her clutches. "You played such a funny prank! I was so hoping our old friend Bran had come to visit, but no! What a shame!"

"Ah," I say. "You're welcome."

I could easily imagine my mom seated beside Mab, unintentionally mirroring the entire thing. Why are mothers like this? Drunk, oblivious, fun-oblivious, yet somehow always able to support their grim existence?

The fairy princess May, bedecked in glam diamonds and an over-the-top, antique, and slightly yellowed button-down wedding dress—yikes—spins on her stylist stool and casts me a carefully neutral look.

"Hello, Samantha," she says.

Her expression is . . . haughty, obviously, but also calculating. I wonder what she did to get Queen Mab off the scent of Bulan's body. Well, shrewd or not, she deserves some respect before being forced to wed a teddy bear of a prince in desperate need of stuffing.

In case there was any doubt, I'm *definitely* still pissed at Hanry.

I curtsy to my enemy. "Your Highness."

Mab gestures to the bats at my side. "Who are these two?"

Possibly she hand waves some form of unseen magic, because at once Jurgis and Gustavo transform and topple into a heap.

"I'm a photographer," says Jurgis.

"I'm a vampire," says Gustavo, rolling over Jurgis somewhat dazedly. "And your videographer, sí. Oh! It is fun to fly!"

"They're here to record the day. In the tradition of human weddings," I remind the room. Immediately, Jurgis leaps to his feet and gets to adjusting lighting, moving furniture, setting up shots. *Click, click, click.* I can't find any sign of Bulan's body—I'm dimly curious what May did to manage that—but I decide to let the matter go and focus on damage control. "Mab, I'm so glad you enjoyed my prank earlier. Unfortunately, it's a one and done. We're going to stay on schedule after this."

The queen mother sighs in disappointment, her long face growing long enough that I want to fix it for her manually. But that would put me in reach of her pointy antlers. Not worth it.

"I'm so disappointed, Samba!" she whines.

I forcibly move Gustavo's hand from his camera to prevent him from recording this particularly low moment. The less that's on film, the less that can come back to bite me later.

"I know you are, and I'm sorry, but—"

"Mandy told me that human weddings have many elements that

must come together," May says for me. Her intervention reveals a concerning degree of understanding. "You want Hanry and me to have a good day, don't you, oh Queen?"

The queen collapses against her furniture. "I do," she says, resigned. "If only human makeup wasn't so laborious!"

Since my new job is to keep Mab content, I take the hint immediately.

"Shaki, can you wrap this up quick? I remember Her Majesty wanted to discuss the florals downstairs. And it's approaching one p.m."

"Oh yes! Our guests will arrive soon!" The queen bubbles up with laughter so effervescent, she has to reach out for my arm to stabilize. "Was it yellow I was suggesting?"

"Purple, actually. Magenta."

"Indeed?"

"Mm-hmm. Here's my phone. Check out the pics. Jurgis, come with us," I command. The newly born vampire, temporarily returned to human form, licks his lips and reaches for my elbow. I bat him off with a strict, "No! Bad vamp! The only thing you get to hold is your camera. I'll give you blood downstairs, okay?"

"Very well," he relents.

Before we leave, I tuck my clipboard beneath my arm and say loudly enough for the whole room to hear: "Oh, and May? One last thing. You're looking great. Freaking stunning."

The fairy princess's eyebrows knot together for a brief moment, likely suspicious at a compliment from her romantic rival. But she touches her hair with a graceful flourish.

"Thank you."

The final pieces of wedding prep move fast after this.

Although Bulan and Mandy aren't close at hand, for reasons unknown in Bulan's case and unmentionable in Mandy's, I still have ample assistance. My borrowed fairy servants toe the line of my hasty instructions, meaning that when Mab sees the State Room, she melts with delight at its completed setup and décor. Jurgis dutifully photographs the caterers' work of setting out the display wedding cake. Queen Mab, jubilated, unearths wedding invitations she sent at the time of Hanry's changeling adoption. Jurgis documents this too. He adds these announcements to a gorgeous commemorative wedding display, contributing loose flowers, moss, and ribbon.

"Photography is so coarse," Mab reflects. "A still life would be nice, don't you think?"

"Mm-hmm. I'll look into finding a wedding painter," I reply, refusing to worry about the practicality of that at T-minus two hours. "Where's His Royal Highness? King Tits?"

"Oh, he's out recruiting one last guest. I *do* hope he'll return on time."

Mab picks up a leaf and watches it flutter down. If I were her, I'd be concerned the king of Fairyland would risk missing his own son's wedding. But, then again, these are fay. If Mab's not having a panic attack, I guess I can't be bothered to have one either.

"Cool, cool," I say. Then I call over a catering fairy. "Add an extra place setting to the head table, will you?"

"No!" Mab commands, halting them. "It's a *secret* guest. We can't spoil the surprise by giving them a place to sit."

"Sure," I say, in spite of the fact that no one will be in the reception area until after the wedding is done. The customer's always right, after all. To move her along, I bring up another topic: "Your Highness, once Jurgis is done in here, he'll head to Princess May's room to photograph the bridal party. Did you still want to do a first look?"

"Do I ever!" she cries.

It takes a good half hour before I rediscover Mandy. Rather, she finds me, as Hanry is being paraded from his rooms by a mime-guard entourage. I refuse to watch as he is walked out beneath the cloudy sky onto the turret bridge to behold his fiancée in her royal wedding finery. I'm too busy directing the first set of guests from their carriages to the courtyard for their champagne reception.

Okay, that's not true.

I see *everything*. The way Hanry holds himself away from Princess May—whereas if it were me, he would've turned his chest in to cradle my shoulders. How he poses for a photo, stiff—whereas if it were me, he would mold himself into my warmth. I notice the closed-lip grimace he makes when a minion with a parasol ushers Jurgis onto the balcony, and Jurgis guides his hand onto the princess's shoulder. The way Hanry jolts when Jurgis clasps their hands together, bares his teeth, and goes for their wrists.

Hanry may be ridiculously conflict-adverse, but he's still Hanry: he holds Jurgis back gently. Kindly. I know these attributes are what let his mother control him so easily. I'm certain a woman like May will walk all over him.

Hanry deserves better than that; he deserves someone who will respect him.

But if he doesn't want to fight for something better, that's his choice. He's shoveling his own grave, so to speak, and I refuse to let myself be buried with him. Swallowing back the hurt, which feels like a clod of dirt catching in my throat, I elbow Mandy softly in the side.

"So." I cough to correct the weakness in my voice. "So, you snagged the Roach."

She squeals. "I know!"

"Come on, spill. How'd you do it?"

"He's impressed with how serious I am!" Mandy squeals again. Because I have literally nothing to say to this, she explains: "He said that I'm always composed and prepared. He finds me very *sensible*."

Rochester's intelligence just dropped significantly in my estimation. But hey, after all the hard work Mandy has done to pull off this wedding, she deserves a reward. Though, frankly, I think she could do better.

I pat her shoulder. "How about you go ahead? Make like a lovebird or whatever and hang with Rochester for a while, if you like. I'll greet the officiant and our DJ on my own."

Mandy's eyes dart to mine, equal parts dubious and excited. "Are you sure?"

"One hundred percent," I say, forcing a smile. The glimpse of my teeth seems to discomfit her slightly, but after hugging me, she skips off in search of her lover. That's fine. Sure, I was planning to ask Mandy to help me find Bulan, but falling in love doesn't happen every day. And if it happens at a wedding, well . . . what kind of a jerk would get in the way of that?

"Samantha, I do not want to say that you are being a jerk—"

"Then don't call me one. I'm not jerking you or anyone else around." It's T-minus five minutes before Hanry's wedding, and I'm trapped in an argument with Rochester. For the most part, the guests are seated. The enchanted DJ is poised at his booth, eyes glazed over, and hands moving frenetically—indicating he's unaware his sound system blew out the room's lone electrical outlet, rendering him useless. At least he's trying to do his job, unlike Hanry's fairy godmother. As our wedding officiant, Rochester isn't supposed to be with me in the antechamber; he should be front and left with Mandy, ready to stride up to the altar. But he is not cooperating with the spirit of the situation.

He is calling me names.

"I do not believe Hanry's heart is in it," he is saying.

"Yeah? Well, one could argue my heart should be broken too."

The stoic fairy appears less than pleased. So basically, he appears as much as ever like a weathered chunk of rock.

"And yet," he says. "You are participating in this scheme. And you seem happy."

"I like what I do," I reply tersely. "Even more than I like Hanry. Which begs the question: What's with *your* change of heart? You should have protested this union ages ago."

His glance at Mandy answers that question.

"You believe in true love now? Aww," I say despite myself. "Well, do you think it's possible Princess May feels truly in love with Hanry too?"

Rochester doesn't answer. He doesn't need to. Last I checked, May knew she was getting a great deal: she was glowing, ecstatic, and kept mentioning facial hair to her bridesmaids. Presumably she's excited about Hanry's hair, not her own. Fairies seem universally smooth-skinned. It really takes beard-envy to new and soaring heights.

Feeling done with our argument—and done thinking about Hanry's good qualities—I paste on my most professional face.

"I'm sure you'll find a way to keep Mab and Tits happy," I say.

With that, I leave the antechamber so I can watch over the ceremony from a respectful distance. This was my last official coordination task prior to the reception—and let's be real, the caterers should be able to manage the bulk of the after-party with only minor oversight, barring major incidents.

"Unthink that, unthink that," I mutter.

Slipping to the back of the Throne Room, I silently evaluate the scene. Sixty rows of chairs splay out before me, gorgeously wrapped in greens and neutral beiges and whites, with occasional pops of magenta. Beyond the guests is a stagelike platform, where May's personal harpist, recently enlisted to replace our DJ, has taken a seat. Above the platform is a raised dais, punctuated by two spectacularly mossy fairy thrones. As Rochester ascends to the lower platform, he nods at the harpist. She lifts her obscenely long fingers to the ceiling.

And so the wedding begins.

To my left, Gustavo clicks on his video camera; to my right, Jurgis begins snapping photos; and before the audience, May's harpist begins plucking a loose version of Pachelbel's *Canon in D*. The melody sounds okay . . . for about five seconds, until it's time to bring in the accompaniment. She doesn't do it. Instead, she keeps plucking the D repeatedly without varying it. Or stopping.

Wait, I was wrong. She's now playing D in *more* octaves.

Okay. Breathe, Sabby. At least the sounds emitted by the harp are technically music. Mandy will still know to prompt the bridesmaids to move forward. And . . . there. Applause rings out from the guests. I assume this means Hanry has entered the Throne Room via the royal entrance. I'm not sure if he's being escorted by his buff fairy servants, if they're miming him in a cage for effect, or if he's walking unaided. And that's because I continue to refuse to look.

Thanks to our vigorous post-lunch rehearsal, May's fairy entourage succeeds in walking up the aisle, arm in arm with the groomsmen. They're steady and perfect. Moved to passion, a few guests stand up and attempt to develop some kind of leprechaun-leaping game of hop-scotch. I snap my fingers, and fairy minion ushers swiftly intervene.

Something else is much more wrong, however. Something less easily fixed.

I cross the room, maximally stealthy, and sidle up to Mandy. "There's one too many groomsmen," I whisper close to her ear. "Or one too few bridesmaids."

She squeaks, reddening. "You're right! What should we do?"

"I don't know," I reply. But I'm going to have to think of something, fast. I leave Mandy to approach the platform, hugging the wall along the way so I garner minimal attention. Thankfully, my well-honed, borderline invisibility skills remain on point. So much so that when I emerge from the relative shadows to signal Rochester to interrupt the music, no one notices. Except him.

With obvious resentment, the fairy-godmother-officiant clears his throat.

"Now that the processional is complete," he says, "we will have the entrance of the ring bearers and flower girls."

Finally, mercifully, the harpist quits ejecting D notes at us. Her music shifts to a folkloric, pleasant tune. At the back of the room, Gustavo smoothly adjusts the angle of his camera, and Jurgis crouches and creeps past me, changing lenses ahead of May's grand entry.

On any given wedding day, it's expected that the bride will float down the aisle, an angelic vision in white. Sure, there are variations on this theme. May's variation is that she's going to do it literally. I wouldn't look, and I don't *want* to look, except I need to make sure her ceiling entrance isn't terribly bungled.

And . . . crap. She's gorgeous, her face shining with a pearlescent glow. The layers of her white silk kimono float up cloudlike behind her, giving her the appearance of an actual angel. Or, I guess, a fairy. I'm aware that she is gracefully descending on wires—not magic, because this is a human wedding—but that's beside the point. She's taking her time with it too, sighing and preening to great applause, her geta shoes dancing in the air.

It is *devastating*. Because at the end of it all, she alights on the platform beside Hanry, looking as pleased as any other bride I've seen.

And Hanry . . . Hanry looks happy too.

I really can't believe this.

Like, two nights ago, *less than fifty hours ago*, I was texting him about how he makes me laugh. I was thinking about the way he'd told me I was beautiful; the touch of his hand pressing against my back, smoothing down my shirt; how it sent frissons into my stomach. And now he's not just marrying a fairy princess, he's actually trying to smile back at her. Wow.

Woooooow.

The officiant begins his opening greetings. "Welcome, welcome, on this happy—"

A deep voice calls out from the front of the room:

"I object!"

I freeze. We all do.

Actually, as far as I can tell, I'm the only one who understands that this word means something. And you know what? That's good. Because *hell no* to anyone objecting to this wedding. I want Hanry to pay. I want him to suffer like I'm suffering. To feel, every day, like there's a dagger sticking out of the center of his chest.

"Go on!" I shout at Rochester. "The vows."

"Yes, yes, indeed, the vows," the fairy godmother says, struggling to recover. Same as Hanry, who searches his pockets. Oh, shit. Mandy checked that Hanry had his vows ten minutes ago. Could he seriously have lost them already?

"I have them," calls out a groomsman. I release a "whew" of relief. Said groomsman, a stocky redheaded fellow, strides over to Hanry, a hand on the back of his neck. He makes a big show of extending the parchment out, one-handedly, to Hanry.

At the last second, he whips the parchment away.

"Aha!" the groomsman exclaims. "Surprise!"

Oh. I get it now—this must be one of the cousin-bullies Hanry told me about. I smile tightly, enjoying the poetic justice.

"Surprise what?" asks Hanry, that pre-wed wussy of a prince. He reaches out again for the vows, but the groomsman doesn't release them. Instead, he turns to face the gathered guests. His laughter booms throughout the room.

"These are not Hanry's vows, but mine!" he announces. "For I too am engaged to May!"

I stagger backward.

How did I not recognize that groomsman's voice immediately?

It's *Bulan's*.

30

RELATIONSHIPS ARE A DISASTER, DO NOT RECOMMEND

MAY'S SHOCKED EXPRESSION IS ONE FOR THE BOOKS. SPECIFically, for comic books. It doesn't belong here, in this royal fairy wedding, which needs to proceed without a hitch.

"Bran!" she exclaims.

"Bran?" I ask the air. "Like *Game of Thrones*? Or the cereal?"

"Bran," says Rochester darkly.

Hanry's more lost than ever, but I understand: Bran must be Bulan's true name. Same as Princess May is truly *hime-sama*, or something else, and I've gone by Sabby, but I've stayed Samantha, the witchy-enough inheritor of the Spük family name, beneath it this whole time.

"Bran, Bran," the crowd murmurs. Close to me, I hear a few "Surely nots!"

So, I'm guessing Grandma's pet head has been epically involved in this fairy family's drama. Damn, I really should have let him tell me his story.

Reveling in the attention as always, Bulan throws his arms—arms!—behind his back and rips a facade of skin and hair off his face in a move stolen from Scooby-Doo. The moment he's unmasked, his face transforms—like it's been under a glamour, I suppose—returning to his more familiar features.

Also, his head pops off his body.

"I was merely in disguise!" Bulan's rolling head announces to a collective gasp. Even Gustavo releases a breathless "ooh" while continuing to record with delight. I push his equipment away and cut ahead of the front aisle to where Bulan's fiery-red head has rolled in ecstatic, chaotic bliss.

"What are you doing?" I growl as I pick him up.

He has the audacity to beam at me. "I'm stopping the wedding!"

"No!" I hiss. "I need this wedding to happen!"

Which is why I'm going to draw attention to myself. I have to if I'm going to save this thing.

"Apologies for the interruption," I announce to the watching room, putting Bulan behind my back. "This was a prank! Everyone, carry on, as you were!"

Unfortunately, Mab isn't falling for that excuse again. She's risen from her seat, apparently in competition with May to show the most astonishment. A hand over her forehead, she's bending backward—kind of like a spring-loaded jack-in-the-box.

"Bran!" she screams with furious drama. "*What* is the *meaning* of *this*?"

"And how did you get your body back?" May chips in. "I checked it was there before leaving my room!"

"You did *what*?" says Hanry from her side. He's visibly revolted. Which is fair.

"I will tell you all!" booms out Bulan/Bran. He wiggles from my arms, then bounces back onstage, ascending several steps so he can be viewed by the entirety of the wedding guests, including the tree staircase.

"A long time ago," he intones, "many centuries past, I was a young man. A burgeoning beacon of masculinity! And I made friends with the loveliest young creature—this Lady May."

Bulan's body, though separated from him, makes a spasmodic gesture at the Japanese fairy princess. She fans herself.

"Now is not the time," I say for easily the thousandth time. But I'm shushed by the entire wedding party and audience.

"Thank you," says Bulan, overwhelmed with gratitude. I throw up my hands, because I know I'm supposed to protest. Even if I'm glad to finally be getting answers too. "May and I promised ourselves to each other on a beautiful solstice eve. She promised me much favor in battle, and granted it to me manifold—I became a great king, with a fascinating entourage—but I did her a terrible disservice. I allowed my head to be severed from my body. And buried for centuries."

"What does that have to do with anything?" asks Hanry.

Bulan's voice is tragic: "It is what kept us separated. It meant we could not marry."

"It sounds like you were separated by . . ." Hanry gestures at Bulan's body. Seriously? Is Hanry actually *arguing* with Bulan right now? Why? This is the perfect out: if Bulan wants to marry May, then Hanry can step aside and retain his dignity—and avoid his mother's anger.

"Since Bran had promised himself to me, I performed magic to ensure he would not die," says May. "I've been keeping his body for years in hopes I'd see him again."

"It's one thing not to be in love, but *hiding a body*!?" Hanry exclaims.

Rochester steps rigidly between Hanry, May, and Bulan. "My Queen," he says to Mab, "mustn't we pause the ceremony to untangle this?"

I can't hear Mab's response over one of the groomsmen.

"I concur!" he calls out. "It is impossible for the wedding to proceed with two suitors!"

"Indeed, that is my point," Rochester says.

But there's no sign the wedding is ending. If anything, the energy is . . . intensifying. Mab un-accordions herself to regale her audience with an overplayed, considering expression. The Throne Room begins to reverberate with primitive whoops and calls.

Shit, shit, *shit*.

Seeing how the situation is slipping out of my control, I approach Rochester from a crouch. "Hey! What's going on?"

"They must fight!" Mab announces at last, her voice ringing out over the ruckus. She pumps an elegant fist in the air. "Fight! Fight! *YARE!*"

"As Her Highness has indicated, there is a cultural imperative,"

Rochester says to me, expression uneasy. "For Hanry and Bran to fight."

If it weren't weird enough that Hanry's own mother wants him to enter a primal mating dance to the death, out of nowhere, Hanry pulls a thin, rectangular object from his pocket. Bulan's head, meanwhile, bounces back to its body. His torso bends down, and his arms extend, reaching for his head. He places it atop his . . . neck bone, I guess. It doesn't attach there well, as you'd expect after a dozen centuries or so. He holds it in place with his elbows pointing outward. Then he turns to Hanry. Hanry, who—while huge—is too kind for his own good. And most likely lacks the battle experience of an ancient Welsh king.

"The fight commences!" Bulan booms out.

"Bring it on!" cries Hanry.

The two men move to meet each other on one of the wider stairs. I clutch onto Rochester's arm as the guests call out a countdown from ten. When they get down to zero, Hanry and Bulan rush each other, and begin to . . . I don't know what you'd call it.

But basically, Bulan is jabbing Hanry with his elbows.

And Hanry is whapping Bulan's head with his slender white weapon. Not stabbing. Bapping. Smacking. It is, I can see now, an electric toothbrush.

It is *incredibly ineffective*.

The crowd's fervor deflates in confusion.

"This is how humans fight?" asks a fairy behind Hanry's parents.

"How strange," says another.

Since all semblance of a typical wedding ceremony has long since been lost, I let go of Rochester and fully ascend the platform to where May watches with a disturbed expression. I place a hand on her gorgeously robed shoulder and lean in.

"You've got to stop them," I tell her. "And choose who you want to marry. Before they hurt themselves."

The princess closes her eyes, calm overcoming her beautiful, pearlescent face. "You're right."

"Thanks."

Having had enough of this, May leaves the altar and places herself between them in a swirl of silk. I skedaddle, removing myself from the scene in time for her to shout:

"I object!"

The wedding guests absolutely lose their shit. And so do Bulan and Hanry, pausing in their weakly attempted displays of viciousness. And me? I don't know whether to pump a fist in the air or to cry.

"What do you mean?" asks Bulan, his voice wretched. Overwrought. And frankly, a bit too Shakespearean. "I've waited a millennium for you!"

Confused, I watch on.

"These displays have been most pathetic. And so I've decided. Today"—May stretches out her arms, and her floor-length sleeves, with grandness—"I am not marrying you, Bran. Or you, Hanry. I am marrying . . . myself."

The princess snaps her slender fingers, and the harpist begins playing Lizzo.

"Most theatrical ceremony I've ever seen," comments one of the fairy guests.

"Absolutely fantastic."

"I want a human wedding someday!"

"Oh yes. I predict it'll be all the *rage* next season!"

I've finally stopped reeling in the wake of Hanry and May's disastawedding. Instead, I'm reveling in it alongside the guests. The reception hall crackles with energy and laughter, in spite of its lack of newlyweds to receive. A party is still a party, after all—particularly if said celebration is filled with alleged "pranks." Because that is the absolute best thing the chaos-happy contingent of Fairyland can imagine.

And, frankly, if Mab and Tits are happy—and Mab, at least, seems euphoric; Tits is still nowhere to be found—who am I to object?

Once I've finished organizing the catering fairies, I wind through the crowds of guests to the lavishly decorated head table. Many guests mill about, having long since abandoned their plated meals for dancing. Overlooking them all, Prince Hanry slumps in his seat, alone. The place settings for his parents and May remain untouched; the chairs to his right and left, unoccupied.

Until I slip into the seat beside him.

Now that I'm off my feet, I'm unable to hold back a gigantic sigh of relief. I've probably done thirty thousand steps today, and my toes prickle as blood returns. My stomach growls even more noticeably. Basically, I'm a bodily orchestra. For better or for worse, I'm too tired to care.

"Mind if I eat that?" I ask, gesturing at Hanry's untouched steak and potatoes.

"Be my guest."

"Already am," I answer, shoveling a fork of buttery goodness into my mouth. I swallow, gratefully, because I am *starving*. I better add granola bars and snack packs to the emergency kit for next time. Maybe water bottles too, because my breath stinks, and that's arguably more important than food.

Plus, you never know when you'll need to melt a wicked witch.

"I know you're mad at me," says Hanry.

Oh, does he?

Bolstering myself with a mega-fast pep talk, I finally allow myself to look at my ex-boyfriend. A few strands of hair have gone rogue from his hair pomade. He has a paper cut on his lip, but otherwise, Hanry has escaped without impressive or dreamy battle scars. His gaze touches mine for a moment, fleetingly—just long enough for me to read regret. Digging into a front pocket of his tunic, Hanry reveals a folded-up parchment. He places it between us.

"I was never going to marry May," he says. "See? I had my wedding vows. They weren't lost."

"How was that going to keep you from getting married?" I ask.

"I planned to seek an annulment. You see, my legal name isn't Hanry. It's Henry. A wedding for May and 'Hanry' would have been invalid from the start."

Despite myself, I laugh, dropping my fork loudly on his china plate. "I always thought Hanry was a weird name."

"No you didn't."

"Okay, fine. I didn't." My assault on the potatoes complete, I attack a slab of meat. Hopefully it's venison and not some other forbidden delicacy, like pixie. Mandy would've warned me if I were eating one of her people; I'm sure of it. "So, why the name change?"

"My birth parents named me Henry. When they adopted me, Mom and Dad kept mispronouncing my name as 'Hanry.' Well, mostly Mom."

Hmm. This fits: Mab definitely struggled to remember my name. And here I thought it was personal. "Why didn't you correct her?"

"Didn't seem worth it." Hanry—or Henry, I guess?—colors slightly. "Anyway. Bulan found me today, and we devised this plan."

"I would've appreciated some warning," I tell him after another bite.

"I know. Bulan only slipped me the toothbrush right before the ceremony. He explained that May doesn't actually want to marry a human man. She thinks she does, because she's convinced we're stronger and more macho than we are. That's why Bulan and I figured if we proved we weren't as masculine as she imagined, we'd both finally be off the hook."

Well played, Hanry . . . sort of. He still hasn't learned to tell his mom no. His lack of courage is a problem, and it's a problem I don't think I can fix.

"May actually seems like a catch," I say, getting up. "I'm kind of disappointed for you."

"Sabby, I'm sorry."

I suck in my lips so I don't say something stupid.

"Sabby, I'm *so sorry*," he repeats, standing. Reminding me how tall he is, how safe I thought I was with him.

"I need someone who can protect me," I say. "Someone who can stand up against chaos. Or at least their own parents. You came up with all these schemes, but at the end of the day, you still couldn't tell your mother the truth."

"I get it," says Hanry.

"Do you? Because when you were standing up on that platform

in your wedding tunic, it felt like you didn't care about me. Like you didn't care I was being humiliated by your own parents, that I was the butt of a thousand jokes. How could I believe you'd ever try to make our relationship work in the future? That you wouldn't give up the first time it became inconvenient?"

Hanry sighs heavily and sits back down with the same air of defeat. "I do care about you, Sabby, and I'm sorry for . . . making your life worse. And not being honest with you. I know I need to do better. I don't know how, but I need to figure it out."

"Strong agree. Grow some balls."

"I don't want to lose you. Again."

I point Hanry's oily fork at him. "You realize that on some level, you weren't totally on the up and up with either me *or* May, right? That's shitty. How could I ever trust you?"

Grimacing, Hanry says, "I don't know."

He keeps saying that.

"Well maybe you need a second Rumspringa. An *Eat Pray Love* journey."

"Maybe." Hanry's gaze moves from me to the party, his expression caught between pleased and sad. "You're serious about this, aren't you? The wedding planning thing."

"More than serious," I reply. "I'm ditching my job in New York for it."

He smiles. "Good."

It is. I survey the State Room, trying to see everything like Hanry does: the room, filled with members of the Community in their wild and fascinating glory. Fairies, mostly, plus a few familiar faces from Halloween. Mandy dances with Rochester. Robert the Sasquatch waves his arms beside them. Crows peck at the wedding cake. A manticore relieves itself on a flower arrangement, and . . . there's May, calling me over to the dance floor.

Beside her stands King Tits and a smooth-skinned fay. I *know* I would've noticed this fairy if I'd seen him earlier—he puts Rochester to shame when it comes to hollow cheekbones and sulky sexiness. Like Hanry, he's looking around, but instead of being sad, he's torn between wistful and angry. Making eye contact with me, his scowl deepens.

"That's Seb," says Hanry unnecessarily. I already recognized him from the photo in Hanry's room. He has the same hooded eyes and scowl. Also, he's Tits's spitting image, minus the antlers and chaotic affability.

"So that's why your dad left this morning. To pick him up," I realize.

Hanry nods unhappily. "He was in the human world. When Mom and Dad adopted me, they swapped us out. I got to grow up as royalty. He had to live with my parents. Except for yearly check-in visits."

"When you found out he was doing fine?"

"No. His home life was shit," says Hanry bluntly. He goes on: "Anyway, Mom first told me about this wedding the day right before we broke up."

"The trip you took before Sidney's wedding," I say.

"Yeah. After you left, there was nothing stopping me from coming home and giving Seb a break."

My sympathy slams to a halt.

"Okay, fine. I had a role in this too. But that doesn't absolve you of being weak. You still could've told your mom that no one was going to marry anyone."

Besides, I wonder why he's so sure Seb would've been forced to wed May. Seb has TikTok-ready dolphin skin. He's shiny-pale and smooth-chinned. All evidence indicates May would sooner marry a gorilla.

Out loud, I say, "I wonder if Seb's a good dancer." Exactly as expected, Hanry glowers. I grin up at him, ready to enjoy his jealous display. But my heart, calloused and angry thing that it is, softens a bit.

"I'm just kidding." Mostly. "See you later, Princeling. Good luck finding yourself."

"I'll find you when I'm done," Hanry says. "I mean it, Sabby. I know it's unfair to ask you to wait for me—"

"Correct."

"—but if you do, I'll make it worth your while."

That's a tall order. I rest a hand on the table and turn fully toward

Hanry. And although I try to find an insult to throw at him—an extra-cutting one, to match the pain I'm still reeling from—instead, my heartbeat skips. I can't help it. I'm reminded of how Hanry smells, like pine or cedar or some other indefinable spicy, nature-inspired wholesomeness. How I find his strength reassuring. His kindness and decency and desire to help others is flat-out impressive—all the more so when I compare it to his royal fairy upbringing. I've longed for weeks to share in his cozy, comfortable world. And now, all our make-out sessions, all the times we lay in each other's arms on his sofa rush back to the front of my mind. We never promised anything to each other. This would be the first time.

More than anything, I want Hanry to be ready to make good on what he's offering—not later, but today. If only his inner strength matched his outer strength. If only he had the spine to support the weight of his noble heart.

I wish I could hold that against him. I want to stay angry. But . . . I can't. I've needed help figuring myself out too. It took extreme measures for me to realize what I wanted. Maybe it wouldn't be so bad if I gave Hanry a chance. After he takes some time to grow. See what happens down the road.

Eyes fastened on his, I take Hanry's goblet and throw back fairy wine.

"If you find any other fairy princesses to marry, tell them I've got dibs. You hear?"

Hanry laughs. The taste of lilac and nettles lingering hot on my tongue, I drop the goblet, curtsy, and leave him for his party.

No—for *mine*.

31

ALL'S WELL THAT ENDS WHALE?

"NO. WE ARE NOT ADDING AN EXTRA BEDROOM."

Bulan, pretending not to hear, bounces around the inside of the cupboard. He's all head and no self-control, so despite my efforts at shampooing him this morning, he's progressively taking on lint and dust.

"It's got a smell back here," he complains. "Blech."

"I don't remember you complaining about the mildew before."

"I had rhinitis. Don't you remember my sniffling?"

"Would you at least stop rattling the shelves? Hanry isn't around to fix them."

Mandy clasps her hands, perplexed as Bulan and I work to determine the master bedroom closet's destiny. After visiting multiple apartments with a real estate broker, we agreed that Grandma Rose's pink house was the clear winner for our shared future abode. It has the most light, lower property taxes than we'd have to pay in rent, and an ambience of familiarity. It will probably require the deepest cleaning, but I'm sure Mandy and I are up to the task. If not, maybe Mandy can convince Rochester to loan us his fairy servant minions. Or maybe she'll continue wringing her hands until she's whittled them down to nubs.

"Mandy, stop."

Embarrassed, Mandy throws her hands behind her back. "Sorry! I just, umm, are you *sure* this is okay, Sabby? Us moving in!"

"I'm sure," I say for at least the tenth time since returning from Fairyland, armored with a fresh plan for business success. "I need my employees to have stable housing. I need to stay in the green myself, and to do that, I'll need renters. If anyone's going to be in my space, I want it to be my friends. Why are you acting so nervous?"

"She's cutting back on sugar, remember?" booms Bulan from deep in the shelving. "Now focus on me again, Sabby. I hate this room. Hate it! Remind me why I can't sleep in the corner anymore?"

I place my hands on my hips. "Because I've seen your whole body. It's too creepy sharing a room now."

"Well, I'm not bringing him out of storage," Bulan replies, his miffed tone muffled. "Every minute I have to wear that torso and legs, I lose a minute of immortality."

"And I lose the opportunity for an extra pair of hands at my weddings. But you don't see me complaining, do you?"

Bulan emerges from the back of the cupboard, nosing forward a tiny key chain with a house key and a whale. This is at least the second whale we've unearthed today.

Grandma Rose, did they mean something to you? Please, *please* don't force me into asking Matilda. Just because I'm living here, it doesn't mean I want your friends. I'll choose my own weirdos, thanks.

"Fine," says Bulan. "My one request is this: if I must share a wall with Mandy, I request you install soundproofing. Lest I hear unspeakable things."

"You won't," I promise. "Rochester is not sleeping over, ever."

Mandy gasps. "But Sabby! You let Hanry stay over!"

"On the couch, for one night. Before he left for his cross-continental *Eat Pray Love* trip. I'm not a monster."

"You made out with him!"

"So what?"

Popping her pinkened hands out from behind her back and shaking them with distress, Mandy cries, "Rochie will just linger outside all night, then! It'll be TRAGIC!"

"He isn't a stray dog. He can get an apartment of his own if he's going to keep acting so besotted with you. Now, listen, Serious Mandy—" The nickname gets her attention. She catches her breath and makes her back go ramrod straight as I remind her: "We have over twenty weddings booked over the next twelve months, and after the show we put on in Fairy, we've got a reputation. We've got to stay on our game. No more winging it."

"Right," says Serious Mandy.

"Also, no more running cheap," Bulan adds. Since I've given up on accounting, I've been cross-training Bulan to handle our shop bookkeeping. It turns out he has a knack for keeping track of things. Which is ironic for someone missing 80 percent of their body composition, unless you think about it: he has more reason than most to understand how every little bit matters.

That said, I'm not ready to give up full ownership of our financial records. Old habits die hard.

Speaking of expenses: I've been in touch with Baldy about how to make my paranormal business quasi-legal. Thanks to his questionable lack of integrity, and a solid start-up investment from Queen Mab, Spüktacular Weddings, LLC seems set to straddle both the human and the paranormal worlds with success.

"Did Baldy seem distracted yesterday?" I ask Mandy as she peruses the kitchen in a transparent search for sugar. I'm clearing out the pantry, which puts the two of us in a favorably symbiotic state. "When we went to his office to close the estate, did he seem frazzled to you?"

"He did! I think it's the gnomes."

Ohhh. Shit. "I forgot to take those off him again, didn't I."

"I thought you left them on purpose," says Mandy. She unpops a cork from a jar and sniffs it. "Oh, look, another whale key chain."

As the three of us begin removing Grandma's crap in earnest, making a competition of who can find the most inexplicably hidden whales, I mentally rummage through the last two weeks. It was a small ordeal moving out of Jane's apartment and getting my room sublet. What else might I have missed on my set-life-back-to-rights-in-Salem to-do list? For one thing, I need to apply for my sale license at the county office and call the floral wholesaler for the mermaids' wedding. Since there's been a change to the brides' budget, I have to adjust my specialty orders. Tomorrow afternoon, I'll meet some elves for a forager-themed wedding food tasting. Do I need to follow up with their caterer? Or their arborist? No, it's something else . . .

Finally, it strikes me: Mom. I need to call Mom. Because it's Friday, and although we haven't managed to talk for two months now, I can't bring myself to stop trying. It's a daughter's duty and all that.

It takes her ages to pick up.

"Sabby, I'm kind of busy," she says before I can get a word in edgewise. "Can you call me back?"

Who knows how long it'll take before we connect again? I'll have to get right into it.

"Mom," I say. "I've resigned from EFG."

She barely misses a beat. "Really?"

"Yes. I've decided I don't want the 2.5 kids, the suburbs house, the normal life."

"Well, that's great, Sabby. It's so important to know what you want."

She doesn't sound upset. In fact, she doesn't sound like she's listening. I click on my video, hoping that'll wrangle slightly more attention.

"I want to be more like Grandma," I tell Mom. "And like you."

"Like me?" I swear I can hear her blinking in confusion.

"A true Spük," I say, though obviously I'm just describing high-level similarities here. "I only need myself and my friends to be happy. I don't need to play it safe and boring. I want to live a life worth living."

Mom's video connects. She's sunbathing by the pool as usual, no hint of a job in sight. She waves up at me and picks up her margarita. And that's when I see the engagement ring on her finger.

"You—you—" I stammer. "What's that?"

"What is what?"

"Are you getting *married*, Mom?"

She rolls her eyes majestically. "I told you I've been busy!"

"To who?! The pool boy?"

"Well, it's complicated."

Complicated? Why would you get *married* to someone if it's complicated? I mean . . . unless he's a fairy prince changeling? And now I'm fighting a bittersweet pang of missing Hanry *and* being worried about my mom. Great.

Not wanting to spook Mom, who seems as innocent and unwary as a desert mouse, I force out a gentle, soothing voice. "Hey, so maybe . . . what do you think about coming home? To talk things through before your wedding. With some distance from Mexico. You know?"

Coming home helped me figure out my life, after all. Maybe it'll help her too.

Mom laughs cannily. "Mi gordita, why would I do that? I love it here!"

I frown, watching her take a sip of her magenta drink. Something feels off. It's just a gut feeling, but it's one I've been slowly learning to trust.

"Mom, how long has it been since you left your hotel?"

"Only a few months," she says casually. She taps her chin. "Maybe three? I'm planning to book a flight back before school starts, Sabby. I can't leave you to muddle through senior year by yourself!"

Shit, shit, *shit*.

"Mom, it's been five years since I graduated high school," I say, horror dawning on me. "Let me call you right back."

I hang up unceremoniously on Mom and poke my head around the corner.

"BULAN!" I shout.

He rolls in atop a Roomba he's unearthed from a pile of decaying newspapers, circa 1980s.

"What is it?" asks the head. "Also, how do you correctly navigate this fair mechanical steed? As your knight-in-rolling-dustpan, I'm elated to divide and conqu—"

"There's no time to clean," I interrupt. "Remember how my mom's in Mexico? In that place called Hotel California? Well, I think she's in trouble."

"Trouble?" Bulan asks, his bushy eyebrows furrowing. Mandy

scoops him off the vacuum and squeezes him like a teddy bear for comfort.

"What's happened!?" she asks worriedly into his hair.

"She's getting married."

"That's all?" asks Mandy.

"And here I was worried," pouts Bulan around Mandy's forearm.

"Yes 'that's all.' It's a big deal," I tell them. "Mom isn't the marrying kind. And she hasn't been dating this guy for any length of time, as far as I can tell. On top of all that, she seems . . . confused. About where she is. What's happening around her. And how long she hasn't been home. I think she might be in some kind of danger." Paranormal danger, I'd bet. Grave danger? Well, if graves are involved, it wouldn't be the first time.

In any case, this calls for an intervention.

Or at the very least: a vacation.

ACKNOWLEDGMENTS

Wait, *acknowledgments?* Does this mean I'm a real author? I guess we did it, team. Thank you, so much, forever:

To Caitlin Blasdell, who *got* Sabby (and me), and just as importantly, kept me sane. To Amara Hoshijo, who fell in love with this book and whose imagination helped release the best version of Sabby's story into the world! To the team at Saga Press who manifested our shared vision: Rachael, Stacey, Jéla, Christine, Ali, and Theresa. Great job! And special shout-out to Ella Laytham and Lucie Corbasson—this cover is a VIBE! Whoo!

To the writing friends who've helped me reach this stage in my publishing journey, including but not limited to Aloha Pens (Sue Wyshynski and Gemma Fairlamb) and MUG (Taylor L. W. Ross, Ana Ellickson, J. C. Peterson, Genevieve Godwyn, and Brianna Bourne). You lot mean the world to me. I'm sorry I'm so late to every meeting; it's my ADHD, I swear. To K. X. Song, Gloria Muñoz, and Heather Dean Brewer for your inestimable professional advice and friendship. Additional heartfelt thanks to writing friends Samantha Landau, Rob Costello, Nora Shalaway Carpenter, Rachel Michelle Wilson, Angela Pham Krans, Amanda Glaze, Seina Wedlick, the CTS gang who wrote Pokémon fanfic with me in the mid-2000s, the 2026 Saga debut Discord group, and to myriad others whose names won't fit onto my allotted acknowledgment pages. You are the community that makes my heart sing (out of tune, but joyfully)! Thank you for your support!

To Briana Hanson of Privé Events, who let me come on board for her quirkiest weddings and checked over my manuscript besides. You are a wedding QUEEN. I miss you, Bee!

To Mrs. Crawford and Mrs. O'Connor, thank you for reading my middle school poetry and believing in me anyway. I've carried your faith with me this whole time. Thank you to Professor C. E. J. Simons, for suggesting I focus on writing prose (again, the bad poetry thing), for supporting my wacky writing club, and for enduring my unscheduled office visits.

To Vivian Chang and Laura Lambert, for being there for me when I nearly let go of my writing dream post-college. For reading manuscripts no one else will ever see. For your friendship. Ugh, I'm teary-eyed. You're the best.

To coffee.

To Coco and Nuts, *meow meow, meow meeeeowll meowlry meow MEOW*.

To my children, because I somehow did all my drafting and edits while pregnant with you two. I'm probably stealing your creative energy. Thanks, I love you, now please skip all the kissing bits. That goes for you, too, Mom.

Oh, right! MOM. I promise Sabby's mom isn't based on you. When I base a character on you, it'll be some form of multitalented, overpowered, humble saint. I love you.

To my family, who can't be thanked enough for all their unwavering, decades-long support, and for never once hinting I might fail to realize my dreams. Cici, I wish you could see this book in print, but I'm so glad you got a copy of the first ARC ever. I miss you.

To The Love Interest, for brainstorming this book with me as we drove through the mountains. For helping me move mountains to get it published. For laughing at my jokes. I love you. I'm sorry I keep writing about things that concern you. I swear I'm fine. I won't poke out your eyes, ever.

And lastly, to you, my reader. Thanks for joining me and Sabby for this party. I hope to see you again at the next one!

ABOUT THE AUTHOR

ALEESE LIN is a fantasy writer who lives with her family in a hillside cottage overlooking Boston, Massachusetts. She is a 2022 Lambda Literary Fellow, a Tin House workshop alumnus, and an educator. This is her debut novel.